WAITING FOR FATE

FATE SERIES: BOOK ONE

YVONNE KJORLIEN

To every writer who has ever struggled:

You are not alone.

PROLOGUE

"She is coming." The words came out in a croak. Her throat was dry and sore. She sat cross-legged on the bare earth, white robes draped around to keep in what little warmth rose from her body.

Had he heard her?

Her hair brushed against her back as she craned her neck to see if her guard was asleep. "Maleor?"

Shuffling came from the shadows between the columns adjacent to the entrance. "Yes, my lady?" The voice was muffled as if a hand was running over the mouth and face, scraping away the sleep.

"She is coming." Repeating the statement suddenly made it real. The implications sprang into her mind, as she had just Seen, and electric excitement danced through her. Gooseflesh rose on her bare wrists. "And the Outerworld."

"I shall make it known." Footsteps; metal scratching as Maleor picked up his sword; the door opened and shut. Silence.

She continued to sit upon the earthen floor, trying to calm her anxious stomach. The bucket holding her regurgitated breakfast was not far and the smell further enhanced her nausea.

Redirect and focus, her training commanded. With uncanny deftness, her mind obeyed.

Slowly -- a little more slowly than usual, she thought – her stomach quieted along with her mind. The light of day, shining through the crystalline ceiling and a lone window, now appeared a little more real as the shadows released their substance and eventually faded. Warmth trickled through her. Inch by inch, her mind gently coaxed it along, bringing life back to her inert body.

With one last violent shiver to release her mind and being from the dark nothingness of the Outerworld, the 29th Seer of Juno unfolded her legs and, when she could feel her toes again, stood to perform the movements her mother had taught her. *You will not be able to sit and See if you cannot stand and walk,* she remembered the 28th Seer saying.

From stance to stance, stiffly at first, her body moved, her mind flowing from muscle to muscle, from limb to limb. Finally, with her mind and body supple again, her pace increased and the energy snapped into the air as a hand, then a foot, released it back into the surroundings.

Then, her arms fell to her sides and her feet came together. She stood and lifted her face to the light. "Much better," she smiled. The sky always seemed so blue after a vision.

Maleor wasn't much of a conversationalist but she had to talk to some-one. Even if talking to herself was crazy behaviour it was better than going insane from the visions. She turned to pick up the wooden bucket full of vomit, but doubt suddenly stilled her. "It had been Juno, hadn't it?"

Yes, it had to be, her mother's voice echoed through her head.

"Yes, you're right. It was Juno." With a self-affirmed sigh, Ailsene placed the bucket by the door then picked up a biscuit from the tray of assorted snacks.

Before the biscuit entered her mouth, wonder confronted her again. This vision had been different. She was so used to Seeing the darkness, so used to the evil. Watching a person die, their flesh ripping as a blade tears through their torso. The shock in their eyes as they stare at the gaping wound; a black fist rips the intestines from their warm cavity. Their hands scrambling to put back the leaking entrails; hopelessness ringing loudly as the stench of the enemy grows. Hopelessness is pushed aside as bulging red eyes and a blood-splattered grin appear. Terror nestles in, finding a new home in the conquered, and communal screams echo across the land as a country's consciousness pleads for mercy. Then, finally, a resounding thump as a disconnected head hits the ground. Maleor was lucky if he had only one bucket of vomit to carry from her chambers.

Ailsene stuffed the biscuit into her mouth, chewed and followed with cold tea.

She had Seen it all this time. Seen it, heard it, tasted it, smelled it, felt it. Although she knew what to expect and anticipated it, the visions never ceased to have the same effect on her. That was what she had a routine for. That's what she had Maleor for.

She refilled her teacup and deliberately turned the handle away so that she could hold the cup in her palm with her fingers curled toward the brim.

But this time, this time had been different. She had Seen Juno.

She picked up a cake and stuffed it into her mouth as she walked across the earthen floor to the stairway.

In her ten years as Seer, she had never Seen Juno in her visions. She was young, but not inexperienced. The Creator was not of Juno, not of the islands on the Ocean Rire and not of the lands in the distant east. The Creator was more than the land and the air, more than the collective consciousness. She was all. She was the Creator.

With her skill and her feet upon the soil of Juno, the Seer could see through the eyes of the Creator. Usually the visions were a hodgepodge of broken images. Nothing made sense and nothing was recognizable. These visions were not to be made sense of. They were not for the Seer. This all changed when the Outerworld drew close to Juno. Evil seeped in. The images became clear and vivid, their interpretation unmistakable. This was a message for the Seer, a warning to Juno: prepare for attack.

That is what perplexed her.

Cup in hand, the Seer climbed the stairway up to the lone window. It was late afternoon. The suns were behind her tower now and the sea glistened in front of her. Pretty soon, the white marble spirals of The Inner City would reflect the pinks and oranges of the maturing day. It was said to be a sight that beckoned men to Juno, leaving their beloveds behind.

She knew these famous towers well. They had become part of her routine, part of her sanity. So had the mountains far to the west, the farmlands on The Northern Plateau, the sandy beaches in the east, and The Plains in the south. The landscape of Juno was her sanity, its soil tenderly cradling her bare feet and sifting between her toes. She knew Juno although she could see nothing past her towers.

"Everything's going to change, isn't it?" The feeling welled inside her unexpectedly.

Yes.

Everything that she couldn't see, hadn't had a chance to see, would change. Ailsene fought to keep the loss from overwhelming her.

She had been to the Plains once. The dead grasses and the blackened ground only added to her instinctual knowledge of the landscape. Her single visit had been enough to feel what that place held. Loss. Desperation. But also pride and love. It was mixed into the soil like the ashes of the dead.

This is what she had Seen. The Plains had been in her vision. The Creator would walk the Plains of Juno.

Yes. Everything will change. She is coming.

It was unprecedented and she doubted her Sight. But she hadn't been wrong yet.

There will be an attack, but not too soon. The Creator will walk Juno's land, but there was something else in the vision. Something she would not tell the Council. Something that would be better left unsaid. Again she remembered her mother's words. *As long as the attacks were predicted, nothing would be questioned.* Fate did not need someone else doing her job, although the Seer often wondered what She was up to.

So why did she tell them of the Creator? Wouldn't it have been more prudent to keep that piece of information until later? Ailsene sighed as she shook her head, "Such is Fate."

Her mother had taught her well. No, she would not tell the Council of the possible circumstances of the young Aristovin's summons. Not yet, at least. The Council too often listened only to the information they wanted to hear. No. She would let Fate have her way in this.

"Yes," Ailsene sighed again and gulped her cold tea, "everything will change." As she stared out her window into the vast expanse of sea, she knew this was the right decision and, for the first time in a long while, felt pride in her position. The Aristovin son will be gone and She will come. There was nothing she could do but wait. Wait for change and wait for Fate.

Chapter One

The dishcloth dripped dirty water onto Simone's sneakers and jeans as she stood rooted at the empty coffee shop's window. Watching.

He wore a black hoodie. Jeans. Possibly knife flashing in the sunlight. Running full tilt down the opposite sidewalk toward her, a pretty blonde girl. Stylish knee-high boots. Skinny jeans. Oblivious to everything except her cell phone.

Oh god, no. Don't. No.

Simone watched, helpless from her vantage point inside the coffee shop. Fear sucked the life from her body, froze her soul, and rendered her a gaping zombie. As the man ran down the sidewalk, Simone could already see his hands grabbing the girl, forcing her down while she struggled against his strength. Would she scream? Would she have a chance?

"No." It came out as a squeak, Simone's lungs working against the terror.

As the dishcloth exuded the last of its water through Simone's clenched hands, the man reached the girl. Her blonde hair flew as he breezed past, brushing her head lightly. The girl looked up from her cell phone as he stopped dead in front of her, "Jonah! You're such a jerk!"

He held his cell phone up to her, "You didn't text me! What up?" He grabbed the girl into a bear hug and she squealed with delight.

Sally burst into the shop. Simone screamed and threw herself against the window. Sally screamed and fell against a set of table and chairs.

"Holy shit," Sally panted as she propped herself up on a wooden chair. "Now that we got that out of the way, what the hell was that about?" Red ringlets circled her head, eye shadow glittered on her eyelids, fading was in the correct places on her jeans; Sally was the polar opposite of Simone.

Breath returned to her body and her mind engaged once again. Simone turned to look out the window. The girl was alright. The guy was a friend. There was no knife. There was no danger.

As the adrenaline fled and left her drained, Simone took stock. She was safe. Intact. Dressed. Unharmed. As she looked over her body, Simone saw that dishwater had dripped down her worn jeans, left a large wet spot on her second-hand "U2" T-shirt, and seeped through her greyed runners. "Crap," she reached down and plucked the fallen dishcloth from the floor. "What are you doing here, Sal?" and headed into the kitchen.

"Karen called me last night. She wanted me to come in early so you could make a few more pies today for the conference."

"Didn't you have any appointments?" Simone kept her back to Sally.

"Not as of yesterday. Sam gave Mrs. McGregor to Sarah again."

"That's bullshit, Sal. Your clients are your clients. Sam can't do that." Simone threw the dishcloth into the sink of soapy, dirty water.

Sally shrugged, "It's his salon. I just rent the chair. So, you wanna tell me what that was about?"

"What was about?"

"You screaming bloody murder."

"You scared me, that's all."

Sally pulled her oversized Prada knock-off and dropped it onto the staff table with a clank. Simone could only imagine the arsenal of cosmetics and hair supplies in that bag. "My turn to call bullshit. I've scared you lots of times and you never reacted like that. You nearly jumped out of your own skin."

Simone deflected: "Do you think maybe we could go shopping some time?"

"You hate shopping."

Simone felt her heart flutter, "Maybe you could do my hair. Maybe Wanda could give me a manicure."

"The day that I let Wanda near your hands is the day I see pigs fly down main street." Sally crossed her arms and cocked an eyebrow. "You're trying to change the subject and it isn't working."

Simone turned. Slowly. Hesitantly. Keeping her eyes on the linoleum floor, in her periphery she could see Sally, arms crossed and leaning against the table: a picture of defiance in miniature. Her fear was not something that she wanted to discuss. Ever. With anyone. Usually she kept it under wraps. It took practice, but she managed it. She really didn't want to delve into her past and her crippled psyche to explain the momentary slip of her mask.

She had one more card up her sleeve. It was a low blow, but it was guaranteed to work. "Mr. Briefcase came in this morning."

Instantly, Sally's demeanor changed. "Oh my god. Did he say anything? Did YOU say anything?" Sally covered the distance between them in a light second. "Tell me!" She grabbed Simone's arms, shaking her.

"He asked for the usual: a coffee, a blueberry bran muffin. He paid, said 'Thanks,' and left."

"And?"

"Your freckles look really big right now."

Sally threw a swipe and reached far enough to smack Simone's ponytail into disarray. Then the bell over the door to the cafe rang. "Shit." A finger was raised and Sally's ultramarine blue eyes burned, "This isn't over, Simone Larken." She turned, grabbed her apron, and ran through to the cafe. "Hello! Welcome to The Only Cup."

"Saved by the bell," Simone breathed a deep sigh of relief, and fixed her ponytail, "Let the chaos begin." She plucked a bowl from drying rack and prepared to make some extra pies.

The lunch rush was more than usual. The annual forestry conference swelled the small town to double its usual size, and sent city tourists seeking a real coffee instead of 'that black stuff they were trying to push down at the arena.' By the time the rush had calmed down, Simone and Sally were taking turns drying the sweat from their shirts out behind the shop in the warm September air.

"How much did we make?" Sally sank down beside Simone on the concrete back step and set down an iced tea.

Simone held up a finger, holding an old wooden top in one hand, as she used the other hand to punch numbers into a calculator and jot the figure down on her notepad. Quick addition to the credit card subtotal, subtraction of the shop profit, "And divide by two is $68.70 each."

"God you blow my mind. Seriously, you got some computer in that head of yours."

"It's not that hard. You just gotta get your thinking straight. Tips are down from last year's conference. Do you know what the turn-out is this year?"

"Haven't a clue. I'll grab the paper." A moment later, Sally returned. "Huh. Turnout is down; 12.8%. Hey, there was a robbery at Mike's Five & Dime last night."

Simone punched some numbers into her calculator. "Tips are down 16%. We must be missing out on some heavy hitters this year."

"You're freakin' me out, whiz kid."

Simone was suddenly self-conscious. "Sorry," and started to put the paperwork together. The old wooden top bounced off the papers. Sally grabbed it before it rolled away.

"You never did say if you applied for university. And, since you're still here, I'm guessing you didn't."

"Yeah, about that," Simone said and plucked the top from Sally's hand. She held it, caressed it, savouring the way it fit into her hand. The wood of the top was soft, almost silky, from decades of use. Sometimes she thought she could hear children's laughter spinning off it. "I was thinking of sticking around for a while."

"You've got to be joking." The acerbity in Sally's voice was palpable.

Simone shook her head, still caressing the top, "No, no. I've got a good thing going here; the shop, doing the books for Karen and Mr. Decker."

A small ringed hand appeared on Simone's knee. "Simone. Honey. There is no future in this town. Seriously. You have got to get out. You are too good to be here. Please say you're not giving up on university all together."

Simone shrugged non-committedly, "I just want to delay it a bit."

She continued to caress the top as Sally leaned against the screen door, "Has your Dad figured it out yet?"

"Maybe. He's back on the 17th. I'll talk to him then."

"Let me see that again." Sally held out her tiny hand. A flicker of anxiety flirted in Simone's stomach. Then she handed Sally the top. "Where did you get this? I've only seen these in antique shops in the city."

"Mrs. Decker gave it to me."

"You should keep it safe. Could be worth a pretty penny."

Simone plucked the top a little too quickly from Sally's hand. "No. It was a gift. Besides, I like the feel of it." It had been a couple days since she'd had time to pull it out and play with it. She made a mental note to take it home with her tonight.

"Maybe I could grab some supplies from the salon and do your hair. Some highlights, and definitely a haircut," Sally ran an experienced hand through Simone's mane of tangled blonde curls.

Simone sighed. "How much?" Sally's touch was melting her steely resolve.

"Mmm, foils, colour....say sixty bucks."

It was time. It had been three years, three months, and twenty-one days. I am safe, she thought for the thousandth time. It was time to step out of her shell.

With determined hands, Simone put the wooden top away and counted out the money from her apron. Sally gathered up the cash. "And maybe when you have a new hair-do you'll feel better about asking out that lawyer guy, Mr. Briefcase, mmm?"

"Impossible things happen all the time," Simone tried to convince herself that she was doing the right thing.

"**D**id you take the pies out?" Simone called to the kitchen.

"Yeah. They're on the counter." She turned back to her phone and continued texting.

Simone propped up the broom and fetched two fresh cherry pies from the kitchen. She smiled as the warm sweet scent tickled her nose. When she swung through the door, there was someone on the other side of the counter. She hadn't heard the bell over the door ring.

It was someone she never expected to see again.

J.D.'s smile was hungry. His gaze was predatory. She felt his eyes draw over her body, an intangible tongue licking her from head to toe. Bile rose in her throat. She wanted to hit him, thrash his face, jump on his eyes until there was nothing left. But she'd tried fighting. It hadn't worked. She was a five-foot three female and he was a six-foot four ape who had hauled around engines in Shop class and beat up guys on the football field. She hadn't a snowball's chance in hell and he knew it.

All that was left was the fear. Raw, sharp fear.

J.D. leaned over the glass display counter. Panic focused her mind to a searing point. She stepped back, a pie in each hand teetering. Sweat down her back turned cold.

His eyes finished their jaunt across her body. "It's been a long time," he whispered.

In a heartbeat, Simone was standing in the middle of the kitchen, shaking and numb, with the kitchen door still swinging in front of her. Her hands were empty.

Sally appeared beside her, "What's....?"

The world grew fuzzy around that searing point of fear. Then a voice called out from the cafe, "Can I buy a pie?"

Escape.

Run.

Survive.

Fear jolted her body into action. She darted for the bathroom.

Time became irrelevant. It passed as Simone shook and shuttered through the fear that numbed her body and senses. Fear was animal that consumed her being. The walls of the bathroom were her shelter. They closed in around her, suffocating her in security. She wanted to stay there forever.

A gentle knock on the bathroom door tempted to broaden her focus, "Simone? It's Dean. That guy is gone. It's okay. You can come out if you want."

There was some scuffling and murmuring, then Sally spoke, "Simone, can I come in?"

The doorknob turned. Simone stared at it. It wasn't locked. Was it supposed to be? She watched as Sally entered slowly, quietly, and looked around, her eyes finally landing on Simone. Then she propped herself against the sink, across from Simone, "Hey," Sally said.

The word, the person, at first didn't register in Simone's mind. Then, slowly, the acute, penetrating focus released her mind and Simone came back to herself.

She felt...constricted.

She'd managed to wedge herself between the toilet and the wall. She never thought a body could fit into such a small space, and now that she was aware of where she was, found she was having trouble breathing.

Simone held out her hand, "Help?"

Sally pulled her out then resumed her position against the sink. "Are you okay?"

"I will be."

"Want to talk about it?"

"No." Her muscles had started to cramp. She stretched a little and, as she leaned back, noted a crack in the ceiling. "Is he really gone?"

"Dean or the guy?"

"The guy."

"Dean's on guard out front. Doors are locked." Sally crossed her arms. "Do I need to call the cops? Did he do something?"

"No."

"Then what?"

"Nothing. Leave it."

Sally stood and stared at Simone. The seconds grew, and so did the distance between them. Simone felt this and regretted it. But the words just wouldn't come. She wouldn't let them; they were conjoined to the fear, and she loathed the fear. That fear was the gateway to the memory of that day, and that was a closet best left locked.

Finally Sally surrendered, "Fine."

"Fine."

"I'll call Karen and tell her we swapped shifts; I'll close. Dean will drive you home. Have a hot bath and relax. Call me if you want to talk." Simone bobbed her head. Instinctively, her hand reached inside her apron and once again grasped the wooden top.

Chapter Two

*ll movement stopped.*

The breath he was hearing, was it his?

In front of his eyes, through the crack in the door, her arms fell slack. The sword slipped from her limp hand.

A metal clang echoed down the corridor, off the awaiting armour.

A gasp rang out, heavy against the silence. White robes billowed as her knees buckled and hit the floor. In a hush, long dark hair brushed across her shoulder as her head dipped. Then he saw it.

The blood. Saturating. A dark organic growth consuming the whiteness.

Then, his mother fell.

A scream.

No.

"NO!"

Cary sat, now awake, stomach clenched, and watched as the sweat from his forehead dripped, making faint spots on his overturned sheets.

He had tried so hard to forget. But now it was back, all of it. Even the scent of roses lingered. He shivered.

Cary pushed the sheets back farther and looked toward the window. It was not yet dawn. With shaking hands, he tidied his bed, then stood bare-foot on the stone floor.

Just breathe, he told himself. Metal clashing against stone echoed through his mind.

Slowly, deeply, the breath flowed through. Lungs expanding and contracting with a practiced breath, a breath that pushed everything away. The shaking eased, his mind emptied, the tension fled with the outward breath. He felt the cool stone beneath his calloused feet, the way his body balanced on each toe, on each heel. Then, Cary raised his hands and began.

Push. Pull. Slide. Breathe.

His body shifted. He stepped to the side; the weight upon each foot balanced proportionately. Hands snapped out. The tension released. Shift again. His body danced the morning routine, stepping in, out, aside, around.

Cary's arms fell in a controlled descent back to his starting position. To finish, he inhaled deeply.

New light in his room dimmed.

The scent of roses caught in his nose.

A scream jarred him again.

You must ask him, the voice in his head said. Fine, I will. Cary gave in. He'd visit Dmitri and put the voice to rest. He threw on his clothes and boots, and burst out of his rooms.

Cary pulled up short at the kitchen and immediately straightened. A hulking figure in black with bright red hair loomed and made the over-sized Household kitchen seem small. His statuesque partner in grey made the room seem dumpy.

"Just making some tea, Master Cary." Denis, Cary's steward and lone remaining live-in Artistovin servant, had a kettle in hand and was about to place it in one of the two stone hearths. Denis making tea in his dressing gown was usual, but Cary could see the precarious dignity in his steward's eyes diminishing by the moment. "Would you like some Mayflour Bake?" Denis knew better than to offer it. Having the two nobles in his kitchen meant two things: the pretense was up and something was afoot.

Everett Fraaml adjusted his belt and bulk causing the various weapons, including a Warrior-weighted sword, to clank. "About time you woke up."

Dominic Roan flashed his famous stare Cary's way, "We were just about to come and get you." A wicked smile dashed across his face.

Cary pushed his racing heart down and attempted to regain his breath. "I just woke up." He pressed a hand against the stone of the kitchen wall, the dream once again banging inside his head. He whispered to Denis, "It's okay. I can take it from here." As Denis placed the kettle over the fire, its handle broke loose. Again.

Water splashed and sizzled in the growing fire. Cary leapt to grab a rag from the far side of the kitchen, but Denis had already plucked the kettle from the fire with the end of his dressing gown. "I got it," Denis said and set it on the stone floor. Cary tossed the rag on the table as he returned to the hearth, ever aware of the two pairs of eyes upon his back, and with sheer will and manual strength, pushed the handle back into place. He handed it back to Denis who set it to boil.

"What are you doing here?" Cary asked crossing his arms as Denis retreated from the kitchen.

"Got anything to eat?" Everett asked.

"You're kidding me." Then the daylight faded and the room went black. A cry rang out. Cary groaned as he attempted to push back the remnants of the nightmare.

"Hey, are you okay?" the voice was far away.

Metal clanged against stone again. Then as quickly as it started, the darkness retreated and daylight streamed in through the windows, illuminating the dust specks dancing in the air. Everett's freckled face loomed in front of him. His hazel eyes seemed like beacons in the menacing blackness. Cary clutched his chest, as if trying to fill the abyss of loss. With a deep breath, Cary re-established himself and began again, "So what are you doing here at the crack of dawn?"

Everett stepped back to his original position, swung a glance to Dominic, then cleared his throat. "We...uh,...we were wondering how you were doing, is all."

Dominic, however, took over smoothly. "Your stableman seems to be absent. We had to take care of our own horses." He tugged his grey trousers and sat gracefully at the old wooden table, swiping half-heartedly at imagined crumbs atop the table.

Cary rolled his eyes and pulled a dish of Mayflour Bake from the cupboard. He slipped it into the hearth beneath the kettle. Cary tried again, "I haven't seen you since spring and you show up at dawn, harassing my staff. What's up?"

Everett opened his mouth then closed it. Then he glanced at Dominic. Dominic was drilling his stare into the old wooden table.

"Come on, you two. Something stinks in here and you cannot blame me. I had a bath yesterday."

Cary stepped up to his flame-haired friend and poked a finger into the solid shoulder. "Spill it, Fraaml. Now."

Terror filled Everett's eyes. Just as his lips parted, Dominic spoke up, "Fine. This is an intervention."

Everett backed off as Cary stepped up to the table, "Excuse me?"

"An intervention."

"And into what are you intervening?" Dominic held Cary's stare, an old battle of wills.

Everett pointed to the hearth, "Kettle's boiling."

It wasn't until Cary pulled himself away from the table that Dominic spoke. "You."

"Me," Cary glanced back.

"Look at yourself, Cary." Cary went to the cupboard and pulled out a canister of tea. He threw a handful into an awaiting teapot. "You look like you were dragged across your fields by a runaway horse." Cary placed the teapot with three mugs onto the worn work table in front of Dominic. "You're still wearing the same grey tunic that was fitted for you, what, three years ago?"

Cary took the rag he'd retrieved before and plucked the fragile kettle from the fire. "Look. We know things haven't been easy. But you really need some help."

Cary turned. Dominic's pale skin was framed by black hair and only made his green eyes all the more intense. "I'm doing fine," and sloshed boiling water into the teapot.

"Cary," Everett said, "You're a warrior, not a farmer."

Cary set the kettle on a ledge beside the hearth then returned to the hearth to fetch the Mayflour Bake. "Says who? Did you see my crop this year? I'm going to have gourds, tomatoes, AND corn." He and Denis had worked so hard this year. Farming was new to them both, but they'd learned so much. The new corn crop and increased yield in gourds and tomatoes was a clear indication of their efforts.

Dominic rounded on him, "And you're going to live on vegetables all winter?"

"No," Cary said as he sat the hot dish on the table. "We'll sell some of it in Mangshek for beef. And I fish too."

Everett plucked a fork from the bowl of cutlery on the counter then sat at the table, "You're not a fisherman, either." He paused before digging in. "Are you sure you don't want some?" Cary shook his head, pushing the rising bile from his throat. There weren't too many things he hated more than Mayflour Bake. "You might need your energy."

"I'll stick with tea, thanks."

Cary took a seat across from Everett and Dominic and poured them all tea. " Look, we came by to treat you."

Cary paused, smelling a rat once again. ""Treat me?"" He could feel the glance exchanged between Dominic and Everett.

"Yeah, you know, a nice diversion." Bits of Bake flew across the table as Everett chewed through his words.

Cary sipped his tea, "I don't have time for a diversion. I have a Household to maintain. I have a harvest to bring in. And I still have a few dozen fish to catch and dry before it gets too cold to swim. If you really want to help, you can chop some firewood."

Dominic pulled a satchel from the belt of his pristine grey tunic. It landed with a resounding clang against the table and echoed in the old stone kitchen. "There are other ways to maintain a Household."

With a fairly accurate estimation, Cary knew that the satchel contained enough silver to get him and Denis through the winter with a bit of fat on their bones. Unlike last winter. He might even be able to fix the kettle.

Dominic turned the full intensity of his stare on Cary. "One day is all we ask. We'll go to the City, visit my tailor, get you groomed, fed, and indulge a bit of friendly camaraderie. We'll return you home a happy, sated man by nightfall." Cary suddenly felt a tempting reprieve from the screaming and the darkness of his nightmare.

He tore his eyes from the satchel and swung his gaze between the two nobles. "Why? Why now and why are you offering so much for so little? What's in it for you?"

The silence that fell spoke volumes to Cary. Just as he was about to rise from the table in disgust, Dominic's hand grabbed his arm. "It is overdue." The tone in Dominic's voice caught Cary off-guard. He sounded sincere. There was sadness, regret in his green eyes. "We should have done this a long time ago."

Cary pulled his arm out of Dominic's grasp. "If I didn't know better, I'd say that you were trying to buy back my trust."

"That was a mistake, Cary," Dominic turned away before Cary could read his expression. "We shouldn't have put you in that position, especially knowing how you felt about the immigrants."

"Not 'felt', Dominic. I still feel that way. And beating up anybody for sport, not just immigrants, is wrong."

"Enough, you two." Everett paused from his eating and looked at both of them. Cary shifted, suddenly self-conscious. "Rehashing the past doesn't get anybody anywhere. Look, we're worried about you, Cary. You look horrible." Cary fiddled with one of his stained, frayed cuffs. "When Dominic and I come round to visit, you're off ploughing, or planting, or fixing something. You're running yourself ragged. Heck, you just about fainted earlier. We want to help," then he resumed his attention on his food.

Dominic leaned back and downed his tea. "It really isn't much, you know."

Cary glanced at the bag of silver. "Sounds like a lot."

Everett scraped the dish clean with his fork, "I had some savings."

"And when my father found out about our little plan, he pitched in," Dominic smiled.

"Mine too," Everett pushed the empty dish aside and belched loudly before downing his tea in one gulp.

"So you're paying me to spend the day with you."

"Yup."

Cary tried not to think of the amount of silver involved in this scenario; it scared him. "Okay, if that's the bribe then who's funding this little 'intervention'?"

Dominic's smile turned wickedly. "We are, of course."

Cary glanced once again at his worn sleeves, his dirty fingernails, felt the tightness of his tunic across his shoulders, the way his trousers rode up uncomfortably. He tried not to look at the cooling kettle by the hearth. His Household, the home of his family for five generations, was falling apart, stone by stone. "It's not that bad."

"Cary," Dominic's hand landed on his arm again, "we didn't want to tell you this, but you do stink." Everett snorted back a chuckle.

Cary glanced behind at the kitchen entrance. He caught sight of Denis' housecoat peeking out from behind the wall. "One day?"

"That's it," Dominic said already basking in the glory of victory.

"That's all," Everett finished, eyes flashing with hope.

Familiar feelings of shared adventure welled inside Cary's heart. It had been a long time.

Cary let himself smile finally, "One day."

CHAPTER THREE

I t had been three years, three months, and twenty-one days. She was finally starting to make progress, to live a normal life, to feel safe. She was beginning to like life again. It had been a long time, patience, and a lot of emotional ups and downs, but life felt like it was finally her own again.

"I can do this." Launching herself from her bedroom, Simone strode through the empty house and picked up the phone. "Hi, this is Simone Larken. I need to get in to see Beryl as soon as possible."

Thursday. Practically two whole days. Two days was a long time. Time enough for her mind to work itself into overdrive. She wrote her appointment on the wall calendar, scolding the way her shaking hand wouldn't hold the pen right. It was a week away from the seventeenth, circled in red ink. A week was even longer. And that was if her father kept to his schedule. It was a long time to be alone.

Had she been deluding herself? Had she been able to feel safe only because J.D. had moved away? Would everything crumble now that he was back?

Then she picked up the phone again, "Hi, Michael. Yeah, all is okay. Any word from my dad? Okay. Hey, do you know the Colemans? They moved away about three years ago. They had a son my age. I think the father was a truck driver, I don't know what the mother did. Yeah, pretty nomadic bunch. Would Marty know them? Yeah, that'd be great. Okay. Talk to you tomorrow."

Why had he come into the coffee shop today? Was it by chance? Did he know she worked there?

She disconnected then dialed the only taxi service in town, "Hi Mr. Decker.....No, Dean and Sally drove me home tonight.....Yeah, they are nice. Can you pick me up at nine-thirty tomorrow morning? ... Just the lunch rush, yeah.....Thanks. I'll have sandwiches for you tomorrow."

Then the thought struck her. Hard.

What if J.D. knew where she lived?

Knotton's Shallow was a small town of nearly six thousand people. Everybody knew everyone else's business. It wouldn't be hard to figure out where someone lived. Even if that person lived outside of town, along a long gravel road, deep in the forest.

The old fear coursed through her body, unleashed its possessiveness grew once again. She ran through the small house and dug into her father's closet. From inside its depths, she pulled out a long case and laid it on the floor. She opened it. And was instantly disappointed. "Of course. Why would he need a handgun living in the forest?" A .333 caliber rifle and a 12-guage shotgun lay in the case. She slammed it shut. She'd need to go shopping tomorrow.

"I ordered a tuna on sourdough. This is ham and swiss."

Simone blinked, befuddled. "Sorry. I'll get you a tuna right away." She retreated and ran headlong into Karen coming out of the kitchen. Ham and swiss went one way, the plate went the other. The crash momentarily silenced the rumble of the lunch crowd, then applause let out.

"What has got into you?" Karen, the owner of the Only Cup, whispered as they both dropped to the floor to gather up the mess.

"I'm sorry." Simone threw the larger plate pieces into the garbage and plucked the broom from beside the beverage cooler. Just then, the phone rang. Simone grabbed it as Karen took the broom from her hand, "Only Cup."

The low thunder of the lunch crowd had returned to normal. Simone strained to hear a voice from the phone. "Hello? I can't hear you. Please speak up." Still nothing. "I'm sorry but I can't hear you. We're very busy right now. Please call back again after lunch." She replaced the receiver then dove into the kitchen to make the missing tuna sandwich.

Karen strode up beside her and placed some empty dishes into the dishwasher. "That was a ham and swiss."

Simone spread mayonnaise onto freshly baked sourdough bread, "It was supposed to be tuna on sour."

Karen lingered momentarily, wiping the sweat from her brow, and tucking a greying lock of hair back into her braid. "Are you okay?"

"Yeah," Simone scooped tuna from a bowl, slapped it onto the bread, then returned the bowl to the fridge, "Just having an off-day."

Karen swung open the storage room door and drew out a box of sugar packets. "Didn't think I'd live to see the day."

"Ha, ha," the sentiment left her mouth as the knife cut through the new tuna sandwich and her thumb. Blood spurt across the bread and cutting board. "Oh shit."

Karen put down the box and sided up, "Yup, when you do something, you do it good, kiddo. Here." Dishpan hands turned on the cold water tap and pulled Simone's thumb under the running water. Karen's long brown braid swung over her shoulder as she retrieved the first aid kit.

"Sorry. I'm a bit of a mess today."

With a gentle, deft touch, Karen pulled Simone's hand from the water, dried it, and encased her thumb in gaze and tape. "It happens to the best of us, kiddo. There. Now don't take this off until tomorrow night."

"Yes, ma'am."

"Ugh. You make me feel so old when you call me 'ma'am'." The forty-something woman scrunched her face and stuck out her tongue.

"Yes, ma'am," Simone couldn't help grinning.

Karen pointed, "Out. Take the sugar. I'll make the sandwich." Simone was halfway out the swinging kitchen doors when Karen called out, "Who was on the phone?"

It had happened so quickly, the phone call had slipped from her mind. "Don't know," Simone said as her mind slowly recalled the event, "couldn't hear."

Karen nodded as her hands flew over the sandwich construction. But as Simone exited the kitchen and entered the lunch milieu, she now remembered. She also remembered that she'd never before *not* been able to hear a phone call during the lunch rush. A frightening scenario began to form in her head.

A few minutes after 3pm, Simone emerged from the back door of the coffee shop, two-day old sandwiches in her pack, and a mission on her mind. First stop, the sporting goods store.

Rick of Rick's Sporting Goods, dressed in the ubiquitous plaid and jeans of rural life, stepped up to the glass display case and whispered, "Simone, what's going on?"

Her palms were sweaty and she drew them back from the glass counter. "I'd just feel safer with a gun."

"You know I can't sell you one without a permit and your dad's permit is only for long barreled guns. Besides there are safer ways to defend yourself. Here. How about bear spray?"

She held the canister offered. It was the size and weight of a large can of hairspray. It had a lever instead of a button release. "I've heard stories about this stuff. Gotta watch the wind direction, distance, etc."

"Yeah, that's true," Rick said pulling at his salt and pepper beard. "But if you're looking to use it on people, I don't think you'd be in a situation where wind and long distances would be an issue."

Simone conceded that Rick had a point. She bought the bear spray. "Outta curiosity, have you got a taser gun?"

From Rick's Sporting Goods, she set a bearing for the senior's home. In Knotton's Shallow, there was only one senior's home. It was called the Shangri La Lodge.

The quickest route from downtown to the Lodge was cutting through the elementary schoolyard. A long bushy area skirted the backside of the school grounds, and a trail ran through it. The trail ensured that she would be safe from little kids should school let out before she made it across the school grounds. Breaching the forest far enough to reach this trail was the epitome of bravery back when she'd been a student here. This bit of forest was a dark musty place full of shadows and goblins and things with claws.

Simone looked from side to side, the trail winding through the trees. She could nearly see the edge of the schoolyard on her left and the chain-link fence bordering residences to her right. All in all, it was probably a thirty-foot wide strip of bush that ran the length of the school yard. So little forest and so much imagination.

A twig snapped. She spun around. A squirrel sprang across the path and darted up an aspen. The wind momentarily picked up and tossed the treetops around.

Simone waited. Watched. Listened. She was alone. She knew it. She didn't feel it.

Did J.D. know her routes, her schedule, her habits? Did he care? Was he following her? How did he know where she worked? When did he get back? She pulled the canister of bear spray from her pack.

He had left. His family had moved shortly after it happened. She'd heard, but she needed to make sure. She'd checked around. People told her that he'd moved to the city. It was all too good to be true. He was gone and she was safe. For three years. Until yesterday. Simone couldn't help but feel that she'd been thrown into an inevitable river, forced to ride the current that would only bring more unwelcomeness.

The school buzzer rang. Simone jumped. Kids erupted from the school like ants bursting from a collapsing anthill. Three fifteen, she thought and picked up her pace.

At #15, Simone knocked. She waited politely but fidgeted. The smell of pumpkin pie mingled with old people smell. Simone looked up and down the hall. The corridor was poorly lit this time of day, with daylight streaming in through open apartment doors, shadows growing dark in between. A TV blared from an apartment further down. Simone glanced down the hall again. Someone was coming towards her. Someone young. Someone male. He was wearing scrubs.

"Mrs. Decker's in the piano room. Do you know where that is?" He was a new nurse, tall, with a mop of dark curly hair. His smile had crooked teeth.

Simone nodded then spun off toward the east.

A group of seniors, two men and three women, sat in a corner room with two walls of windows overlooking a garden. An upright piano stood against the wall to the left as Simone walked into the room. Simone recognized one of the men and two women. She stood to the side and waited to catch someone's eye.

Mr. Blane in his cavalier red blazer and winning smile notice Simone right away. "Hello, darling. Come for another visit or the pumpkin pie? It is Wednesday."

One of the women turned around. Liliana Decker wore her hair in an old-fashioned way. She had long silver hair and wore it up in a loose bun. A shawl always hung about her shoulders with a cameo pinned at her throat. She was a lady out of her era. "Of course not, Steven." Her smile widened, "Simone has come to visit me." Mrs. Decker flashed a wise eye at Simone and seemingly surmised everything Simone had experienced within the past 24 hours. "Bring my chair, Simone. Steven, help me up."

They said their partings and Simone pushed Mrs. Decker from the piano room. The overwhelming need to run to safety itched at Simone's feet. "We will get there in good time, my dear," Mrs. Decker said. "No need to rush."

Simone pushed the chair toward the window in #15, spun it around, then returned to close the door. "So, my dear, are you going to talk to me or am I going to have to threaten you with that torturous concoction they call pumpkin pie?"

Simone dropped her backpack and sank to the edge of the bed. Slowly, the shaking began. It had been lurking, waiting since J.D. had left the shop. It had been waiting for Simone to let down her guard. If it had the space, she knew the shaking would take over. She pushed it down.

"I see," Mrs. Decker said. "I trust you brought the top."

Simone unzipped her backpack and pulled out the old wooden top. Her fingers caressed the smooth wood, almost as if they could sink into the organic tree-flesh. There were times she thought she could hear the pulse of the tree, long dead and carved into a hundred toy tops.

Without a word, Simone pulled off her jacket and sat cross-legged at the small coffee table. She cleared off the magazines and crosswords puzzles then positioned the top, ready to spin. Simone closed her eyes and took a deep breath. "Ready?" Simone nodded. "Time." The word was spoken softly, as if urging an old horse down a new path. Simone spun the top, then sat back and watched.

The shaking had become her life before she'd started seeing her therapist, Beryl. About a year ago, the shaking had turned into a panic attack. The adrenaline spike and fear found Simone running the six miles from her home into town. It was like she'd been sleepwalking while awake; she had no control over her body. The fear had completely taken over and all she could do was watch. Finally she came to her senses in the middle of Knotton's Shallow. She'd called Mr. Decker and, like before, he hadn't asked any questions. Except one. "Do you mind if we stop in and see my wife first? I haven't seen her yet today." Simone walked into #15, curled up on the bed, and didn't move. No amount of apple pie, blueberry pie, or peach cobbler could get her to move. Only the top had piqued her interest.

The world ceased to exist when the top spun. There was no time. There was only Simone and the top.

"It is an act of meditation," Beryl had said. Mrs. Decker, however, said something different. "It's mind over matter, my dear. If you feel you can do it, you can."

Then the game began.

"Seventeen seconds. Again." Simone grabbed the top and spun it again.

"Twenty-once seconds. Again."

"Sixteen seconds. Not good. Again." Mrs. Decker clicked and reset the stopwatch.

The average over the year, minus the false starts, was 18.67 seconds. The longest time was 23 seconds. Simone fought for 24 seconds.

"Don't fight. Breathe. Again." The stopwatch clicked.

The top spun. It wavered, skipped, fell. She spun it again.

Breathe.

It spun, wavered.

Breathe. Just breathe.

The top spun. And spun. The spots where paint had flecked off the old top blurred and the yellow stripe around the middle became whole.

Breathe.

The age and flaws of the top faded; it became a new red top with a yellow stripe humming its resonant song on the table.

Breathe.

The table vibrated with the hum. The hum worked its way into her hand, up her arm. Soon she felt the vibration of the spinning top in her teeth. She heard the hum, felt the hum throughout her body. There was only her and the hum.

"I thought I might find you here."

Simone started. The top skipped and jumped from the table.

"Oh, really Louis," Mrs. Decker exasperated. She clicked the stopwatch and tucked it into her pocket.

Simone blinked and came back into herself, heart pounding frantically. The stillness of the moment faded. As reality returned, she wondered what exactly had happened.

Louis Decker bumbled into the room, his nylon jacket rustling, and kissed his wife's offered cheek. He pushed back his hat and sat upon the bed. "I had a break. Thought I'd stop in."

Simone finally turned her eyes to him. He was looking at her. Dark blonde five o'clock shadow lined his face and peppered tufts of hair sprang out from underneath his hat. Salt had gathered in the corners of his eyes from his afternoon nap. He had a ketchup stain on his blue checked shirt. "I'm going to go to the library." Simone breathed reality back into her brain. "Call you for a ride home?"

Mr. Decker's sagging face bunched up into a generous smile, "Sure. The forestry conference is keeping me busy, but I'll fit you in."

Simone pulled her backpack across the bed and pulled from it a plastic bag. "Two ham and a chicken salad."

Aging hands pulled at the loose knot and the taxi driver looked inside. "Yum. Always get lots of ham but not much chicken salad. Thanks."

As Simone ducked behind the table to pluck the top from where it had disappeared, Mrs. Decker tugged her sleeve and whispered, "Twelve minutes 34 seconds."

With the top grasped in her hand, Simone stepped back. Liliana Decker looked her square in the eye.

Twelve minutes 34 seconds.

Not seconds. Minutes.

What the hell had happened?

Chapter Four

Cary had been washed, scrubbed, soaked, tugged, measured, and appraised by the time the twin Juno suns were high in the sky.

Deep within the City walls, the three young men were lounging around a table laden with cold meats, cheeses, fruits the likes Cary had never seen, and an assortment of prepared dishes from which steam was still rising. Cary was about to suggest that they return to the tailor to remeasure his expanded waist when Dominic broke the comfortable silence. "You know what we could do, just for kicks? Drop in at Trium. Surprise everyone."

Cary felt the bottom drop out of his day. His gut trembled and the voice in the back of his head grumbled softly. Everett's fork had paused midway. "Dominic, nothing's new there. What's the point?" Then Everett's fork continued its journey, plunging the slice of beef into his mouth.

"The point, Everett," Dominic threw down the apple core he'd been finishing off, "is that our Cary hasn't seen his friends in years. It'll do him good to know there's people beyond his Household walls who care about him."

Cary's gut tightened. "You know how I feel about Trium, Dom."

Dominic turned his fiery gaze to Cary. "You've become a recluse. You have friends. You have colleagues. And you need help. Remember, this is an intervention. We're here to help you."

"I don't want that kind of help."

"Despite what Everett said, Trium has changed. You should drop round and see for yourself."

"I can live without that sort of information."

Dominic leaned over the table toward Cary and locked his gaze. "Maybe you're afraid."

The voice in the back of Cary's head grumbled again. *Are you afraid?*

He heard this voice often. Mostly when he was locked into the depths of his father's wing-backed chair, watching the sky darken around his home. In the emptiness of his Front Room, Cary could feel the first steps of the enemy's horses upon the sandy shores six miles east; he could hear the clang of swords as battle began; and he could feel each body fall and hit Juno's soil. Fear kept the cast iron frying pan in Cary's hand as he waited for the Outerworld to once again burst into his Household and rip away everything he held dear.

"I'm not afraid of Trium," he said.

Dominic and Everett exchanged a familiar glance. "Then show us."

Trium Hall sat nestled within forested hills, about ten miles south of the City, near the eastern coast. Various shades of grey stone shone in the morning light. A pillared entrance was dwarfed on either side by large, arched windows overlooking the formal gardens. Practice rooms were in the anterior with study rooms in the center and living quarters above. Stables, pastures and Greens were to the east of the main building, training grounds to the west. The rear and front of Trium were meticulous formal gardens containing ornamental as well as medicinal herbs and plants.

Trium Hall was home to Juno's Mentors and these Mentors trained the Warriors of Juno's army.

Shouldn't be here, Cary thought as he assessed his surroundings.

A younger cohort of Sons was out in the arena practicing horsemanship. Horses trotted, galloped, walked, all crisscrossing the grounds with Sons atop; some were seated backwards, kneeling, some standing, some on one foot. Though it had been one of Cary's favorite lessons, he knew how difficult it was. "As the sword is a weapon so is the ability to ride a horse," he remembered Petri say. Horse and rider must be one: they must be Companions.

A memory flashed. Immigrant boys lying on the ground. Beaten and bloodied. Surrounded by Sons. Laughing.

I should not be here, he thought again.

Tailored slate grey tunics adorned every well-groomed Son, younger and older. The white cord wound around their shoulder displaying the Council's acknowledgement of their training. Cary distinctly remembered the day he had ripped the cords from his tunic. They had, for the umpteenth time, caught on the wagon hitch as he hooked up their old plow horse. He had torn them off in a rage. In truth, he had been looking for a reason to remove them.

Cary dismounted, removed Marcus' bridle and slung it from the saddle, then left his Companion to wander the grounds he knew so well.

His every sense screamed rebellion, a need to escape. Why was he here? Maybe he was afraid of Trium.

The accusatory voice in his head was silent.

A tall figure in white robes appeared from around the far corner of Trium. Grand Master Sesmon's grin was obvious from a distance and painful up close. Cary felt ten years old again and guilty of lighting fire to the armory shed.

"It's good to see you again after such a long absence, young Aristovin." His grin grew. "Would seem that you are not above your lessons as some of the Sons had thought."

The old man drew closer. His breath smelt of Hagwort. Did he chew the herb just to make the Sons cringe? "Perhaps we'll have to see if, and what, you've learned in your absence from Trium." Long white cloaks fluttered as the man turned and strode away with a grace unnatural for his age. Whatever his age was.

Cary stood rooted, shocked. Then turned on the two Sons behind him. "What is going on?"

This time Dominic and Everett didn't mask their motive. "It's your Test today, Cary."

"My Test? But they can't....it wasn't announced.... I didn't see..."

It was too late. Practice had stopped. Younger Sons were gathering around, whispering. And then, from around the far eastern corner, more Sons appeared. The latter ones were older, and their presence demonstrated the entire compliment of Sons at Trium. Their pace slowed instantly. They recognized him, and he them.

Cary caught the faces of some of the older Sons. Would they beat him the way they beat those two immigrant boys? He didn't put it past them. The older Sons were filtering through the crowd of younger Sons, measuring their paces. Some held his eye, but some refused to meet his gaze.

Cary shuddered. Yet for another reason.

He registered eighty-seven Sons; a far cry from the hundreds that should have stocked the roomy building. Juno's perpetual enemy was slowing laying waste to the country's army. Ten years ago, there had been two hundred and forty-seven Sons at Trium. Cary still remembered how the halls had echoed with empty rooms even then. How could they hope to continue to defend their country when resources were so thin?

Cary continued to scan the crowd of onlookers. There were no training Warriors and no Mentors other than Sesmon. If this was truly a Test, there should be witnesses. His potential peers should be present to bear witness to his transition from Son to Warrior.

Where was everyone?

No, Cary wasn't afraid, not really. If he was afraid of anything at Trium, it was precisely this -- being manipulated. This is what Trium represented to him: a political game of manipulation played out amongst the nobility.

He turned back to Dominic and Everett. But he would find no help there. Dominic wore the grey training tunic with pride and was following in his father's footsteps. His father was Count Roan, Commander of strategy, and one of a triad of Warriors that had kept Juno safe for a generation. There had only ever been one path for Dominic, and Dominic believed there was only one path for Cary, son of Lord Cale Aristovin, the late Commander in Chief.

Everett, however, seemed to shrink from Cary's eyes. It was no wonder that even though Everett had been Tested and wore the black tunic of battle, he'd yet to see actual battle. "I'm sorry," Everett mouthed as he and Dominic backed away into the crowd of Sons.

Think, Cary, think, he scolded himself. It was his owned damned fault he was in this mess. He should have known something was up when Dominic and Everett showed up in his kitchen. He should have known this day was too good. Why didn't he see it? Think!

Cary turned, looking for an escape. A wall of grey uniforms had formed a circle around him, all eyes on him. A Warrior in black leather armour broke through the wall of Sons. A Warrior-weighted sword hung from his hip. He carried another in his hand.

Leather creaking, Xan strode two paces and stopped. He held out a sword to Cary.

Cary groaned. He should have known this day was too good. There was only one reason he hadn't seen the rot in the apple: Fate. Some said Fate didn't exist. Cary knew this wasn't true. He'd been Her plaything since he was eight. She was more than an absent deity to Cary. To him, She was a nemesis. He could smell the tampering, the weaving. It was more vivid than the roses from his dream. And the only thing Cary, or anyone, could do when Fate intervened was take matters into his own hands.

Cary shook his head. "I walked away from Trium, from the training, and the battle. I refuse the Test."

Xan smiled and plunged the sword into the earth. "You are here. That is acceptance," he spread his hands. Then he withdrew his own sword from its scabbard and started toward Cary.

Fate's bowels, he thought. Think, Cary, think!

"If you can survive your Test and first battle, then you are worthy of being a Warrior." These words were burned into every Son's brain. "If you can survive" were the words burning in Cary's brain. He had no intention of dying today.

There is more than one way to kill an Outerworlder. The voice sprang from the depths of his mind.

More than one way. Another way.

Cary ground his teeth then turned from Xan, looking for another way. Locking eyes with every Son he could see, Cary tallied what he saw: doubt, fright, awe, expectation, confusion. Then, as the moment stretched and Cary stood, his height drawn up and his eyes drilling into them, he began to see it.

The waiting. Despite the undersized and stained training uniform, the gauntness of his face and frame, the Sons of Trium Hall were waiting for orders from him, their Commander in Chief.

Cary finished his breath and bellowed, "Four rows! Watch your spacing! Berringa's Compliment, Levels One through Five. Begin your counting on my mark."

Cary clasped his hands behind his back and let his feet feel the earth, feel the tension grow as the Sons stood staring at him, not sure if they believed what they were seeing, hearing. All at once, the perimeter of grey tunics ordered themselves into four rows, shoulder length apart, stretching the length of the training grounds. Cary called "Mark" early to increase the confusion and then waded into the sea of grey tunics.

"One!" the ranks called. Arms lifted and slowly the Sons fell into unison and began counting through the movements of the drill.

Stalling was surviving and he needed time to think. He'd just bought himself a 134-count span of time. Skirting around the first couple rows to the back then swerving to the end of the first row again, Cary fell into count and waited for Xan. And a plan.

"Seven!" The Sons called as the ranks spun and kicked. Their feet landed, they took a neutral fighting stance, then continued to Level Two. "One!"

A Son stumbled, third row, fourth from the far end.

"Two!" The Sons stepped forward and shot both hands out from their chests.

Out of the corner of his eye, Cary saw the armoured Warrior walk cautiously between the ranks as Sons performed the maneuvers.

"Five!" Cary stepped back to the second row as the Sons stepped back, ducked and spun on their knees. Before the Sons stood again, Cary grabbed the shoulder cords of a blond Son nearest him and broke them off. To Cary's sour delight, the Son did not break his concentration. There was a slight flinch but the Son continued, standing, then blocking, "Eight!"

Using the landscape was a natural and effective defense if the enemy wasn't familiar with the territory. If he could use the Sons as his landscape, Cary figured he might just be able to corner Xan and walk away from all this without lifting a finger. *A victory without fighting is the best victory.* Inside Cary's mind, the pieces of a strategy fell into place.

And it was beautifully simple. Now, all he had to do was move around and alter some of the landscape.

The Sons feet hit the ground together. Along the second row, Cary kept pace with the Sons' drill. The Sons turned on the three-count, and he heard Dominic's voice, "You're nuts!"

They turned to face front again and Cary whispered back to his friend, "And I have you to thank."

"How long to you expect to keep this up?"

"I don't know."

Dominic shook his head, "Typical," then, on a ten-count, threw a left hook and right undercut. Cary continued down to the end of the row. He heard some confusion with some of the younger Sons. Good, he thought. As the levels ascended, more and more of the younger Sons would not be able to keep up.

Cary heard the cordless Son at the end of the row gasp as Xan pulled him up from the eight-count lunge of the end of Level Three. Cary stepped toward the third row. However, his foot didn't move as expected. He stumbled then went backwards but caught himself and stepped back to keep up with the forward step of the ranks. Drawing himself up, he fell into count again and faced the saboteur.

If Fate was Cary's intangible nemesis, Langrid Tolonel was his nemesis incarnate.

The golden haired Son smirked as his fist shot forward and his foot kicked up, aimed at Cary's face.

Xan turned and approached Cary's direction.

"You can't avoid it, Aristovin," the Tolonel hissed. Cary turned from Langrid's smirk and fell into unison with the third row.

"Fourteen!" The Sons shouted, approaching the end of Level Four.

Langrid spat, "You always were a coward, just like your father." A neutral stance was reached and Level Five of Berringa's Compliment began. Amidst the confusion of the younger cohorts, the older Sons jumped, kicked and fell back to attention. All but Cary.

During the jump kick, Cary felt the ball of Langrid's foot push into his back. He hit the ground awkwardly and hard, his trousers and tunic splitting wide at their seams. So much for camouflage.

Xan halted in front of him. Cary stood, attempting to hold himself up to the Warrior's stern appraisal. An uncomfortable silence grew and Cary became increasingly aware of his bare backside gleaming in the late afternoon suns. Finally Xan called out, "Back to practice." The Sons broke from ranks. Xan remained face-to-face with Cary as the Sons dispersed. "Follow me," he said to Cary.

Inside Trium Hall, their soft-soled boots tread quietly across marbled floor mosaics. Xan's leather armour creaked. They passed tapestries of great battles and portraits of Warriors generations old.

The door to Sesmon's study creaked as Xan pushed it open. Suns' light shone red through the stained glass window overlooking the back Greens. Sesmon's white robes rippled like pools of blood in the odd light as he stood looking over the back Greens.

The Warrior stopped several paces from the Grand Master's elaborately carved desk and awaited his orders. "Thank you for your cooperation, Lord Menk'len." Xan bowed curtly at his dismissal and left without so much as a glance in Cary's direction.

The door clicked softly.

He was alone now. To hear the verdict from Old Man Sesmon. "You will not join the Warrior sect but will you join the battle?"

Cary frowned. Sesmon turned from the window and walked around the desk. Silence stretched as the Mentor came to stand directly in front of Cary and wait. Cary didn't answer; he was struck by the feeling that the Mentor was searching the air around them for an answer to a much larger question.

"There are other ways to fight than with a sword," the Mentor continued. "This is something usually not practiced until after the first battle. The question is will you exercise those ways against the Outerworld?" Sesmon broke his icy glare and returned to his viewpoint at the window.

"The Test of your convictions has not released you from your obligation, Cary Aristovin. If anything, it has demonstrated all the traits instilled in you here, at Trium Hall. The Council has not given up on you and I certainly have not. You *will* be brought to battle, with or without a sword in your hand." Sesmon turned to his desk and opened a drawer. He withdrew a small silken pouch and delivered it to Cary's hand, "You may now leave and be well, *Lord* Aristovin."

Cary shut the door to Sesmon's offices and stood with the small cloth package clutched in his hand.

He didn't want this. To Fate's bowels, he really didn't want this. He had tried to reject it, tried to turn away from events, but it seemed it was all beyond his control. He was just a pawn in Fate's weaving.

And now he could add Sesmon's comment to the mix: 'Brought to the battle regardless'. The whole thing really made no sense. He wouldn't fight and he wouldn't take his father's place as Commander in Chief.

How did they expect him to engage in battle if not to fight? Would he be dragged to the battlefield, stood in front of the Outerworld, and made to watch as his comrades fought and died around him? Would he allow himself to die without lifting a hand to defend himself? What did they expect of him? What did he expect of himself?

There was so much more going on here than he could see, and he resented everything about it. It reeked of manipulation, of being played, and of not having control over his own bloody life.

Bile rose in his throat and a bitter rage began to course through his body.

Shoving the silk package containing a gold Crest into his trouser pocket, Cary walked down the corridor and toward home.

CHAPTER FIVE

Twelve minutes and thirty-four seconds.

It was too much to believe. Was Mrs. Decker lying? No. Simone wiped the thought from her mind as she passed through the nursing home doors. Why would she lie?

To get your mind off what is bugging you, Simone thought. And that was something that Lilianna Decker would do. This brought Simone to a dead halt at the curb.

She pulled the top from her jacket pocket. In those spinning moments, whether they were seconds or minutes, Simone felt peace. But more than that. It hit her that she felt rested, relaxed. It felt like J.D. hadn't come into the shop yesterday, that there'd been no strange phone call today. It even felt like she'd slept last night. If she could spin the top longer, more frequently, would J.D. disappear from her life all together?

Simone stuffed the top back in her pocket and struck out back across the elementary schoolyard, toward downtown. If she could stretch the seconds into minutes, why not minutes into hours? Was it possible? She wanted to believe. The twelve minutes and thirty-four seconds of peace was fading. But its affects lingered in her body, urging her to trust. To hope.

The library had grown smaller and less adventurous, much like the schoolyard forest. A small town library only got so much use and Simone figured she used it enough for at least a quarter of the town's population. She knew the place of each book by sight rather than by its catalogue number. Today, the mothers and their tots had already cleared out. School-aged kids would be showing up soon.

An internet search found that 12 minutes, 34 seconds wasn't long at all for a top to spin. The world record stretched into hours. Simone smiled to herself. There was hope.

She next wound her way to the New Age section, fingering her way along the spines, looking for something on meditation. Voices burst into the quiet, bouncing off the high ceiling, then abruptly hushed. Simone froze. These weren't little kid voices. They were much older. Familiarity teased at her mind.

She peeked through the shelves at the newcomers. Two guys and a girl. Teenagers. Freshmen, by the looks of them. Simone relaxed, but continued to peer. They'd picked a table by the bay windows and were spilling out their binders and texts. The girl had long brown hair with sparkling ruby barrettes. Her smile flashed of lip-gloss, her nails were trim and painted. When she faced each of the boys, they smiled shyly and couldn't meet her eyes.

Simone pulled back, catching sight of her own dish-drowned hands and bare fingernails.

"Can I help you ...?"

She spun reflexively and threw herself as far back from the voice as possible. Into the bookshelf. It shook above her, casting a book or two to the floor. Any remnant of the twelve minutes and thirty-four seconds of peace evaporated.

He was a little older than her. Dark hair, clean cut, a boyish face, wearing a green polo shirt. He was now crouched, surrendering and ready all at once, expecting either the bookshelf or Simone to fly. "Whoa. Sorry. Wow. I didn't mean to scare you. Are you okay?"

His nametag read, "Hi, My name is Alex." Alex was new.

Simone gulped down her raging fear, "I'm fine. You shouldn't sneak up on people."

Alex straightened and ran a hand threw his neat hair, "Sorry, I didn't...I mean, I didn't mean to, um... is there something I can help you find?"

"No. I know my way around. Thanks." Simone beat a hasty retreat, winding her way to the fiction section, as far away from Alex as possible. Then waited, listening, to make sure his footsteps traveled away from her.

Eventually, Simone found her way to the new releases, sizing each one up by reading the first few pages. "The new Robert Ludlum is pretty good. If you're into that sort of thing."

Simone didn't look up from page four of Tom Clancy. Instead, she shifted her gaze to the floor. His shoes weren't runners like the usual part-time student crowd working here; they were leather lace ups, not new and not yet old, just well-worn and comfortable looking. Still, she didn't look up, "I'm not into spy novels." The shoes hesitated but finally moved on. Simone continued reading.

"The library will be closing in five minutes." Mrs. Harper's voice whispered over the loudspeaker.

The Clancy novel was returned to the display and David Eddings was plucked. Out of the corner of her eye, Simone glanced the leather shoes hovering at the end of the nearest bookshelf, books sliding back and forth, the metal bookends clicking out of then into the shelf slots. Hovering. The back aisle was messiest. But yet the leather shoes hovered near the front.

Words on the first page of the Eddings book blurred.

Click of the metal bookend. The soft shuffle of books sliding along the shelf. Another click as the bookend was pushed into place.

Shit.

Simone snapped the Eddings book shut, replaced it, then strode to the check-out counter. Leather shoes raced up the behind the counter.

Double shit. Could this get any worse?

"This it?" The books were slid across the counter and their back covers flipped open.

"Yeah," she said keeping her eyes on her books, on the counter, on the flyers on the counter.

The computer beeped as the books were logged in one by one. "You have pretty diverse interests." Beep, slide. Beep, slide.

"Yeah."

"I bet you're in here a lot, huh?" Beep, slide.

Finally Simone turned her eyes to him as the last book was checked out. He wasn't bad looking. Tallish, nice smile. And he had nice eyes too, maybe had a bit of intelligence behind them. Too bad they were giving her a puppy-dog stare. "You're new in town."

"Yeah," he smiled and the blue puppy-dog eyes grew above the smile.

"Welcome to the shittiest place on earth," the voice that emerged from her mouth fell flat, smacking the hard edge of reality into his face.

His smile vanished. And somehow sound evaporated, the resulting vacuum sucking the beating of her heart into her ears.

Simone picked up her books and left. Outside the wind was cool against her face, washing away her regret. Darkness was descending and the streetlights cast away their initial pink for their night orange glows.

As the doors swung shut behind her, she spied a car in the parking lot. It was the only car in the parking lot and it wasn't empty. That was also the moment Simone remembered that she'd forgotten to call Mr. Decker for a ride home.

Simone spun around and yanked on the library doors. They were locked. "Shit." Her gaze raced up and down the street, peering at the door fronts, looking for someplace open, someone to help. A witness, even. At six o'clock, Knotton's Shallow not only shut up for the night, it vacated.

She pulled the bear spray from her pack and used it to bang on the library door, Fear crept up into her throat and wedged its fingers into the base of her brain. "Hello? Can you open the door, please? I need to use your phone."

The car behind her started. The engine revved. Headlights came on and blinded her with their reflection in the library doors.

Panic tore into her body. The bear spray dropped. She pounded on the glass doors with her bare hands, "Please! I need help." A snap resounded in the glass. A crack appeared between her palms, shooting from top to bottom and splitting the glass into two halves inside the doorframe. In the primal corner of Simone's mind, she saw this as escape and shifted her fists to the crack, enlarging it.

"Please. Help me!"

Alex appeared and raced to let her in. Simone pushed open the door and fell inside, panting, sweating, shaking. "Geez, are you alright? What happened?" He was looking for blood, broken bones.

"Phone. I need to use your phone," she finally managed.

Alex did a visual sweep of the world beyond the glass doors. Simone glanced behind. The car was gone. Great, now she was hallucinating. The canister of bear spray lay on the sidewalk. So much for that brilliant idea.

Alex knelt down in front of Simone, his puppy-dog blues now wide with concern. "Okay. Phone. Can I get you anything else?" She was so sure he'd view her as crazy, crying wolf for attention. But that wasn't the way he looked at her. The tone of his voice had changed too. There was no anxiety, no judgement, only assessment. He waited, like one of Tom Clancy's soldiers: patient and calm, but ready to spring into action.

Simone struggled to get her breathing under control. "Maybe just some place to hang until my ride gets here."

Again, he nodded, assessing her one last time. "Okay. But if your ride doesn't show, I can give you a lift home. My shift is done in half an hour."

It was Simone's turn to appraise him. "I don't know you," and reached to pick up her abandoned backpack. He beat her to it and threw it over his shoulder.

He stood suddenly and held out his other hand, "I'm Alex."

Simone pushed herself up, avoiding his outstretched hand. "Yeah, I got that," she nodded at his nametag. "What I meant was that I don't know anything about you."

He stuffed his hand into his pocket. "Like, if I'm a serial killer, or something. We have only just met. Valid point." Simone reached for her backpack. Alex pulled away. "I have a proposition: I make you a tea; you calm down; I keep you company while I finish my shift, all with Mrs. Harper in attendance. If you don't feel comfortable around me by the end of 30 minutes, you call your ride. Deal?"

"Why do you want to give me a ride home without knowing where I live?"

Alex shrugged, "Doesn't matter where you live if you need a ride."

"I live out of town."

"So?"

"It's long way."

"And?"

"There are lots of gravel roads."

"Driven lots of those."

Simone suddenly felt a desire to lash out. "Why are you doing this?"

"Doing what?"

Simone could feel her mouth open. No words came out. No words ever came out when they were supposed to. And her frustration drilled a cavern into her soul.

"Got anything else?" He was giving her that calm expectant look again. "Look, if you need a ride home, I'll give you one. That's it, that's all." Alex walked back into the library, her backpack over his shoulder. "And don't forget your bear spray."

Simone flipped the door lock, the broken glass rattling in the pane, and plucked the canister from the sidewalk. No more revving engine, no more headlights.

Simone waited until Alex had gone into the kitchen to put on the kettle then called Mr. Decker. Ten minutes, he said. Alex gave her a mug of chamomile tea then disappeared around a bookshelf. Soon, familiar headlights appeared through the library windows, then picked up her backpack and left without saying goodbye. She felt bad for it.

During the twenty-minute drive home, the only noise was the radio softly playing an Oldies station.

"Can you wait until I'm at the door, please?" Mr. Decker nodded. He was silent just like that day three years ago.

Simone opened the car door and paused, one foot out, one foot in. The cool evening breeze rustled the leaves of the surrounding aspen trees and sent the pines swaying. A loon called from the pond behind her garden. Stars glistened against a velvet sky, the Milky Way a striking band across the cosmos. Simone let the environment of her home envelope her, seeking security, yet also straining to hear a foreign sound.

She shut the car door and listened as the gravel crunched underneath her feet. Each crunch was her own. The smell was familiar. Halfway between the car and her home, the yard light burst its yellow light across the front lawn, and she wanted nothing more than to bolt. The wooden front door of the single-storey, two-bedroom bungalow was too far away. The concrete front step was miles in the distance. It would be an eternity until her key turned the dead bolt.

A tiny leap up the single step to the door brought her home, the warmth of the day still radiating off the stucco. Her house key had cut red dents into her palm. With a determined thrust, Simone shoved the key into the lock, passed the encroaching shaking.

The door opened. Both the house and Simone sighed.

She turned a meek wave to Mr. Decker; listened as the car retraced its course down the gravel road; waited until the car was completely gone. Then she waited, listening, reaching out every sense to judge the familiar. Just in case. Just in case.

Simone reached up to the yard light above the front door and flicked the switch from Auto to On. She closed the door, deadbolted it, dropped her bag, then headed to through the kitchen to the back door. She opened it, locked the screen door, deadbolted the wooden door, then wedged a kitchen chair under the knob. Retreating, she grabbed another kitchen chair and did the same to the front door. Then she made the rounds through the house and snapped shut all the curtains.

She plucked a small blanket from her bed, the one her grandmother had made her as a baby, and wrapped it around her shoulders. Wedged into the farthest corner of the house, upon her bed, as the shaking worked its way through her body, Simone listened.

Silence.

She let it settle in around her. Feeling the security of nothingness.

CHAPTER SIX

As Cary broached the last set of hills between the forest and his lands, his home, FarSee Cove, almost appeared restored to its former glory. Shadows masked the needed restorations and missing décor. He could smell his mother's neglected rose garden in the ocean breeze from the Southwest.

He had practiced swordsmanship with his father on the Greens to the Southwest overlooking the cliffs. Sometimes, when he walked there, feeling the grass beneath his bare feet, Cary could still see the upturned soil from where he'd fallen, dug in his blade or his toe. "Again," his father would say and they would continue.

He had practiced dancing and courtroom protocols with his mother near the gate, where the Aristovin crest hung and shone in the morning light. Sometimes, on his way to the cliffs in the mornings, Cary would pause at the gate. He would imagine a ghost's hand on his shoulder, "Here, my love," the soft voice would sound in his ear, "you must direct the lady like this." The breeze would blow the scent of roses to his nose and the ghost would solidify for only a moment.

It was all memory.

Sometimes Cary thought that memories were all he had left. Most of the memories, the really vivid ones, he tried hard to forget. The good ones were clouded by time and were fading too quickly. On days when he couldn't picture his father's face, he would venture into the dusty old study, stare at the leather-bound volumes, the shelves crammed with crumbling maps and parchments, smell his father's soap and all the memories would come flooding back. That room alone sustained him.

He was startled to hear Denis' so close, his weathered face peering up at him from beside Marcus' shoulder. "So? Was it worth all that silver?"

Denis had discarded his jacket at some point and his sleeves were rolled up. "Weeding the garden?" Denis didn't answer but maintained his stern gaze. Cary slid down from his Companion and tried to find a way to break the news. "I've been Tested."

The old man drew back from Cary. "Tested? I know you didn't hold a sword so what's the catch?" Cary sighed. Denis' old, calloused hands turned him round. "And you're a disaster. Your trousers. Ah, your tunic! What happened?"

He and Denis walked Marcus to the stables. "I was Tested without a sword." Another suspicious look from Denis. "I was Tested on my conviction."

"Well, you hardly needed to be Tested on that."

"It was a formality."

"Let's see." Denis held out an old and calloused hand. Cary pulled the silk package out his pocket and gave it to him. From inside, Denis pulled a Crest. The double suns were embroidered in yellow and orange and outlined in gold thread. It was a simple design but the colors were striking and brilliant. The Crest was made by Council demand and by the same set of families that had been making them for generations. "Yes, it's just like your father's." He thrust it back at Cary. "I was notified about it."

Cary missed a step in the wooden corridor of the stables. "But I was also informed that if I attended, I would be removed from service and put to scrubbing pots in the Inner City kitchens." Denis eyed Cary as he unbuckled the saddle and removed Marcus' blanket. Cary could feel his stare, his probing questions, and his suspicions. He took the brushes from Cary's hands and, with Marcus looking on, asked, "So what is going on?"

Cary jumped up to sit on the half stall wall and adjusted his split trousers. "I don't know." Denis, again silent, kept the suspicion fresh in his expression. The man stood and waited. Cary sighed, "If I had to make a guess, I would say that now everyone will assume I'm taking my father's position."

Denis tsked and resumed brushing Marcus. The horse shifted uncomfortably under the hard strokes. Cary leapt down from the wall and took the brushes from his steward.

"So if you're a Warrior without a sword, what are you going to do?" Denis leaned on an empty barrel at the far end of the stall with a stern look, and his strong, lean limbs crossed.

Cary finished brushing Marcus' belly, cleaned the brushes, and put them in their place. He leaned against the barrel next to Denis. "I don't know. But I do know, as I have always known, there are other ways to fight a battle. There is always more than one way to do something. I thought I taught you that?"

Denis glanced at Cary and broke into a grin. "Yes. You have taught me many things, Young One, but most of all you taught me that there are always alternatives." With the tension broken, they sat, old man, young man, and watched Marcus munch his oats. "So what are you going to do?"

"I'm going to visit Dmitri tomorrow." He heard the rebuke before Denis spoke and cut him off. "Dmitri may have some suggestions, and he may even have some answers. Denis, he's the only chance I've got to understand what's going on here. My choices are limited. I don't want to lose you or the Household. I'm doing my best without sacrificing everything."

Denis reached a sinewy arm around the young Aristovin and squeezed his shoulder. "I know, Young One. You are doing your best. Just don't do your best to get in trouble."

"Have you walked the corn yet?" Denis shook his aged head. "It's okay, I'll do it. Go put the kettle on. I'll be inside in a little while." The man nodded and walked stiffly out of the stall. Cary sat looking after Denis. He was getting old. Too old. He shouldn't be serving any more, Cary thought, and now he was weeding gardens. But Cary just couldn't bear the thought of giving Denis up. It would devastate them both.

Cary walked the abbreviated family fields with a spade, dug weeds, and cleared the irrigation channels he had made last year. The corn stalks were tall and strong. Cary peeled back the husk of one. A cob of bright red kernels greeted him. He cut it and another down for a sampling that night.

The orange gourds would be the last harvest of the season and it looked as though they would have enough to sell in the City. They were growing well in the loamy soil of the hills. Fist-sized orange balls peaked out from dark vine-like leaves. They would mean a little more money to buy staples to see them through the winter.

Cary ducked inside the kitchen and was surprised to see someone standing at the hearth. She was plump, with arms like logs, and frilly cap upon her head. The kitchen smelled divine. Olivia Maklinari turned, "Hello,

Young One. You look famished." She dished up a bowl of stew and placed it on the table. "Sit. Eat. Now."

Cary put the corn on the counter and did as he was told. As he ate, he felt Olivia's gaze on him, or rather his torn clothing. "Don't ask," he said.

"I'm not," she said and turned back to her chopping. "But you will leave that tunic and those trousers here after yer done eatin'." Cary began to protest. Olivia held up a gnarled hand, "I don't want to hear it. I have a husband and three boys. I have seen male backsides before. Yer not stepping outside this house with yer pants flapping in the ocean breeze."

Despite his embarrassment, Cary was secretly glad Olivia was there. He had no talent with a needle and Denis was only slightly better.

With a full belly and wrapped in a blanket, Cary stepped inside his father's study. By lamplight, the leather-bound books danced on the floor-to-ceiling shelves. The desk jumped into and out of shadows. The wing-backed chairs by the fireplace held dark ghosts who ducked from the light. It had been ten years but Cary could still detect the smell of his father's spiced soap.

Father, what should I do?

Something out of place caught his eye. He brought the lamp down to the floor, looking closer at the foot treads on the dust-laden rugs. As a matter of routine Cary would visit his father's study, sometimes more than once a month. But he wouldn't let Denis clean it. Cary preferred to keep everything as is. Tonight it was to his benefit.

Smaller foot-treads were on the rugs beside his larger ones. They led to a low cupboard behind his father's desk. Anxiety crept up on Cary. He opened the cupboard. It was empty. "No, no, no, no."

Denis had caught their previous cook stealing from their coffers. They barely had enough to feed themselves and she'd nearly cleaned them out. As Cary looked at the empty cupboard with tears in his eyes, he figured she had, in fact, succeeded.

The only things that Cary valued were in this room: the smell of his father, his father's knowledge, and the contents of the cupboard. "Fate's bowels, that women had no decency!" Granted, he wasn't planning on using either his father's sword or his mother's wedding gown any time soon. But, it was the sentiment he clung to. Unfortunately, the gown may not be as easy as the sword to find.

Cary arrived in the kitchen the next morning unsteady, with the scent of roses still fresh in the halls of his mind. The suns' light was bright and flour dust floated in the air like the nightmare in his mind. Olivia was at the counter making bread and Denis at the table pouring over the Household ledger. Olivia pointed with a flour-covered finger, "Yer clothing is there. I suggest yoos find another set that fits ya proper-like. That set has been resurrected for the last time."

Cary pulled the pants on under his night shirt, "Genica stole more than our money, Denis. The cupboard in the study is empty."

Denis closed the ledger and pulled his eyeglasses from his face. Olivia asked, "What was in there?"

"My father's sword and my mother's wedding dress."

"Only a native would even think of such of thing," she spat, then stopped, "Sorry. No offense."

Cary found himself beaming. Denis glanced at her before saying, "Then it is doubly good that we have the silver from yesterday. We will need it to buy them back. If we can find them."

"I think we need food more, Denis, but I appreciate the offer." Cary pulled on his boots and sat down as Denis poured him a mug of tea. "Olivia, for how long are you helping us?"

"As long as you need me," she said, her back to the pair of men as she placed the bread into the hearth. Cary raised his eyebrows to Denis who shrugged his shoulders in response.

"Then, tomorrow I'll stop in and visit your husband. Maybe Reid can figure out a way to find a Warrior's sword without a cash transaction."

Olivia turned back to them, hands on ample hips, "You'll be needing supplies. I'll walk into Mangshek and ask around about yer mum's dress." The village of Mangshek was about three miles northeast of the Aristovin Household and was one of the few places where immigrants were welcome.

Cary downed his tea and rose. "I should see you in the afternoon. We need to fix the hole in the roof before the winter rains start."

Cary made for the back door to the stables, but found himself at Olivia's hands, pulling, tugging, and inspecting.

"Let me see your teeth."

"Olivia, please," but she continued. "For Fate's sake, I'm fine." She eyed him viciously.

"If ya don't stop yer cursing Fate, Young One," Olivia said, her voice bending under her native Southern Rire accent, "mercy on yer soul when she finds yoos."

So, he showed her his teeth. It had become a game. It had started after Cary's parents had died and Reid still worked at the Household. Olivia had taken on the role of surrogate mother. Cary hadn't complained.

Denis poured himself another mug of tea and settled in at the table to watch the show. "I can't believe you've been letting him out of the house looking as he does," Olivia said. The rising mug did not hide Denis' grin.

"Well, I don't care if yer the mythical Emperor of the Inner Rire." Olivia pulled away from Cary, "Yer going to be looking presentable even if I have to scrub ya me own self." She rolled her eyes, "You'll be having a bath tonight, young man, and I'll be bringing back some soap from Mangshek. For both of yous." She wagged a finger at Denis. "Now, off ya go. I got work to do."

The usual whistling and howling of the dark forest fell on deaf ears. Focused and determined, Cary and Marcus emerged from the depths of the forbidden woods to find Dmitri waiting. Sitting at a table on the edge of the clearing in his familiar long blue robe, hands on knees, looking straight at Cary, he was smiling. Cary recognized the smile and relaxed.

"What took you so long? I was half expecting you to wake me in the middle of the night ranting and raving about your future and obligation."

"You knew too?" The Mentor shrugged.

Cary dismounted and let Marcus roam. Dropping the bridle on the scarred table, Cary dropped into the chair opposite Dmitri, "The Council's going to call me, isn't it?" A cold sweat ran down his back. "My eighteenth birthday is in two months. That's it, isn't it?"

The Mentor stood and walked to the cave.

"The Council can't call on me." Cary strode up and down the length of the clearing, each step fueling an anger he hadn't felt in years. "I wasn't Tested, not really. I didn't hold a sword, and nobody was there to witness it, and the Council can't acknowledge it. It just can't.

Then the foundation of the anger reared up and turned over in Cary's stomach. "The Council can't make me fight, it can't call me to battle, it can't make me take my father's position. It can't make me pay taxes, and follow rules, and stupid traditions that don't make any sense. They're not going to feed me and fix my roof and mend my britches and till my fields. I am!"

Birds chirped in the distance. A breeze set the treetops swaying.

"To Fate's bowels with the Council of Eight. To Fate's bowels with the Council, the City Guard, the Warriors, nobility and all their bloody snobbery. To Fate's bowels with the Council and its stupid rules and laws. And to Fate's bowels with the Council and its traditions!" Cary kicked his chair.

"You're scaring the wildlife," came a voice from inside the cave.

"I don't care!" Cary kicked the dirt. His hand swung down and plucked a stick from the dead campfire, "I don't care what they think, or who thinks what, or who's what whenever." The stick jabbed the air, marking each point. "I won't do it!" he swung the stick around, hearing it push the air unlike a sharp sword. "I am not a Warrior and will not let them make me into one." He turned back to the cave. "Being a Warrior is not good or right or noble. It only gets you killed. Don't you care that the Council is ripping Juno's youth from their parents' arms and turning them out to the Outerworld for the slaughter? And those people who do want to fight -- the immigrants -- aren't allowed. It's all stupid!" Cary turned and threw the stick from his practiced hand. It lodged into the trunk of a nearby tree, vibrating like the anger coursing through Cary's body.

Then Cary's anger solidified and settled. "Somebody needs to do something," and he stepped to the east.

"Stop right where you are." Dmitri was leaning against the cave entrance with a casual air. His hooded cape was gone. Cary was reminded that the Mentor was hardly a feeble old man despite the silver hair. The loose fitting blue trousers and tunic draped over a lean commanding body and made the Mentor seem twenty years younger. But twenty seasons younger than what?

Cary stopped and turned back to the Mentor, "Why?" His body quaking.

"The Council didn't kill your parents. The Outerworld did. You know this." A scream erupted from inside Cary's mind. The scent of roses filled his nostrils.

"Now comes the hard part, my dear Aristovin heir. Do you want to save Juno from the forces of the Outerworld?"

Without hesitation he answered, "Yes."

"Do you wish to take up the sword again?" Cary instantly replied to the negative. "So how do you plan to go about making your way in the world?"

Again, Cary replied without hesitation, "I haven't the foggiest idea."

Apparently his answer amused Dmitri to the highest degree. Gleaming white teeth shone in the early morning suns' light and a huge laugh erupted from the man's throat. "I believe that's the first coherent thing

I've heard from your mouth in nearly a year." Cary mumbled and waited for the Mentor to stop laughing. "Ah, things were becoming entirely too tense anyway." He looked directly at Cary, those bright ice blue eyes freezing Cary's spine.

"If you're up to it, we'll start your training immediately. Your father sensed, as I, that your ways parted from his in relation to the sword. Circumstances only made you realize this fact sooner than he anticip ated....."

"A Mentor?!" The words fell from Cary's mouth. "This is the choice I have? A Warrior or a Mentor?" He found himself across the clearing from Dmitri, knees trembling and palms sweating.

Dmitri folded into his chair at the table, "The Mentoring profession has much to offer a person and to Juno, Young One." Dmitri almost sounded offended. But his tone suddenly changed. "If you don't want to do it, you can return to your fields and stables and remember every time you cut into Denis' Mayflour Bake that you passed up your last chance to save your land, your Household, and yourself."

Dmitri was right. What choice did he have? Taking back the sword was out of the question and ploughing fields, well, that was slow going. There was a certain sense of accomplishment in seeing a garden growing and prospering, but it wasn't the kind of fulfillment Cary had been searching for. Frankly, he'd begun to wonder if he'd ever find fulfillment. He knew more of what he didn't want to do and what was wrong with the country than what he wanted to do and how to fix it all.

"Being a Mentor affords a certain amount of freedom." There was a flash there in Dmitri's eye then. Freedom, Cary thought. Freedom from the Council. Freedom to be his own person.

"But the Mentors started the civil war." The Aristovin paced the length of the clearing across from the reclining Mentor.

"About that. It was a long time ago and you need a re-history lesson. There used to be female...."

Cary continued to pace, caught in his own thoughts, "Can you make me into a Mentor within two months? I'm under a deadline here."

Dmitri smirked, "I have been training you in the ways of a Mentor since your departure from Trium over three years ago."

Cary hesitated at this admission, then continued to pace. "So we can do this?"

"Mentorship isn't taken lightly, Young One."

Cary threw his hands up. "Stop with the riddles. I need straight answers now."

"How long did you train to become a Warrior?"

And as soon as he'd said it, Cary knew what Dmitri was implying. He'd been at Trium Hall since he was four years old. Warrior training started early, to ingrain the teachings into the foundation of the mind and body. Still, training wasn't complete until the first battle. "So what am I going to tell the Council when they call me in two months?"

Dmitri sighed. "The Council only needs to hear that you've started your apprenticeship and that you're training for your tests."

"Tests? What tests?"

"You will need to demonstrate your abilities to a group of Mentors. If your abilities show promise, you will be allowed to continue in your apprenticeship."

Was there ever going to be a time when he wasn't living up to someone else's expectations? Cary ran a nervous hand through his newly cut hair. "Okay. What do I have to do for these tests? Mix a poultice, make a love potion, what?"

Dmitri smiled, "Actually, you are already acquainted with the first." Dmitri rose and placed a foot upon the chair.

Cary groaned. "How could imagining a chair in my mind be a test?"

"All in good time." Dmitri stood tall and asked, "Do you accept the apprenticeship?"

The Mentor's smile was gone. This was it. The turning point in Cary's life. He could almost see his life pass before his eyes. His childhood disappeared from view and the future stared back at him. Only to go forward, he thought. He couldn't go on with the way he and Denis had been living. The silver Dominic and Everett had given him yesterday would only last so long. He and Denis would be boiling their boots for soup by next winter if things didn't change.

Cary nodded to the old man. "To be a Mentor and a Civil War conspirator." It seemed he just couldn't stay out of trouble.

Dmitri nodded, "And a re-history lesson..."

"Re-history?"

"There is more than one side to the history you've been taught at Trium."

"That's sounds like a very long and daunting story. I have a harvest to tend to, chop wood, gather enough fish to last the winter...."

Dmitri sighed as Cary called to his Companion. "A Mentor's income isn't as much as a Warrior's. You will begin to earn a small wage upon declaration to the Council of your apprenticeship. And you might want to change you grey uniform for a black one," Dmitri said as Cary mounted Marcus.

"Why? What's wrong with this one?" He rose in the stirrups so that the mended tears of yesterday's Test were visible to the Mentor. When Cary looked down, he could see that the stitching was already parting on his backside.

Dmitri cleared his throat, "Among other things, it's too small."

"Yeah, so?"

"Just a suggestion. Come back in the morning and we'll start your training. Formally."

Cary sighed and ran a hand through his new haircut. It felt strange to have his hair so short. "I have a harvest, Dmitri. I don't know how I'm going to do all this and live."

"It is 56 days until your eighteenth birthday." Cary did a doubletake at the Mentor's memory. Dmitri smirked, "You should know, however, that the law is often misquoted. The Council may call upon a male native any time *by* his eighteenth birthday, not necessarily *on* his birthday." A cold sweat broke out between Cary's shoulder blades. "My dear Aristovin, you've been fair game to the Council since the day you were born." And the Mentor slapped the horse on the rump sending Cary homebound.

CHAPTER SEVEN

With her thumb bandaged, it was difficult to wash dishes. Another plate slipped and hit a glass in the sink, shattering it. Simone cursed. Tears welled without warning. Geez, she needed some sleep.

"Hey, Simone," Sally burst through the swing doors. "I brought in a list of movies we could watch on Saturday." Sally's bag hit the table with a loud clatter.

Simone remained at the sink, fighting to see through the oncoming tears, and picked out the pieces of glass.

"I don't know what you like so I thought a list would be a good place to start." Sally appeared at the counter. "I was thinking of getting a couple of...Simone?"

Tears sprang up as Simone sliced open another finger and blood blossomed in the dishwater. "Shit."

"Hey, it's okay. It's just a cut." Simone grunted as she skirted passed Sally and fished the gauze and tape from the first aid kit. Sally followed. Sally was the one person Simone just couldn't face right now. Bloodshot eyes with dark circles, her hair a knotted mess. And Sally would see it all in a single glance.

Gauze slipped from her wet hands. Simone cursed again. Tears flowed. Sally's hands caught the gauze and then placed a towel around Simone's finger. "Hey, it's okay." Her finger was dressed, but the tears continued to flow. They just wouldn't stop.

Sally displayed an uncharacteristic show of strength by grasping Simone's shoulders and gentle but very firmly turning Simone to face her. "Hey, what happened? Simone, please tell me."

If only to stop Sally's blue-eyed concern, Simone finally said, "I just didn't sleep, that's all."

At last Sally pulled back, "Bullshit. Look at you. You're a mess."

"I just need some sleep. I'm an eight-hour person. Maybe it's the phase of the moon. This is me without sleep." It was hard to keep the raw edge out of her voice.

Sally straightened her back and planted her hands on her hips, "Double bullshit. You look like you've been chased all night by something out of a horror movie and now you're lying to me. No way. I'm not leaving it this time. Something is up, Simone Larken, and you're coming apart. If you don't talk to someone, you're going to implode. And I really don't want that to happen.

"Does it have something to do with that guy on Tuesday?"

Simone had been through all of this before. She knew the reality of implosion. It had begun to creep up on her after the 'incident.' She'd quit school and locked herself in her house for a month. With very little food, losing ten pounds, and no contact with the outside world, Simone had deteriorated physically and mentally. If her father hadn't called to say he was coming home in a week, Simone figured things would have got pretty ugly. She'd turned on the computer and found Beryl. With Beryl's encouragement, she'd enrolled in an online matriculation program. A few months later, she'd got this job. And, as far as her father knew, it was life as usual.

She'd thought she'd managed to cope with it all, put it behind her. That apparently was not the case. Sally was right. Elements of the 'incident' were suddenly popping up and showing her that it hadn't left. She hadn't outrun it. It would be there forever. Staring at her through J.D.'s eyes no matter for how long she spun her top.

She just had to make it through today and make her appointment with Beryl tonight.

"I'm talking to someone, okay? I'm dealing with it."

Sally seemed to take this in as Simone noted the water stains on the ceiling. "I'm not sure your methods are working, Simone." Sally grabbed Simone's shoulders, "Look at me. Something has happened, I can see that, but it's eating you alive. You need to *do* something about it. Don't let it eat you. You're too good to lose." Simone guffawed, "Seriously. I've never met anyone like you -- you're insanely smart, funny, gorgeous, and you've got this big heart that you never show anyone. I'm worried about you, Simone. I want to help, but you have to let me in."

Simone tore her eyes from Sally's, "Yeah. Okay. Sure."

"'Yeah. Okay. Sure.' That's one hell of a response." Sally took a long look at Simone then left for the front of the coffee shop.

Simone slumped with relief against the counter as the tears threatened to rise again. She hurried over the sink and splashed cold water on her face. "Come on, Simone. Get a hold of yourself. Get a hold of yourself!" She toweled off and went to the back door. "Just breathe. You have work to do. Just forget it. You can think about it later. Now, just breathe. Just. Breathe."

By noon, Simone had managed to regain some sanity. The nightmare retreated, the panic calmed, and the shaking stopped. At one point, she noticed how brightly the linoleum of the kitchen floor shone as the late morning light filtered through the back screen door. It was a moment that let her see that beauty was possible. Sometimes.

"Hey," Sally slid up to Simone at the kitchen counter, a gleam in her eye, "I know something that will cheer you up. Mr. Briefcase came into the studio yesterday for a haircut."

"And?" Simone finished pinching the pastry around the edge of the pie and pushed it aside.

"Have you talked to him yet?"

"Nope." Simone pulled a glass of water from the tap and walked toward the back door.

Sally began her melodramatic routine, "Ah, come on, Simone," her hands flew into the air, dropped and slapped her thighs, "He's cute! Why don't you at least try?"

Try as she might to halt the conversation with monosyllabic responses, Simone found that, as usual, Sally liked beating a dead horse. Simone wrinkled her nose, "I just don't think it's worth it."

"What? You think Mr. AB-SO-fucking -LUTE-LY Right, is going to walk right in here and know all your secrets and exactly what to say, whisking you off your feet in the process?"

"No," and Simone paused. She paused because she delighted in how Sally's pupils dilated and her mouth gapped whenever Simone threatened to exit the confines of her character. Simone milked it.... then continued, "Actually, I'm not waiting for anyone. I plan on being alone forever."

Sally rinsed out her glass then turned back, slow realization spreading across her face, "Wait a second, wait a second. That's it."

"Oh God, here it comes. The revelation of the century," Simone downed the rest of her water as she rose and attempted to put her glass into the sink.

Sally blocked her way, "No, that's really it, isn't it?"

"Move your ass so I can put my glass in the sink."

The smile growing on Sally's face was sickening even if Simone didn't yet know this incredible revelation. Sally didn't move. "You really *are* hoping for Mr. Right to come sweep you off your feet." Simone gave up and put the glass on the counter. "Holy shit! That's it." Simone walked back to the back door and sat down on the step. Sally followed, "You have some guy in your head, some made up dream guy, and you're waiting for *him*."

"Jesus Christ, Sally. Will you let it rest already?"

"So, does he look like Brad Pitt? No. Wait. How about Jude Law? I know you like Jude Law." Sally's eyes were dancing now. Dancing with the thrill of the kill.

"Will you shut up?"

"What colour hair does he have? Is he muscular," she growled, well-groomed eyebrows dancing, "or a lean machine?"

Simone pointed a firm finger to her friend, "I'm gonna hurt you if you don't stop."

Sally dodged the finger and slid conspiratorially up to Simone's side, "You know that's dangerous, comparing everyone to someone in your head," she wrinkled her nose, "doesn't work. You'll always be disappointed."

"I'm used to disappointment." The wind had come up and she could smell the burger joint a couple blocks down.

Sally stood again and blocked her view, "Come on, live a little! Explore. Be adventurous. Try someone new."

"Isn't it possible that I just don't like people, guys in particular?"

"You're human, Simone." Sally sat again, her $80 jeans hitting the cement beside Simone's $20 butt. "Besides, I know you." Sally nudged Simone's shoulder with her own, "You don't hate people THAT much. Hello, you work in the service industry."

Simone snorted, "Not like I want to."

Sally slapped Simone's thigh, "What am I going to do with you, Simone?" The little redhead smiled, ringlets dancing about her head, "I'll find you a man," a sparkled fingernail rose to point-of-fact. "Don't worry. And he'll be at least as cute as Mr. Briefcase, if not Jude Law."

At two-thirty, Sally's boyfriend, Dean, came to pick up the little fiend. "How's it goin', Simone? That weird guy been around today?" He wasn't the cutest guy on the block, with shaggy brown hair, an acne-scarred face, and a long, lanky frame, but Dean had a sparkle in his eyes that even Simone admitted wasn't entirely undesirable.

"Which one? There are too many in this town."

"Ah, the one who sings while listening to his earphones."

"Yeah, he was in about an hour ago."

"Hasn't asked you out yet, huh?"

"Oh, yuk, yuk," Simone swiped at him but he diverted in a much-prac-ticed move. "If you weren't her boyfriend, I'd beat you black and blue."

"Gotta admit though," Dean settled his elbows back on the counter, "he is pretty freaky."

"Who in this town isn't?"

Sally came from the kitchen, hair in place, cheeks rosy and a fresh coat of lip gloss on her pouty mouth, "You want me to come back at five-thirty and help you close up?"

Simone rolled her eyes. "No. I'll be fine."

"You sure? They still haven't caught the guy who robbed Mike's."

Simone pointed. "Out."

Sally shrugged then blew a kiss, "Saturday, Chiquita. You. Me. All day," she called as she made for the door. Dean tossed a wave in Simone's direction and at last, the coffee shop was quiet. Simone turned on the stereo and went to the back closet to fetch the mop and bucket.

The bell over the door rang.

As Simone approached the front of the coffee shop, a moment of clarity hit her. If she had psychic abilities, they would undoubtedly allow her to avoid these situations. She'd be able to see them coming and run the other way. Instead, all these crumby situations were burned in her mind. Whenever she closed her eyes, they would pop up and haunt her, taunt her, and leave her quaking.

"Oh my god! Simone?"

Pushing a frizzy lock of hair aside, Simone stood face-to-face with a voice she hadn't heard in nearly three years.

Tanya had changed but not in ways Simone had predicted. 'Filled out' would probably be the appropriate expression. Tanya hadn't really been scrawny when Simone had last seen her in high school, but now Tanya could definitely hold her own. In a school hallway, a bar, a swanky hotel, wherever. And Tanya had discovered that cosmetics consisted of items other than glitter and blue eyeshadow. All in all, she'd turned into quite the package deal and, in a place like Knotton's Shallow, that's really all that mattered.

"Hi Tanya," Simone managed to say and pushed a smile to her face.

Tanya's smile grew. Simone added teeth whitening to her list of Tanya's weekly maintenance. "It's been a long time, Simone. I thought you'd moved or something."

"Nope. Still here."

"Well, how are you?" Simone cringed. Sum up three years in two sentences or 10 seconds. How does anyone do that?

"I'm doing well, as you see." Simone felt the sweat drip down her back and knew it beaded on her forehead too. She was a dirty, wet mess and a part of her wished she could hug Tanya only out of spite.

"How long have you worked here? Do you make these?" Tanya's eyes began to eat up the pastries in the glass cabinet.

"Um, a year and a half and yes."

Tanya broke her gaze at the pies and giggled at Simone. "You always were quick, Simone. Speaking of, I didn't see you at graduation in June."

Simone scanned the cafe. Only three tables were occupied. Nothing needed to be tended to. Simone grabbed a cloth from the counter behind her and started wiping down the cash register. "That's probably because I wasn't there."

"Oh." Tanya backed away as the cloth wiped the outer edge of the register. "That's too bad. I always thought you'd go to university or something."

The bile in Simone's throat rose as her pulse soared. "I didn't say I didn't finish. I did. A year early. With honours. I chose not to attend that parade called graduation. And I'm working this job to save for university." Simone threw down the cloth and then looked directly into Tanya's perfectly outlined eyes. "Now. Is there something I can get for you, or is there some other reason you're here?"

Tanya regained her distance from the counter. "Simone, I don't.... what do you mean?"

"Why are you talking to me now, acting like we're the bestest and oldest of friends?"

"I just wanted...." Tanya shrugged. "I guess I wanted to see how you were doing. J.D.'s back and he said you worked here."

"You *talked* to him?"

"Yeah, he wanted to know how you were."

"You told me we couldn't be friends and now you're here, at J.D.'s bequest, to inquire after my welfare?"

"I'm sorry."

"'Sorry' doesn't cut it. I felt like a leper in school because no one -- including you --would talk to me. I don't know what the hell you said to everyone but it stuck. Now either buy a pie or get out of my shop."

Tanya managed to swallow before turning and exiting the shop. The shaking had resumed, but now Simone relished it. It wasn't a reaction. She'd taken control and felt life fill her in the wake of the rage. Revenge was feeling awfully good.

She left the customers to their tea and cakes, letting the kitchen doors swing wide and proud.

Chapter Eight

"And again." Dmitri sat on the wooden table, feet on a chair, reading, as Cary flowed through the movements again. Cary pulled his hands to his chest, breathed, and pushed outwards. One foot rose, thick with tension and pushed out to the side to release the built-up energy. Then the other side. Breathe. Arms pushed out again. "Feel the tension flow through your limbs and then push it out as you push the air away." Dmitri didn't even look up, not that Cary was looking. He had his eyes closed, trying to imagine each muscle tensing, contracting and then relaxing, releasing. Beads of sweat trickled down his forehead. He had long ago shed his tunic. His shirt was soaked in sweat although the afternoon breeze had come up. Muscles expanded and contracted, lengthened and shortened with every movement, all as Dmitri commanded.

"And again."

Cary hadn't done drills for a long time. The swordplay and fighting drills, like the ones he'd used at his Test, had once toned his body to a lean, responsive machine. They'd been absent from his life for nearly three years now. Strange how his muscles, once sore from a day's chores, now pulsed effectively.

Cary clenched his eyes shut, picturing his hand rising to the sky. His feet planted, balanced. The movements were similar to the fighting stances taught to the Sons, but he felt different. His body felt alive. Tension flew from each hand and foot as it struck the air. Breathing became easier as he now felt a sort of energy flowing throughout his body. Each movement, at first clumsy, was now swift, deft, and all flowed together to become a dance. His mind seemed to fall into a state of stillness. Focused. His mind was blank.

"Stop!" Cary nearly fell over as the voice reverberated through his mind. He had forgotten where he was. "You are no longer a Warrior. I realize it's been a while since we've practiced, so let me remind you. The Warrior's drills require a blank mind, a separation between you and the environment." Dmitri had closed his book and was giving Cary that icy stare.

"Here, the drills I teach you are used to keep your mind alert and connected to everything. You must be conscious and aware at all times. Do you understand?" Reluctantly, Cary nodded. So many years of training and he had to either erase or alter them all, it seemed. Two measly months wouldn't scratch the surface. If he had the luxury of two months. "Now start again. Slowly. And this time keep your mind about you."

Again, Cary started the movements. But this time, as his mind began to meld with the movements, he pulled away and regained the image of each limb moving, each bone. The blood pulsing through his veins. His heart beating against his ribs. Expand, contract. Expand, contract. Up, down, across, through, up, over. The wind came up again and tussled his damp hair. He heard the wind play with the leaves of the trees just off his right, then felt each hair on his forehead being picked up, tossed, turned and set down again upon his skin. Each time, each hair. His arms moved across his body and out. Grasses trembled in the breeze, clashing against each other.

Relax, he heard Dmitri whisper from the recesses of his mind. *Relax and let it come.* Like a stream of water, the energy trickled in a minute flow of tiny rivulets. With each breath he breathed in synchronicity of his environment, the flow grew stronger. The blackness of his mind's eye had depth, it seemed alive. No, it was alive. He was the trees, the grasses, the insects, the moss, the birds, the deer running past. And they were him. They were one and giving freely of each other to each other.

The flow grew and as the current strengthened, somewhere outside his mind's eye Cary though that if it wasn't for Dmitri, he might not be able to handle the force. It was so strong but he felt no strain, no pressure. It was effortless. It was almost scary.

And in one fluid moment, it all changed. He gasped forceful breaths under the strain. The air seemed to thicken. And his once friendly environment turned to shadows clinging to the daylight, sucking his life in what seemed like sheer desperation.

A reassuring pressure on his mind lead him back to the clearing outside Dmtiri's cave. Cary opened his eyes. "Why is it so different?" he gasped as Dmitri stretched his legs out from the chair.

"It's different due to the approach and the results." The Mentor rose but continued to stretch, his limberness surprising Cary. "If you are one with the universe, as I've shown you, the flow is easy, like it's being granted. There is no resistance and therefore a stronger connection is made and you can ultimately focus more energy. Being a singularity, as a Warrior is trained to be, only limits the flow. The universe is forced to redirect energy to an outside presence rather than being persuaded by an internal form."

"Persuasion is better than force," Cary echoed as he remembered Dmitri's previous lessons.

"Now that you know the difference, I will allow no excuses," and with a raised finger, Cary had been given fair warning. "And I will know when you do it the wrong way."

Cary smirked. He didn't need to know how or why and in a way he didn't care. As far as he was concerned Dmitri could remain omnipotent in his mind. Things would be less complicated then.

"Now," Dmitri slid down the length of the table and rested his booted foot upon the other wooden chair, "We'll get you started on your first test. I know you remember the difficulty, but do you remember the objective?"

"Place the image in my mind."

"Correct. I want you to look at it from every conceivable angle. Once you have done that and stored it in your mind, retrieve the image. Do these steps again and again until you are sure you have every hue, every knot, every corner of the chair fixed in your mind." The Mentor leapt from the table to stand in front of Cary. "Good luck, Young One. This test is tricky. Don't get frustrated. If you do, return to the movements to release the tension and regain your concentration, then try again to picture the chair. I am going to collect some Tanker's root and lattertot." Dmitri grabbed his shoulder pouch from a hook near the cave entrance.

Cary called out after him, "Is this it? All of the test? Or is there more?"

Dmitri turned back from the shadows of the forest, "It's only part of the first test. To complete this test, you must turn the image." Then he was gone.

"Right." In his higher state of consciousness, Cary stepped around the chair, knelt to look at it, stood on it and stepped back again. "Right." He closed his eyes.

By the time Dmitri returned, the suns were below the mountains. The shadows had lengthened across the clearing to Cary's feet. He had thrown off his shirt. As Dmitri emerged from the forest with a full pouch, Cary was sitting on the chair, head in hands and sticky with sweat. "Three years," he mumbled.

"I see you've been busy."

Cary sprang up. "For Juno's sake, you scared the daylights out of me."

Dmitri paused, a contemplative look on his face, then handed Cary his shirt and tunic and a bag of coins, "I have heard that your old stableman's son is quite the blacksmith. I would like a sample of his latest work."

As Cary dressed, muscles screamed and his skin was raw with sunburn. He glanced into the bag. The coins were gold. It'd been a long time since he'd seen that much gold.

"How many tests are there, Dmitri?" He followed Dmitri to the cave.

Dmitri hung the full pouch of herbs on the hook by the entrance and looked at Cary. "Five and we'll take them one by one. I have every confidence in you. Now go home and rest. I'll see you in a few days. Practice when you can."

Cary whistled. Marcus trotted to the clearing from the path through the forest. With much effort, Cary saddled his Companion and departed Dmitri's abode. The ride back to FarSee would have been painful if his mind wasn't so numb from the 'chair exercise.'

Practice, indeed. He'd never needed to practice anything. It had always come so easily. By watching a task he could pick up the basics, and then with little instruction and hands on experience, Cary usually could accomplish the task, within two to three repetitions. Languages and tracking were as second nature as battlefield strategies and fighting while on horseback. Practice. He'd never needed to practice. Perhaps it was a good thing, too. He lost patience too quickly.

Cary arrived home after dark to find a young boy splitting wood in the courtyard by the light of a single torch. It was Emil Maklinari, Reid and Olivia's youngest son. A wagon sat next to the stables. Relief swept through Cary. Leave it to the Maklinaris to look after him and his decaying Household. The boy trotted over and took Marcus' reins from Cary. "Tough day, Master Cary?" His face was brown from a lifetime of outdoor labour.

"You could say that," was all Cary could muster. Harvesting the corn and tomatoes would have to wait another day, he thought.

"A package came for you today. It's in your rooms." Cary thanked the boy and headed to the kitchen.

The kitchen was empty. A note from Denis told him that Emil would be staying on, free of charge in return for keeping him out of trouble. Olivia would be back the day after tomorrow. Supper was in the hearth.

But he was too tired and frustrated to eat. Cary made his way to the Front Room. He opened the three large windows that overlooked the southern cliffs then sank in his father's chair.

Instead of his mother's scream and the scent of roses, water rose up in his dream. He fought to break the surface, gasping for air. A hand reached out. He grabbed it and looked for the face that had saved him. He saw only long blonde hair.

The room was dark when he opened his eyes. He had managed to curl himself into a tight ball within the confines of the overstuffed wing chair. Wind from the sea whistled into the room and chilled him. Cary untangled himself, flexed his sore, stiff limbs and rose to close the windows and doors. He ran a hand through his hair, wrapped his arms around himself and retreated to his rooms, shuffling his feet all the way.

A package lay on his bed. It contained two uniforms, one of black wool and the other of blue silk. But Cary didn't have the energy to curse Dominic and his meddling. The new uniforms ended up on the floor as Cary fell into his bed exhausted and fully dressed.

CHAPTER NINE

"We need to do that headphone thing again," Simone blurted as she dropped into the lounge chair.

"Want to tell me about it?" Beryl sat in her own lounge chair and crossed her trousered legs.

Simone chewed on her lip, trying to think of some way around saying it. Beryl waited patiently as therapists do.

Simone was about to start counting the ceiling tiles again, when Beryl said, "You came here for help. I want to help. Telling me will help."

The shaking started anew. Her mouth opened and closed, her tongue thick and dirty. Finally, the words fell out, "He's back."

"He's back?"

Simone nodded feeling the panic seize her heart, "He's back and he came to the shop. He found me and he's following me."

Beryl put down her notebook and slid forward to grasp Simone's hands. "It's okay, you're safe here. Tell me what happened."

Words fell out of her mouth again, tumbling and bumping into each other, as the old fear ground its gritty teeth into her heart. The minutiae of J.D.'s hungry grin slipped through her brain and jumbled up her thoughts. His voice echoed in her ears and bounced against her own voice. His image gripped her mind like the hands that had once held her down, stapling her to the ground. Suddenly Beryl grasped Simone's shoulders, "Simone, look at me. I need you to breathe. Okay? Just breathe. Watch me." Beryl's green eyes locked with Simone's while she took deep, calming breath after breath. "There. Better?" Simone let the air flow through her lungs one more time then nodded. "I don't think J.D. is following you. I think that phone call was just a coincidence. He's back in town. Okay. We can do the headphones, but we need to do something else first." Nod. "I need you to tell me about that night again."

Shit. "I don't....."

Beryl clasped Simone's hands and locked her gaze again. "If J.D. is back in town, you need to deal with that. You haven't been dealing, Simone, you've been running. Unfortunately the only way to deal with the fear is to confront it." Simone violently shook her head. "The first step to confronting it is to talk about it."

This was where her 'university fund' was going. Therapy. These sessions that had managed to strangle the nightmares from her mind. A year and a half in, Simone was very happy that her sessions had decreased to every couple of months instead of twice a week.

But thanks to the event in the coffee shop two days ago, the nightmares were back with a vengeance.

Beryl's blue eyeliner was bright against the blackness of her lashes and green eyes. "You don't have to do this if you don't want to, but I think it's for the best. If you never confront it, you'll never truly be free of it. And I know you want to be free." Beryl squeezed Simone's hands then gently let go.

To be truly free.

No more dreams. No more fear. No more shaking.

That would be nice.

With a deep breath, Simone nodded.

"Okay, take me back to the day it happened. Start with earlier that day."

It had been a good day. Friday. "Dad was out beyond Blue Ridge. Wouldn't be back for another week. I wanted to go to the library." Simone smiled. "Tanya said she couldn't believe I was going to spend the weekend with my nose in a book, so we instead walked around town a bit, phoned a couple more girls who lived in town, then headed to the Burger Baron on 50th street. It was a nice night."

"Tell me again, who were the girls?"

"Jenny Matheson and Melissa Jones. Jenny was in Tanya's class. She and Melissa had been best friends since kindergarten."

"Right and Tanya knew them better than you?"

Simone nodded again. "Yeah. I didn't really hang around in their circle."

"Did you hang around with anyone other than Tanya?"

"No. I sat with a couple of girls in class, but nobody really interested me."

Beryl made a note on her writing pad. "Now, after you got to the Burger Baron what happened?"

Simone sighed and pushed her reluctant memory onwards. "A couple of guys from school started chatting up Jenny and Melissa. Said there was a party down at the river later."

"Tell me about the boys."

"They were a year ahead. I knew who they were, but I never talked to them."

"Tell me what you were feeling when you found out about this party."

Simone shrugged; the shaking was creeping up. The Fear was readying itself. "I don't know. I mean, I'd never been to a party. Well, not one down by the river. I'd been to sleepovers and stuff. But this was a real party, with guys and everything."

"You said before you were excited."

"Yeah, I guess so. I'd never done anything like that. They invited us."

"Simone, I want you to pause and remember that excitement. I want you to remember what it felt like to be singled-out and recognized as special."

Simone pushed her memory. The orange fiberglass seats of the booths at the Burger Baron suddenly hard against her backside. The descending sunlight glared on the laminate tables. Then the emotion hit her. Excitement. One of the guys had looked right at her. He'd been smiling, chatting with Melissa, but then looked right at Simone. And smiled. "Come on," he'd said, his blue eyes sparkling and the product in his hair shining in the daylight. "Come to the party with us. I'll be fun."

"It felt nice," Simone finally said to Beryl.

"Okay, keep going."

"We got in their cars and drove passed the campground by the river to a spot further down. There were already some people there and a fire going."

"Was it dark now?"

"The sun was setting. It was getting cool, especially since we were down by the river."

"Okay, keep going. You arrived; the fire was going. Who did you talk to?"

"Nobody at first. I kind of stayed around with Tanya because I didn't know anyone else. I felt out of place. I sat down by the river and watched the sun go down. It was nice down there." Simone let her mind wander there, in that safe place. "A couple of ducks played in the water and I remember wondering if ducklings had already grown-up and flown away."

"Did Tanya come find you?"

"No. She was talking with the guys."

"How did that make you feel, that she wasn't talking with you?"

Simone shrugged. She hadn't really thought about it and Beryl hadn't asked this question before. But through the lingering Fear, through the encroaching shaking, deep resentment waited at the fringes. "I guess I felt kind of betrayed. She'd brought me down here but she was off hanging with everyone else. Yeah, I guess I was kind of pissed."

"So you were angry sitting down by the river?"

"Maybe. Yeah." Simone checked off that box -- that would explain her outburst at Tanya earlier.

"What happened next? It was getting dark."

She pushed further. "I was getting cold. I wanted to go home and started looking for someone with a vehicle or a cell phone, when...."

"You can do this, Simone." There was a polite pause as Beryl waited.

Violent shaking started from inside, deep inside Simone's stomach, and was working its way out. She was cold and feverish all at the same time.

"Say his name, Simone."

Her eyes began to blur, filling with tears. Fear was sinking its teeth into the base of her brain. She grit her teeth and pushed again. "J.D. It was J.D."

"What did J.D. do?"

"Nothing. It was just....." Simone pushed against the Fear, breathed back the shaking, and wiped away the tears. "He said I looked cold and I should come to the fire. He'd let me use his cell phone."

He'd been so nice.

"Fuck, I was so stupid," the words spilled out. "He was so nice. He gave me a beer. Talked to me. Smiled at me. Said he liked that I was smart. But he didn't care. He didn't care about books, or music, or school, or me. It was all a ruse. He made a big show of saying his cell phone was dead. It was a fucked up ruse and I played right into it. God, I was so stupid. How could I be so stupid. Why didn't I see what was happening? Why couldn't I see?" The cold sweats turned into a fevered rage. Her jaw clenched, and strained under the pressure making her head hurt.

"I don't even remember how many beers I drank while he pretended to ask around for a cell phone. All I know was that I finally had to pee and I'd barely pulled up my pants when he was there, fucking asshole. I thought it was funny. Funny! How fucked up is that? I thought it was nice that he'd come looking for me. Nobody had ever come looking for me. Then suddenly he was there, close. Too close. He was holding me, and pawing me, and pushing me, calling me a bitch and stuff, then he was on top of me, on the ground and I was shocked and scared and I didn't know what was happening and then suddenly it all hit me, what was happening."

No.

"It was like suddenly everything became clear. No beer. No fuzz. No fog. It was clear and happening and dark and scary and I had to get out of there and I had to do it NOW. And then I was running and running and I don't remember how I got on the road, I didn't recognize where I was, but my legs just kept running and I kept moving, and moving, and running, and away from him. And then I was home. And I was shaking and scared. I locked myself in my room and shoved my desk and chair against the door. I was so scared." The Fear had full control over her body; shaking, seizing, clenching, sobbing, and vivid tears of terror and rage flowed as she pushed herself back into the chair.

"How long were you there, in your room?"

The darkness abruptly fled Simone's vision. Beryl sat across from her. "I don't know. I fell asleep."

"And when you woke up?"

"I was sore. I tried to stand and my feet hurt, and my legs hurt, and my insides hurt. That's when I knew it wasn't a dream. I thought maybe .....I'd moved the desk against my door because, I don't know..... but I hurt so bad. And then I got scared again because what if .....he'd got me pregnant. I didn't know anything about that then, I'd never done it. And I didn't know what to do, or how to deal with anything or who to talk to."

"Is that what made you go to the hospital?"

Simone nodded, the shame flooding and drowning out the Fear. "I called Mr. Decker. He drove me. He didn't ask me anything. He was really nice."

"What did the doctor say?"

Simone felt a foot tall in the big lounge chair, like she'd bitten into an Alice in Wonderland cookie and shrank to a quarter of her real size. "He didn't say anything. He just kind of looked at me."

"How about the nurses?"

She shrugged again. "They were nice, but it was all so cold in there. I didn't like them all touching me and looking at me. I was so sore. I felt all bruised and torn and battered down there. The doctor said I was fine and gave me a couple pills. The nurse gave me a card but I lost it."

"Did the police talk to you?"

"No."

"Did you ask to talk to them?"

Simone shook her head. "There was nothing to tell. It was my own damn fault. I should have known better. I was stupid."

Beryl set down her notepad and slid her chair up to Simone. "I want you to listen to me, Simone. Listen hard. I've said this before and I'll continue to say it until you believe it. It wasn't your fault. You are not stupid, not then, not now. J.D. raped you. HE did this to you. It wasn't your fault."

But the wall had descended. Simone was numb now. It had been too much, reliving it all again. Beryl's words ricocheted off the wall leaving Simone safe and contained from all outside influences.

"Have you talked to Tanya?" Simone shook her head. "How about your Dad?" No. "Anyone?" No.

Beryl slid back her chair and regained her notepad. "Have you enrolled in that self-defense class?"

She felt herself sinking further into her container, wanting only to be at home. "I'm saving up. Hopefully next month." The truth was she'd gone to one class and was so disappointed she hadn't returned. They focused on technique when all Simone wanted to know was how to pummel someone into the ground.

Beryl nodded again. She was good at that. Simone figured they taught that in shrink school. Whatever. "I'm glad you're looking toward that class. I think it would be very constructive for you. But you need to tell your Dad and at least one friend about what happened. Keeping this secret lets the fear fester and grow. That's your homework. Next time I want to hear who you've told." Simone could feel Beryl watching her, wondering what to do with this poor, sad, confused case. Simone only wanted to leave. To be alone. She didn't care about the nightmares any more. She just wanted to go home. "Are you still calling into your Dad's friend, Michael, everyday?" Simone nodded. "Good. Keep doing that. Have you found something new to do, like we talked? Have you found a way to break out of your routine?" Simone shook her head. She didn't want to tell her about her girl's day date with Sally on Saturday. "The self-defense course isn't just for defense, it's to help out get out, socialize, do something for yourself. I want you to know that this experience hasn't crippled you. If you let fear win, J.D. has won." Simone felt herself meld with the chair, erecting the wall higher and higher. Simone nodded weakly only to make Beryl stop. "So homework is to talk to someone and break out of your routine."

"Now tell me about things that makes you happy and safe."

Simone breathed a sigh of relief. She knew why Beryl was doing this. This was their pattern. First, the prelude, then the dark. Then Beryl would have Simone shift her thoughts to lighter ones. This is the note upon which they'd end the session. This is what made the hundred dollars an hour worthwhile. And this is why Simone stayed.

"Books," Simone began, already feeling the tension leave her shoulders. "Books, books, books."

Beryl smiled. "And?"

"Hearing the wind in the trees. The smell of my Dad's soap."

"Good. Keep going." Beryl switched on the headphones and placed them on Simone's head. Buzzing and beeping alternated from one earphone to the other as Simone went through her list.

"And there's this guy...."

Beryl nodded and smiled. "Tell me about him." She pressed a couple of buttons on the stereo and the buzzing turned into music, alternating between Simone's ears.

"He's smart and strong, but he's nice. He's very nice." Simone could feel her body grow heavy and meld into the chair. "And he's beautiful." Her eyelids began to lower.

"What's his name, Simone?"

Simone had just enough time to answer before Beryl turned up the music and Simone sank into an hypnotic oblivion. "Cary Aristovin."

Chapter Ten

The corn, the second crop of tomatoes, carrots, potatoes and orange gourds were all ready to harvest. Thankfully Olivia was back. With her and Emil, Cary and Denis finished the harvest and loaded up Milner's borrowed wagon. As they loaded the last sack of corn, the stitching on Cary's old grey trousers gave way. "It seems that your new set arrived just in time," Denis chuckled as Cary removed his ripped tunic and tied it around his waist. "Though I don't think you should be farming in a battle uniform."

As the early afternoon breeze rode up under his tunic and found his bare backside, Cary waved as Denis and Emil nudged the wagon onwards to the nearby town of Mangshek. "We'll be lucky if we make enough to buy a side of beef," Cary mumbled.

Olivia walked with him back to the kitchen's side door. "Why don't you go with them? You look like you could do with a break and they might be able to get a better price with you at their side. You could ask about yer mum's dress too."

"Actually," Cary opened the door for Olivia. "It's the exact opposite. If the townsfolk saw it was my produce, they wouldn't buy it at all. They wouldn't speak a word to me except to grovel at my feet."

"Don't they know Denis works for you?" Olivia took a pot from the hook beside the hearth and set it on the table.

Cary smirked. "Yes. They just pretend he doesn't." Olivia frowned and opened her mouth to ask another question, but Cary held up a hand. "It's complicated and doesn't make any sense, I know. But that's how it works. Is Tivas working in Tolonel's smithies or with the Household itself?"

Olivia had begun to slice carrots and put them in the pot. "He's in the smithies, with a fellow named Bektman. Why?"

"I'm going to go visit your husband and then your son, Mrs. Maklinari. I will return the day after tomorrow. Because, as you said, I need a break." Cary winked at her and she beamed.

The new black wool encased his lean chest. The white collar of the silk shirt scratched against his midday stubble. The black trousers didn't ride up in uncomfortable places. While his old grey set had been worn out and too small, it was his and it was uncomfortable in a familiar way. It felt strange to be wearing new clothes, especially black battle garb. The package had been completed with a couple sets of small clothes too. Now, even if he did split his trousers he wouldn't be flashing his white backside to all the lands. Maybe Dominic hadn't done too badly after all. A final brush of his shorn blond hair and a pull of the stiff collar and Cary felt ready to face the future. He had to admit, too, that the new soft black leather boots fit much better than his old ones. And they didn't have any holes.

Cary made it to Reid's before dark. The Village was a loose composite of huts and houses that lined the main road up to the City's gates. Immigrants lived here because it was the closest they could get to living in the City. The Maklinaris had lived on Juno for nearly ten years; the closest they could build their small house was a quarter mile from the City gates. Cary handed off Marcus and the blacksmith stripped the horse of his tack and saddle before they headed indoors. "I'll look at the repairs in the morning. My wife, your cook, has left us a small feast. So tonight, we eat, drink," Reid leaned in and whispered, "and you tell me why you're wearing black."

Nursing a bit of a hangover the next morning, Cary awoke on one of the small beds in the Maklinari Household. It was warm here. Everything was made of wood. And the nightmare didn't invade his sleep. Maybe he should drink more often.

Reid took a look at Marcus' tack and shook his head. "It needs some solid repair work. I'll loan you some replacements. I'll be done by the time you're back through from the north."

If the Creator had broken a mountain range and scattered the pieces over the Rire Ocean, Juno would be the tallest piece and the one furthest out. Cliffs and broken mountains lined the majority of the island's coastline with only the southeast corner dipping sandy shores into the ocean. Juno was split by a gorge, the Tmaz cavern, which separated the north from the south, and the City sat poised on the eastern lip of the cavern, greeting the twin suns and incoming merchant ships from Inner Rire nations.

Juno's north was currently home to five Commanding Households. Captain Signan Stats, Commander of Juno's Navy, had a Household overlooking the rocky cliffs of Juno's sailor town on the farthest north coastline. Within spitting distance to the City, Lords Arissio Silva and Colin Darine organized and maintained supplies for the Warriors. Darine also had paddocks and stables full of horse as his family trained the Warrior's Companions. The Tolonel Household was nestled just behind the northern reaches of the Jire forest on the Western cliffs.

The suns had just touched the tips of the mountains in the west when Cary breached the expansive outer reaches of the Tolonel Household. Like the northern country with its vast forests and parklands was so unlike the southern pastures and farmlands, the Tolonel Household was so unlike any other Household. It was more like a village in and of itself. The main Household was surrounded by blacksmithies and metallurgy shops, stables, wood mills, leather shops, and drilling grounds.

This was the testing ground for Juno's armament. The temperature rose swiftly on the interior of the Household's outer walls. Smithies cooked the open air as products of their craft - swords, spears, shields, chains, armour - hung outside their workshops.

Though the road followed straight through to the main Household, Cary didn't intend to follow it. He dismounted and ducked into a smithy with axes, long, heavy, and double-headed, leaning against the brick wall. Two smiths, the master and apprentice, presumably, were bent over the fire adjusting its temperature. "Now, too hot and the metal won't bind. The blade will fall apart at first strike."

Cary stepped up and cleared his throat. The two jumped. The master, a large man, balding but with a keen eye and not too old, instantly took in Cary's black attire and bowed deeply. The apprentice, a young lean and wiry lad of perhaps thirteen years, followed suit. "My Lord."

Cary hesitated at the recognition, then cleared his throat. "Ah, fine workmanship you have displayed outside, Master....?"

The man and bedazzled youth both rose. "Uh, Labelin, my lord Aristovin. Thank you, my lord."

"And you?" Cary looked straight at the apprentice. The wide-eyed youth wrung his hands inside his leather apron.

"Uh, Van....Vantaren, my lord," the apprentice had begun to sweat.

"And how long have you been apprenticing, Vantaren?"

"Since spring, my lord."

"You look to be in good hands with Master Labelin." Both master and apprentice beamed. "I'm looking for a young immigrant smithy, Tivas Maklinari. Very good from what I hear."

Master Labelin spoke enthusiastically, "Aye. He is good. Some of the best work I've seen, even around here."

Apprentice Vantaren piped up, "He's working on an alloy to take on the Outerworld."

"Aye. I think he's almost got it, too." Labelin leaned to Cary with a keen smirk and a gleam in his eye. "Put the rest of us to shame."

"He comes from a good family. Where could I find him?"

Labelin pointed a large finger down the side path to the north. "Four shops down and in the back. He is with Master Bektman. Good with metal but not so good with flesh, if you follow."

Cary nodded and bid the two good day. The fourth shop was a small wooden shack that was likely to fall over in the next storm. Cary left Marcus and strode into the darkened smithy. The tall man hammering turned a discerning eye toward the entry and growled. He squinted against the light from outside. "What do you want?"

"I've come to inquire after Tivas Maklinari." Bektman's eyes must have adjusted for the sneer disappeared. The suspicious glint in his eye didn't.

"He's round back," and resumed hammering, watching Cary out of the corner of his eye as the Aristovin thanked him and strode out of the darkened shop.

Through a short doorway, a small room enclosed a hearth the size of a stable stall. The room was as hot as an oven and, if it hadn't been for the ill-fitting slats holding up the roof, the heat would have been unbearable. The room was bright with the coals of the hot hearth and the daylight filtering in through the slatted walls. A shadowed figure was hunched over the far anvil pounding a sheet of metal. Cary noticed that in the past two years, Tivas was looking more and more like his father. His shoulders had broadened with a little more height added to his stature. His arms weren't as thick as Reid's, but the veins and tendons on his wiry frame stood out as he worked. Dark hair stuck out from under a handkerchief wrapped around his head. Tivas was mumbling. Just like his father, Cary thought.

"I've heard you're getting a reputation of your own."

Tivas jumped and spun. "Cary?" The frown disappeared. "Fate's mercy, it is you!" He threw down his work and grabbed Cary's hand and shoulder with strong hands, a broad smile shining through the soot and sweat on his face.

"How are you my friend?" Cary asked. "Your mother told me you were here."

"I am well. Came here last winter thanks to Da. He spread the word and Tolonel personally came to see my work."

"I'm glad to hear old fuddy can still see good workmanship even if it is from immigrant hands."

"Actually, I get more flak from his Sons and the other smiths combined. What are you doing this far North?"

"I come on an errand. But I also have a problem."

"Wait a second," Tivas stepped back from Cary, "You're wearing black." Then Tivas' face suddenly went ashen. "How?"

Cary shook his head. "I'll tell you all about it if you and Daant will sup with me tonight."

Tivas crossed his arms and regarded Cary. "Okay. Deal. Now what's the errand and this problem that brought you all the way north?"

"First, I would like a sample of your work."

Tivas gazed suspiciously at Cary. "My work?"

Cary nodded. "Apparently, your work is getting noticed."

Tivas didn't budge. "By whom?"

Cary didn't want to bring Dmitri into the conversation. He knew the Mentor would only confuse things. Cary decided to gamble. "I heard you have a new alloy. I'd like to see." He jiggled the coin bag. "I can pay."

Tivas' steps were tentative as he moved to take the coin bag. He gasped, "Fate's eyes! I've never before seen this much money. Where did you get it?"

"You ask too many questions, Tivas."

"This is too much."

"I'm not going to argue any more. Please can I see your work? Give me an axe or something."

Tivas dropped the bag onto his counter then pulled a breastplate from the rafters. "I don't have any weapons yet, just this. I haven't given it a real test. Daant and I have been playing around and it stopped the blows we threw at it."

Cary held the breastplate up to the light. He could see the hammer marks in the steel, and the rivets from where Tivas had joined the front to the back. He could see it was a steel alloy, but it was amazingly light. There were no marks from a blade or axe in the plate.

"What were you using?"

"An Outerworld blade."

Cary did a doubletake at Tivas' words. He brought the plate into a slit of daylight to examine it. Nothing. Not a mark other than that which helped make it. "Let me see that blade."

Tivas' enthusiasm was evident. So was his nervousness. He pulled the heavy Outerworld sword from behind the counter. Cary placed the breastplate on the ground and accepted the sword. It was the first sword he'd held in nearly three years. It was ill-balanced for his hand, for his skill, his height. But it was well taken care of; Tivas had oiled it and sharpened it with loving attention. "Do you have another plate? A control?"

Tivas again moved excitedly around the shop and pulled a thick plate of steel from beside his counter. The plate of steel hit the ground beside the breastplate with a dull thud on the dirt floor.

Tivas retreated as Cary felt the balance of the sword in his hand. He switched it from hand to hand, feeling gravity pull the weight of the blade, which way the hilt shifted. Feeling how his hand, initially grasping the hilt strangely, now fell into an old routine. The familiarity traveled up his arm, his muscles and tendons remembering how to move, when to constrict, and when to flow.

Then Cary raised the sword and swung with practiced grace into the steel plate and then the breastplate. The ground beneath the steel plate showed through the gash. The breastplate was unmarked as before. Cary's hand ached with the reverberation and effort.

"Wow." Cary turned at Tivas' gasp. But Tivas wasn't looking at the experiment. The look of astonishment, of wonder, of worship was for Cary alone.

Suddenly self-conscious, Cary placed the Outerworld sword on the counter with the marred steel plate, then broke the spell. "My father's sword was stolen."

Tivas snapped back to reality. "What? Who?"

"A native girl we had cooking for us. She took my mother's wedding gown too."

Tivas snorted then. "Only native would do that."

Cary rolled his eyes. "I wanted to know if you'd heard or seen anything. Tolonel must acquire weapons coming through here all the time."

"Daant would know. He's a stable boy up at the Household. He hears all the gossip and gets to drool over the Ladies." Tivas slipped the leather apron from around his neck and pulled the handkerchief from his head. Black hair stuck out from all angles. "Are you staying at the Household or the Inn?"

"I was going to stay at the Inn."

Tivas nodded and dipped his head into the barrel of water. He scrubbed at his face and hair, then reappeared water dripping over his bare chest and face. "Okay. I'll go find Daant and meet you there."

Cary stashed the breastplate in his saddlebags then walked down the main road from the Household, Marcus following behind. Cary rounded the corner by Labellin's smithy and stopped. A golden haired man in a golden tunic stood before him. Tall and lean with curly locks, a jeweled hand and a Warrior sword at his hip, Lord Durlan Tolonel locked his gaze on Cary. "To what do I owe the pleasure of the Lord Aristovin's Son and heir?" he said through pursed lips.

The deliberate omission of his title was beginning to sting. "Just come to visit some friends, my lord."

Tolonel's eyebrow rose. "Congratulations are in order." He nodded at Cary's new tunic. "I look forward to seeing your father's sword in action once again."

"Not likely, my lord. My father's sword was stolen. Along with my mother's wedding dress." Maybe it was a good thing the sword had been stolen.

Durlan Tolonel's face was difficult to read. Cary didn't know if he saw shock or disbelief in his eyes. "I will inform Fermes of the situation. Both are unique items and cannot go unnoticed. We will find them and put all to rights." In more ways than one, I'm sure, Cary thought. Lord Tolonel nodded and then with cat-like grace, proceeded past Cary to the Household.

Cary remembered Langrid Tolonel's foot in his back during his Test and wondered if something similar hadn't happened between his father and Durlan.

It was dark by the time Cary reached the doors of the Feather in the Hat Inn. He'd left Marcus to be stabled and entered the large bright common room. It was packed. Cary hadn't seen so many people in such a small place in a long time.

The innkeeper took one look at Cary and his black uniform and ushered him to a table already packed. The short, fat innkeeper swished a towel at the table's occupants and after they, too, took one glance at Cary, quickly relinquished the table and bowed as they left, mugs in hand. "There you are, my lord," as he wiped the table clean with his ever-present cloth. "Don't often get nobles in here. All stay at the Household."

"Just come to sup with some friends tonight, Master....?"

"Ah, Hedgeworth, my lord. We have a fine pork roast on the spit tonight."

Cary threw a couple of Dominic and Everett's silvers on the table, "And I'll be staying the night."

Master Hedgeworth waved the rag as he shook his head. "No, no, my lord. None of that, now." And he disappeared.

Cary had discovered, much to his dismay, that when a noble was among commoners the place was no longer common. Things and people changed. A stunned hush was the first thing to happen. Refusal of all money from the noble was the next. Then, bowing and groveling. Despite what the Maklinaris thought about the native disregard for the Warriors, there was still enough reverence to make Cary nauseous. What made it worse was the colour of his tunic. It didn't matter that the Crest wasn't on his chest. He was a Crested Son of the Lord Commander in Chief. Everyone was going to have something to talk about tonight.

The minstrel was singing a woe begotten song of a love gone wrong. Several girls in red petticoats swayed amongst the crowd of guests and villagers slapped their bottoms, laughing loudly as the girls yelped and pretended to not like the attention.

He could disappear here, or at least feel like he was sunk behind a wall of people unseen and unheard. Although he knew only too well that too many recognized him and watched his every move. They were all native Junoans. And like a native's bright hair and light eyes, part of their common knowledge was the Aristovin legacy.

"Anything else for you, my lord?" The serving girl had appeared in front of him. So had a plate of the pork and a mug of ale. She was plain but the gleam in her eye told him she wasn't as dumb as she made out. She flung her long auburn plait over her shoulder and gave Cary a distinct look-over. "Pork is fresh, m'lord. From Master Korrow's farm, it is."

"What's your name?"

The serving girl looked over her shoulder then whispered, with a blush, "Maryta, my lord."

"Thank you, Maryta. I am expecting two young immigrants. One is a black-haired smithy, the other is a brown-haired stable boy." At Maryta's frown, he pushed one of the two silvers her way and added, "They are my friends." Maybe she was just another female vying for Cary's noble attentions. Maybe she had sense.

Maryta took the silver and nodded. "They'll find their way here, my lord." She swung her hips away. Cary watched as her red petticoats swished against her legs, legs neither too long nor too short, and a shape he found not unattractive. His eyes traced the curve of her shoulder under her flimsy blouse and followed her long plait down to her waist. She rotated her hips to squeeze between some men and Cary found his eyes on a laughing man. Each freckle, each wrinkle seemed to somehow leap from his face to Cary and, like he was seeing everything for the first time, the passage of time slowed. Everything was a detail. Everything, a nuance. A twitch of a cheek muscle. The flick of a finger. An itch inside an ear. The laughter reverberated through a dense cloud of time as if the very air itself had thickened. The music bounced within the noisy room. The gap between Maryta's teeth, as she laughed mightily with the group, seemed to swallow his entire vision. Across the room, the hand that slapped another serving girl's backside moved slowly through the thickened air. Her expression was exaggerated and just as slow as Cary watched the pantomime play out. A match was struck, the snap hitting the air, echoing as the sulphur smell slowly gave way to the rich, pungency of the tobac in a pipe and mingled with the scent of pork in front of Cary.

And there, beneath everything else, they lingered. Like solitary pinpoints of light in the darkness, he felt each of them, each person in the room as a unique and independent essence. Yes, essence, that's what it was. Each core of being, unaltered by their dress, the food they ate, the miasma of the sight, sound and smell of the common room, each stood out.

The man smoking his newly lit pipe faded from Cary's eyes, the clothing disappeared along with the skin, muscle, and bone of the man. Only the essence remained. Happiness. The man was genuinely happy at that moment. Worries had been temporary forgotten and the good-natured and quiet cheesemaker reveled in the merriment of the surroundings.

An overpowering sensation took Cary as he saw the crowd of the inn, not in the flesh, but as their souls. Pride, envy, greed, some contentment that would quickly fade as they stepped out the door later that night. In the crowded din their essences seemed to mingle.

All together there were over thirty people in the common room and he could feel each. His Warrior-trained mind had calculated the odds the moment he'd stepped into the room; now that calculation was a knowing he felt throughout his being. The essence of these people called out to him, he didn't need to seek them, tally them. They just were.

It was overpowering. Cary looked down at his hands. The hands clasping his mug seemed not his, the fingers wiggled slightly. He tried to shake his head, shake this sudden sense of the surreal. An idea struck. Turn, he thought. He released his hands from his mug.

Turn. His eyes closed against the muted din. *Turn.* The image of the mug sprung into his mind's eye. *Turn.* Every detail was there. Every curve, every shadow, every crack. *Turn. Turn.*

In his mind's eye, the mug slowly rotated.

He opened his eyes. The mug handle now pointed away from him. Maryta appeared before his table again. For a moment, her hair was short and blonde, and she wore trousers in place of her red petticoats. She was a completely different person.

A bag of coin hit the table with a bang.

The room snapped into view. The music grated, the smoke billowed, and the laughter again boomed. It was all back. It was all gone.

Tivas and Daant collapsed onto the bench opposite Cary. A redheaded Maryta appeared beside them. "Something to drink, boys?"

Cary pushed a silver to Maryta. "Ale and pork, please."

Tivas and Daant each whipped out a silver. Maryta took the immigrants' silver and left.

"When will you learn?" Tivas shook his head as Cary pushed his silver toward the two. They pushed it back.

"I've got to keep trying." Maryta appeared again with mugs of ale and plates of pork; his room would be ready when he needed it.

Daant started in on the pork, his eyes shining under the mass of freckles. "I asked around after yer Da's sword and yer Ma's dress. We'll keep on the lookout. I got me an ear to the ground at the stables."

"I met Tolonel on the way here." Both immigrants stopped eating and stared at him. "I told him too."

Two sighs collectively escaped the immigrants. "He really doesn't like you, does he?"

Daant burst out, "Is it really 'cause yer Da got the Chief posting instead of him?"

Cary shrugged and played with his food, "I guess so. I never heard the full story." It was true. Even his father hadn't been able to explain Tolonel's hatred.

"So are you going to take your Da's post? You are Crested, right? You're not just parading around in black for your own good." Cary told them the story of the past few days, minus the bit about being a Mentor's apprentice. At the end, he could tell they were waiting for him to say he'd take the Chief post just to put Lord Tolonel in his place, but instead he said, "I don't know what I'm going to do," and shrugged.

"But that just doesn't make sense. They're going against tradition," Tivas said, pushing his empty plate away. Maryta appeared again, took their empty plates, and topped up their ale.

Then the music and the room quieted as the voices rose. "And I say it's our land too. Who are they to say, nay, we cannot fight to save ourselves? I say we have to fight for our own freedom and not depend on a bunch of richies."

A chorus of shouts in agreement broke out. "If you attended to your farm as much as you think of fighting, Aharon, you'd have a fine crop, indeed!" Laughter and then a voice from the side.

"Have you seen an Outerworlder, Aharon? I say let them face those beasts. Let them die and not us!" More shouts of agreement.

"And wha' happens when they're all gone?" Aharon retorted, slurring drunkenly, "You know there are only a handful left. And then t' Outerworld will march right to your doorstep to slaughter your family."

"I say we ask the lord in the corner why natives armed with swords and pride cannot fight."

And Cary froze.

All eyes in the silent room turned on him. He would have borne Sesmon's glare again if only to have those eyes turn away from him. A man -- Aharon, Cary's instincts said --squeezed through the crowd, ale sloshing over the lip of his mug. His bloodshot gaze was stuck on Cary. Aharon stood at the end of the table, and the rest of the crowd seemed to gather in and perch on his shoulder. "So, m'Lord Aristovin, whatdaya say?" Aharon demanded as he swayed slightly. "You have the Chief post left vacant so many years, you now have Command. Explain it so that we, peasants, may all un'erstand; why do you deny us the fight?" His fist slammed down on the table making Tivas and Daant jump.

An old instinct had braced Cary. "Your fathers denied you the fight when they declared you to the Council. It is upon them you should place your blame."

Aharon took a swig of his ale. "I want to change my father's decision; I want to change my destiny and fight."

To change destiny. It has been so long.

"Again you are making demands of the wrong person, my friend," he replied. "I have only recently earned the Crest and have not taken the post to which you refer. There is no Commander here and no sword. Take your query to the Council."

A shout from within the crowd, "And what would the Council do for us? They hide behind their high walls. They do not know what is going on in their own land."

Aharon nodded and turned to the crowd, "We cannot depend upon the Council. We must depend on ourselves. We must rise to the fight, defend our land to the last." He turned back to Cary after the cheering subsided. "We only ask your 'pproval, your direction. We will fight. We want to fight."

It has been so long. There seemed to be an edge of sadness in the voice. Did this voice in his mind also resent the Council's authority?

Cary felt a lump lodge in his throat. What was he to say? He could do nothing but refuse. He couldn't grant them approval; not only was he not in a position to do so, but they, also, were in no position to fight. They weren't trained. They would be defenseless against the enemy, and they'd last only minutes. All of them. "As I said, my friend. I am in no position to grant approval. I am only here to sup with my friends and enjoy good company."

Aharon, perhaps for the first time, saw Tivas and Daant. He sneered, "I heard the Lord Aristovin had a soft spot for immigrants."

Aharon's opponent yelled through the crowd, "Better to let them fight and die than us!" The common room was vindictive in their roar of approval.

Daant was suddenly on his feet and nearly on the table. "I'd fight, I would. Fight and die for Juno. Juno is my home!" Tivas pulled his friend's shirt, but couldn't drag him down.

Aharon roared a great laugh and gestured to his audience, "And there you have it! We will have people fighting for a land that is not their own and us depending on them to succeed." Suddenly his face was in Cary's. "Is that the way you would have it, m'lord?" he growled. "Shall we place our hope in their hands instead of yours?"

A calmness settled through Cary and he met Aharon's drunken glare. "If it were mine to give, I would grant the order for all to fight for their freedom. All of you." Cary rose and stood to face the crowd, hoping desperately to dispel an impeding riot. "You," he pointed, "you, all of you. And my friends here, who have lost so much more than any of us will ever know," he gestured to Tivas and Daant. "But it is not within my power. I am not in Command and I am no Warrior. As for hope, I suggest you place it in yourselves."

Cary regained his seat, the murmur returning to the room when suddenly Aharon's mug knocked his own. "I take that as an oath, my friend." He drank a gulp and left. Cary sighed and pushed away his ale, no longer thirsty.

"Still the same Cary," Tivas raised his mug. Daant cheerfully joined his friend's toast and slurped his ale.

"I was just sitting here. What did I do?"

Daant's mug hit the table empty, "She's still after ya, my friend." He licked the foam from his lips. "Ya know that as long as ya hold yer vendetta, She'll come after yoos."

Cary pointed a finger across the table taking them both in, "Just stop that talk. It's nothing I do."

Tivas raised his mug, "You just told these men to take fate into their own hands, Cary. That's blasphemy." And the mug was emptied.

Cary rolled his eyes and signaled a maid for another round. "I don't have a vendetta. I'm just angry."

"For ten years?" Tivas asked. "For anger to last that long, it's got to be pretty strong."

"Vendetta-like strength," Daant chimed in.

"It's Fate, friend. She wants the hairs on the back of your neck." Tivas grinned.

Cary ground his teeth. Daant continued, "Ya know the stories. Ya have to settle with Her or yoos get no peace."

"Peace won't bring back my parents," Cary mumbled. The mugs of ale arrived. One directly hit the table with a bang and a slosh, right into Cary's lap. Cary's teeth clenched amidst the apologies from the maid and the suppressed smirks from his friends.

Against his insistence to spend the night at the inn, Tivas and Daant headed back to the Household and let Cary to his room. The Aristovin snickered on the way. He had left the silver initially offered to Master Hedgeworth on the table the entire night hoping it would be used to pay the tab. But, at the end of their night, it still sat. Cary had left it there, still hoping someone needy would pick it up. He smiled at the thought of a serving girl finding it and buying herself a new dress.

His hand came upon the doorknob as Master Hedgeworth's voice came down the hall. "My lord! My lord!" he said hardly louder than a whisper in the sleeping hall. He trotted up to Cary. "My lord," he panted. "Your silver," and he held out his hand. Cary received it, smile disappearing as Hedgeworth retreated, and sulked into his room, the silver heavy in his pocket.

Morning saw Cary fresh, only slightly hung over, and ready to make the long trek back to the south. Marcus' saddlebags were packed full of rations thanks to a dutiful Master Hedgeworth. Villages were sparse, he said then pointed to the incoming storm, "There's the end of the season. Best you make good time back south."

By suppertime, Marcus was wearing repaired leatherworks and Cary was bidding a regrettable farewell to his former blacksmith. "I need to get back before the rain sets in."

The rains swept in suddenly as they often did closer to the end of autumn. Quick and fierce, short bursts of pelting rain soon petered out to nothing at all. Soon winter would be here; too cold and too dry to do anything. Cary and Marcus were drenched but neither minded. Cary was glad to wash last night's sticky ale from his trousers.

Just before the suns set and darkness settled in, Cary found himself on the Plains. It happened sometimes. An instinctual pull brought him here. No amount of resistance could avoid the call.

Passed the bridge over the Tmaz Cavern.

Passed the east road to Trium Hall and Cannor Manor.

Passed the western forests and mountains in which Dmitri lived.

Cary rode south and crested the last set of hills.

Burned grassland stretched out to the south and down to a sandy coastline that rounded to the east. Fragments of an old stone wall lay like broken teeth from east to west. There was nothing here except the wind, salt air, and echoes of battles past.

Water droplets bounced catching what was left of the light. Streaking rain made the openness of the Plains seem shadowed. Humid air lifted the smell of the dead from the ground.

Cary sat astride Marcus, both of them silent on the open ground. Listening.

Chapter Eleven

"Karen, I'm here," Simone called as she walked through the swing doors into the kitchen.

A forty-something woman sat at a desk in a four by four foot closet that acted as their office. Karen rolled out her chair into the kitchen, her greying brunette hair tied in a perennial French braid. With glasses perched on her nose, Karen attempted to focus on Simone, "Hey, hun. How you doin'? How's the thumb?"

"Okay," Simone nodded noncommittally as she hung up her backpack. "I need to run over to the library for a drop-off. Be back in ten."

"Sure," Karen rolled back into the closet cum office.

Simone grabbed a couple of books and a cheque book from her pack. She'd stepped back across the kitchen linoleum when Karen called out, "Before I forget, your boyfriend dropped by this morning."

Simone froze mid-stride. Fear lurked, but craving to put it all aside, she willed Denial into its place.

She backtracked. "What did this boyfriend look like?"

Karen was hunched back over paperwork and a keyboard. "Dark hair, nice smile, tallish." Simone continued to pull at Denial to keep Fear at bay. "He was nice," Karen finally pulled up from the paperwork and glanced back at Simone. She did a double-take then spun the chair around, "What's wrong?"

Blood rushed out of her head and straight into her feet. Suddenly the location of everything in the kitchen became the most important yet the least important thing in the world. "Did he say anything else?"

Karen rose, slowly removing the glasses from her nose. "No. He said he was looking for you and didn't know your schedule."

Denial finally broke then and the shaking began anew. "Did you tell him?"

"Do I need to call the police?"

Her voice broke too loudly in the cafe kitchen, "Did you tell him?"

"No. I told him you'd be in later." Simone swore under her breath. "I thought he knew you. It sounded like he knew you. He seemed nice."

"He isn't. I don't want anything to do with him. Did you tell him anything else?"

"No. What happened? Are you sure the police shouldn't be involved?"

"No, just don't talk to him again, okay?" Karen finally nodded.

She thrust the books back into her pack, on top of the bear spray, and threw her pack over her shoulder. She left Karen staring after her. Now both Sally and Karen were worried. Three years and she was finally approaching a normal life. Now it was all coming down around her. All because of J.D. He'd ruined her life three years ago and he was doing it again.

Her pace shifted from race-walking to jogging. Across the street, down the block, her eyes darted to every corner, every car, every face searching for J.D. expecting him to pounce when she dared to blink.

The crack across the library's glass door shone in the late morning light. Simone burst through the entrance and strode directly to the desk, yearning to get the day over with so that she could barricade herself in her house all over again. And in that instant Simone made a decision: she'd tell Karen she'd finish out the day, then take a couple weeks off. Maybe she'd go back, maybe she wouldn't. She only needed the money to pay for her sessions with Beryl. There was a large part of her that felt guilty at the prospect of leaving Karen stranded, but it needed to be done. Everything would be sorted out later. Right now, she just needed to get out of town and go home. Where she was safe.

There was no one at the desk. Simone strode toward the office at the back of the library when Alex stepped out from between the stacks, "Hey," he smiled and advanced.

Simone pulled up reflexively then slowly retreated, "I was looking for Mrs. Harper."

Alex paused, standing straight. "She's on her break."

The entrance/exit was behind her. The desk was to the left. The stacks were to the right. Where was the emergency exit? "Sorry. I don't know her schedule. I don't come in during the mornings."

"Can I help?" As Alex stepped to the left, behind the desk, Simone saw the 'EXIT' sign glowing in the recessed interns and allowed herself to relax.

"I came to pay for the door. From the other night."

Alex looked at her then, as if his blue eyes were recording and analysing her image. He was re-assessing her, revising his initial assessment. Then his smile grew to a grin. "I knew you were good people the moment I met you."

And then the claws of Fear clutching her heart and stomach eased. The coldness that shot through her spine didn't drill so deeply. A warmth blossomed inside her gut and began to radiate out to her limbs.

Simone held out the folded cheque. It was damp from her sweaty palm. "I, uh, didn't know who to make it out to or for how much."

Alex slid over a piece of scrap paper and placed a pencil beside it. "Write down your phone number and I'll have Mrs. Harper call you." She placed her open pack on the desk and accepted the pencil and paper. "Returns?" he asked, lifting his chin toward her pack.

She nodded.

He took the books from inside her pack, the canister of bear spray clanking against the counter. Simone paused, waiting for comment. But none came. Alex turned the pack back to her and scanned the books, his gaze flitting to her. She was self-conscious this close to him. He smelled good. Sliding the paper across the desk, she asked, "Did you come into "The Only Cup" this morning?"

Alex finished the scanning the returns and smiled, "No. I don't know where that is yet. I'm new, remember? Why?"

Simone tucked the blank cheque into the pocket of her pack. "No reason. Just wondering. Bye."

As her hand grabbed the door handle, Alex said, "Bye, Simone." She froze, the Fear back and turning her spine to ice. It was strange hearing her name coming from him, like a cat speaking in her father's voice. While she may have been panicked two nights ago, Simone clearly remembered not telling Alex her name.

Simone turned back. Dark hair, tallish, nice smile. Just like Karen said. Shit. No.

"How did you...?" she managed to squeak.

Alex waved the scrap paper. "You wrote it down. It was nice to see you again. Bye," then pushed the book trolley across the library floor and disappeared between the stacks.

Chapter Twelve

Denis looked up from the Household ledger as Cary walked in. "You're going to go blind crunching numbers," Cary said as he strode to the hearth and pulled off his drenched tunic. He threw another log on the fire.

"I see you got caught in the storm."

Feeding the fire another log and shivering, Cary asked, "How far will Dominic's silver take us?"

"Beef is at a premium at the moment; autumn prices. We didn't buy much in Mangshek. I thought we might try adding some more vegetables to our diet."

Cary paused midway through pulling off a soaked boot. "More?"

A smirk appeared on Denis' face. "The silver allowed us to buy an entire side of beef and replace many of the staples that we'd depleted this year. I also bought a new rooster and a hen. We have a bit left over for emergencies."

"Eggs?"

"Eggs," Denis beamed.

A wave of relief swept over Cary as he stuck a dry dishrag into his soaked boot and then pulled at the other one. Denis removed his spectacles and placed a package upon the table. "Olivia has worked her magic once again. Your mother's wedding dress."

He paused midway through pulling off the other boot. "How?"

"I didn't ask. It's back and that's all that matters." Denis closed the ledger. "There is fish stew in the cubby hole and apple pie in the cupboard. I suggest you eat." He plucked the kettle from the counter and opened the kitchen door to dip it into the rain barrel. "Your bathwater's lukewarm by now. It'll need to be refreshed."

"I had a bath…" he paused, counting in his head, "three nights ago." Cary pulled out the dishrag he'd been pushing into his other wet boot.

With shaking arms, Denis placed the kettle on the hook over the fire. "I suggest you have another. Dominic's Test is tomorrow morning at Trium and you are expected."

Cary groaned and padded back to the roaring hearth, the fresh heat making the fish stew fragrant. "Dmitri will have unkind words with me if I don't return tomorrow. I was supposed to be back today."

Denis nodded. "You've been Crested, whether you wanted it or not. Until you find a way to give it back or void your Test, there are now expectations of you."

"Not that there weren't before," pulling the pot from the cubbyhole with the dishrag in hand.

"I'm sure that you will find a way to make this all work. There is more than one way to do something, isn't that right?" Cary snorted as his own words were spoken back to him. He hadn't yet told Denis that he'd accepted an apprenticeship with Dmitri.

Denis bid goodnight and left the kitchen. Cary called after him, "But I'm not wearing the Household colours!"

A crowd had already gathered east of Trium Hall. Beyond the confines of the practice grounds and the gardens, a field opened up across the hills, the Ocean Rire stretching out across the horizon. Rain from last night had turned to a frosty white in the cool morning air. Flags bearing Household colours snapped in the mid-morning breeze. The crowd was a plethora of grey uniformed Sons and their distinctly attired families, from Inner City whites to the Commanding Household vivids.

Cary approached on foot having left Marcus at the stables. He wore his new black wool and he tried hard not to feel self-conscious at the looks and whispers.

Dominic, in his own grey uniform, approached. "No hard feelings?" He asked as he grasped Cary's shoulder.

Cary grunted and leveled a glare at him. "Let's just say I'm trying not to hold a grudge." Dominic laughed heartily. Cary recognized it as a burst of anxiety and wished for the old times when they all laughed freely together.

Dominic led him back to the rest of the Roan family, a study in the dark burgundy of their Household. Only Dominic's younger brother,

Frej, stood out in his grey uniform. Count Goran Roan, a man of only thirty-nine years, sat in a wheeled chair, hunched and wheezing with each breath. Cary held the frail hand, "It is good to see you, Count Roan. At last you will have a Warrior son to whom you can pass on your vast knowledge."

The count coughed and rasped. "Yes, my dear Young One. I fear I will not last to see Frej's Test. The least I could do is see Dominic a Warrior, even if the event killed me!"

"As you can see, my dear, my husband's humour has not changed in your absence." The countess, petite and brunette with the burgundy of her dress accentuating her alabaster skin, extended her delicate fingers to Cary.

Cary took her fingers and kissed them, "I apologise for my absence, Countess. I have missed your company."

"Tosh," she commented. "You have been exercising your individuality. I know that even if no one else will say it."

Cary suppressed a smile as he turned to acknowledge Frej and his younger sister, Mika. He stood back and scanned the crowd. The green of the Fraaml Household was absent from those present. "Where is Everett?"

Dominic opened his mouth to answer but stopped as the crowd began to murmur.

Lord Brask Fraaml appeared at the far edge of the crowd. A chill ran down Cary's back. The Warrior was not wearing the green of his Household. He was wearing black. This was why the Fraaml family was not in attendance; their patriarch would be Testing Dominic.

It had been many years since Cary'd last seen Brask Fraaml. The lord had a larger than life quality made possible by his stature and the muscles straining the seams of his tunic and trousers. He had a voice that could bellow drill orders across the Plains and reach the gate of Cary's Household. But the hands that had played with Cary and the laugh that rumbled in the man's chest revealed that the man was a kitten inside. And, as he delivered the news of Cary's father's death ten years ago, the look in Brask Fraaml's eyes spoke a sadness that could never be fully expressed.

The man who now strode across the field was far from the one Cary had known as a child. His stride was fluid and strong, each foot placed deliberately and precisely. His presence had a frightening grace. Cary had been witness to Tests in his youth, had seen Warriors display their skills while teaching at Trium. But watching Brask Fraaml stride across the Green to meet Dominic sent him into a terrifying realization: this was one of the greatest Warriors Juno had ever known, just like his own father. And, as strong and skilled and powerful as this Warrior was, the Outerworld was worse. If the Outerworld could kill his father, they could kill Brask and Dominic and everyone.

Brask stopped centerfield and bowed, his dark auburn hair flitting in the ocean breeze. A glint of gold around his neck caught in the daylight. The Warrior straightened and focused on Dominic.

Cary heard Dominic swallow heavily and take a deep breath before stepping out to accept his Test. Two steps out, Dominic hesitated. Brask had drawn his sword. It had happened lightning quick and soundlessly.

Disgust mingled with terror in Cary's throat. Dominic had no weapon. He was defenseless against one of the best Warriors in history. And everyone was standing around to cheer them on.

If you can survive your Test and the first battle, then you are worthy of being a Warrior. The voice reminded him of the popular saying handed down through the cohorts.

Cary had witnessed Sons being slashed, cut, beaten to a pulp. Some had been seriously wounded during their Test. But, like him, they'd all been offered a weapon. They'd had a chance. This was more than allowing or endorsing the beating of immigrants. This was injustice condoned and performed by his own peers, and he chalked it all up to the elitism of the nobility, the Warrior tradition, but above all, the Council. All in the name of getting killed.

Bile rose in his throat. Cary wanted to leave. He wanted to turn and leave like he left Trium Hall three years ago. But he also desperately wanted to do *something*. To retreat or fight?

Dominic had engaged in an evasive protocol. He had no choice with Brask coming at him with a sword. Dominic ducked and rolled, barely missing a descending blade. Brask spun and swung as Dominic rose, blocking Cary's view. A gasp rang out on the far side of the crowd. When Cary saw him again, Dominic was sporting a slashed sleeve and blood was running down his hand.

That was the last straw. Time to retreat. Cary backed away from the clearing. As he turned to leave, he saw something change in Dominic. His eyes. His manner. Cary recognized that change; he felt it to his core. It was exactly the way he'd felt when he'd walked away from Trium's Greens that bright sunny afternoon three years ago. Exactly as he felt now.

"Time to take matters into my own hands," he'd thought. He had acknowledged Fate by denying Her efforts. And a week ago he'd chosen to fight, but in his own way. Now Dominic was choosing to fight, choosing his own course of action.

Brask's blade descended. And in a moment that Cary would remember forever, the air seemed to thicken and he saw each movement as an eternity. The sword sliced through the air with a sound he'd never fully realized. The black wool around Brask's arms tightened around flexing biceps. The grass under Dominic's boots sighed under his shifting weight. It was like the Feather in the Hat Inn all over again. The mug had turned that night. Should he attempt to alter the course of events here? Could he?

A wise man knows when to take action and when to watch the action.

With two palms Dominic caught the blade with just enough force to push it aside and down, throwing the momentum to the ground. Using Brask's force upon the blade, Dominic compounded the inertia of the blade and his own force to kick the Warrior's abdomen and send him off balance.

Cary had never seen such a move. It was an act of sheer confidence and stupidity. And of conviction.

The sword plunged deep into the ground and Brask fell to the side as Dominic regained his feet and stood, waiting.

Brask rose, pulled his sword from the ground, cleaned and re-sheathed it. Through deep, easy breaths, he spoke, "We are finished," and bowed to Dominic, Grand Master Sesmon in the distance, and the count and countess respectively. He walked down to Trium to leave Dominic loaded with adrenaline and gasping for breath.

Cheers went up. Cary stood in shocked amazement. This was not what Tests were about. They went on for hours. There was blood and sweat and lots of fighting. Cary thought his own Test was a one-off, a technicality to force him into a position. But Dominic had just been Tested on the very things Cary had demonstrated three years ago and at his own Test: the ability to act upon free will. Dominic didn't need to be forced. He was a willing participant and subscribed to the Warrior belief system. This could only mean one thing: something had changed.

Cary bowed out of the celebrations for Dominic's successful Testing. With wheels turning in his head, Cary found himself at Dmitri's cave with the Mentor absent. "No matter," he said as he tied Marcus' reins about the horse's neck. Then he stripped off his tunic and stood in the clearing. The leaves of the forested country had turned a brilliant yellow almost overnight. "Do I watch the action or make it?" Cary raised his arms and began his drills.

The petals on his mother's roses had long since departed. Harvest had taken up so much time; the autumn experience had all happened too quickly to savour. Cary opened the kitchen door to find the hearth still glowing, the kitchen a welcoming warm.

A piece of parchment sat on the kitchen table. Even before he opened it, Cary knew what it was: the Council had summoned him.

That night, Cary found himself wondering the halls of his home. His appearance before the Council the next day loomed.

Sleep would not come. His breath seemed a blue smoke in the cold dusty air. After several fitful hours of contemplation, his room had cooled; the fire was now only a tiny glow in the fireplace. Cary donned his old worn boots and pulled a thick wool sweater Olivia had knitted over his nightshirt. He stepped out of his rooms and began to tread the empty halls of his home. One by one, the old wooden doors of the south wing flickered by his eyes. Grey, polished stone then dark wooden doors silken to the touch from generations of use. The iron hinges on most of the doors had not yet turned crimson with rust, but in the ocean air, it was only a matter of time. Even Denis couldn't keep up with time's inevitable pace.

Cary rounded the corner and proceeded down one set of the pair of grand stairways flanking the Great Room. He spied a figure standing at the large windows overlooking the sea at the back of the house. As a silhouette against the bright moon, Denis resembled the agile man Cary knew as a child.

The moon was nearly full. Cary stood next to the old man, "I have been summoned."

"I know. When?"

"Tomorrow."

"What will you tell them?"

Cary tensed and decided to tell Denis. "I've accepted a Mentor apprenticeship with Dmitri."

Denis sucked in a breath, "Not exactly your father's footsteps."

Cary hugged his arms tight about his chest, "Not like I've ever followed my father's footsteps, Denis."

The old man's face turned toward him. The light bounced off Denis' eyes and their blueness seemed suddenly chilling. "I know," he said before turning his gaze back to the waters. "You should read this," and Denis pulled out a parchment from the pocket of his dressing gown without meeting Cary's eyes.

Cary carefully unfolded the aged paper.

Lord and Lady Aristovin, It is imperative that you take every precaution in the next nights. Your lives are in great peril. May your son see your faces together again in the light of day.

It was not signed.

"The next day your father was killed and then that night your mother. The Outerworld retreated after that. It was the shortest and most devastating battle Juno has seen since the Civil War."

Cary handed the letter back to Denis. "I was born a servant's son and was destined to be a servant. The night this letter arrived, your father changed my life." He paused, perhaps to consider his words, then continued, "He gave me instructions: I was to place you with your mother, and put you in possession of an amulet that he put pulled from around his neck. He was very explicit, however, that the amulet rather than your mother was to be protected. At all costs."

Cary suddenly felt faint then gasped for air. He hadn't been breathing. Every word Denis had spoken beat the air from his lungs. Cary collapsed into the lone piece of furniture in the expansive room, his father's chair, and let its supple leather and the scent of his father's soap surround him.

Denis continued, "I was terrified after your father returned to the battle. I delivered the amulet and you to your mother and I then patrolled the castle, sword in hand, though I had little idea of how to use it. I was in the north wing when I was hit from behind -- I don't know why they didn't kill me. I awoke to screaming and a chaos of metal." His voice faltered. "I picked up the sword and ran as I have never run. But I was too late. The Outerworld was everywhere. I have never seen the enemy before or since, but I knew what they were: the black armour, the stench. Bodies and blood were everywhere. I didn't know where to look. It was carnage. At the end of the hall, I saw you. With your mother." Cary dared to glance at the large front doors, the doors that hadn't been opened since his parents' deaths. There was a lump in his throat but the sadness he felt was for Denis. His mind reconstituted the scene regularly in his nightmares. He didn't know if Denis shared the same dreams. "I didn't know how you were still alive. I didn't care. I did the only thing I knew. I put you on your horse and sent you away, to a person who could protect you: Dmitri."

"You did the right thing, Denis. You did all you could do. My father could not have meant for you to do more."

Denis turned away from Cary, shame painting deep crevasses on the old man's face. "No. There are rumors about the history of Juno. The immigrants talk of the Mentors being something else, capable of things unimaginable."

"It's just talk, Denis. Migrants believe in fantastical things..."

Denis shook his head and turned back to Cary, "You father asked one thing of me: protect that amulet at all costs. He valued it more than his own family. *His own family*. I should have appreciated that. I should have heard the meaning in those words. Instead, your mother died and the amulet is gone.

"I failed your father and this family."

Cary opened his mouth but could not find any words.

"During the ten years since that night, I have sought to find a way to atone: I was ignorant; I hadn't listened; I was too entrenched in my own beliefs. I believe the path to atonement is through knowledge." Denis pulled out the letter from his pocket again. "Master Cary, I believe there is a reason that amulet was so important. I believe there is a reason why Dmitri is and has always been closely associated with this family. I believe it all has to do with how you, an eight-year old Son, survived that night and how you were Tested without fighting. I believe you are about to learn a truth that few know, and one that I can only imagine."

Chapter Thirteen

The phone rang again, "Shit." Simone balanced the plates on her arm and grabbed the receiver. "Only Cup, make it quick."

The line was quiet amidst the roar of the lunch crowd.

"Look, whoever you are, stop calling and breathing at me. I don't have time for this shit."

"Ah, could I talk to Simone?" a female voice finally descended through the phone line.

"Sorry, this is Simone. We've been having crank calls lately. What can I do for you?"

"This is Jean Harper from the Public Library." Oh shit, Simone thought. "I understand you stopped by this morning to pay for the door."

"Yes. I didn't know who to make out the cheque to or for how much."

"It was very nice of you to accept responsibility for the damage, but I don't believe you were at fault. Alex told me what happened on Wednesday night. I think the door had a crack and you merely exacerbated an existing issue. The glass is very thick; there's no way you could have broken it."

Simone remembered how the crack appeared in front of her. She'd watched it grow and lengthen. It was possible that a crack had already been there. But she'd pounded on it, encouraging it to break open. In that, she was at fault.

"I feel I contributed. Will you at least let me pay the deductible?" A man in a grey suit and pink tie was waving at her, wanting his bill. Simone nodded back and shifted the plates on her arm.

"If you insist. It's very kind of you. I will accept $200. You can make it out to the Town of Knotton's Shallow. I'll send by Alex to pick up the cheque."

"Between two and six would be great."

Simone signed off. Her heart fluttered. She was going to see Alex again. But then the man in the pink tie waved again and she forgot about Alex. She even forgot about the crank calls and her fear. She forgot about everything except the lunch rush. Sometimes she wished everyday could be a 12-hour lunch rush.

Simone sat in the closet cum office, ledger and cash pushed aside. She spun the top again and started the stopwatch. The top sputtered, staggered, and fell. Eight seconds. Now, when she needed it most, the top wouldn't cooperate. The wind banged debris against the back screen door and made her jump.

She could really use that resounding peace right now.

Reset, spin, start. Twenty-one seconds.

Reset, spin, start. Eighteen seconds.

Reset, spin, start. Twenty-four seconds. The top caught on the ledger Simone had pushed aside and darted off the desk and behind the door. "Shit." She dove into the dusty sliver of space.

A knock on the door. It was Karen. "Hey, there's a guy here who want to see you. He isn't the guy from before. He said he's from the library. Are you here? Do I need to call the cops?"

Simone leapt from her awkward stretch behind the desk and ran through the kitchen to peak through the crack between the swing doors. Alex stood in the sparsely populated cafe, hands in pockets, observing every nook and cranny. She gave Karen the thumbs-up, "All is good. No cops required."

"Okay, then I'm going to go get some milk." Karen pulled her jacket and purse from the coat stand. "Is the deposit ready yet?"

"Nope, not yet, but we could use some change."

Simone ducked back into the office and pulled a few bills from the deposit. "One-forty should be good."

"Can you man the front for twenty minutes?"

"Sure. It'll cost you."

"Tack another twenty bucks onto your accounting fee, O Supreme Number Goddess." Karen pulled open the back door. "Lock this door after me."

Clouds were coming in, dark and billowy. Looks like snow, Simone thought as she flipped the deadbolt on the backdoor. Okay, time to do this. She was sure her pounding heart was making her T-shirt quiver. She stepped through the swing doors. "Hey, Alex."

Alex brought his gaze around to her and smiled. And suddenly Simone felt hope. "Hey, Simone. I came to pick up that cheque, if now is okay."

"Sure, I'll get it for you."

With shaking hands -- nervous, happy hands -- Simone dug out the cheque from her wallet, filled in the blanks, and headed back. Alex was patiently waiting, leaning against the end of the counter, neither in the cafe nor in the workspace. "So this is 'The Only Cup.' I like it." He accepted and pocketed the offered cheque.

"Want a coffee?" Simone attempted but squeaked in the process. "We make a pretty decent cup. It's on the house."

"Sure," he said after a moment's reflection. "It's Friday. I can bear a late night." Simone turned and ducked to dig out the takeaway cups from deep inside the cupboard. "Speaking of Friday, I'd like to take you out sometime, like tonight. For a movie maybe."

Simone froze, still buried in the cupboard. He's not J.D. It's okay. Gotta face my fears. Gotta try something new.

Struggling to breathe and think, she pulled out a paper cup and lid and tried to sound calm, "Um, yeah. Sure. I probably won't be done until about six though."

Alex beamed, relief dripping off him. "I can work with that. Meet you at the theatre at about six-fifteen then?" Before Simone could catch herself, she was nodding, "I'll give you a ride home too. You don't have to worry about that," he said, accurately anticipating her rebuttal. Then he leaned in and whispered, "You can even bring your bear spray, if you want."

She didn't remember pulling the coffee for him, but saw as he reached to accept it. "Thank you for the coffee. See you later." He retreated from the cafe, holding open the door for a couple of women on the way out.

He'd been wearing khaki pants and a blue dress shirt. His dark curly hair had glistened with product. Why hadn't she noticed all this at the library this morning?

Simone extricated herself from her reverie. The cuckoo clock showed five after five. It was then that she looked down at herself. And groaned. Her favourite Cowboy Junkies T-shirt was threadbare with mayonnaise down the front and her jeans had dried flour caked in streaks along her thigh.

She grabbed the damp dishcloth from the counter by the coffee pot and furiously went after the blemishes. "You look fine," a voice from the corner of the shop said. "Don't worry about it. He doesn't care."

Preston was the projectionist at the local movie theatre and frequented 'The Only Cup' to work on his great Canadian novel before work every night. He wore his dirty blond hair collar length and tucked behind his ears. It added to his writer persona.

"I'm a mess. I am not date worthy. Maybe I should call Sally..."

Preston's gaze remained glued to his notebook, an empty plate and bowl in front of him, "You're not Sally. You're you and he asked you, just the way you are. Dust bunnies and all."

"Oh my god, my hair. Sally didn't...." suddenly remembering the promised haircut and highlights.

Preston finally lifted his eyes from his notebook. "It's been a while, hasn't it?"

Like a deer caught mid-highway in oncoming headlights, she was rivetted. "You have no idea."

Preston placed the pen in the notebook's fold and tucked a lock of hair behind his ear. " I haven't seen you in the theatre for a couple of years."

"I'm a homebody."

"Uh-huh. Listen, your guy there has given this a bit of thought and done his research. The show starts at six-thirty tonight, he knew you'd still be here, and he knows you don't have a vehicle. He knew all this and still asked you. He asked you, not your clothes, not your hair. You." Simone fidgeted, searching for a fault in his logic. "Tell you what. I've got an extra shirt at the theatre for when I bike in for matinees. It's not pretty but it's clean. Come up the back way and you can borrow it. I'll leave the door open."

Relief flooded through her. Then bewilderment set in. "Why are you doing this, Preston? We barely know each other."

"I see you nearly every day."

"That's not knowing someone."

Preston shrugged, his shoulders traveling miles to his ears, "Sometimes it can be. I know enough to know you're a good person and that you deserve to be happy."

Simone flopped down into the chair opposite him. "Why are you still here, Preston? In the Shallow, I mean."

"Instead of....?" He leaned back and stretched, as if letting Simone's tension out of his body.

"Instead of moving to the city, getting a real job, going to school, doing something with your life."

"I am doing something with my life."

"Sorry, I don't mean...."

He smiled again, "S'okay. I know what you meant." He shrugged, his bony shoulders poking through his polo shirt. "I did some traveling and working in cities. I like it here. It's quiet. There's no expectation. I can do what I want and how I want it. There's freedom in that."

Simone snorted and was reminded of all her un-ladylike qualities, "Pretty wise for someone who's, what, twenty-four?"

"Twenty-six, but I'm not counting." He smiled lop-sidedly. "Why are you still here and not in school somewhere?"

Suddenly the frayed edge of her favourite T-shirt was all-consuming. "I guess for kind of the same reason, I suppose. I've got a good thing here."

"Uh-huh. Just make sure you're not here because you're afraid to leave. It's okay if you want to stay, not okay if you don't want to go." With Sally and now Preston seemingly able to read her like a book, Simone was beginning to think she was transparent.

"More coffee before I return to the land of accounts receivable and payable?"

"No, thanks." Preston rose too. His lanky six-foot two frame seemed to go on forever. "I gotta go."

"Out of curiosity, what's playing tonight?"

He tucked his notebook into a messenger bag. "We're running the original 'The Day the Earth Stood Still' then the new one."

"Cool. I'll see you in a bit. Thanks again."

Preston left, messenger bag slung over his shoulder. Simone picked up his plate, soup bowl, and empty mug and circled around to clean up after a group of women. The shop was now empty and she breathed a sigh of relief. Fully loaded with flatware, she'd reached the pie display when the bell over the door rang. She turned.

A man was suddenly there, in front of her, within her personal space. So close. Too close. And so black.

She didn't see the handgun until it flashed in front of her eyes, his voice thundering in her ears. It was all happening so fast. Just like that night. Just like J.D. She had no control. Her mind was fighting to control the speed of the action and couldn't. It couldn't keep up and things didn't make sense. "What...?" Her backside found the edge of the glass display case. She slid along its edge.

"I said open the cash register!" The empty dishes rattled in her hands. The handgun waved in front of her eyes again.

"My hands are full," for once she wasn't being sarcastic.

A swipe stung the back of her hand. A snap resounded behind her, disarticulated from the action in front of her. Dishes shattered across the tile floor. "Open the cash register." The voice was anxious and growing louder. Her hand stung, like the sting of J.D.'s hand across her face. Shock. What had happened? Her spinning mind spun faster, unable to clutch onto reality. She remembered looking at his face but not really seeing it. The eyes in the balaclava, were they brown or black? Or, had everything suddenly become very dark?

"There's no money...." *in the till,* Simone wanted to finish, but her mind was constricting. Get him out of here. Get out of here. The Fear was growing, slowing working its talons into her nervous system, shutting everything down, constricting her rationale. Everything had become so dark, so confining. He was too close. Everything was just too close. Get off. Get away. Get away. Too close.

He came closer. She could smell his breath but later she would not be able to remember what it smelled of. The bear spray was in the back. Not here.

"Just open the fucking cash register." They were black. Those vicious, threatening eyes were black. They could only be black. Evil people had black eyes. Black and beady.

Something smacked the front window. A crack snapped through the café, originating behind her. Simone jumped, Fear's icy claws digging deeper into her spine. A paper bag flew off into the wind. If she'd been able to think, she'd have thought about all the things that man could do to her, alone, in the shop. It was the one thing her mind should have been able to think. It was experiential learning. But, to her benefit, thinking was not possible. The Fear had completed its conquest. Only one phrase spun through her stricken mind.

Too close.

Simone saw her finger rise to the register's keyboard but could not find the key to open the drawer. Panic rose in her chest.

Think, think, where.... why?.....don't know.....

"Come on, come on." His voice was deep in her ear, rubbing her innards with a vicious and cruel, rough hand.

She cringed behind the panic.

Think, think...breathe...just breathe...

Far beyond reason, her mind fought to drive the panic into an easier pace. Finally, her finger found the correct button and the register drawer flung out with a loud 'bing'. The man flung Simone out of the way, her back hitting the glass cooler. Glass splintered behind her and showered the floor around her shoes. The display case in front of her spontaneously cracked into a cascade of webworks. The man flinched like a startled cat, "What the....?" If her mind had been clear she may have registered the strangeness of the splintering glass.

Once the shock of hitting the cooler faded, physical pain set in and dislodged her mind from its panicked rut. She opened her eyes to the ceiling - the invader was not there. Simone caught a single breath of uninvaded air and prised a finger of Fear from her brain.

The man turned back to the register and plunged his hands into the cash drawer, scooping a couple of fives and tens. "Where's the rest?" He growled, then turned on Simone. "Where's the deposit?"

Simone kept her eyes glued the ceiling...breathe, just breathe...and reached beside the cooler. Fear clenched tighter, squeezing her rational brain. Fingers reached, searching. Searching. As the display case in front of her continued to crack and fissure like a lake in the depths of winter, her fingers reached.

"*Where is it?*" He grabbed her T-shirt and Fear pulled her eyes back to his.

The display case shattered into a torrent of glass. The man ducked, "What the fuck...?" Simone's fingers grasped the broom handle. It swung out from between the cooler and the counter, and caught the man between the legs. The man collapsed. Simone ran.

Dust smacked her face, blinding her. She ran. Pavement disappeared under her feet and gravel appeared. Seventh door down the alley, a metal door was propped open with a concrete block. Simone dove inside, raced up to the stairs. Preston jolted from the film projector as the door flew open.

"Cops," she gasped, hands on her knees when she was tucked safely behind a large, worn armchair. "Have to call the cops."

"Simone," Preston knelt down to her after he shut the door, "are you okay? What happened?"

"Man with a gun in the shop. Robbery. Have to call the cops." Preston nodded and retreated to the phone.

Simone's legs crumpled beneath her, the shaking turning into shock.

Chapter Fourteen

Clouds hung thick like old blood on a stone wall. The air stank of burning flesh. Screams echoed against the hills. Fires in the distance were Households, not campfires.

As he stood amidst the trampled Plains, the thunder of hooves vibrated up through Cary; loss flooded his body. All hope had died with the new strength of the Outerworld.

His clothes, torn and soaked with blood. The smoky horizon began to dance with the growing silhouettes. The silhouettes remained black as the horses drew nearer. Black armour, black horses; bottomless in their ideal darkness. Closer and closer they raced, but Cary did not move. Hopeless. It was all hopeless. Tears ran down his face, his heart bled. Cary stood as two horsemen lowered their blades in line with his heart.

The Outerworld raced passed. Cary collapsed to the ground. Loss hammered through his body. He was not dead. They had removed their swords within inches of his life. There on the surrendering earth, he could smell their passage, dank with rotting flesh. A guttural yell erupted from his parched throat, and he curled around his hopelessness. As he shivered in the depths of his emptiness, he felt a body beside him. Cary rolled over.

Her hair lay in a tangled bloody mess of blond curls. His hand reached out. She was cold. With her blood on his hand he touched her hair. Soft and still warm. He suddenly felt a need to apologize to her. He felt to blame. "I'm sorry," he breathed. *I'm so sorry.* Tears ran renewed. He drew himself closer to the coldness of her corpse and laid his face in the warmth of her hair. *I'm so sorry.*

A rap on his door. "I'm sorry," burst from Cary's mouth as sprang awake.

Denis cocked an eyebrow. "It's time," said the old man. "Tea and oats this morning. No protests."

Against his sleepiness, Cary hurriedly dressed to escape the cold morning air. He washed his face, cleaned his teeth, and placed a comb to his hair when he suddenly froze. His image in the gilded mirror; blue eyes wide, ringed in dark purple circles, light hair rumpled and wet, and his hand frozen above his head. Before the girl, before the Outerworld, before the hopelessness, he'd seen this. Staring at himself. But his hand hadn't held a comb, it had held a sword. An intricately engraved long-bladed sword that blinded his mind's eye even now. It was double-edged and of lighter weight than a Warrior's sword, but the Warrior's Creed had flashed along the length of the blade. He had been in battle with himself. That hardly seemed possible, but he remembered the fear. The fear as his opponent matched him inch for inch, move for move. What sword had he held? Had he held one? Cary couldn't remember. He couldn't even remember the duel itself or the outcome, only the fear. He shook his head and pulled the comb through his hair. He plucked up the amulet and dropped it over his head and inside his tunic as he headed downstairs.

A mug of tea and bowl of oatmeal sat waiting on the table, steaming. Olivia was already behind the counter, a mixing bowl in her arms. Denis sipped his tea and nodded as Cary sat. "With Emil here, we should look at repairing the old chicken coop and the drying shed." Cary nodded as he fed oats into his parched mouth. "We could even expand the drying shed so that we could dry tomatoes and onions on one side with fish on the other." Cary nodded again, sipped his tea. "Olivia knows a man in the Village who's a drying expert, got several drying sheds."

Cary nodded, "Seamus Black."

"Right," Denis continued. "You might stop in to see him on the way back today. His help could save a lot of time, money, and effort for us."

"Yeah. Sure." Cary took his empty bowl to the washbasin.

"Don't worry, love. I'll look after it," Olivia said, so Cary left the bowl and turned back to the table. "Now, now," Olivia's voice stopped him. "You've a big day today. Turn around. Let me have a look at you."

Cary turned back and stood. Olivia pulled, brushed, and examined him. "You should have worn your Household blues. Denis, don't you agree?" Cary blinked and she was facing him, finished. "What? No protests today? You're white as a ghost. I should have fed you meat this morning. Got your circulation up."

"Big day," Cary said and downed his cooled tea. "Seamus Black. Back for afternoon tea."

Cary strode to the kitchen door. "You will do fine, Young One," Denis spoke from the table. "You always have."

Marcus bounded happily across the hills to the Main Junction. The City was in sight within three hours. Cary rode through the immigrant village to the City gate. He passed the circles of chanting migrants who came to Juno for both refuge and communion; passed dwellings that ranged from hastily constructed sheds to houses of lumber and thatching; passed smithies, candlemakers, bakers, weavers; passed gardens, children running, dogs barking, and newly fallen leaves. Cary waved several times at the familiar faces.

So many people in the Village now, Cary thought. What if the Outerworld did get this far north? Through the Plains, passed the southern Households. Passed Trium Hall. Passed the Main Junction? So many people now. Were the battles taking longer than they used to? Was Juno losing more lives than before? Was the Outerworld retreating more easily? Cary doubted this last one since discovering the Outerworld had his father's amulet. What would it be like? Killing. Living while he watched others die. Would running his blade through an Outerworlder feel good? Cary shuttered at this. How could killing anything feel good?

The tall defensive wall enclosed the City. Outside, only the gleaming white domed towers could be seen. Inside, the City felt like a country in and of itself. Well-built cottages and houses of brick and mortar dotted the spaces between gardens and parks. Merchants strolled behind carts of thread, cloth or pans, while gardeners collected the last of this year's harvest. Wagons full of gourds and corn were a common sight on the stone laid streets. It looked to Cary that the City was still doing well while the rest of the nation suffered. The City still collected the standard tax and for those Households without a Warrior or a Son, it took a devastating toll. Cary reminded himself to visit Seamus Black on the way out so that they, too, could preserve this year's harvest.

The City gates stood wide and, after opening at dawn, the guard stood and watched. White leather creaked as the guards nodded to Cary. Their shields stood propped against the edge of the City wall. One caught the morning light and Juno's emblem, two matching suns, shone brilliantly against a white background.

As he nodded at the City guard all dressed in his brilliant whites, Cary stifled a groan.

There posted for all to see was the announcement Cary had been dreading:

> *The Council of Eight is pleased to announce the Cresting of Cary Aristovin, son of Lord Cale Aristovin, Commander in Chief. For Juno may he live, for Juno may he die.*

As he made his way through the gates, he saw more parchments of the same announcement dotting the inside wall of the City.

The main road leading to the inner City was lined with tall slender trees, and it wound around blocks of shops, inns, and houses. Cary hadn't forgotten how beautiful the City was. White house fronts, green trees, red banners, fruit filled stalls, brick and marble faced inns; and he also hadn't forgotten how closed in he felt. So many people going about their business, drunkards already stumbling out of the inns into the stinging light of the morning. Cary could almost feel the City walls looming above the houses behind him, he didn't have to turn to see them.

Finally, with the Guardsman Inn to his left and the guardhouse to his right, the inner City gates loomed high, sheltering his eyes from the gleam of the white towers inside.

Cary dismounted as a large bellied guard emerged from the guard's house. Cary smiled largely as he clasped the guard's hand and shoulder. "It's good to see you again, Merek. I see the Council treats you well."

Merek barked a laugh and squeezed Cary's shoulder. "It is good to see you, Young One, though it seems you are not so young anymore." He disengaged from Cary's embrace and roughly spun him around taking in the black uniform. "And, it seems the stories I have heard are true. Come inside," he motioned to the inn across the way, "and tell me everything. Are you still lighting small houses on fire?"

Cary had to force himself to stop and turn back toward the gates. "I'm very sorry, Merek. Perhaps another time. The Council is waiting."

The guard sighed, "I know, I was just hoping to calm your nerves first. You are a smart lad, always were." He barked another laugh and rubbed his large stomach. "I didn't think you'd chose my company over the Council's. Just remember that a pint of good company and strong ale awaits outside the gates and then you will do fine." Cary smiled and handed him Marcus' reins. "What's his name?" Cary told him and Merek looked over the gelding, ear to hoof, and then gave Marcus a good slap on the thigh. Marcus whinnied and eyed the guard closely. "A good steed. Maybe as good as your father's. I'll feed him oats while you're inside."

"Not too many. I don't need him fat, just satisfied." Cary stroked the gelding's nose to calm him and then began to walk to the gates.

"But fat is satisfying." Merek called back to him.

As Cary raised a hand to knock at the immense gates, the lock clicked and a door in the gates swung open. Cary stepped through and was greeted by a guard dressed in the same gear as Merek. He was almost difficult to look at, shining from head to foot in the morning light. "The Council is expecting you. Up the stairs and straight ahead."

Several white marble stairs that were perhaps the width of his Great Room at home lay ahead of Cary and were at the base of his view of the Council towers. A continuous cascade of white hung before Cary.

Marble stairs, up to the seemingly ceaseless columns and finally, squinting to see against the bright blue sky, Cary could see the spiral towers. He eased his neck back to normal level and glanced at the side gardens flanking the stairs and continuing around the inner walls. Cary gave the guard a brief smile and noticed the guard hadn't taken his eyes off him. I wonder if everyone reacts this way when they step through the gates, Cary thought, proceeding up the steps.

The wide metal embossed doors stood open to the dimness of the halls inside. Cary stepped cautiously inside and let his eyes adjust. The whiteness continued. White-on-white marble floor mosaics were part of the sparse fashions decorating the long hall. Doors were interspersed between columns that held up a ceiling that was so high it seemed not to be there. By the time Cary reached the end of the corridor, he was glad to break the monotony of the redundant door after column décor. Fifty-seven. There had been fifty-seven doors and he couldn't believe he'd remembered that.

As he approached the end of the hall, two guards opened a set of doors and nodded to Cary. Inside, two attendants flanked a door opposite. Two suns in yellow marble were inlaid in the center of the floor. The room was otherwise bare. Cary nodded to the guards and then he proceeded to the door opposite. Both attendants each took a large door handle and pulled the doors open.

Only a step inside and the door shut behind Cary. Darkness enveloped him. All composure he had managed to emit on the long walk in, he felt quickly melt away on the marble floor. Unable to move – he didn't know where to go -- his vision adjusted. Or, at least he thought it had. Just as panic began to well in his chest, a voice rang through the darkness, "Cary Aristovin come forth." But where, he thought. In answer, the draped darkness drew back. Here goes nothing, he thought and wiped his palms on his trousers and straightened his tunic.

With as much confidence he could muster, Cary strode out of the draped anteroom and out into the Council's audience chamber. Windowless, but brightly lit by wall bracketed torches, the eight white robed figures opposite him held the room with their presence. Cary nearly tripped over his own feet once his mind finally registered who he was looking at. He walked across the seamless floor, halted and self-consciously knelt and bowed his head to the floor. A story leaped to mind. A story Xan had told him. Dueling men had come to a stalemate. The two came before the Council for a judgment. One man failed to address the Council properly. His sword was removed.

A shiver ran through him, the coldness of the marble biting into him. With head low, the young Aristovin proclaimed, "Giving Juno life, the Council of Eight reigns high. For Juno I live, for Juno I die."

"Arise, Young One." Cary obeyed though his mind reeled at the informal address. Cary looked into the face of a man he felt he should know, but also felt this same man had lived a thousand years. It was this man who spoke. This was The Lauch Shinhan, the head of the Council. "I knew your father well. He was always a welcome visitor here, though he seldom came without our summons. It is good to see his son after such a long absence. We have heard much." To Cary's amazement, a twinkle appeared in the man's eye.

One of the others spoke, "Why do you not wear your Household colours?" Every Son is taught the names of the Eight, their histories and their duties, but right now the ability to recall what he once thought was useless information eluded him.

All right, you expected this. "I do not wish to wear the Warrior Crest that is now part of my Household tunic."

"But you earned this Crest by reason of your peers and teachers." One to the left of the center man spoke.

"I was denied an audience of my peers, my family, my friends." Eyebrows rose. "Grand Master Sesmon granted me the Crest."

To turn the conversation would be trying to will the impossible into existence.

Yes, yes, Cary thought back to the voice but continued, "I didn't earn the Crest nor do I feel I deserve it."

"It is not for you to decide whether or not you deserve to be a Warrior."

Another spoke: "You are expected to take your father's post; you have been trained as such."

Cary could feel his face heating. *Calm. Down.* But before he could embarrass himself and his Household, The Lauch Shinhan spoke, "Why do you feel undeserving of the Warrior crest?"

"I have forbidden myself to fight."

The Lauch Shinhan leaned back while the others conversed quietly amongst themselves. The short man on Cary's far right finally admitted, "We'd heard you'd not taken the sword for some time but assumed that since you'd received the Crest that you'd renounced your previous vows. There is much hope riding on you, Young Aristovin." All nodded in agreement. All except the man in the center. For the first time since entering the room, Cary felt some semblance of security. The Council wasn't omniscient after all.

Conversation began between the Council members with voices low enough to remain a mere mumble to Cary. However, The Lauch Shinhan's eyes had locked with his. The man was clearly thinking but kept his thoughts from his face. The face was that of a Warrior, Cary decided as he also kept his gaze fixed. A Warrior, yes, but another kind of Warrior. One for the court. How had his father done it? Fighting battles on the Plains as well as in this enclosed space where words were wielded like swords. Suddenly a newfound respect blossomed within Cary. Respect for a man he had barely known and a position he was now beginning to realize. Yes, a truly great man indeed. He could never fill those shoes.

Silence crept upon the room as the peripheral Council members finished their private conferences. As Cary was beginning to wonder how long this game of tenacity would last, The Lauch Shinhan, with the deep green eyes and perfect teeth, laughed. And not a mere bark or a chortle but a loud laugh straight from the belly. It made Cary want to join him and, for a brief instant, he felt a chuckle begin to tickle his throat. Especially with the looks on the other Eight's faces. "My Lauch Shinhan?" the one on his right questioned. But the laugh was stifled. It was just nice to see that at least one of the Eight was human.

"It would seem that you're living up to the prophecy your father proclaimed." Regaining himself, The Lauch Shinhan continued, "Your father said you'd be a handful -- a good lad, but a handful."

"My Lauch Shinhan, I don't think..."

"It's alright, al'Mahan," he consoled the short one to Cary's far right, "in this case, I think it is alright to tell this Son of his father's prophecy. He may even need to hear it.

"As you may or may not know, all children born on Juno soil are, at some time, brought before us." Cary nodded. Yes, he remembered. "It is on that day that the name of the child and its destiny is proclaimed. You were to be destined for Trium Hall. Your father consented, as all Commanding Households do, but your father also added a comment that I found quite comical at the time. He said that, although you had a good head, your heart may not allow you to pass through Trium's curriculum without incident, if you completed it. I thought it was quite unforgiving for a Commander of high esteem to say such of his heir but now I see he was quite correct."

Cary found this surprising because Dmitri thought the exact opposite of him – good heart, wooden head.

The Lauch Shinhan leaned forward and looked Cary squarely in the eye. "My fellow Councilman is correct: there has been much hope place on your shoulders. Therefore, I'm not going to ask if you've found the right path. What I would like to know is have you found *your* path?"

His path? "To tell you the truth, My Lauch Shinhan, I don't know what my path is."

"You have forsaken the sword and the fight, how do you justify yourself to us?"

"Master Dmitri has shown me a path, but I do not yet know if it is *my* path."

Dmitri's name seemed to resonate in the Council room. To Fate's bowels, he was no good at this! Should he just keep his mouth shut? Could he walk away from this? No. Not this time. He'd have to play along while revealing as little as possible. Whether he said the right things or not, the Council was questioning his existence.

"You were right to suspect his involvement, My Lauch Shinhan." This Council member had just spoken volumes to Cary. From the look in The

Lauch Shinhan's eye, he also knew that one of his fellow members may have given up the game.

However, the center man merely hummed back a response. Now Cary was beginning to have an idea of what his father may have gone through on a continual basis. No wonder he hated coming here. How far would they play his father's son? That wonderful, though strange feeling of security fled and left only the voice in Cary's mind uttering defensive comments. After a brief pause with his freckled and aging hand on his chin, The Lauch Shinhan asked, "Have you accepted the path offered by Dmitri?"

"I have agreed to an apprenticeship."

The Launch Shinhan paused, seeming to take stock of all the implications in Cary's acceptance. "Then we look forward to receiving word that your Testing has been completed. Grand Master Sesmon will be notified that you will not be returning to Trium Hall."

Suddenly the eight men rose and bowed their heads to Cary. Cary was shocked and instinctively jerked a step back. "Swift and true. Guard Juno with your life. For Juno may you live, for Juno may you die." They turned and filed out of the room.

Left alone, Cary's mind spun. He turned back the way he'd entered.

The black curtains dropped back into place, leaving Cary in a velvet darkness. Instead of the double doors opening, a hand grabbed his wrist. A small metal disc was inserted into his hand. "The next battle will be lost unless you have this." The voice was female and it disappeared into the darkness with her hand.

The double doors then opened. Light from the white, mosaicked anteroom assaulted his eyes. Blinded and backed by darkness, he couldn't see a retreating figure. Two attendants stood aside each door, waiting. Cary placed his hand with the disc into his trouser pocket and retraced his steps down the long hall.

Chapter Fifteen

A security camera, that's what she needed.

Simone drew the curtains back from the living room window. The motion-triggered light above her front door was still switched to ON, throwing its light against the impenetrable darkness.

The RCMP officer had kindly taken her statement in the projection booth with Preston going about his business. The Mountie had left upon reaching Karen on her cell phone and met her at 'The Only Cup.'

A security camera and another light, she thought. She let the curtain fall back across the window. The country was so dark compared to town. Headlights barely made a difference on the highway, only illuminating what was directly in front.

The clock read 1:13am.

Every light in the house was on. Simone sipped her brandy and noted that her hand was now steady.

At one point, Preston had said, "Your date was downstairs. I had to tell him what happened and that you were alright to get him to leave. He was pretty concerned." Preston had been looking at her, assessing her, she knew. She'd tried to hide the shaking -- sitting on her hands, crossing her arms and legs -- but it wouldn't stop.

A thought burst into her mind: "My top." She'd leapt to her feet and ran down the alley back to the cafe. The Mountie and Karen were still there. There was glass everywhere.

The Mountie held up a hand, "Simone, I need you to go back to the theatre."

"My top," was all she could manage as she maneuvered past the Mountie, glass crunching under foot, and into the kitchen.

Her hand plunged behind the desk. Karen, the Mountie, and Preston stood behind. "My top," she proclaimed. Relief, as she held the smooth wooden toy.

Her living room was wonderfully small and familiar. She'd grown up here, knew each piece of furniture by touch and smell.

Preston had escorted her back to the theatre. The Mountie had returned with her backpack and Karen. "Go home, Simone." Karen had said. "I'll call Sally. I want you to take a few days off."

The Mountie nodded and placed his notebook into his cargo pants pocket. "Do you need a lift home?" He'd asked. Simone caressed the top. His nametag read Mitchell and his eyes read concern. But Simone didn't know him. He was new in town. Only been here a few months.

Simone nodded. Karen left. Preston remained silent. Mountie Mitchell gave her a ride home.

Simone rose from the sofa and placed the empty brandy snifter on the coffee table. Her other hand still held the wooden top.

Living in the country. Her father knew country living because he worked in it. He knew it held dangers. Simone remembered a bear wandering through their yard when she was about five years old. It had been searching for something to eat and had smelled their garbage bin. "Stay here." The urgency in her father's voice and stare had jolted her. He'd retreated to the back of the house then through the back door. Then she'd heard a massive shot. It was loud, but mostly it was unexpected. She'd run to the living room window to see the bear, dead, and her father venturing up to it, shotgun in hand.

She'd felt nothing for the bear. Its appearance was tacked up into her memory. It was large, possibly taller than her father, and had huge paws. Its claws were like daggers.

Her father had stood over the dead animal and assessed it. A paw lay next to her father's foot. Excluding the claws, that one paw was larger than her father's foot, maybe even larger than his head. Suddenly everything was put in perspective.

Simone ventured into her father's bedroom. She opened the closet and pushed aside the few shirts and jackets that hung there. She pulled out the gun case, grunting with its weight, placed it on the bed and opened it.

Her father may not be here, but the guns were. And if a gun could take down a bear, it could keep her safe from robbers and rapists and murderers.

She took out the 12-guage shotgun and curled around it on her father's bed, a hand still clutching the wooden top. Sleep drifted in and with it, a vision of Cary Aristovin walking white marble halls and bowing before a group of men in white robes.

Chapter Sixteen

Merek took one look at Cary and knew. "I've seen that look before. No need to talk. I'll fetch your Companion."

Alone, Cary pulled the object from his pocket. It was a necklace with a large metal disc as an amulet. The disc itself was embossed with Juno's two suns, much like the Crest that now adorned his blue uniform. Denis' confession from the night before sprung anew into his mind and he strung the amulet from his neck, tucking it under his tunic and shirt. He patted his chest, "It is returned, father."

Hoof steps from inside the cavernous stable sounded as the clatter of a canter sounded from down the cobblestoned street. "Lord Aristovin!" Cary turned to the summons as Merek emerged from the stables. A messenger pulled his horse up in front of Cary, "Lord Aristovin, I have a message from Warken House. Your presence is urgently requested. Count Roan is dying."

The suns shone brightly over top Warken House as Cary finally descended upon Dominic's home. Just as he was under the shadow of the castle he heard the flapping of the Household flag and looked up. It was at half-mast. He was too late.

As he rounded the corner and rode toward the stables. From inside, he heard familiar voices. "I know this is no time for such questions, but I need you to be aware of it. First, Cary's father and now yours. I need you to consider the state of command. I need to you consider accepting your father's post."

Cary dismounted and looked for a stable boy so that he didn't have to face such a conversation. "I thought I heard someone ride up," Lord Fraaml emerged from the shadows. He had shed the black battle attire from Dominic's Test. A forest green wool uniform made his auburn hair and beard seem to alight in the mid-day suns. A memory caught in Cary's mind: the day his father died. The battle was in full swing with the enemy's darkness oppressive and dank. Lord Fraaml arrived, blood-soaked and armoured, and delivered the news. Cary's mother collapsed into the Warrior's massive arms, her soft white robes a beacon of light against the gory evidence of battle. As his mother sobbed and shook, Lord Fraaml stood holding her, steady, true, and patient. Cary remembered the Warrior turning to him then. The man didn't have to say it. *I'm sorry.* Whether it was guilt that he'd seen it, or couldn't stop it, or that Cary would now know loss, it didn't matter. It was all there in his eyes. And Cary knew that if Brask Fraaml could have died instead, he would have. In an instant.

"It has been a long time, Young One," the Warrior reached out and grabbed Cary into fierce hug. How could he have made himself forget this, this source of protection that didn't involve a weapon or a shield? For a heartbeat, Cary regretted every day for the past three years.

"Are you here out of friendship or duty?" Fraaml said once he broke his hold.

Cary spied Dominic a pace behind, still lurking in the stable's shadows. "Both. But I didn't receive the news in time to say goodbye. My condolences, Dominic."

Hazel eyes found Cary's as the lord grasped his shoulders, "I need to talk to you before too long. Later today. But now, let's inside." The Lord whistled and a stable boy appeared.

"Thanks for coming, Cary. It means a lot." Dominic walked abreast as they made their way inside.

Inside, livery bustled about. The death of a Warrior meant many travelers from near and far would be descending upon Warken House. Cary was suddenly glad he'd got here when he did. A familiar voice issued directives: "Henry, we'll need the Long Room set with refreshment as well. We've just received word that Captain Stats is on his way." Cary glanced into the parlor as they made their way to the stairway. Laurina Fraaml, Brask's wife, caught his eye and bustled over. "My dear, thank you for coming. The countess is upstairs. Darling, I need you to fetch our daughters," she raised a finger to Brask who studied the woodwork of the doorway with great interest.

Released, the three continued their way upstairs. Cary glanced at where Dominic was injured during his Test, "How is your arm?"

"Healing well thanks to the Mentor's treatments. Another week or so and I'll be able to lift a sword again. What about you? I heard you were summoned."

"I'd rather not, Dominic. I have a lot to think about."

"Cary, I need to know. We need to know. That's why Brask needs to talk to you. He's now the only one left of the Great Three. You, me, and Everett are the next generation and we need to step into our posts."

"Dominic, I'd rather just give my condolences to your family right now."

Dominic knocked gently and opened the door. Though it was mid-day, the room was dim with lamplight, the curtains drawn. Count Goran Roan, a crippled yet young man, lay still and pale in the bed. The countess was at the far side of the room talking in murmurs with Grand Master Sesmon. Mentor Saul nodded to Cary and company as he left the room quietly.

Cary bowed over the count and kissed his cold forehead. Sesmon broke off the conversation with The countess and excused himself. The countess crossed to embrace Cary, her burgundy taffeta rustling. "I'm sorry I didn't greet you downstairs. It seems there is so much to consider now that Goran is no longer here." Long fingers bent Cary's head down to her petite height, then she kissed his forehead. "It's very good of you to come. This week I have seen you more than in the past three years. I hope you will again make a habit of visiting." She held Cary at arm's length and ran a gentle hand along his jawline. "You have become a handsome young man, my dear. The three of you will soon be the most eligible bachelors on the Rire."

Cary shifted self-consciously, "If there's anything I can do, please just ask."

"Thank you. I believe Frej and Mika are downstairs with some of the Inner City men. Darine and Tolonel should be here shortly. Laurina is helping coordinate, thank the Creator. We'll be transporting Goran to the City at sunset."

As they filed out of the count's bed chamber, a large hand pulled Cary aside. Dominic glanced back but continued downstairs after his mother. "I heard you were summoned," Brask whispered.

"This morning. My lord, I don't...," Cary began.

Brask stepped up and grasped Cary's shoulders. "Since when have I been 'Lord Fraaml' to you? Cary, just tell me what's going on. I need to know."

Cary sighed and tried not let familial emotions bias his response. "I know you want me to take my father's post. Everyone does."

Brask stepped back, still towering over Cary, his hazel eyes drinking in every word. "But you don't want to."

Cary ran a nervous hand through his hair. "It's not so much that I don't. I can't."

Brask stood a moment. Cary could see the man was thinking, perhaps of things outside Cary's sphere of knowledge. Brask paced away and leaned against the banister overlooking the Front Room below. He finally pulled a pipe from behind his belt and took a pinch of tobac from a pouch on his other hip, then struck a match on his boot sole. He pulled a couple draws before saying through the sweet smelling smoke, "Is this a personality thing or a Mentor thing?"

"Both."

Brask nodded and hummed through the pipe. "I know you've been trained by Dmitri. Your father told me. It was his idea, or so he said. Is that your path?"

"I guess so. I'm still not sure. I don't have much choice here. You know that."

Brask hummed through his pipe again. "Difficult situations make for difficult decisions." Smoke billowed from his nose and it's sweet scent brought back images of playing on the Fraaml staircase and racing through the halls. "Just know that I will support your decision, whatever it may be." He plucked the pipe from his mouth and waved, "Are you going to be social?"

"I'll make an appearance in a few minutes. I need some time first." Brask nodded and descended.

Cary wandered down the opposite corridor looking for a bit of solace before meeting up with the family again, and the mass of visitors that would likely be arriving soon. A few steps down the corridor toward the guest bedrooms, he heard voices. Familiar voices. He leaned into the door.

"No, no, Nina, like this. See? Watch again." Footsteps shuffled across the carpet, irregular and under strain, as if someone was pushing something awkward. "Now you try again."

Cary opened the door. Inside, Everett's two younger sisters were dressed in their finest dresses, hair elaborately plaited, and were holding swords. "What is this?" Cary entered the room fully and closed the door.

Both girls spun, hiding the swords behind their skirts, and stared pale-faced and guilty at him. "What would your father say if he found out you, his daughters, were holding swords? Especially since he's a Commander." Cary strode in. Teasing Min and Nina had been a much-favoured childhood past time. It had been too long since he'd had an opportunity. This was too good to pass up, even more that he suspected that Min was hiding more than just the sword.

Min relaxed into her guilt, "Cary, please. Don't tell father. It would break him. They'd send him away."

The sword had slipped from behind her skirts. It was a light sword, double-edged, built for a smaller hand. He glanced to the sword that Nina held. It was the same. He'd only seen a similar sword once before

- in his dream last night. Breath caught in his throat. Cary interrupted Min's plea, "I won't tell anyone. On one condition."

Immediately Min reverted to the personality Cary knew and cherished: she leaned on the sword hilt, cocked a hip and an eyebrow, and placed the other hand on her hip. "Oh yeah? What? I haven't got any money, Cary."

Cary pushed aside his racing thoughts and tore his eyes from the sword. "I don't want your money, Min." Cary grinned and leaned in, "I want information." In a flash, he grabbed the sword from Min's grasp and pushed her backwards into an awaiting settee.

"Hey, give that back!"

With a quick wrist, Cary held the sword at Min's throat, effectively pinning her to the plush furniture. "Information, Min. Nina, please come forward where I can see you."

Nina shuffled forward. "Now, please. Where'd you get the swords?"

"The Old Ones," it was Nina who replied. She was shaking, obviously terrified, but whether for being found out or because Cary was holding her older sister at sword point, he didn't know.

"Hush, Nina."

"The Old Ones are dead."

Nina shook her head, eager to please. "No, there are four. They live in the city."

Min had crawled out from under Cary's half-hearted threat, grabbed a pillow, and lodged it at her sister. It struck home. Nina cried out. With the distraction, Cary saw from the corner of his eye that Min was winding up to kick him. He spun, tripped her onto her stomach, and pinned her with his heel.

"How did you find out about the Old Ones?"

"Don't hurt her!" Nina yelled from behind him.

"Nina, how did you find out about the Old Ones?" Min wriggled and slapped at his leg, as the toe of his boot dug into her spine.

"Please, Cary. You're hurting her!"

"Nina, tell me."

"Don't tell him, Nina. Don't!"

Nina's watering eyes looked from Min to Cary and back again. "Mother."

Dumbfounded, Cary let his foot slip. The Old Ones should be dead. They'd fought in the Civil War and that was over 200 years ago. How could they still be alive? But more shocking than the Old Ones was the fact that they were teaching females to fight. Females. Only Warriors were allowed to fight. Not immigrants, and certainly not females. Females in battle were the reason the Civil War happened in the first place.

Was this part of the "re-history lesson" to which Dmitri was alluding?

Cary's mind spun as Min scurried away and motioned to Nina. He held up the sword, Min's sword, and looked at the markings along the blade and on the hilt. He recognized the old language from books he'd borrowed from Dmitri years ago. He also recognized it from his father's sword. "For Juno, we live. For Juno, we die." It was the Warrior creed. And it was here, on a non-Warrior sword. Just like in his dream.

Females were being taught to fight. By the Old Ones. Cary's head spun with the implications, good and bad, when an image from last night's dream popped into his mind. A young woman lay on the scorched battlefield. Loss renewed in his heart and seized his body.

Cary gasped under the sudden weight of the loss. A memory flickered -- pulling the amulet over his head and tucking it under his tunic -- and he lifted a heavy hand to his chest.

Cary's hand didn't reach the amulet. Min hit him over the head with a vase of flowers.

Chapter Seventeen

It has been so long.

Darkness dripped through the worn canvass of a sky. Smoky sunslight seeped out from behind the torrential storm to play a dangerous game with the shadows in the grasses. This is the way it is; Cary's mind registered the picture. This is the way it has been and will be. The bleakness was normal. The vacancy, commonplace.

It was the Plains but, at the same time, it wasn't. Cary looked at the ground around his bare feet, at the landscape. It looked like the Plains, but it felt.....different. The burned ground, the disturbed grasses that only greened after a long spring rain. The sandy hills to the east. But something was missing. He had had dreams of the Plains, dreams filled with battle cries. And sometimes when he rode Marcus in the consciousness of day, he would hear them. This was not the Plains. There were no voices. There were no echoes of the dead, of battles, of community, of Juno. It was silent here. Silent except for the raging wind.

The wind whipped his hair against his face, stinging his skin. He felt....

...desperate.

Desperation mixed with a sense of duty. Desperation. The word quizzically rolled around in his mind. Why desperation? He didn't know, but it was growing. Uncontrollably. That ever-present hole in his chest was nothing compared to this. His stomach began to clench. The word stopped rolling and seized his brain. Why....?

Don't!

Breathe, just breathe.... He looked down at his hands. His dirtied, calloused hands framed by frayed grey cuffs were now shaking. Without a sword, a bow, a spear, a knife, a mace, without a weapon for nearly three years, he felt the absence of one here.

It has been so long.

And no horse. Not even a horse. Now the shaking grew into a vibration working its way up his arms.

Too long.

A knot in his stomach formed and the desperation turned to fear. His hands clenched. No... must stop this...

Through the penetrating fear he knew. He felt it. It wasn't emptiness here, on this plain. It was loss. It was thick and pungent like a smell. He would fight for what would be lost.

Lost.

Everything.

Fear grew into panic as the stench of deprivation seeped into his skin. His fingernails dug into his palms.

Why?!

Through the mounting panic, somewhere, far off to the right, his memory tugged again, and he knew the irrationality of it all. But right now, *right now*, as his stomach churned and the fear cramped the air from his lungs, all he wanted was a sword. He wanted to free Juno, he wanted his family, he wanted, he wanted....

Don't und....stan..... Can't... brea...the...

The panic drove his heart into a race. But from what? Or to what?

Can't breathe...No...NO! "No!"

In less time it took his anxious mind to blink, he was standing on the Greens of his home. And they *were* the Greens. A vivid, suns' lit green, not the blackness of an unknown desolate plain. His eyes traced the vibrant expanse: the communal field to the east, rich in the season with Mixflak; the hills to the north over which he could just make out the stone walls marking the outlines of his family lands; and then, slowly, he turned to the west and let out a tortured breath.

Home.

It was there, intact. Whole. Unharmed. Untarnished. And more so, it was the FarSee Cove of his childhood. The grey stone, finely cut, shone in the midday suns. The stable roof was new with no holes. The well-pruned roses rustled and sent their fragrance into the ocean breeze. The family crest hung, freshly polished, above the gate to the left.

Though he knew not how this could be, he checked his fighting stance and cautiously took solace in the familiar sight. Slowly his hands released, tight and stinging. Breath filled his lungs; he inhaled the sweet fragrance of his memory. While the fear had fled, the voice in his head had not.

It has been so long. So long without breath. So long without....

Eyes closed against the calming breeze, tears welled. It was here. It was all here. Salt in the air, the pungency of the rose garden, a full stable, Mixflak maturing...

It has been so long.

But yet.... A smell he'd almost forgotten. Soap.

He spun around.

"This is for you," the Lord Aristovin was holding a sword in his hands, a sword of Warrior weight, the Creed flashing along the blade. "Take it and guard Juno. The survival of this land is the link between total collapse and ultimate salvation."

Cary blinked. It had been so long. So long since he had seen his father. Too long. The sight of him was shocking. He blinked again. The tears would not clear. Was it...?

So long...

The man stood in full armour, suns' light gleaming off the silver helmet. Still now he was larger than life. And perfect. The armour was so well made no hammer marks caught the light. It was like silver silk. Chainmail scratched against the metal tunic and, underneath, a black wool collar hugged his neck. A moustache and beard peeked out from under the hood of the helmet. The eyes were piercing in their brilliant blueness, framed by drooping eyebrows laced with a touch of gray.

The memory, once faded, was there; it had been triggered and reconstituted. Every detail, everything he wanted to remember but couldn't. The memory was solid. All that had faded in the days, months, years since that night came flooding back. It was really, truly perfect.

His father was standing before him. And Cary longed to hug him.

It has been so long.

"You must do this for your people, for the land, for the universe. For me."

A protest began to form on Cary's lips but it didn't emerge. If only to touch his father, this image that he'd only had in his mind, plaguing it until, finally, fading, fading.

Cary felt his hands leave his sides. So very long. Just to touch him. Just to touch....

...the sword.

His father vanished.

"So you have chosen to accept your responsibility." Cary jumped and whirled around. A lone figure stood out from the surroundings and piqued Cary's nerves. Perhaps seven feet tall, he seemed a giant, or Death as he was clothed in a long-hooded billowing cape.

"Who are you?"

The figure loomed closer. But still his face eluded Cary's eyes and the suns' light of the dream. "Someone that has a purpose in the place. You are trespassing. I knew one day someone would come to break the boundary but I didn't expect one so young or inexperienced."

"My name is..." Cary began.

"I know who you are, Cary Aristovin. I have been waiting for you to accept your responsibility."

The surreal words left his mouth as if, after playing hide and seek, they gave themselves up and were revealed. "I have chosen a path but I do not understand my responsibility."

The quantum leap astonished even him, but yes, he understood now. He had figured it out. The Council summons had been the final piece. Even here, on this strange, yet familiar façade of a dream, he knew. He had felt it.

Since his parents' deaths, or perhaps it had been since his departure from Trium, he had felt it, saw the signs. The longing in people's eyes. The desperation in their voices. The pleading in their gestures.

So long it has been.

He didn't want to believe it. The Council had made him believe. He had seen it there too. But they hadn't hidden it behind stolen glances. Without words they had confirmed what he had suspected.

So long without hope.

He was a just one person. The son of a great man. His *son*. But however he viewed himself didn't seem to matter. He had begun to see the situation for what it was, to see the hope in people's eyes. What he believed didn't matter. It was what they believed. And the lingering expectation of a great man's son fulfilling his duty was a hope they could grasp.

It has been so very long.

"Your responsibility," the man smirked as he strode around the Green toward Cary, "Your responsibility is to the future, to the past you've yet to create, and the destruction that you will incur." The man, clean-shaven and unwrinkled, yet ageless and formidable, stopped only feet away from Cary. "You're already in way over your head and you've only just begun.

"Our world, including the oceans, the air, the other lands across the seas, the stars, the suns, and the moon are all linked," the man said as he broke his stare and strode again across the Greens. "This should be no surprise to you if you've managed to listen to anything Dmitri has tried to teach you. Any one thing cannot be without another. The reliance is like a tapestry: each thread is essential to the whole. It is what makes up the structural integrity of the Universe. The destruction of one thread is the beginning of total collapse. Anything that appears to die is simply reborn as another form elsewhere. That thread is moved or rewoven.

"Your parents are not really dead. Their threads have been rewoven into the sky, the earth, the stars, and the communal consciousness."

Communal consciousness? His brain stopped. His parents not dead? Question, must question, but how? Why? …

…It has been so long…

The man continued, "Our land, while part of the greater whole, is also key to maintaining the equilibrium of that whole," he motioned with outstretched hands. "Juno is special. More special than even the Council, present or past, ever suspected." The dark cloak billowed as the man again stopped and hovered inches from Cary's face. "Ever wish you could converse with your ancestors, the ancients?" An eyebrow arched, "Your parents?"

The question Cary was attempting to form lost all coherence.

So long… so long!

His mind spun. Blank. The man's eyes were shining. "Yes. It is possible. Here. Here, we can view the threads." The grin grew. "Move them."

"How?"

The man casually paced the Green, "Rumors abound. Shiploads of people come to Juno to die, to commune with the dead, and to foretell the future," he sniffed loudly into his moustache, "as if this were possible. A person must be trained to tap into the communal consciousness and even then, the amount of access is severely restricted.

"The amulet. The air, this soil, the water, the power of Juno can be accessed by the amulet. I made it so."

So long.

This man, D'Ono Felari, was one of the Magicians that fought in the Civil War. The war that ripped Juno to its foundations. This man helped cause that upheaval. Could he be trusted? "But the Outerworld has....," Cary tried.

The voice in his head screamed. *Hope...so long without hope!*

"The amulet is useless from Juno's shores, but if the Outerworld were to have one, there would be an end to all."

Hope...

Cary was bewildered. "But if everything is related and if nothing can be destroyed....?"

Felari strode to within inches of Cary's face. Blue eyes glistened with a rawness Cary had never witnessed and, for an instant, spiked his heart with fear. "The Outerworld is not of this universe. It is not us. It is if nothing was. The Outerworld eats up reality and leaves nothing in its wake. It is the opposite of Juno's essence: hopelessness, desolation and darkness. It is nothing."

"Why are you telling me this?"

...hope....

Felari smiled an omnipotent smile that solidified Cary's fear. At that moment, Felari was more than ageless. He was boundless. "Because you needed to know. *Now!*"

Cary awoke with a start. Sweat trickled down his brow and stung. A hand on his forehead found dried and glistening blood. A glance at his palms saw marks where his fingernails had dug in. His head ached suddenly but due to the injury or the dream, he didn't know. The blanket had been thrown back in his hasty waking. A chill was taking him. He looked down. Naked. That was strange wasn't it? *Wasn't it?* He didn't know. It had been so long.

In drawing the blanket around himself he took in the surroundings. A campfire, once lit, was now dying. A few lone flames licked the charcoaled remains. Trees and underbrush surrounded the clearing where he sat. Through the trees he could see a body of water glistening.

Then it hit him. It was more than his surroundings, more than his physical state. There was something else. A warmth that filled him. A comfort.

He pushed against the ground to sit up but found the attempt took a lot more effort than anticipated. The dizziness overwhelmed him to the point of nausea. A concussion, he thought and lowered himself back down. A sound in the distance caught his ear and he turned to look. As dizziness took him, he saw nothing. But that sound was familiar. A shuffle muffled by leaves. A footfall. Yes, a human footfall.

Cary lay his dizzy head down and waited. The dizziness subsided and slowly he turned. It was only a shadow, but he could see the faint outline retreat from his glance. A guardian, a captor perhaps, or maybe his rescuer. His memory was a blur. It had been so long. Only a darkness and a fleeting glimpse of his father dotted the sparse remnants of his thoughts.

He turned his head back toward the fire and sank into the blankets to fall asleep. *So long.*

The comfort faded too.

He awoke with a dreadful sense of just remembering something that he had previously tried so hard to recall. Cary sat slowly trying to jog his stubborn mind but the furthest he got was the shadow in the forest the night before. The daylight was bright against that memory. His hands pressed into the ground to raise his torso. They were sore. He looked at them again. Four half-moon grooves on each palm. His fingernails had dug right through the calluses. The raw wounds stung and he, again, tried to remember. *So long.*

Just then he heard footsteps behind him.

"Please wait." His own voice reverberated inside his head and brought the dizziness back.

At the edge of the forest, over a hundred feet away, a figure appeared. Cary could make out that the figure was a female and young. There was something in her posture that told Cary she was on comfortable ground; this was her ground. She dressed in trousers and dress shirt. Her short hair was softly curled, and hung about her shoulders.

She stared directly into his eyes.

A calmness came over him. Warmth radiated through his chilled and nauseated body. He felt... whole, complete, fulfilled. But how?

Her skin reminded him of white marble; white with a translucence that hinted at hidden colours underneath. Her features were balanced and soft.

"Hi," she said. Her voice had a tremor. He should have recognized it.

An involuntary smile tugged at Cary's mouth. It was a dream, all a dream. But it was better, because he was floating upon a pink cloud of ....*love*. Yes, that's what it was. Love. Pure, unadulterated, and fulfilling. It was beautiful and terrifying all at the same time.

And there was something else too. What was it?

Wait.

There.

In his chest. Wholeness.

Yes. This must be a dream. It was all perfect. The day was bright and he was whole and loved.

Chapter Eighteen

Waking up wrapped around a shotgun was not normal. Her hand had cramped from clutching the wooden top while she'd slept. She was stiff, sore, aching, and had a headache from the half bottle of brandy she'd downed in an effort to get some sleep. All in all, a fitting way to wake up after the events of the night before.

As the coffee perked, Simone made her belated daily phone call to Michael -- sorry, the cafe was robbed; yes, she was alright; good to hear that the hearing is over and that her father would be home soon. Then, steaming coffee in hand, Simone donned a jacket, slipped into her dad's summer shoes, and went for a walk in the crisp September air.

Life up until that point was normal, or within the normal range of experience. Simone figured if life was a bell curve of normality, her life would have likely dwelt near one of the extremes. However, within a few dozen steps of her home, her life took on a whole new curve.

"Cary."

Her coffee mug tilted limply in her hand and dropped. Her mind went blank. She retreated, numb, and paced. The pacing continued, wearing a neat path in the grasses beside her garden as her mind spun on its axis. Despite what reality told her, despite what common sense was driving her to believe, Simone couldn't deny her eyes, her ears, and, most of all her gut.

"You live in the middle of nowhere and then one day you find a guy in your backyard, unconscious, naked and looking a helluva lot like some guy you'd only ever seen in your dreams? This can't be real."

Real or not, she just couldn't leave him there, naked and cold. He was a person. Maybe.

"Cary." The name, said a hundred thousand times in the past, was now strange and potent in the air between her lips. She backtracked with a blanket and some matches. The blanket was large enough to keep him hidden from Simone's view. Grunting and sweating, she pushed reality from her mind and managed to drag his limp form from the pond's edge. He didn't stir. She built a campfire then retreated again.

"Oh, what the HELL IS GOING ON HERE? This is insane!" She yelled at the trees, her garden, the sky. "There is no way! No way. I'm delusional. I'm still in shock. I got knocked on the head. I'm dreaming."

For most of the day, she walked the path to the clearing. There and back. There and back. Each time she returned, he was there. Still. Unmoving. Not disappearing. Anxiety pulled her back to the house. Doubt drew her back to the clearing.

Late afternoon, he awoke. Simone froze, caught like prey. But his eyes found hers.

A beautiful plume of realization suddenly exploded in her chest. Tears came to her eyes, warmth washed over her heart, and, for one brief and sublime moment, she believed it could all be real. That the world wasn't such a cruel place, that people actual had hearts and cared about what others felt and thought. That evil didn't exist or, at least, if it did, it could be conquered. In that moment, it had all been real; hope, beauty, harmony with nature. The warmth that had washed through her and calmed the sea upon which Fear sailed was like the sun's heat upon her face in the height of winter. She wished for it to happen again, to make her believe, beyond all doubt, that it was all real. She wanted confirmation.

He passed out again. A concussion. She didn't have the strength to drag him indoors. Calling an ambulance was probably prudent, but she couldn't yet face the possibility that all this was real. His presence was hope, it was escape, and it was exactly what she needed. At nightfall, Simone retreated, leaving a campfire blazing to hold back the frigid night.

The shrillness of the phone pierced her silent contemplation. "Hey, honey. I heard what happened. How are you?" It was Sally. It had only been a matter of time.

"I don't want to talk about it." Simone downed a gulp of brandy.

"Okay. I'm going to bring you some food tomorrow."

"I'm fine. I don't need...."

"I don't care. Karen asked me to bring you some. We made some extras today."

"Today?"

"Yeah. We cleaned up and opened for the afternoon. It's the last weekend for the trade show. I'll see you tomorrow after my shift, about 330."

Shit. Simone raked a shaking hand through her hair, the bandages on her fingers catching on strands of hair. She couldn't handle much more of this. Was she handling it now?

She spent the night laying atop the covers of her bed, looking out her window at the stars.

Morning arrived. Cary was awake but groggy. He was unsteady as he put on the clothing Simone had pulled from her father's closet, then followed her back to the house. He fell onto the sofa and slept. It was an instantaneously deep sleep and, despite her desperate desire for information, she was happy for that.

Simone stood. The emotional toll of recent events was working its way through her body. Shock was leaving aches and pains in its wake. The adrenaline surges had left her weak. On shaking legs, Simone took her brandy glass to the kitchen. The glass slid along the bottom of the stainless steel sink sounding like how she felt: raw and course. She filled the glass with water, drank, then put the glass on the counter this time. "What do you do when the man of your dreams appears in your backyard and falls asleep on your sofa?" Out the window to the back garden, Simone saw her garden in general state of disarray. "You get him to help fix your garden, that's what."

She needed distraction, but she couldn't leave him. She didn't want to leave him. The draw was magnetic. It had taken all of her will to deny that attraction when she'd found him by the pond yesterday morning. Perhaps she should have been grateful for the shock and pain of the last few days. If not for J.D. and the robbery, she might have made a complete fool of herself and thrown herself at Cary.

She poked her head around the corner. "Cary?" her voice was loud, invasive. "Are you still sleeping?" The body on the sofa didn't move.

She crept up, that all too real sensation in the pit of her gut getting stronger as she closed in on him. That should have been enough, but she had to see for her own eyes. Yes, he was still breathing.

Simone stepped back. *Of course, he's still breathing, you idiot. You knew all along.* But she looked again.

His hair had parted unevenly and flopped over his head; streaks of ash and blond falling over the sofa's arm. The unmarred side of his forehead was up and uncharacteristically uncreased. His blond eyelashes fanned out against the circles under his eyes. Strong, yet acute cheekbones drew up from a long, straight nose. Dark, curved eyebrows framed his eyes. All of that put together would have made a rigid, sharp individual. But there was a softness in his eyes and mouth, a softness made intense by the acuity of other features. Even his hands, with their strong and long fingers, held a gentleness within them. It was so hard to think of what he was. He was so quiet now, so serene. How could anyone so beautiful be so deadly?

Her hand was above his forehead then, reaching out. If only to touch, she thought. If only to touch him and know that he is real. To feel his hair, his skin, his pulse. To feel what she'd only ever seen in a dream. But her hand hovered there, inches from his head before finally drawing back.

She withdrew to the kitchen again and peered out the back window, collecting herself.

She was so sure that upon first sight they would know each other. Wasn't that why she'd felt that warmth, that completeness? It had felt so right for that to be the truth. She needed it to be the truth. Now she didn't know what was true and what was real.

A shrill ring cut through the silence. Simone grabbed the phone off its cradle. Michael was worried and checking in. All was good, she assured him.

Simone felt a gentle push on her gut. Cary walked into the kitchen.

"Hey, how's it goin'?" as the words left her mouth, Simone cringed. *How are you? You are supposed to say 'how are you?'*

There was only a beat missed. "It's....*goin'* well." She watched as his mouth and mind worked around the vernacular. "At least, I think it is," he said as he sank into a kitchen chair.

"You definitely seemed to sleep well," she cringed at the small talk. God, why was this so tough?

Cary nodded and yawned. As if the yawn brought new oxygen to his brain and triggered new thoughts, Cary stopped. His face was suddenly ashen. There was no twitch of an eye, no tremor of his body. Only a momentary colour change. If her eyes hadn't been on him, she could have missed it. Then she felt it. Shock. "What...." Even his own words now seemed foreign. "Where am I?" His eyes found hers, his emotions an open book. Overpowering, growing shock.

Simone did the only thing she could, "Do you know me?"

Cary nodded without hesitation, "Yes, you are...," he faltered, and the shock continued to fester.

Through the emotional onslaught, a small beam of hope shone down upon Simone and she smiled. "I'm Simone, that's right. What else do you remember?"

Simone flinched as Cary tried to recollect, then stumble. The shock grew. Disbelief, bewilderment, and then back to shock. Simone's gut did somersaults with each new leap of his emotions. Finally, she reached out her hand and grabbed his, "Please, Cary. Just calm down." As soon as her hand landed on his, a stab of panic flew into her gut and she nearly blacked out.

He ripped his hand away, breaking the connection, "How did...?"

"It's as plain as day. You're scared shitless." He continued to stare at her. Distantly now, she could feel the light-headedness, the disconnected thoughts, the panic. Then her own desperation kicked in. She was going to lose him to Fear. She couldn't let it win. Not this time. "Cary," she dared put her hand upon his again, "look at me." The eyes. That's what did it. Holy shit. It was beyond calm. Amidst a universe of thousands upon thousands of reflected images, there were only the two of them. Everything else was gone. "You are safe. I promise." Slowly, Fear melted; a small spike of shock remained.

"Do you remember your name?" and while looking in his eyes, she heard her own voice through his ears echoing back to her.

"I am Cary Aristovin. I am Cary and you are Simone."

This was all real. *He* was real. Simone beamed, in spite herself. "Good," and though she knew it was inappropriate, tears welled in her eyes. "That's a good place to start."

"Where am I, Simone?" She could feel the wheels turning in his head, trying to recover some memory to attach to his surroundings so that he may feel within the familiar.

"You are in my home."

He drew away from her; the small space between them felt infinite compared to their closeness a moment ago. "I don't recognize your home."

Simone could feel his mind searching for the answers, questioning, hunting. This was Cary. This was who he was. And suddenly the very real reality of the situation crashed down upon Simone: none of this could last.

Cary continued to stare at her, waiting for answers. His touch was electric, and it fueled her craving to hold him. She looked down at her dishpan hands; pulled them from his beautiful touch. Then Simone did something she'd never be proud of: "You don't recognize it because you just got here. You are an exchange student, just arrived here from Ireland. You are living with me while you visit my country."

Cary nodded. Accepting. Trusting.

Disgust and Shame cuddled up beside Fear in Simone's heart as she let the lie flow. "I don't know why you don't remember anything, but it's sure to come back soon. We'll just have to wait."

"I didn't bump my head or anything, did I?"

"Actually, you did." She stretched out her hand toward the healing bruise on his forehead. His hand followed hers and felt the ragged bump.

"How?"

"I don't know. I found you unconscious." Again, Cary nodded.

Simone waited while the wheels in his head turned and hoped that she was masking herself enough to hide the lie from him. Finally, he turned to her, a bleak smile on his face, and said, "So we are friends, this is your house and I just got here when something happened."

Simone nodded, waiting for him to accept.

"Well then, I guess it's just a matter of time." He paused: the wheels were turning again. "Can you show me where you found me?" Fear shot up her spine. "What?" Cary's hand reached out and grabbed hers. It was warm and gentle. "What's wrong?" He was just as much in her mind as she was in his. This wasn't good.

Simone shook her head while she pushed and shoved Fear into the back closet with her lie. "Nothing. I found you by the pond." As much as she didn't want to, Simone slipped her hand from Cary's and led him out back.

Chapter Nineteen

A voice boomed through FarSee Cove. "Cary Aristovin! Present yourself and report!" Olivia screamed, Emil ducked under the table, and the mug of tea jarred from Denis' hands.

That's when Denis began to worry.

Cary had been absent for three days now. Denis tried not to worry. But even a day without a message was too long where Cary was considered. Denis tried to console himself that the lad had gone on a soul finding journey. The Test and Count Roan's death would have hit the Son hard, Denis knew this even if the boy didn't show it. His summons would have been icing on a very unpalatable cake. But three full days?

Footsteps echoed down the corridor to the kitchen, drawing nearer. Olivia hustled out the kitchen door tugging a resistant Emil along with her. The door drew closed as a red-faced Lord Fraaml entered the kitchen, "Where is Lord Aristovin?" Denis feared the worse. What could Cary have done now? What had happened? Where was he?

"I do not know, my lord. He isn't here," decreed Denis as he rose stiffly to fetch a cloth. "I haven't been given the privilege of his presence for three days. Since the count's death."

The table shook as the giant-like Warrior slammed his fist into the wooden top, "For the Council, I will have his heart!"

Denis wiped the spilled tea from the tabletop. He had been witness to scenes such as this before, not only from this lord, but many others. It was usually due to the Aristovin Son. The roaring, destruction, and violence held no threat to him. As a servant to these men, Denis knew them and knew their constraints. He imagined that if he were in their place he would feel the same, especially since he knew firsthand just what his master was capable of. "What did he say when you last saw him?" The Lord Fraaml towered over him, sweat dripping from his forehead. Yes, perhaps he would be reacting the same way given the circumstances.

"He did not say anything, my lord. I last saw him leave for his summons to the Council. A messenger arrived not long after bearing the news of the count's death. I presume Lord Aristovin went straight from the City to Warken."

Denis tacked on, "And I have seen neither your son nor the count's." But the allusion to the instigating event the week before missed its target. Instead, the lord sank to the bench. His colleagues didn't know where the Aristovin was either. Cary was alone. Somewhere. A coldness ran over Denis' neck.

At times, the late Lord Aristovin's expressions had been difficult to read, but Lord Fraaml's were not. The Warrior was confused. And, there, in the crease of his lip, worry. This man was deeply worried. Maybe as much as Denis himself. The lad had gone too far this time. But was the worry for the Young Aristovin or for the others he would affect?

"If I may ask, my lord," Denis returned to the bench opposite, "when did you last see Lord Aristovin?"

As if from a daze, the Warrior replied, "At Warken." The gaze broke and he seemed to find a perplexing spot on the table. "His Companion has been in their stables for three days."

The coldness took a seat in Denis' heart. Too much was being piled on to the youth's shoulders too quickly. He had seen this coming and feared its consequences.

"Well, he can't be far. What happened just before he left?" Denis knew he was being bold but more than Cary was at stake. He had a hunch that between the two of them, they could figure out not only where Cary was, but what he was doing.

"I spoke to him of his obligation."

"And how did he respond?"

"He refused it."

"On what grounds?" The crease in the lord's brow deepened. It wasn't anger at Denis' insubordination; it was understanding. Whatever had happened just before the Aristovin's disappearance, it was only the trigger. The Council had told him something, of that Denis was sure. But what had the Council told him?

"Dmitri." The name resonated in the stone kitchen; it bounced off the flagstones, the cast-iron pots, and set the air aquiver.

A shadow fell over Denis as the Warrior rose abruptly and headed for the door. "You will sent word to me immediately if you see him?" The question was more a demand as the lord pointed a large finger at the servant.

"Yes, my lord. Most assured, I will."

"His horse is out front." The Warrior turned and strode back through the Household to the front entrance.

"You're welcome, my lord," Denis raised his mug to the empty corridor.

He glanced toward the door. Emil's wide eyes stared back, "Was that Lord Brask Fraaml, one of the Great Three?"

Denis nodded. "And not on one of his better days."

Emil stepped from behind the door as his mother pushed him out of the way. "That's enough of yer Warrior worshipping. Best yoos be fetching Master Cary's horse, now." She swept her son out the kitchen door. "Were you talking of Dmitri, the Mentor?"

"Yes," Denis nodded as he placed his tea mug into the washbasin.

Olivia sided up to him and snatched the mug from the water. "But the Mentor couldn't have anything to do with Cary's disappearance. You suspect the Council." A dishcloth appeared in Olivia's hands and she began washing up.

"It could easily have been either planting ideas in the young man's head."

With smooth efficiency, Olivia washed, dried, and put away their breakfast dishes. "Cary's smarter than that."

"Yes, he's smart. Usually that's the problem." Denis left the kitchen to see about putting their new drying shed to use.

Chapter Twenty

It was only morning and already the day was beautiful. Insects buzzed around in the still air while birds called out among the trees. The forest, he thought suddenly. Should he remember that? It wasn't that he didn't remember it rather, it was that he was asking this particular question. The mere act of asking was an implication. But he had no answer, neither to the question nor the assumed implication.

But he had a hard time understanding why he wouldn't remember certain things. Like his parents, his home. These were things intrinsic to a person. Unless, of course, that person didn't have a home and his parents were absent from his life. If they were present, had they been so awful that he had gladly forgotten? The more he thought about it, the gloomier the outcome seemed to be. By the time they reached the pond, Cary was almost convinced that he didn't want to remember.

"Over there," Simone pointed to the south shore.

She followed him then as Cary began the inevitable walk. He sunk down to his knees and let his fingers trace the marked ground, the pockmarked mud, and the drag marks. Her footsteps. All was all here. It was all true. Why wouldn't it be, he thought. Had he been expecting something else?

No. He was expecting nothing because he had no expectations.

Cary stood again and surveyed the view. Over the open fields of grasses, across the distance evergreen forest, along the fence line, back to the aspen forest behind him, and Simone.

Simone. How could he forget her? Especially if he'd just arrived. He knew her by sight, felt like he'd known her since birth, but everything else was gone. Had something so horrible occurred that he'd want to forget her? The bump on the head didn't explain it all. If the accident had been recent, he'd still be nauseous or dizzy and the wound would still hurt. Instead, there was only the healing line. Even the bump was nearly gone.

Something must have happened.

There wasn't any one thing that was attractive about Simone. It was everything. That he'd never felt like this toward anyone was a severe understatement, especially considering his current condition. He couldn't keep his eyes off her. It wasn't just the way her hair caught the light, the way her face lit up when she smiled, or the way she spoke her halting jargon. It was the sum of everything. Including the fluttering in his chest. It wasn't anything remembered, it was just a feeling. Involuntary and profound. He couldn't help but assume it was all normal. The way his eyes followed her, the way his ears savoured every sound from her lips, the way his heart leaped and threatened to explode in his chest when she smiled at him. It all fit together so well and felt so wonderful, it couldn't be wrong.

Something horrible must have happened to block out why he felt so utterly completed by her. If only to regain those first moments with her, how they met, how she'd looked then, he would gladly have back those memories of whatever tragedy now held his mind blank.

She looked at him, concern in her eyes, but behind it, there was a sense of worry. Was she, too, worried that he would remember that horrible occurrence?

Cary shook his head. "I don't remember anything," and the worry in her eyes faded.

"I'm sorry." The intonation carried a deeper apology.

Even though she tried to hide her shame beneath a mask, he could still glimpse it. It was too strong. He approached and held her hand. "Simone, did something happen between us?" The shame threatened to burst from behind the mask.

Her brow creased, "No. There is nothing between us."

"I don't think so," and he let the implication weave into her heart.

Her hand slipped from his again that morning, "There was never anything between us." She turned and walked back down the trail. Cary followed, intent on making amends.

It was night and day. The difference astounded Simone. In her gut, she knew this was not right. This was not Cary as he should be.

They returned to the house and a ringing phone. Mountie Mitchell wanted her to come in to follow-up on her statement. She glanced at Cary, who, at sensing her discomfort, stood ready and wide-eyed. Could she leave him alone in a place completely foreign to him? He'd figured out a way to close off his emotions. She didn't know if that was good or bad. He'd also figured it out a lot quicker than she. Events were flying by her, like trying to see the rifling on bullets as they shot by her.

In the end, she chose to deny that she wasn't yet ready to leave his presence; instead, she chose to focus on keeping him distracted. If he distracted her, she likely did the same to him. It would keep him from figuring out her lie, and keep him around a bit longer.

"I have to go into town and give a statement to the police."

She hadn't even finished talking, when he said, "Can I come with you?"

It seemed distraction was going to be easy.

It was nearly 2pm by the time she finished her statement about the robbery and departed the local police station. Mr. Decker had dropped Cary at the cafe at Simone's request. Sally had greeted him with a delicious smile and Simone wasn't sure which was safer for him, Sally or a swordfight. When Simone entered the shop nearly two hours later, Cary was waiting on tables like he'd been doing it for years. Again, her mind stumbled trying to comprehend the ease and speed with which Cary processed and adapted to his surroundings. This should all be only myth or dream -- her dream -- but he was here, a trained solider and noble waiting tables.

Cary's presence at the shop had been a good thing. The cafe was full, Karen was up to her neck in dirty dishes and sandwiches, and Sally was run off her feet. Simone stripped off her coat, re-stocked the soft drinks, and made some more coffee. "You shouldn't be here," Sally tried to say.

"You need help."

"But you need some time off."

"I'm here and you need help," Simone glared at her friend. Sally nodded then. It was too busy to deny help.

At five o'clock, the cafe finally quieted. Karen went to buy supplies. Simone sipped a glass of water and propped herself against the back counter as Sally wrapped up leftover pies. Cary had flipped the chairs onto tables and was mopping the floor. He made it seem natural. But she knew it wasn't.

"Sal," the word leapt out of her mouth, "if someone you knew was acting differently, not necessarily like they should, but much better, would you let it be or attempt to make things right?"

In the instant that Sally turned, large green eyes fixed on her, Simone knew it had already gone all wrong. "If things are good, Simone, don't rock the boat. Especially if things weren't good before. I don't think I could stand seeing you like that again."

"Sal, it's not…"

"Nope," a small hand shot up in front of Simone's face, "don't say anything." Sally threw down the plastic wrap. "Anything to keep you safe and smiling. If that other guy did something to you and this one loves and protects you, don't question it. It just is." Sally's eyes were probing just a little too hard. Just a little too close to Fear which threatened to paralyze her.

"Why don't you open up to him?" Jolted, Simone stared, then cursed herself for her knee-jerk reaction. "I know you like him; you wouldn't have brought this up if you didn't. And he obviously likes you. Hell, I'd be willing to lay down money that the boy pretty near adores you." Simone snorted in disbelief, looking at anything other than Sally's face inches from her own. "Have you seen the way he looks at you?"

"Sal, you've seen us together a total of five minutes."

"It's not rocket science, Simone. I don't know where you've been hiding him or how long it's been going on. I don't care. When these things are there, they're obvious." But Sally's smile quickly faded. Tiny, ringed fingers grabbed Simone arms, "Why is it so hard to believe he likes you? Why is it so difficult to hope that things could be good?

"Simone," she stared as Sally shook her arms, practically begging for something that Simone was not in a position to grant, "If you could just open up and let him in, you two might have a chance at something really good. Don't you want that?"

Fear had wedged into the base of her brain again. This time its fingers were cold, so cold it made her numb. She'd never felt it like that. She wanted to cry, she wanted the pain to course through her, to let her know that she was alive, if only to ease some of the pain she saw in her friend's eyes. But there was nothing.

"Simone, say something. Please."

Simone shrugged. "It won't last. They hurt you and then they leave, so what's the use? There is no hope."

Sally reached up and grabbed Simone in a tight hug. Still, tears did not come to Simone's eyes.

Chapter Twenty-One

"The Young Aristovin gone?"

"Is he dead?"

"Has the Outerworld got him?"

"I heard he left to seek out the Outerworld homeland."

"It is not true. I saw him only yesterday, walking out in the fields."

"If the Aristovin heir is gone, all is surely lost."

The news was not so new anymore. Rumors ran abound in the immigrant village. Most were not willing to believe that their adopted son and homeland were lost. Worse, that rumors were true and both were lost to the Outerworld.

The chanting circles outside the immigrant village grew in size and volume.

"Cary's gone? What do you mean 'gone'? He's got to be somewhere, you know Cary," but he could hear the fear in his father's voice. What scared him more was the fear he saw in his father's face.

"Tivas, Magshda confirmed it," the older blacksmith said.

Magshda. Back on Dell 'Aire, she had been their village's healer. It was said she could hear the voice of the wind and read the earth. "Have you ever known Magshda to be wrong, father?"

Reid shook his head, "Even before my grandparents, Magshda had established her reputation. No one has ever known her to be wrong, son."

Tivas' world collapsed. Images of darkness flashed before his eyes, images he thought he had long forgotten. On Juno he was safe – correction - had been safe. They had emigrated to Juno when he was seven, but he still remembered. Tivas had tried long and hard to forget. He had put his faith in what his parents, his parents' friends, and other immigrants had said about Juno – they would all be safe. Safe. It was all gone now.

"Is he," the words lumped in his throat, "dead?" The tears welled in his eyes.

Again, the older blacksmith shook his head. "Magshda just said he's not on Juno."

Hope sprung anew. "Well, then he could still be alive!"

Tivas looked at his father. The lines in his face seemed deeper somehow, the circles under his eyes darker. Age had crept up on Reid Maklinari in the minutes since the conversation started. In that instant, Tivas knew his father felt it too. The images continued to taunt him too.

"You know how he started fishing at the bottom of the cliffs a couple years ago? Well, maybe he's just fishing." The older blacksmith shook his head.

"Even before Magshda came to tea last night, Emil came to tell us two days ago. Cary is missing."

"No, Father. He just got picked up by a fisherman. He just drifted out too far. He can swim back. He's a strong swimmer." His palms were sweating and tremors began to run up and down his legs. It had been so long and he had nearly forgotten. Those images, those voices, those screaming voices. It was so dark....

"Shouldn't you be working on the new alloy, blacksmith?"

The voice took them both by surprise. Tolonel wore a look of cold boredom only noble-born arrogance could wear.

"My lord," both blacksmiths bowed and father and son swiped hands across their faces in the process.

"My lord, this is my father. He is also a blacksmith."

"Yes," the golden-haired lord spoke in a drawl that matched his languid eyes, "I know."

If Tivas had spent most of his life around nobility, like his father, he would have picked up the shift in cadence in the Lord's voice. Tolonel had only barely concealed an emotion that, revealed, would have been wholly improper in present company -- sadness, and a hint of fear. Instead, Tivas caught a slight flash of light in those deceptive eyes. "The alloy, blacksmith? Is it ready yet?"

"Yes, my lord. I completed the formula last night."

"Then start on breastplates. I need enough to fit all Warriors. Day after tomorrow. Ronal will be by later with the numbers and measurements."

"But my lord, it takes three days for the alloy to be mixed and then tempered correctly."

"Then you had better get started. Maybe your father would help." The Warrior left, soundlessly.

Without a single word, Reid donned a leather apron and set to work beside his son.

For the love of the Creator, he hated this place. It sent shivers down his spine. Brask's Companion twitched under the saddle, pulled at the reins. The Warrior glanced about with weary eyes as the Jire Forest howled, cried, and sparkled blue in the height of day. How did his late friend and Chief do this? How did Cary do this?

From the shadows of the forest's evergreen depths, Brask finally emerged into the sandy clearing fronting the Mentor's cave. He dismounted, his Companion tight against his shoulder, as the old man appeared at the cave's entrance. "To what do I owe this pleasure, my lord?"

"I've come in search of the young Aristovin. He has gone missing." Brask reviewed the circumstances as he and the Aristovin steward had discussed, then waited.

The Mentor peered at the Warrior. Brask didn't know if the Mentor was trying to divine his thoughts or other Outerworldly depths. He focused his mind as if in battle, regardless.

"The Aristovin is not on Juno," the Mentor finally stated.

"Then he has been taken or has traveled across the Rire."

"Unknown."

"Where...how do I search?" Brask stumbled. He had not been prepared for the Mentor's declaration. "Am I able to search?"

"Please leave his search with me. There are avenues I can employ that might bear fruit."

Brask hesitated, then asked: "Should I worry?"

The Mentor's gaze changed then. "Worrying when you can do nothing is wasted energy. If you act when you are able, then worrying need never factor." Brask nodded, resigned. "I do, however, have two questions. Do you know what was discussed at the Aristovin's audience with the Council?"

"That is information privy only to the Council and to the young man himself."

The Mentor nodded, accepting. "Was the Aristovin in possession of an amulet?"

Brask started. Once again, the Mentor had caught him off-guard. He started to shake his head adamantly, then paused in thought. "He has not accepted a posting so there is no reason for him to be presented with one. As far as I know, his father's amulet is still housed at the Inner City. "

"Kindly check to ensure that your and the count's Son have their own amulets in their protection."

Acknowledging, Brask turned to leave and perform this latest task. "Cary told me of his apprenticeship with you."

"You know that his path would divert from his father's."

A cold sweat broke down his back as Brask thought more about Cary's absence and it's possible ramifications. "The Outerworld.... I fear that ...." He paused and started again. "Our army is weak and growing weaker every year. We need every resource that we can lay our hands on. Cary is a very valuable resource."

A curious thing happened. The Mentor smiled. "Yes, he is a very valuable resource. Only the best and most promising Sons are invited into an apprenticeship." In all of Brask's life, he'd never heard of anyone being offered a Mentor apprenticeship. "Please, my lord, leave this with me. I will be in contact with you." And with that, Brask Fraaml finally mounted and left, worry causing chills to settle in his boots.

Chapter Twenty-Two

After a meal in which Simone taught Cary the mechanics of a gas stove, she confessed to him her need to tend to her garden. The effort of harvesting felt familiar. By sunset, the weeds had been pulled and a generous pile of potatoes awaited transfer to the kitchen pantry.

Tires crunched on gravel and the light bending around the small bungalow was like daylight. Cary felt Simone's hopes suddenly soar. "Dad," and she raced around to the front of the house. As her legs froze and her feet ground into the gravel, Cary felt her happiness flip to fear and he raced to catch up.

There were two trucks facing the house, drowning it with their headlights. Men yelled and staggered around the vehicles. Shadows danced and disappeared on the tiny house. Gravel spewed with a deviant kick. Arms flailed as words were issued with violent gestures and a spattering of spittle. "Come on, Larken. We know you're in there." A slight man in a blue jacket and hat bellowed as he retrieved a heavy stick from the back of the truck.

"Yeah, come out and face the music, you bastard," yelled a stout man in a checked shirt and boots. Drunken laughter erupted. All the men were staggering, some more than others. Cary could see five men and all looked and sounded like they'd had more than their fill of alcohol that night.

A low growl entered from the recesses of his mind's fog but it was too late. Striding up toward the men, he asked, "Is there something I can help you with, gentlemen?"

"We've come to see Bill." A tall blond man in a red jacket and boots staggered round a car. His hair was straggly, looking to be much in need of a wash.

"Yeah, we need to talk," snickered the stout man in checked shirt.

Cary could feel a prickle on the back of his neck and knew Simone was behind him, moving toward the house. "Mr. Larken isn't home at the moment," however, the prickle was accompanied by an itch in his palm. The growl became an audible voice.

Their fear has been drowned in ale. They are full of bravado and drunken stupidity. They are not worthy opponents.

Cary blinked and waited.

The voice, too, seemed to wait.

Cary regained his footing, "Would you like to leave a message with me? I'll pass it along as soon as he arrives." He heard Simone murmur either a warning or a shocked statement, but his concentration was fixed on the movements on all five men in the dim light. Every step, movement, and breath was being stored and monitored. *Diplomacy will only delay the beginning, it will not win a battle.* The itch was beginning to burn. There was truth and familiarity in the voice. He felt it.

"Yeah, you could pass on a message," the red-jacketed man pulled himself together and strode up dangerously close. He was close enough now for Cary to make out the details of his gaunt, ruddy face and smell the alcohol. More than just his hair needed a wash. "Tell the bastard that we're out of jobs because of him and that he shouldn't stick his nose where it doesn't belong!" Brown eyes glared drunken fire not a hand's span away from Cary's face.

Simone murmured from behind, "He was just doing his job." Cary could hear the anger in her voice and feel a throb in his head. Too many intrusions into his mind. All conflicting.

Against a sudden desire to lay a fist into the man and ease the burning in his palm, "I'm sure he'll be happy to receive your message. Now, I bid you goodnight, gentlemen."

Beware.

A voice from inside one of the trucks spoke calmly. "No. We're not leaving."

Then the stout man suddenly shouted, "Uh, yeah, we're not leaving!"

"An eye for an eye," the voice in the darkness continued.

A chorus of agreement ran through the others along with, "Right, right. An eye for an eye," and, "Give him what he deserves, yeah."

There is a moment during which instinct rules, a moment when logic and reality are distorted towards fight or flight and judgement has no value. If indulged, this moment can be prolonged and enveloping. If it can be endured, it will pass. After it passes, reason again becomes the way of the mind. For a Warrior to survive in battle, he must understand that instinctual moment and endure it. Each Son is trained to use this moment, to manipulate it not only in himself, but also in others.

Cary acknowledged and waited. The moment passed. There was no sound. No movement.

Prepare.

The itch in Cary's palm was a longing. A longing to fill an absence too long endured.

The man in front hadn't backed down nor reduced his glare at Cary. "I don't think you get it, *boy*." It stung. Viciously. A lifetime of patronization. Prejudice. It began to swell up like a sick pond in a winter thaw. "We're not leaving until we make ourselves clear. An eye for an eye, right men!" he shouted over his shoulder without withdrawing his glare from Cary.

Simone's thoughts were tightening his stomach and her muttering grew until Cary put a hand behind to silence her but, in doing so, brought attention back to her. In that instant, he realized he didn't regret this action. He savoured it.

Here it begins.

The man's glare flickered to Simone. "Then I offer my services to resolve your quarrel. Leave her out of it." Cary moved to shield Simone from the men. Her fury was hot on his back and burned his mind.

An additional man -- a young man -- stepped from the darkness. Simone gasped; her hands clutched the back of Cary's shirt. "J.D." The name leapt from Simone's mind to his with a fear so deep and staggering Cary nearly buckled.

Swaggering, J.D. stepped up beside the red-jacketed man. There was a family resemblance, Cary noted. A smile crept up J.D.'s face, "Maybe we'll take her as a hostage until Larken gets home."

J.D.'s hand shot out.

Calmness. Centeredness. Breath flowed deep and easy as the culmination of his analysis of the men peaked. A firm grip of J.D.'s wrist confirmed his assumptions. There was something there. He could feel it. It was as if the sound of the wind suddenly had a voice and it was speaking to him. Only to him. J.D.'s wrist tingled within his grasp. It was circulation, not of the blood. A circulation of energy. Cary saw J.D.'s eyes change. Within his skull, the brown eyes sank away. A gleaming whiteness poured out and the physical man disappeared.

Cary saw it all. But, moreover, he also felt it.

The ground was a continuum of movement, coursing with life and life giving materials. Trees sucked their storage from the leaves and rerouted their life back to him. Life from his surroundings flowed through the ground, through the air, to him. It was given. Generously. And, yes, the wind did have a voice. Its voice filled him with reassurance. It overran the voice in the fog of his mind.

This was life.

Simone's presence altered within him. He could feel the energy flowing through her as well. She was a conduit, channeling it from the earth to him. And she was completely unaware.

J.D.'s whiteness shimmered and the tingling changed. Anger, the energy labelled it and the trees, the earth agreed. Must return the energy to balance. And with that singular thought, Cary spoke, "I think you should return home. *Now*."

The anger signature of J.D.'s energy intensified. So the energy flowed and Cary began to move.

J.D. twisted and attempted a punch. Cary pushed Simone back and dodged. With J.D.'s wrist still in his grip, Cary shifted his weight and laid him heavily upon his stomach. The others were advancing. Cary knew J.D. would get up again so he drove his palm up and broke his nose.

J.D.'s father lunged. A twist and a dive to avoid him. *Is that wise?* The voice in his head questioned. Cary pushed it away as he ducked and twisted. The other four men were now coming up quickly. A rolling diversion. They scrambled after him.

Cary glanced around, looking for Simone. She was at the door of the house, entering, disappearing within. Cary put himself between her and the men.

His foot shot out nailing the blue-jacketed tall man in the gut and sending him and his heavy stick through the air. Had he felt his foot hit? No matter. The release of tension snapped in his toes.

Three down. Will they stay down? Cary wondered back to the voice. *No, they won't.* They could hurt Simone.

Cary's fist shot out and rammed into the face of J.D.'s father. Blood streamed down his face. Cary added another and sunk the man to the ground. Again, Cary had felt no physical contact. A tide of renewed energy quickly flowed to his hand. He should have added another blow to the downed man's face, but the stout man and an accomplice then jumped at him. He ducked then jumped and spun. The stout man crashed into his accomplice. J.D.'s father began to rise. Cary drove his hand into the man's face again. A crunch sounded across the forested night. The movement was seamless. No air resisted his passage. The man landed with a loud thud and did not move.

That's better, he thought. He could turn his back on that one.

The blue-jacketed man returned with a hesitant accomplice. This time each had a weapon, one with a long piece of wood and the other with a metal pipe. The ground beneath Cary's feet felt real, solid, and comforting. He let any anxiety left within his body flow into the ground and took from the earth a calm strength.

Protect.

The word echoed within his head, sent a wave of energy through his body, and seemed to reverberate through the night. In that instant, Cary knew how this night would end.

The wood swung down upon Cary, whistling by his head. He stepped back, turned, as his foot struck out, crushing the man's ribs. Cary turned again, tore the pipe from the blue-jacketed man's hands and whipped it into his gut. Four now down that won't be getting up.

No, there is....

Finding the leverage point of the metal pipe, Cary returned his attention to the rising stout man and his accomplice. This would be finished.

A spike of fear shot through him. Simone. The night was suddenly torn apart by a thundering blast.

The men stopped. Cary stopped. He turned.

"Don't," Simone's voice quivered. "No."

J.D. stood, blood dripping from his face, not ten feet from Simone. Simone stood upon the threshold of the house. Gun. Cary made the connection between the word and object. It was pointed at J.D. "Go," she said.

In the moment of torrential silence that followed, the voice and the clarity disappeared back into the unknown. Amidst the sudden vacuum, Cary regained his footing and stepped gently across to Simone.

The men began to pick each other up. J.D. backed away, looking longingly back at Simone. Her fear spiked in Cary's mind like lightning across a dark sky. The vehicles roared before finally disappearing into the dark forest.

"They're gone," he placed a hand upon her hands. "You are safe now." Focus crept back into her eyes and she lowered the gun.

Wide-eyed and shaking, Simone dropped the gun and embraced him. Her tears soaked his shirt. "He's going to come back. Don't leave. I can't do this alone. Please don't leave me."

What had he done? No voice answered. Cary looked at his hands as Simone hung onto him. These hands had caused harm.

There was numbness. No fear, no relief.

Who was he to have caused this? He couldn't remember having ever done something like this but somehow he knew. His body knew. His hands. His feet. His legs. His heart. Every part of him knew how to inflict harm. How to protect. He had defended himself. He had defended Simone. And as he continued to stand still with shock, the fearful realization hit him -- he could have killed. Just as Simone could have.

Nothing he knew or felt made sense with what had just happened. Who was Cary Aristovin? He was the kind of person who knew how to inflict harm. Effectively and very efficiently.

Simone had saved him, stopped him from becoming something he didn't even know he was. Did she know that he'd been on a fast path to kill? Would she ever know how indebted he was to her at this moment?

Cary kissed her head and whispered a promise.

The night air blew in a touch of frost.

Winter was coming.

Chapter Twenty-Three

The messenger had come that night. Four merchant ships had been attacked in the past week. No survivors. Only the debris in the tide and their absence in the expectant ports indicated the tragic outcome.

Brask knew that his wife's sister was on one of those ships, but worse, his wife knew too. They had been holding on until the last minute, not wanting to leave their homeland defenseless. If they, the duke and duchess of the Parity in Madelen of the East Rire, had finally fled, then it was sure they fled only from the Outerworld. There was no longer a Madelen. And now no longer a Duke and Duchess of the Parity.

He had done worse. He had told mothers their children had been killed, fathers that their Sons had fallen in battle, but the thought of telling his wife that her only sister had been taken by the Outerworld was crippling him. He could already see the look in her eyes. Tears welling, sorrow mixed with empty rage and laced with the all-encompassing, "Why?" He had seen it all before. It was part of his job. A part he had tolerated until the day his best friend died. The look on the Lady Aristovin's face had nearly broken him. The look on his own wife's face surely would.

To make matters worse, those ships, two from Madelen and two from its sister country, Cergenon Isle, had also been bringing more nobility and soldiers willing and able to fight, along with new minds on battle strategies. The duke had been a good strategist, not as good as the count, but better than Brask. Both he and Dominic agreed that new ideas were needed and welcome. Now, not only did the bodies of all those people, immigrants, soldiers and nobility alike litter the sea, so did the materials, goods and another bit of hope for Juno's future.

Brask took another swig from his wine. He wiped the drippings from his beard and let the goblet drop onto the parchment, adding another red ring to the smeared text. In the past fortnight, only six merchant ships of an expected twenty-one had made it into Juno's ports. Cedric's letters were getting shorter. The Captain of the City ports only cited each ship's manifest, the informalities of old now useless and mundane. Twenty carts of orange gourds, one hundred and fifty bushels of Mixflak, eight-three kegs of wine, two rounds of cheese and one hundred and sixty-three immigrants. They had more immigrants than supplies. That endless statement ran through his head: *we're not going to last the winter, we're not going to last the winter, we're not going to last the winter.....*

Underneath that parchment lay yet another wine stained report, that one from Darine. The informalities again were laid aside, whether it was because of Brask was still Acting Chief or the intemperate air, he didn't know. While crop yields had been good this season, most of it had to be sold to the City for the increased immigrant populations. They couldn't have exported it anyway. The little coin brought in by immigrants and foreign nobility, the crops, whether Mixflak or lumber, was pittance compared to what exportation would have brought.

The country had too many people and not enough food or coin. They needed the sea trade. The Outerworld wouldn't need to attack again. Just keeping the merchant ships from Juno's ports would be enough.

Brask knew they would attack again and soon. It was an instinct. He could almost tell it in the way they attacked. It was as if they held back just a little so they would have something left to fight later. His skin crawled with the knowledge.

.... not going to last the winter. We're not going to last the winter. We're not going to last...

Instead of bellowing for another pitcher of wine he grabbed two parchments and marched through the growing menagerie of papers and books on his study floor. While Laurina would find out about her sister eventually, Brask knew he had to be the one to tell her. So he would tell his wife the terrible news, comfort her, console her and then ride to the City to sit and wait and smoke more tobac as he waited for another audience with the Council.

There were still errands to run, avenues to try, men and forces to organize and while that desperate voice still ran in his head, Brask Fraaml still had a little hope. A little hope that the Young Aristovin would return, someway, somehow. That hope, if only that hope, kept him alive and fighting.

"Opi? Are you here?"

Ailsene slipped a bare foot out of her boot. Her toes had just touched the sandy soil of the forest clearing -- sending shivers of relief through his body -- when a voice descended, "Put your boot back on, child. You know the rules."

Ailsene jammed her foot back inside the boot and skipped across the clearing. "Opi! Opi!" She flung off the long black cape and draped it over the old scarred table. "Where are you? Come out and see me!"

Dmitri finally emerged, a finger holding his place in a tattered book. Ailsene flung her arms about the Mentor and gave him an enthusiastic bear hug. "I came as quickly as I could. There's going to be a battle soon, Opi. But I came as soon as I let the Council know."

Dmitri patted her back as he broke away, "Anything new or different with this one?"

The Seer danced around the clearing before settling on a bench at the scarred table, her white robes floating to rest in an aura around her. She waved a hand dismissively, "Nope. Nothing new. Same as always."

The Mentor nodded and placed the book upon a shelf at the cave's entrance. "So why the summons, Opi? I haven't seen you in ages. I was beginning to think you'd disowned me."

"I'd like to know what you told Cary Aristovin."

Ailsene froze, then attempted to recover. "Which one is he?" Dmitri cocked an eyebrow. Even across the clearing, his disappointment was clear. "I had a vision a couple weeks ago. One that concerned him. I felt he should know."

"Elaborate."

The Seer rolled her eyes and sighed deeply. "Really, Opi. It's nothing special."

"Special enough to breach the Council's chambers."

"How do you do that?" She was more amazed than ashamed for being caught in the lie. The Mentor, however, was not in a patronizing mood. "Fine," she shook out her long black hair as if preparing herself for the story of a generation. "I saw that the Aristovin would be leaving Juno." She took a gamble and told Dmitri something he likely already knew. "I didn't know how, but I thought he should be prepared."

"In what way did you suggest he prepare himself?"

"I merely presented him with the information. That's all, Opi." At the last, she turned her blue eyes on the old man and gave him her most endearing look.

"Need I remind you that your position is precarious. Female Magicians were executed during the Civil War for demonstrating less skill than you. The Seer is only allowed to exist commensurate with several agreements between the Council and the Mentors, one of which is that you are never to contact anyone other than those approved. Cary Aristovin is not one of those individuals."

Ailsene stood and smoothed her silk robes. She hoped her carefully chosen words would work. "Opi. Great-grandfather. I know all this. I know I took a risk. But I greatly felt the Aristovin should be in possession of this information." She closed the distance between them and touched the Mentor's shoulder, "Opi, I only did what I felt was right."

The father of her father's father looked her straight in the eye: "And that was the premise underlying the Civil War." He retrieved his book from the nearby shelf. "Ensure that you are not detected re-entering the Inner City. I don't want to have to cover for your absence again." The Mentor turned, leaving the 29th Seer of Juno quaking with relief.

Chapter Twenty-Four

Blue and red lights flashed in the night ahead of her. "Teach me." It came out more as a demand. Her terror was showing. She was still shaking. But here, in front of her, stood Hope. She clutched at that hope with everything she had left.

He was so calm and self-assured. It was unnerving to be around someone so confident. She felt then that her whole life had been one big guess after another. There was no rhyme or reason. Things just happened and tended to happen poorly and beyond her control. Seeing Cary stand there seemed to say that there is a path, a way to be in control of one's life, to know that guessing is only one option. The other way is to know. Cary's every nuance, his very stance and presence stated that he knew; if he didn't know now, he knew that he would know eventually. Serenity blossomed around him at this knowledge. How did anyone become so self-assured?

That assurance cracked as Cary seemed to take stock of what was accessible in his mind and what wasn't. "You shouldn't.... There must be someone who could.... "

"There isn't anyone."

"But these men, tonight.... It isn't likely... " he tried again.

She dug deep and found a kernel of courage. "It will, Cary. It already has."

She could see a ripple of shock weave through Cary, but he didn't ask. He drew close and held her tight. "Okay."

Simone would learn to protect herself. Cary would stay, teach her, protect her. She needed that to happen at any cost.

"If you thrust your hand this way," Cary demonstrated, "you can hit the kidneys and avoid the ribs, causing more pain to the victim and less to your hand."

It should have shocked Simone that he knew so much about inflicting pain. It didn't. Instead, she saw the shock flicker across Cary's face at the words that spilled from his mouth. "Um, let me show you," then opened his mind to her.

His fist touched her lower back. Through her mind, she could feel what his fist felt. It moved and she felt the firmness of bone. It moved again and she felt the softness of flesh and fat.

Here, he said and pushed his fist against a place not bone and not cushy flesh.

-- You try.

She made a fist, remade it, feeling it in her mind and in Cary's, then placed it on Cary's back.

-- Higher. Here.

She repositioned her fist.

-- Good. Now hit me.

Simone hesitated. "I can't."

You can. You need to learn. The voice at the back of Cary's mind erupted.

Simone gapped. "What was that?"

Cary stood stunned and slightly embarrassed. "I don't know, but I feel he's correct. If you want to learn how to defend yourself, you need to learn how hard you need to hit and how much you need to exert yourself." He smiled then, "I can take it. I think."

But try as she might, she just couldn't provide more than a weak push or a faint tap.

She'd washed the sweat and fight from her body. The soreness felt good, it felt like progress, like strength.

The shower stopped and Cary emerged, clean and shaven, into the kitchen. How did her dad's soap smell so different on him? He was wearing the same flannel shirt and jeans she'd pillaged from her father's closet. They were huge on him. She would have to take him shopping soon. How would he look in well-fitting jeans and a T-shirt?

But amidst the generous gushing Simone was running headlong into, her head hollered, and her heart screeched to a halt. Why bother, Fear sneered. He wasn't going to stay. He couldn't. None of this would last.

Was Sally right? Could she allow herself to hope? Just this one time?

"So, what are we making for supper?" His grin was contagious. Despite her desire to keep him at a safe distance, she craved to return his smile.

She turned away, "We are going to make steak. It's one of my dad's favourites. I figured it wouldn't be as easy as pot roast, but it would be quicker." She pulled out a package from the deep freezer along with some frozen vegetables.

"Steak it is."

"Do you like steak?"

"Haven't a clue."

Simone had an uneasy moment when she couldn't decide if he was learning from her or doing something more. The way he looked at her -- one minute adoringly, the next like they'd known each other since infancy -- was shocking. She felt herself bracing for the blow, that it was all just a farce, a façade. But the blow didn't come. Maybe Sally was on to something.

"Simone?" His eyes probed a second more. She could feel his mind's fingers gently caressing her own, but her wall was now firmly in place; the pain of those memories was pushed into the closet with Shame. She would have to make an effort to keep it there. All of it.

Shaking her head, she forced a smile, "Nothing. All good."

From then on, it seemed that he was trying to distract her. He'd ask about her work, about her father, her friends, all in such a way that made her pleased with her circumstances instead of dwelling on the usual dreariness that was her life. Once, at the beginning, did Simone pause to ask herself what he was doing, what was really going on. It was a brief moment as he was quick to notice her hesitation and distract her again. His questions, his distractions, his smiles, his eyes, his closeness.

"I'll have it like yours," he said, beside her, watching the steaks cook.

Simone ran the knife along the steak and peeled the sides back. "Medium rare. It's the way I like it." He nodded his assent and she found her eyes drifting to his lips, his mouth, his smile.

"**D**id you grow up in this house?" Cary picked up the wooden top from the coffee table as he sat on the arm of the sofa, mug of tea in hand. He'd given her a small reprieve from the questions over supper, enough for her to chew her food between bites. And breathe.

She nodded, sitting on the sofa. "We've lived here since I was five, when my dad started working for forestry."

"He works for forestry?" His expression betrayed so much of him.

"He picks locations from which to harvest or clearcut trees. Those men last night, they think my dad is trying to put a stop to clearcutting, that he got them laid off from their jobs."

Cary nodded, but his expression stated things hadn't completely settled. "Does he live here?"

Simone nodded again, "He's at a court hearing right now. When he's at work, he's often gone for several weeks. More in the summer, less in the winter."

"Where's your mother?"

Shit. She wished she'd seen that one coming. The thought of her mother hit her blindsided. It was subtle, like a punch in reverse; the throbbing numbness and nausea overpowering before the climatic blow.

"Gone." It was all she could manage while bracing against the emotional blow. She plucked the wooden top from his grasp, flinching at the sudden flash of electric connection when she grazed his fingers.

"How?"

"She left." The emotion about her mother and her disappearance used to be all-consuming; ugly and angry. Instead, Simone found herself bewildered by the top; it was throbbing, pulse-like.

"Why?"

Fear reared up and she quickly placed the top on the table. "I don't know." She picked up her mug and sipped her tea. Inside, she shook with the effort of pushing the emotion back into its home in the black recesses of her mind.

"I'm sorry," he said.

"It happened a long time ago."

"Did it?"

Simone's eyes rose to meet his. *Don't*, she thought without projecting it. *Please don't. Just leave it.*

And then he smiled, still holding her gaze, "Read to me."

"What?" Amidst the relief, her mind gasped at the hairpin turn of topic.

Cary leapt up and grabbed a book from the shelf. "Read to me. A bedtime story."

"Okay." *How did he do this? How did he know without asking?*

He leapt back down onto the sofa with a grace that was both cuttingly precise and breathlessly beautiful. A shiver swam through Simone as she was reminded of who he was, what he was. Cary landed next to her and the shiver turned into waves of apprehension as he slid closer to her. This close, the electricity between them was anxious; a circuit waiting to be formed. She could see the grey flecks in his blue eyes. They shined when he smiled. She forced herself to look at the book he'd slid into her hands. "You picked *Persuasion*." *Did he know it was her favourite book?*

"Persuasion." She felt the faint fingertips of his mind in hers. "Wait," his fingers touched her hand holding the book and the spark between them jumped. Simone wavered. "Look at the title again and hold it in your mind."

Her eyes found his. The urge to run was choking her. But run from what, really? What was so dangerous here? *Everything*, Fear told her. Instead, she dug her heels in, heels with 'HOPE' stenciled on each sole.

Simone nodded and turned her eyes back to the book, his fingers still resting on her bandaged ones, tempting that circuit into exhilaration. *Persuasion.* "Sound it out for me and concentrate on what you're doing." Cary closed his eyes.

"Pers. Ua. Sion." She envisioned the lettering as she spoke the syllables.

"Do it again, but by letter." She complied.

Cary beamed and, in the instant before he opened his eyes, Simone's heart blossomed. "I saw it." His finger stopped over each letter sounding out the word just as Simone had. "I love our connection, don't you?"

How did he know exactly what would make her happy? Was it because it made him happy, too? Was it that easy? That simple? Simone let herself begin to savour the blossom of Hope in her heart. Could it be that good? "It's a little scary," she said then.

"Ah, that's why you keep your mind blocked. It's okay. I understand." His hand grasped hers; the connection made, the circuit firing, she nearly gasped at the rapture flowing from his body back to hers. Was it adoration, as Sally said, or the connection? It was easy to doubt. Too easy.

She looked into his easy gaze again. His eyes were dark blue, and she remembered that colour. Storms came into Knotton's Shallow from the west. The sky would still be bright and cheery in the east and made the deepening blue of the western sky seem that much darker. Simone could feel the pull in Cary's eyes, the desire beyond the racing electricity. She wanted nothing more than to sink into him, his eyes, his arms, and let herself open up. But she knew nothing about him. He wasn't even from her reality. Sure, he'd just fought off several drunk men and kept her from shooting J.D., but did that mean she was in love with him? Even infatuated?

She didn't know any more. After J.D. and her mom, Simone no longer trusted her judgement. But as they sat on the sofa, holding *Persuasion* between them, Simone knew that Cary was the one person she knew better than anyone else. Maybe even herself. She didn't know his favourite colour or his favourite food, but she knew his soul. She knew that he would give someone in need the shirt off his back, that he would work his fingers to the bone for what he knew to be right, and that he would never intentionally hurt her. As many times as she ran the fingers of her mind over the texture of his soul in her dreams, right now Simone wanted nothing more than to run her fingers through his hair, across his eyebrow, and along his lips.

"Shall we read?" The circuit faded as his hand left hers, and then the music of her life suddenly stopped. It rose again, as his fingers fell upon her shoulder. It thrummed through her body, affecting Simone in ways she'd only read about. She fought down the rising heat in her face, in the lower regions of her body. Then she began to read.

By 11:30, Simone couldn't keep her eyes open. Cary was leaning back into the corner of the sofa, arms crossed, a hand caressing the wooden top once again, and long legs propped up onto the coffee table. She was lying into the opposite corner, her feet, too, propped on top of the table, touching his. She couldn't feel anything from him. She broke contact and sat up. "Are you ever going to let me have my top back?"

Cary shook his head, a smile creeping cross his face. "I like it. Your image of Kellynch Hall matches the book, but your image of Captain Wentworth isn't at all how he is described."

"You're supposed to come up with your own images."

Cary opened one eye and peered at her. "It's hard when I don't remember anything."

"Fine, you can borrow mine. Just don't complain."

Cary sat up. He was so close that she could feel his warmth, smell mint tea on his breath, and the way her dad's soap smelled different on him. His musculature was lean beneath her father's shirt. His fingers found the book and he eased it from her grasp. "Maybe I'll try to read to you tomorrow night."

"Do you like it?" *Persuasion* hadn't always been one of her favourites. It had grown on her. She figured it was a book you needed a bit of experience to fully appreciate.

"Yes, I think I do. It's about people and I like that. Don't much care for the politics, though. But I suppose where there is one, there will always be the other." His thin smile seemed somehow resigned, tragic almost.

"I know what you mean. I don't know why people just can't be themselves: I don't understand why they feel obligated to play games and manipulate."

Cary nudged his shoulder against Simone's, the temptation to lean into him rising uncomfortably within her. "It's kind of hard to play games when you can see inside the other person's mind, huh?"

The laugh that erupted from her mouth sounded like a cackle. She bit it back, the discomfort growing into embarrassment. "Yeah, kinda hard." She could feel the air between them grow thick. It was more than the strange electrical attraction, more than the physical attraction that hungered inside her. It was like he knew. Knew everything. Knew more than she could ever articulate to him. But yet, there he sat. Next to her. Talking to her. Wanting to be with her. How could he know everything and still want to be with her? Simone rose suddenly. "You can sleep in Dad's bed if you want. It's probably much more comfortable than the sofa."

Cary thanked her and wished her good night. She didn't hear him again. He was too quiet. But it didn't stop her from straining to hear him -- undressing, breathing, shifting, turning, dreaming.

Chapter Twenty-Five

"C ary?"

He spun. On the green expanse, he saw, smelled, felt, heard everything.

And there, robed in grey wool, draped in silver hair and beard, was a man.

"Are you alright, Young One?" The old man strode toward him with frightening grace. Cary drew back. The man stopped and hummed pensively to himself. A finger, long and slender, was brought to an unwrinkled lip then down to stroke the long beard. "What do you remember?"

"What do you mean?" Cary was vaguely surprised to find he had a voice here.

"Juno?"

Juno. The word rung in his mind like a phrase of music. It taunted him. Reaching out familiar fingers to his heart. Familiar like the air, the scenery, the voice, the man.

"Your home."

Home? "But I am home."

Again, the man hummed to himself. After some time spent scrutinizing Cary, the man finally said, "Do you feel as if you trust me?" Cary merely shrugged, unable to sort out the fogginess of his emotions. "I suppose that will have to do for now. Dream pleasant dreams, Young One. I will return soon."

The green and blue landscape darkened. Horsemen in black armour raced across the interns of his mind, scraping their swords across the insides of his skull. Their laughter was tinny inside the iron helmets. Horses whipped around making him dizzy. Finally, Cary felt his body collapse within the dizziness and he sunk to the dead grass, nauseated. Before he passed out within his dream a face looked down upon him. He saw enough to know he didn't recognize the owner.

The next day he let his mind run free. Through his body, his emotions, noticing how everything sat. It felt normal to do this analysis, appraising the current state. Obtaining the status quo.

It was interesting now how phrases would just pop into his mind, to see what was familiar and what wasn't. There wasn't a whole lot that was familiar. Simone was familiar but not as familiar as the taste of an apple. There was something about the taste of an apple that beckoned him to somewhere behind that locked door of memory. He let his mind run to where it might, just in case it stumbled onto the key that would open that door.

There were moments when Cary felt an instinctual urge to worry, that there should be something to worry about. He wanted to worry. Tried to worry. But since he couldn't remember what to be worried about, he tacked it up to all the other strange feelings that just couldn't be attached to a reason. Like why he felt a compulsion to stretch in the morning. There was the obvious, common sense reason – that it improved general health and vigor – but there was another hidden reason that lay behind that door. So, Cary awoke, stretched, moved in a way that felt natural and familiar and then got on with the day.

What happened between him and Simone? The question gnawed at him, but the pain in her eyes was still too apparent. An itch to touch her was growing. If he could figure out what happened, would he be allowed to hold her?

Simone woke, with apparent effort, well after dawn. She appeared around the corner to a kitchen table full of food. "Sorry, I didn't know what you wanted to eat. What do you eat for breakfast?" Restlessness coursed through him.

She smiled then, hesitantly at first, then fully. He watched her eat spoonful after spoonful of yogurt and fruit, her lips curling around the curve of the spoon, her tongue dashing out to lick errant spots on her lips.

"Hurry up," Cary finally sprang up from his chair. His thoughts had begun to swerve to places in his body he didn't know existed. Or, at least hadn't operated until now. "Let's go outside and get you started on lower body defensive moves."

Simone smiled again. How could he forget a smile like that? Today. He would get to the bottom of this today. And today he would get that smile back permanently.

"When you do it, it always works."

"Here. Knock it here." Cary reached down and put her foot on the back of his knee.

— There. Feel that?

Simone nodded.

— Push your foot.

Cary's knee gave way.

— See? Easy.

Simone pushed harder. As his leg collapsed, Cary grabbed Simone and pulled her down with him. She shifted and caught her knee beneath his abdomen. They both grunted as they hit the ground and slammed into each other.

"Ow."

"It would have been better if you hadn't got your leg in the wrong place at the wrong time."

"Maybe I like it there."

Inches from her face, Cary paused, assessing the situation, her present fear, the distance to that smile. Simone stared back at him. Her wall lingered. He didn't push, but she also didn't offer. He pulled himself up and then her, "A caught leg is a useless leg."

"Note to self," Simone nodded.

— I should have kissed you when I had the chance.

"What?"

Cary froze. "You heard that?"

Simone was agog and blushing. "Yeah, I heard that. It was really loud."

"How," he began and stumbled. "We're not touching."

She shrugged. "Haven't the foggiest."

Cary took in a deep breath and let it out. He thought

-- Can everyone do this?

Simone smiled again, this time catching his eyes in a shining glance.

-- No. I'm pretty sure that we're the only ones.

-- Why?

-- I don't know. I don't have any answers.

"Now that we've got that out of the way, can we get back to training? I'm on a mission here." Simone smiled at him, but her wall was firmly in place now. Cary inwardly sighed. So close, yet so far.

The night was clear. There's the Big Dipper, he noticed wordlessly.

Look at that moon, she pointed up. It was big and orange.

-- It's so close, like you could touch it. He smiled and caught her eye.

They sat on the fence by the pond, jacketless. Today had been warm. Summer still had a hold but its grip was waning. The leaves had all turned.

Simone returned his smile.

-- I used to dream that, on nights like this, with a wish, I could jump and land on the surface of the moon.

Stars reflected their faint light upon the water of the pond. Mosquitoes danced across the surface, ripples marring a glassy reflection of the rising moon.

The night air felt so good. Just enough coolness to bring gooseflesh across bare skin. Cary closed his eyes. He could feel the breeze on his face. The shadow of air created by the rise of his nose. Eyelashes moving ever so slightly on their short base. The brush of his hair as it bounced off the collar of his shirt. The rush of cool air into his lungs. The way the fabric of his shirt snapped occasionally. His heart pounded slowly, purposely. Pounding life-giving blood through his body, through his center, through his entire being.

Charged with the night's electricity, he lowered his feet to the ground. A tremor ran through his legs and into the soil, grounding him and exciting him all at once. It was beautiful. This peace. This comfort. This wholeness. The night welcomed him. A comforting invitation to wallow in the insatiable crisp openness that only a starlit landscape could offer. Now tasting the sweetness of the evening's vigour, a laugh erupted from his belly. Unable to contain himself any longer, Cary raised his arms and greeted the nocturne with abandon. Jumping up and down, he just couldn't help it. I am a fool! he thought. "Ha, ha! But I don't care."

"Should I be scared...?" Simone dismounted from the fence, but she smiled hesitantly. Cary grabbed her by the waist and arm, swinging her. His joy was infectious. The swinging melded into a fast waltz, Cary singing loudly and Simone giggling. With her hand in his and the palm of his other touching her back, they were a circuit. Electricity cycling between them, through their bodies. Energy charging with every pass. Growing stronger and stronger. Cary's feet quickened, making the waltz a trot. Simone's giggling grew into uncontrollable laughter. The night whirled by, spinning, spinning. Cary's singing bounced off the trees. The very air he breathed seemed to spark. Simone's laughter grew breathy.

Loss.

Cary drew them to a halt.

Loss? Why loss?

Still within his grasp, Cary felt her energy. Her lightness. Her happiness. Her mind. Breathing hard, she was still laughing. Cary found he couldn't help it. He stood, savouring the energetic connection. Then, so delicately, his focus shifted.

He would lose her. How? They were tied together, that was as certain as the sun rose and set.

There. The softness of her skin in his palm.

And there. The way her laughter was becoming a hum in her lungs.

And over here. How the blueness of her shirt darkened into black amidst the shadows of her body.

Here, too. The way his shirt dampened under her hand. And her hand. He could feel the texture of his shirt through her fingertips.

Cary traced her outline. Then the shadows. The curves. The highlights. The fall of the fabric across her shoulder. The hum of her breath. That floral scented soap she always used. He burned her image into his mind. Her laugh. Her intense, electric stare. The way her brows furrowed when she was confused.

It all made Cary think, over and over, of what her loss would do to him. He couldn't escape it. It chased him down and sat on his mind, suffocating it with dreaded thoughts of nothingness, loneliness, and emptiness. To have her disappear from his view was becoming a desperately distressing thought.

Burn it. Burn it into his mind. Burn it in so it would not fade or disappear.

And then he saw his own body through her eyes. His own shirt. Up, her eyes lifted.

His eyes found hers and the images reflected again. Infinity. Her eyes. His. Him looking at her. Her looking at him. Openness filled him. The mesmerizing sensation that both scared and excited. Complete choice in a place of infinite possibility.

Choice.

His hand left hers to trace a finger down the outline of her face. Shadow. Highlight. Shadow. Her breath smelled of peppermint. And honey. Cary pulled himself closer and inhaled her slowing breath. Had he made a choice?

"Cary, I don't...."

"Shh. Don't talk." Under dark eyelashes, her eyes glistened back at him. Flickering between eyes, he watched as she blinked.

A tremble. Just there, he felt it and let warmth flow to her, comforting her. The wholeness he felt was intoxicating. To have her in his arms. This was....it was enveloping. Completeness. It was.... was this love?

He could feel the warmth flow back to him through the hand on her back. The trembling subsided. His hand moved further around Simone's waist and pulled her closer. Foot to foot, thigh to thigh, the warmth rose between them. Cary let his fingers run through the curls of her hair. So soft. Against his chest, he felt the beating of her heart. So strong. Yet so vulnerable.

The air from her mouth was so sweet. Intoxicating. It drew him closer.

His lips met hers. She trembled and pulled up her wall. Savoring the electricity raging through their circuit, Cary let his lips brush hers, tempting, caressing, asking.

With a small sigh, Simone pressed into him, her wall weakening, and let his mouth fit onto hers. Steadily, the electrical pulse grew, cycling through them, their bodies, their fingertips, their lips. Cary had tucked the wooden top into his trouser pocket the night before and now felt it pulsing as their connection raged.

He finally let his restraint fade. Cary wrapped his arms around Simone and let his lips part against hers. Wholeness, completeness unlike anything he'd ever known enveloped him and led him to believe that he had been empty until now. A black abyss lurked inside his chest. Simone filled it. Perfectly.

Her wall began to slip. Her lips moved against his. Her fingers ran up his neck and through his hair.

A car horn. Gravel crunching.

Simone froze and withdrew, then relaxed. "Dad!" Then ran back to the house, leaving Cary standing amidst the starry sky, content and fulfilled.

I am home, he thought to no one in particular, and strode to catch up.

Chapter Twenty-Six

For days now, the darkness crept closer across the sea. The southern horizon was a black wall for as far as the eye could see. Like a dark sheet, the wall wavered and rippled as the ocean tide beneath it surged toward Juno's southern shore.

Rumors ran rapid throughout the City and the countryside. No one had ever seen anything like this. No one had seen the wall before. Storms preceding an attack were expected and considered normal, if only in hindsight, but this....? The Warriors were tight-lipped and those merchants who ventured to ask an opinion didn't get a response. There was fear in the air. Everyone could smell it. Everyone felt it.

Then, on the eighth day, as the suns rose in the eastern darkness to shed a bleeding light on the waiting landscape, the black curtain crested Juno's shore.

The Warriors waited, Brask at their helm. The younger and newer Warriors shuffled in their armour, under the moral burden of their Crests. Perhaps the newly Crested didn't sense it beyond their own fear.

Brask steadied his unusually nervous mount and drew a deep breath. Yes. He felt it. It was as tangible as the black curtain surrounding the land. *If Juno survives this it will be a miracle.*

Fear rippled momentary waves through the ranks.

There was no room to think of the lost Aristovin heir, the heir of their hopes, dreams, and Juno's salvation. He was here now, on the Plains, with the Outerworld again about to defile his land. He had only one thing to think about: "Protect." And with that one word, they were bound to their training, to the soil, to each other.

The Lord Fraaml was no strategist, no Chief. He was one of the Great Three, but only one. The one leading this battle, and they had one chance. The count was gone but he left a legacy of unfinished plans and strategies. There was one strategy, one that might work...if they were a hundred Warriors richer. But he had had no choice. Even the newly Crested Roan Son admitted it was their best hope. Their only hope.

The distance between the Households had grown since his friend's death. Though Durlan Tolonel only received tolerance for the most part, his presence was once frequent at gatherings. Now the Northerners sought company amongst themselves, if at all. Brask glanced down the ranks again. The Tolonels, Silvas, and Darines were to the east, the Southerners, sailors and enforcement from the City to the west. He had had to beg the Council for the City guard to fight.

Yes. His friend had been a great Commander in Chief and a fine diplomat and he would not be able to match that skill here, now. No one would. The one that would complete the new Three had vanished. Their was hope lost.

Brask caught a glimpse of the count's protégé to his right. He could feel the Son's fear as he felt his own. *Creator, be kind to us today.*

Then as the Outerworld mounts stepped their hooves upon Juno's sand and their black armour caught the last fragments of the vanishing morning light, Brask muttered under his breath, "This is going to be a good one," and smiled.

The chanting rose in volume as the fires blazed, engulfing the three pyres. Was Durlan Tolonel laughing now, Brask thought. No. No one was. He glanced around the encompassing circles of Warriors and nobility. Warriors in ceremonial garb, swords polished to a bright gleam. Household flags snapped in the evening breeze. The Ladies dabbed their eyes with handkerchiefs and grey-clad Sons stood proud not knowing the horrors they would eventually face. The face of every Warrior, including Petri's, was stolid. And the faces of the eight Council members looked on, a calm stare painted on each.

It had been three this time. Petri's nephew, Chistof, had been just as good with the sword as his uncle. Lancet, one of Orsen Mikel's remaining sons, had a sense of humor that matched his late father's, and Lucas Silva, cousin to Lord Arissio Silva, could slice and dice the Outerworld with the best of them. Lucas had only just seen his thirtieth year.

Brask had not the unanimous consent from all Households. There had been no native non-Warriors on the battlefield; only the sailors on the firing range and the City Guard helping the Warriors fighting hand to hand. It was a sorry situation. A mere hundred or so Junoan Warriors fighting hundreds of invaders. It was the Council. Inside his mind, however, Brask didn't have the luxury to be furious. He feared for his land, its existence, his family and his friends. The fear rose in him like a sickness and he began to tremble.

CHAPTER TWENTY-SEVEN

A white truck with a green emblem was parked in a bright circle provided by the yard light. The front door stood open and Cary could hear voices from inside. He rounded the corner of the house to meet this man others despised. But once inside, Cary nearly fell over.

Knees weak, he tried to blink but didn't want to.

His mouth was so slack he could not even form the word.

Father.

His head seemed to open up. In a blinding flash, it all came back. All of it. The scent of his mother's roses, D'Ono Felari, the Outerworld and their swords. And after checking his palms for the scars created by his fingernails, Cary took a deep breath and continued. Slowly. Cautiously. Where was that forsaken voice when he needed it?

This man. Cary drew in the man's appearance as he would draw in a long awaited breath.

Broad shoulders, wide chest, and height only made the hidden physical strength more palpable. And the face. Even the moustache drooped the same. The tone and timber of the man's voice was exact, "Hello." He stuck out his large hand to Cary.

An image flashed. *For the universe. For me.* The Lord Cale Aristovin, fully armoured. With a sword.

Cary blinked in response.

"And you must be Cary. Simone's already told me all about you. You're welcome here as long as need be." Cary weakly grasped the man's calloused hand and stared wide-eyed as his father's twin proceeded back outside.

Cary stood, a steadying hand on the wall, and watched as the man rummaged in the truck.

Granted, he hadn't seen his father face-to-face in nearly ten years, but how ...? By the Creator, where to begin? Am I myself again? A sudden urge to let his hands run over his body, to check. Yes, he was still all there. Clothes...? Need my tunic. Focus, Cary told himself.

The voice in his head was silent, just when he needed it.

This is not Juno. That much Cary could piece together. How to reconcile everything he'd seen over the past.... what? How many days? Weeks? -- Denis will be worried to death -- this has to be far from Juno -- how am I going to get back home? -- but this? To have his father's image looking at him, responding, talking to him? But he is Simone's father...

The voice was still unresponsive. His head was spinning. Cary took a breath and gathered his senses.

With two large bags, Mr. Larken strode to his bedroom. Simone stood in the corridor staring at Cary. He could feel nothing from her. Her eyes remained on Cary as she relayed a message to her father, "Michael said the hearing went well. Did it?"

"It's over and that's all that matters." His voice seemed to erupt from the back of the house and then he emerged carrying a pile of garments. Perched against the corner of the wall of the kitchen, Cary felt his eyes affix to the man as he dumped the clothes on the table and opened the washing machine.

Cary desperately tried to find a flaw in this image.

But there was no flaw to be found. The man was as immense as Cary remembered. Blond tussled hair topped a head resting on massive shoulders. Eyes like blue crystalline peaked from beneath bushy blond eyebrows and the voice grumbled from beneath a large drooping moustache. His hands could have crushed Cary's skull with little effort. The man seemed out of place in the tiny house. Instead of powdered soap and soiled garments in his hands, the man should have held a sword and shield. Cary could even detect a scent. The same scent that clung to the leather chair in his father's study. "Are you going to tell me about the shotgun by the front door?"

A chill shot down Cary's spine. That tone. The man could have easily said, "Are you going to tell me about the fire at the armour shed today?" Never a raised voice. It was the tone that insinuated disappointment. Which is why Cary was amazed when Simone shot back, "I put it there. Makes me feel safer when you're away." Her father grumbled. Did he sound condescending or was he merely probing for her explanation? "For how long are you home?"

"I leave for Blue Ridge in the morning."

"*Tomorrow* morning?"

"Simone..." her father growled.

"And you wonder why I have a shotgun by the door."

"We made pot roast," Cary blurted.

Both Simone and her father paused. "Pot roast it is," Mr. Larken smiled.

After walking along the remembered slopes of southern Juno, the dream suddenly flickered and became intensely vivid. A young woman in white robes stood opposite him in a round room. She had raven black hair and eyes like gems. Her hips moved slowly under the white fabric as she walked toward Cary. Her hand rose as if to touch his face and then she disappeared.

Cary shook his head and made to run his fingers through his hair. He lifted his hand to find a light-weight sword in his right hand and the other hand bloodied. Whose blood? And the sword was not one from Trium, in fact, he'd never seen another like it. Or had he? Faint traces of another dream, another time whispered in his ear but he couldn't make out their words.

He dropped the sword.

Screaming. The terror. The pain. Again, the horsemen rode by on their black snarling horses, leaving their stench hanging in the air. Laughing, they again passed their blades within inches of Cary's heart and this time he begged them to come back.

Cary's eyes snapped open. Scanning the front room with eyes and ears open, motionless he waited to see the shadows, hear the footfalls, the scrape of metal on metal of the Outerworld soldiers come to kill him. But there was nothing. Nothing.

Then it struck. A blow to his heart. Dark and heavy. Cary clutched his chest in a feeling that was beyond nausea; it was pain. Unlike the remnants of his recurring nightmare, this pain was distant. It was in him but outside him. However, the terror-induced pain felt very familiar.

The blow faded to a dull throbbing. He got up from the sofa and attempted to walk it off. What was this feeling? Was he sick? The voice was quiet.

Instinctively he walked toward Simone's bedroom, but as he raised his hand to turn the doorknob, another blow hit.

Desperation.

Clutching to a fragment of reality, a fog of loneliness crept in. Cary's mind went blank as his knees buckled and he fell to the floor. Again the pain grew in his chest. He felt like purging himself but a hollowness enveloped him.

And then he could breathe again. The instinct to check on Simone grew. Something was wrong.

Through her door he could hear it. Sobbing. Desperate, deep, throat wrenching sobs. Cary's hand reached for the knob, he was blinded again.

Fear.

His mind clutched a precipice, dangling over a dark bottomless pit.

Loneliness.

Emptiness.

Nothing.

He was covered in it, engulfed and enveloped by it. The feeling was so tangible Cary believed that if he held his hand out in front of his closed eyes he could touch the nothingness.

Dmit...Dmit....Fath..er...FATH-ER...!

The threat was close. Absolute loneliness, absolute solitude, and absolute desolation. Even that ever-present continuum of appraisal inside his head was gone. It was all disappearing and he would be alone.

For an eternity, the black pit loomed under his feet and Cary clutched his stomach, eyes clenched, curled at Simone's door.

Until, finally, it ceased.

Warmth filled Cary's soul again. That sense of otherness went with the fear, the coldness and the solitude. The memories flooded and flourished again; Dominic, Everett, Brask, Tivas, Daant, Denis, Marcus, Count Roan, Dmitri, his father and his mother and all the others. He was complete again. Relief tickled as the Warrior's voice scolded.

Cary limped to the sofa and collapsed.

Dmitri was in front of him and suns' light filtered down through the blue sky of the dream. Cary stood, grasped in Dmitri's strong arms, trembling for a few moments before he felt he could stand on his own. Dmitri held him fast at arms' length and without saying a word, searched Cary's eyes. With the rise of a single silver eyebrow, Dmitri's grip tightened momentarily, "Are you alright, Young One?" Cary nodded and gazed with a bit of wonder at the once again familiar face. "Do you know who I am?"

Again Cary nodded and Dmitri released his grip. "I don't know how long I'll be here with you, so I'll try to sum up my findings for you." At last,

Cary's feet felt firm on the green grass and the smell of salt air in the wind grounded him. He breathed deeply and nodded to the Mentor. "From what I have gleaned so far, I've determined that, with the power of the amulet, you have somehow been, um,.... *transported*, I guess would be the word. I am presuming that you had an amulet in your possession..."

A nod.

Dmitri cleared his throat, "Anyhow," and began to pace, "since I was unable to find any record of this *transporting* you seemed to have accomplished," he paused momentarily to dart Cary a glare from beneath his hood, "I'm trying to come up with a few ways this might have happened.

"First, what exactly were you thinking just before you, um, relocated?" Dmitri stopped and pinned the apprentice with a cool hard look. "Quick boy, we haven't got all day!"

"I don't remember." He did remember -- Min, Nina, their swords, the Old Ones -- but he was reluctant to produce this information pending dire consequences to the girls. Though Dmitri's glare actually seemed to sharpen, Cary didn't know what else to say. "All I remember is being at Warken. I'd come out of the count's bed chambers and talked to Brask."

"Let me put it this way." Dmitri drew near enough that the sky was occluded by his hood and Cary could see the grey flecks in the Mentor's eyes, "If you had been thinking about your conversation with Brask Fraaml, you wouldn't have relocated here ... there... wherever you are ...where are you exactly?"

For reasons unknown, Cary felt again reluctant to divulge information. "I'm with Simone."

The Mentor poked the air, eyes flashing. "And who is this 'Simone'?"

Cary shrugged under the long finger of the Mentor, "I don't know. Just a girl, I suppose."

"'Just a girl'. Hardly." The old man spun and flung his arms to the air, then suddenly stopped and turned, "Had you seen her before? On Juno?"

"No! I've never met anyone like her." He was tossed between relief and hostility. How could he explain any of this to Dmitri when he didn't understand any of it himself? "I saw D'Ono Felari, uh, in a dream a couple nights ago. He told me some things..."

"D'Ono Felari, eh?" Dmitri took Cary's shoulders in a squeeze and began, "I have an idea, but there are no guarantees. I need not remind you that nothing like this has ever happened or ever been attempted.

"I'll try to be brief. The amulet provides a doorway to the collective consciousness. You must have somehow created a doorway to this 'Simone' to get to her. To get you back, we need to create another doorway."

Cary remembered how the amulet had burned against this chest when he'd recalled the dream of Simone while at Warken. "You make it sound so easy."

"Yes, I suppose so. But the main problem is that you don't have an amulet and thus cannot create your own doorway. It will have to be created for you."

"How would I know when to step throgh?"

"Theoretically, you wouldn't need to know. When using the amulet, you just have to ready your mind with the suggestion and everything should fall into place."

Cary eyed the Mentor. He trusted the old man but sometimes begrudgingly. The man never seemed to tell Cary all the details. And that usually prompted Cary to enter into another bout of troublemaking. Cary now knew enough to be suspicious. "So what you're saying is that you'll open a doorway for me and all I have to do is step through, which should happen automatically?"

"Yes."

"But you said the amulet opens a doorway to the collective consciousness. I'm not in the collective consciousness because when I talked to Master Felari, he said I was trespassing which means that I need to get to the collective consciousness to get to the doorway which you would have waiting for me." Regardless of whether or not he was dreaming, Cary was out of breath.

"You will need to find a way back to the collective consciousness. Unfortunately, I cannot..." Dmitri's mouth continued to move but the sound ceased. Then, with a jolt, Dmitri vanished and Cary awoke to a yellow light piercing the darkness of the small house. He lay still, listening. Breathing and the soft rustle of movement in the kitchen. Cary rose and trod softly.

Mr. Larken turned, a bag full of sandwiches in his hand. "Sorry, I didn't mean to wake you." He said with a sheepish grin.

Cary smiled weakly, "No matter. You're leaving?"

His father's twin nodded. "No rest when there's a job to be done," and sighed with a smile under his moustache.

Cary smirked and shook his head. "That's what my father used to say."

"Pardon?"

"Nothing. I hope you have a safe journey and harvest many trees." Mr. Larken again smiled but then paused, his lower lip perched on the tip of a word. Nothing came out. Cary recognised the glimmer of something he had seen so long ago in his father's eyes.

Longing.

Cary couldn't help but stare at Simone's father. And for a very brief moment, it seemed as if father and son had cut through the expanse of time and memory to come face-to-face once more.

"Well," the moment passed, "I hope to find you well when I return. And Cary, I don't need to tell you that Simone is my daughter. If anything should happen..."

Cary held out his hand, "You have my promise, sir. I will protect her with my life."

After a handshake and a nod, a man the image of one larger than life, cracked the door into the wee hours of the morning and left.

Red taillights turned into the darkness beyond the yard and stillness once again descended upon the Larken household. Cary sat for a few moments at the front window, watching the moths flutter at the yard light. They were so close to the light, yet could not touch it. He ran through the events of the past few days -- his father, Simone's dreams, the amulet, the voice in his head, and Dmitri -- and slowly things began to fall into place. It wasn't like everything fit. He was basing the fit on instinct rather than evidence. But that instinct strongly suggested that everything fit better than evidence would ever show. The light he needed was just a doorway away.

Morning came all too swiftly. Dawn awoke him early. Birds chirped their morning song.

That's it, the Aristovin thought. I have to do this. Cary rose from the sofa, washed, and dressed. He plunged a hand into his trouser pocket; the wooden top was still there. Unable to bear it no longer, he gently knocked on Simone's door. "Yeah, yeah. I'm up."

"Simone, I need to talk to you." There was a sudden stillness on the other side of the door.

"What about?"

To be direct is like a double-edged sword; the entry is clean and precise but so is the exit.

"Could you come out here? I'd rather not talk through a door."

Shuffling and, after a moment, the door opened. Hair wild, circles under her eyes. Her gazed darted to the empty bedroom across the hall. "Gone already and not even a goodbye." She ran a hand over her face and sighed. Cary felt a waver run through her composure before he refocused the wall around his own emotions and thoughts. "God, I need a shower and some coffee. What's up?"

He waved her to the front room. Her growing anxiety threatened to permeate his focus. They sat and Cary found her eyes; amazing blue eyes that usually sparkled in his presence. He knew that after what he was about to do, they would no longer look that way.

He pulled out the wooden top and grabbed her hand.

— Dmitri?

Nothing. No answer.

"Let go of me!" Simone jerked in his grasp and beat against the wall of his clarity.

"Cary?"

Simone paused. She was listening too.

"Young One, can you hear me?"

— Yes, I can hear you. His mind seemed to echo with his own conscious voice.

— I need to tell you that I saw Simone in a dream before I relocated. I don't know what that means.

"I will take it into consideration." The old man's voice was distant but clear in his mind.

— Father? Are you there?

Master Felari was unconvinced that you would fit together the pieces. I knew otherwise. Well done, son.

"I want my top back." Simone snatched her hand back and rubbed it.

"Did I hurt you? I'm sorry."

She didn't answer. Instead, she raised an eyebrow; her anger false. There could be a couple of reasons she wasn't really angry. He took a stab at the least likely.

"You knew," Cary stated.

The mystery of what she'd been keeping from him opened up. She averted her eyes. "I knew."

"How much do you know?"

The silence lengthened so much that Cary thought she wouldn't answer. He didn't know which was worse, the silence or her answer. "I had a dream of you once, a long time ago. You were swimming in the ocean. It seemed forever and all I could feel was determination. I could see the rock you were heading for, and then the cliffs once you touched it and turned back. I saw ships, huge and sailed, filled with men in strange clothes and loaded with weapons. They cheered for you as you passed. You reached the dock and the waiting crowd of boys cheered for you."

Cary fell back into the sofa.

"The Wayward Rock." He'd nearly forgotten. He had been seven and the Son of the Commander in Chief. Some of the Sons had been especially mean to him over those past few months. Cary finally got sick of it and challenged them. They insisted that if he was to use a sword; he had to show his bravery and courage. He had to face the ocean. They demanded he swim straight through the ports, touch the Wayward Rock five leagues east of the coast of Juno, and swim back into port.

Exhausted, he touched the Wayward Rock and turned back, determination pushing each stroke. By the time he'd re-entered the ports, word had evidently spread around and all the ships were crowded with people. Banners were raised and cheers were echoing in the cavernous City ports when Cary climbed the docks.

"My father took me out of Trium for a week and made me clean the stables every day." But when he had returned to Trium, he was practically a hero. Even his teachers seemed to view him differently, perhaps with a bit more respect than usually dished out to a seven year old Son. Only it was the beginning of a downward spiral that eventually fell flat with his parents' deaths. No wonder he'd forgotten it. Would everything have been different if he hadn't swum out to the Wayward Rock?

The Son's mind was spinning. "But how did you know ...?"

"I don't know." She was rubbing her wrist, making it red. "You're not the only one who dreams."

Cary shuttered at the coincidence. This was not right, the concept springing up like a dead fish popping up to float on the water's surface. This was not right at all.

"Give me back my top." Simone's eyes remained on her injured wrist. "It's the only thing I've got."

"I don't want to leave," he began but didn't know how to continue. She had the wall up between them, stronger than ever, shielding her from him and everything. "I can't stay. It isn't right."

"And you wonder why I lied. You were always going to leave. You were never going to stay." Cary could almost taste the venom in her voice. He winced at her words. "You're the same as everyone else. You only care about yourself."

"I never lied to you. About anything. At any time," he placed his emphasis carefully hoping that she'd hear through her rage.

"Do you know what? Just go. Leave. I don't care. I can take care of myself. I don't need you or anyone else. Ever."

An idea struck. Cary stood. *Remember the training.*

"I won't leave you defenseless. Go, shower and eat. I'll meet you by the pond. I won't go without finishing your training, and I won't leave without saying goodbye."

I t was a wary truce. Cary avoided the grief of separation that threatened to tear out his heart, and he avoided looking at the one thing that could collapse him. Simone's wall was rigid, almost offensive in its defensive stance against any impending emotion or thought. She, too, sought to place her eyes everywhere but on him.

Simone brought her hands up and assumed a fighting stance, "Bring it."

Cary let his mind go blank, felt down through his body, through his feet, and into the soil. As his mind connected to her physical body, he threw one word at her.

PROTECT.

A torrent of training and implication slammed into Simone's mind and broke through her wall. Her posture changed, her fists loosened and reshaped, her legs shifted and her weight grounded through her soles.

Then he attacked.

She deflected Cary's fist, spun, and kicked his legs out from under him.

Good, both Cary and his father said. *Good.*

They continued sparring until Cary, and his father, were satisfied the training was intact. Cary pulled the wooden top from his pocket and held it out. "It's time."

"NO." Simone lunged at him, trying to rip the top from his hands.

He twisted from her grasp and flung her to the ground. Her new training kicked in, and she kicked out his legs. He spun and let himself fall, pinning Simone to the ground. Cary held down her arms, the wooden top awkward in his hand, and kissed her fiercely.

He broke away, "I love you," and dared look into her eyes. They were electric blue today and filled with tears. Cary held her gaze though the agony pulsed through his veins. The electrical circuit of their connection raged and nearly drove him to the edge of what he knew would be forever. Instead, he savoured that warmth, that electricity that seemed to pulse between their bodies. Cary knew he'd never feel it, or anything like it, again. Already he missed it.

— Dmitri, Father, I'm ready.

"For this to work, I need you to picture Juno. Picture a place that you know and can replicate in your mind." Cary knew precisely the place.

"Goodbye." He kissed Simone again, feeling the wooden top pulse and their circuit race into a burning frenzy.

Then, quite suddenly, as the last details of his mental picture fell into place, he felt it. The soil upon his cheek and the warmth on his back. And without opening his eyes, he knew. He could smell the salt air and he knew he was home.

Chapter Twenty-Eight

S obbing.

Uncontrollable.

Gut wrenching, throat stripping, soul tearing.....Was her soul torn or was it merely returned to its previous deprived state?

To die. That would be easier than this.

Two terrible claws ripping her soul, strip for strip, ounce for ounce, from her body. The serrated edges of her soul swung freely, hitting the stinging tenderness of her heart.

Could she feel pain? Was there pain?

Shock. Numbness. Overwhelming disorientation. If there was pain, it could no longer penetrate. Maybe a soul was needed to feel pain...

Still she cried.

Sobbing beyond the need for remorse. Mourning, instead, the loss of self and wallowing in the slowly enveloping anger. Dry tears savoured the comfort of the heat beginning to burn within.

Through all the resounding 'whys' her crackling voice managed to ring against the forest and grassy fields, for all the unasked questions her mind waded through, and however she wanted to plead, to make it all stop, Simone did not feel solace in the growing anger. Only dreams of stolen happiness flooded her conscious.

Spent. Empty. Wasted, Simone pulled herself to the house and slept. Awakening reenergized, the loss overtook her reason again and again. Purging her sorrow, tears expended, hollow sobbing exhausting her once again. And again. And again.

Finally, she crawled to the bathroom and vomited. The toilet rattled its ceramics under her shaking hands. She waited, watching the brown and white contents of her stomach twist down the drain.

Standing, propped against the sink, she threw water into her mouth, unsuccessfully ridding her mouth of the taste of bile. Her legs were incredibly unsteady.

Against her will, Simone whimpered. A small thin sound barely escaping her trembling lips. The terror, with the vibrations inhabiting her limbs, was making resounding progress through to her more interior layers.

No. Please. Stop.

The fist of her will beat upon the terror, and forced structural energy to her limbs.

Stop shaking!

The trembling stopped, first in her arms, then slowly faded from her legs.

Now, walk.

Energy had only stopped the shaking; it had not reinstated her strength. Simone nearly collapsed at the bathroom door. She grasped the jamb, white knuckled. "Just get to the brandy. You'll be fine." Fingers trailing along the hallway walls, step by step, Simone pulled her feet and legs back to the living room, terror nipping at her heels. She grabbed the cabinet door, tore it open and picked the first bottle her hand hit.

Liquid fire ripped through her throat and belly sending the terror sulking, banishing the shaking and doubt to a dark corner. It was then that the situation suddenly became very clear. Too clear.

Tears came to her eyes. And this time, without Fear wrapping its scavenger's tail around her soul, Simone cried. Sadness at the emptiness she felt, that she saw around her, that she couldn't conquer. She let it all flow through her.

A mild tap hit upon her mind and made her wonder if the emptiness had always been there. No. Couldn't be. This is new. Must be. And it was the exact opposite of how she felt when he was here. She hadn't really noticed it before, as it had always been there: that hole, that emptiness inside her. She had attributed it to her mother's absence. But with him, it had disappeared.

Now he was gone. She was alone. Again. So, as before, she stuffed away the emptiness, the fear, and the hopelessness.

Only forward. Can't change the past.

Simone put down the bottle of brandy and picked up the phone. "Hey, it's Simone. You need help tomorrow? I'd like to come back."

Chapter Twenty-Nine

Breathing deeply for what seemed like the first time since he was born, the Young Aristovin smelled it.

Salt air.

New tears fell slowly across his cheeks and down to the smile sabotaging his face.

Home.

He was home.

And there was hope.

Hope, the voice agreed. And to the lone Aristovin Son, even the plague-like voice sounded suddenly hopeful and happy to be home. The resonance of that sound warmed him, and Cary let the familiarity of it mingle with the familiarity of his surroundings.

He was in a clearing. It was Dmitri's clearing. Stars overhead; the constellations at once recognized and worshipped. Evergreen treetops danced at the periphery as the Son searched for the moon. It was merely a sliver tonight, perched in the north to tempt the sailors into alcoholic dreams of mermaids and of silver fish that sang.

A song of a different sort began. Rustling trees, starting at the canopy and whistling down to the underbrush, the ghosts of the Jire came alive. Whistling turned into moaning and once subtle whispering became a thunder. The metallic branches of sparsely growing Tika's rose smacked the odd stone on the forest floor and sent a blue glow traveling through the woods. Groaning of mad horsemen riding their enraged beasts through the forest and slashing their enormous swords at unwelcome visitors suddenly seemed a likely story.

But there was no fear. Once there had been a time when he dreaded getting caught in the Jire at night, but now the Aristovin Son instead felt his smile grow and he let the ghosts ease his heart.

A nearby campfire flickered in the increasing wind. Grouse, Cary thought as he peered closer, his mouth watering. But the Mentor was nowhere in sight. As Cary sat up in the brisk, cool night air, he felt somehow strange. But before thought and reason took over, the questions were pushed aside. He was on Juno. He was home.

Just let it be.

Cary arose and shuffled to the fire to investigate the immediacy of a meal.

The groan took the Son a moment to register. It was weak. But moreover, it had come from behind him. Just another sound of the forest, he thought and poked the grouse with a stick.

When the groan drifted his way again, Cary took notice. It was human. And it was female. Simone? No, he couldn't let his mind go there and pushed her memory away.

The Son attempted to focus his attention on the forest, beyond the ghosts, but the enveloping noise was difficult to hear through. Where was Dmitri? He scanned the clearing for a weapon but the stick in his hand was the best he could do.

A blood curdling scream nearly caused Cary to lift out of his skin.

He mumbled silently, asking what voice would not: *What is going on here? And where is Dmitri?*

Brandishing the stick, Cary edged to the cave's opening to listen. Snuggled into a space between a desk and the cave's wall, he could only hear more moaning from within the cave's interns.

Anxiety rising, Cary turned to step beside the desk and begin his path through the interns of the mysterious cave. A hand landed on his shoulder and instantly stilled him. "I am right here, Young One."

A tirade of colourful curses escaped Cary's pursed lips before he turned. A sigh, "It's good to see you, my friend." Silver hair glowed golden in the sparse light of the campfire and cave interior and gave an additional sparkle to the Mentor's already dancing eyes.

"And I you." The grasp on Cary's shoulder firmed, "You look, um, different," the Mentor nodded to Cary's attire. He was still dressed in Simone's father's clothing -- jeans and checkered shirt. That was one question answered. "Are you well?" and the apprentice brimmed with unexpressed gratitude at seeing the concern in the old man's eyes.

"I am getting better every moment. Thank you."

But the man's hand lingered a moment longer, the concern still evident and Cary had to wonder what the Mentor saw in this young heir. However, Cary's thoughts were not allowed to wonder long, "You have stepped over the boundary, Apprentice."

Cary's toes inadvertently began to wriggle inward, but then they stopped. An explanation bumbled through his head, but it, too, was ceased. "Yes. I have."

Not only surprising Cary, this new conviction also seemed to surprise Dmitri. The Mentor's eyes danced a moment longer and just when the Aristovin thought the Mentor would send him to sit at the forest's edge, Dmitri instead said, "You are welcome. I have someone to introduce."

Treading softly, Cary followed Dmitri further into the cave and felt an enormous amount of privilege beneath an insurmountable awe. Passed the table and old bookcase that stood in the entrance blocking curious glances from outside, they filed back, dodging chair after chair and desk and bookcase after desk and bookcase. Shelves upon shelves of herbs, containers and packages made the inside of the cave seem an endless maze. It was a chaotic library of medicinals, conjurings and texts. Every few steps the shelved maze was punctuated by a candle or a lamp. The cave ceiling was low, but above the shelves hung pots, sticks, bones and other objects Cary couldn't quite place.

Finally the shelves ended and the light pooled. Dmitri kept walking into the open area of light but Cary stopped. Where the shelves ended, a living space began. There was a small cot, a washbasin, stove and counter space along with a hearth; the chimney seeming to go up through the endless mountain rock above. But there on the cot, on top of a thin feather mattress, dressed in a robe of white linen, was the young woman who had directed Cary in a dream a few days ago. Long straight, raven black hair spilled across the blankets and her shoulders. Her skin was so fair that her white robes seemed pale in comparison. To Cary, she seemed to be the most fragile yet the most frighteningly beautiful creature he'd ever seen. Her face contoured in some unseen pain and she emitted another blood curdling scream.

Cary inadvertently threw himself back into the darkness of the shelving. "What's wrong with her?"

Dmitri was bent over the hearth making a broth from the herbs he'd brought in. "Go fetch that grouse and I'll tell you a story." Cary did as he was told, weaving his way back inside to the living pool of light deep inside the maze. He sat at a small corner table next to the hearth with the grouse and a cup of wine.

Across the small space, he watched Dmitri feed some of the herbal broth to the woman. She held his hands while the cup was gently tilted to her mouth. She was conscious, or more likely in some sort of trance, still aware of her surroundings. With a gentleness Cary had never seen in the Mentor, Dmitri laid her head back on the thin pillow and looked upon her face with deep concern. The Mentor broke his gaze from the woman and instead turned his eyes to the hearth. Cary could feel the air tighten in the small living space but could not make out the cause. The young woman's moaning subsided but still her face contorted periodically. The air seemed to return to normal and Dmitri spoke, "What I am about to tell you only a handful of people know. Including the Council.

"During the age of the Mentors, a sect of the female line discovered within themselves the ability to see or sense the evil we have come to know as the Outerworld. These 'Seers' were invaluable to Juno as they could 'see' the strategy of our enemy and therefore warn us of impending attacks. But to do this, these women paid a heavy price. They had to look into the face of evil. Very few survived their initial trance. Many more died after slowly going insane. Generation after generation, each woman learned more and more and passed it on to the ones still sane. Slowly they began to segregate themselves from the rest of the population, concentrating on their specialized knowledge and, then, eventually finding that certain women, time after time, could withstand the terrors of the trance. They discriminately breed themselves to secure this immunity. Unfortunately, their voluntary segregation coincided with the growing distrust of the female line.

"Consequently, in the past, several assassination attempts on any one Seer's life were commonplace. This, along with the growing countrywide paranoia of female Mentors made 'Seeing' a dangerous profession. Since then, their existence has been denied and held secret and sacred in the hands of a few.

"This young woman is the 29ᵗʰ Seer of Juno. And to her, both you and I are indebted. Without her help, I would not have you sitting here."

Cary was dumbfounded. This was his home but it felt as if he was a stranger. "But what's wrong with her?"

Dmitri rose and washed the cup he had used for the herbal broth. "As I said, the Seer must look into the very heart of terror and evil to predict the Outerworld's actions. This is what she is doing now. However, the visions are usually not so painful and so enduring. I'm beginning to worry."

"How long has she been like this?"

"Since you arrived back. About midday." Dmitri stretched out his long legs as he sat on a lopsided chair.

The Seer's hand rose toward Dmitri, "Opi? Where are you?"

Dmitri took her hand, "Here, child."

Sweat glistened across her face, her voice a croak. She was shaking. "Two days. At most. They will come in more numbers than any seen on Juno soil. It will be bloody and devastating. That is all."

Dmitri rose, pulled a pouch from a shelf, and poured it into the cup with water left in the kettle. He fed this to the Seer, slowly. Then she lay back, quiet and content, with her breath relaxed and deep.

"Dmitri? Is this what I think...?"

The Mentor pulled a thin wool blanket over the Seer. "Yes. You'd better finish eating that grouse and change. Your clothes are in the cupboard by the entrance. We have a duty to let the country and Council know that the Outerworld will be on our doorstep in two days. We best not fail."

CHAPTER THIRTY

"What are you doing back?" Sally came to an abrupt halt inside the kitchen swing doors. "It's only been...," she ticked off days on her fingers, "...three, four days. Almost four days. You shouldn't be here." Her handbag hit the staff table with the usual cacophony of beauty products clashing inside.

Simone turned from the sink. Sally stood, hands on her hips. Waiting. It almost made Simone smile. Almost.

"I need something to do."

"Okay. I get that. But, I don't know. Can't you do someone's books at home? I'm sure Karen would be good with that. Don't you do that for Mr. Decker?"

How do you say that you were afraid of the walls without sounding crazy, Simone wondered. "I don't feel safe at home."

Sally's frown became embedded. "And you feel safe here. Huh. Okay. Whatever."

"I'm only doing half days, in case you're wondering."

Sally threw up her hands, "Hey, I got no beef with my shifts. I'm just worried about you collapsing or going bonkers on me."

A chill shot through Simone's gut, "Do you think I'm going crazy?"

"You going crazy is about as likely as the Dali Lama coming to Knotton's Shallow." Dressed in her green apron, Sally slid up to Simone at the sink. "I'm just worried that...I don't know..." Sally's green eyes searched Simone's, "I'm worried that you don't talk and I know stuff is going on."

"Shit happens, Sal. That's just the way life works. There's nothing we can do about it."

Sally picked up a dishtowel and began to dry the dishes Simone washed. "There's much to be said for talking, whiz kid. It bonds people through communal venting."

"Since when have you become a psychologist?"

"I work in a hair salon, duh! The blacker the dirt, the tighter the bonds. Trust me; I've heard it all," a conspiratorial tone had crept into her voice.

"I don't want to hear it."

"Oh, come on, Simone! I heard something about Mr. Briefcase. I know you wanna know."

"No." Simone pointed to the cafe. "Go!"

"Why? Cause you got Mr. Beautiful Blond in your back pocket?"

But before Simone could fake a reliable response, the cafe bell rang. She pointed again, "Go."

Sally flashed a devilish smile then disappeared. However, the reprieve wasn't for long. She reappeared carrying a large vase of flowers. "Speak of the devil! These are apparently for you." Eyebrows waggled and she growled, "Someone's aiming for some action. Let's see if there's an incriminating card."

It took a full thirty seconds for Sally's words to register in Simone's brain. When they did, her gut froze -- either it was J.D. taunting her or Cary was back... somehow. Hope or hopelessness; the extreme contrast seized her.

"'Hope you are doing well and hope to see you again soon, Alex.' Alex? I thought his name was Cary."

Alex. Relief and disappointment ran through her in equal measure. The shaking rose. Tears welled in her eyes. A cold sweat trickled down her back then dried an instant later. Simone attempted to push it all away. "The library." It came out with a half laugh; a burst of relief. And somewhere inside, she knew it wasn't about J.D. It was about reality. It was back. And reality was something she could handle. The last few days with Cary could be chalked up as a fantastic delusion then she would move on with the known world of cold and desolate reality.

"What? You've got TWO guys chasing after you? When did this happen? Where was I? What does this 'Alex' look like?"

Simone couldn't help but smile briefly, "He works at the library. He's nice."

"That's not what I asked. You're diverting again." The cafe bell rang. Simone was safe from Sally for the time being. "Ack. Don't let me forget to ask you your bookkeeping rate. I'm thinking of going out on my own," and with that, and a waggle of well-groomed eyebrows, Sally left to attend to the lunch rush.

"I'll be back in twenty minutes."

"If you're going to the library, I'll give you thirty!" Sally called as Simone ducked out the back door of the cafe.

Books. A safe haven of paper and imagination. Books were limitless, with endless possibilities and knowledge. As her hand grasped the library door, Simone felt her defenses slip, her mind open up, and a happy light creep into the darkened recesses of her soul.

Then the glass library door stopped abruptly. She looked up and saw a large muscular hand holding the door above her. She ducked and turned. Her eyes rose up and up -- passed the black leather jacket, the tight black T-shirt and bulging pectorals, a gold chain that strained across thickly-corded neck tendons -- until finally she looked into his face.

J.D. loomed. Cheap aftershave wafted and threatened to choke her breathing. "Shouldn't you be at work?"

A tidal wave of icy Fear shot through her body. She backed away, into the library lobby, mind racing, eyes searching for an exit. A meaty hand grabbed Simone's jacket, "You're not going anywhere."

Time stopped and altered. Fear dropped away. Focus fell into place. She had only one objective. Just like when Cary was there.

Protect.

The word and its implication overwhelmed her senses. Ten years of Warrior training at Trium Hall flooded her being. Her feet grounded.

Her weight shifted. Her body relaxed. There was only her enemy and his weaknesses.

Attack.

Her foot shot out, slamming into J.D.'s groin. An instant later, the heel of her hand thrust into his nose. A crack. J.D. began to crumple. "You fucking bitch," but Simone had already rounded the library desk and was racing to the rear EXIT, passed a bewildered Alex who was only just emerging from the stacks.

Chapter Thirty-One

Two days.

Breathing in the sea breeze from the east, a new strength surged into his pace. Frost had covered the hills that morning. Patches of wild grass were brittle against his boots and the hills were turning a yellowy shade of green. Winter. The dry, cool season that marked the passing of yet another harvest. The harvest was over and food would become scarce without imports. It all happened so quickly. And now the Outerworld was approaching. There was so little hope. Juno would crumble with or without the Outerworld on its shores. It was just a matter of time. The Outerworld would just make Juno's end a bloody one.

In two days.

Emil was in the fields tilling the last of the silage into the soil. The lad looked up and on a second take nearly dropped his hoe. He sprinted to meet Cary in the stable yards and was yelling for Denis the whole way. "It is good to see you." Emil vigorously shook Cary's hand. "We...we... thought you were dead." The young man's last words were whispered.

"It is good to be home. Is everyone well?" But Denis appeared in the doorway before Emil could respond. Cary let go Emil's hand and hugged the aged servant tightly. The old man was weak but rigid with shock and Cary dared not let go. When he felt the old man's grasp lighten, Cary pulled away and looked his faithful steward full in the face. "I've missed you, Denis."

Happiness had replaced shock and Denis had tears in his eyes. "I had hoped that somehow…. My dear boy, I have missed you too."

After another hug, Cary finally pulled away. "Denis, there is going to be an attack. This one's going to be really bad." Cary looked steadily into his friend's eyes. "Day after tomorrow."

He heard a gasp behind him, "Another one? So soon?"

Cary froze. "What do you mean? When was the last one?" The last battle known to Cary was nearly a year ago, a long time between battles. Smithies specializing in weaponry and armour didn't know if they were lucky or not. Cary suspected it was probably yet another Outerworld tactic.

Emil spoke, "Only about a week previous. Really bad. I heard that the Outerworld made it to the old defensive wall. They almost started evacuating the City. Bad strategy is the rumor around the villages."

"How long was I gone?"

Confusion washed over Emil's face, "Nearly three weeks, my Lord."

"We arrived back to FarSee about two weeks ago," Denis offered.

Cary shook the dread from his mind. "You'll need to move out again and tonight. We're expecting the Outerworld back within two days, and in greater numbers yet." Denis' countenance re-firmed and the old man nodded. "You'll have to be resourceful." With final nods from each, Cary headed for the stables.

A sudden wish to stop time seized him. How many men had been lost in the last battle? Who had died? Dominic and Everett would have fought in that last battle...and he hadn't been here. He had let his friends fight for him. Instead of him. Cary threw the blanket on this horse, the anxiety mounting in his chest. Dominic, Everett, Brask. Who had died? How many? He cinched the saddle under Marcus' belly. He would not be leaving again. He would not let his friends fight without him. He would not let Juno fall. Especially not while he was Commander in Chief.

The decision to fight, the knowledge that he would fight, just was. It didn't involve any protracted lists of pros and cons, shoulds or ought tos, it just was. Like it had always been.

He was Commander in Chief. It was his responsibility. And this was his time.

Cary rode his Companion across the Plains. He glanced across the battlefield and found the sense slightly surreal. The deadened grasses. The turned, burned soil. Ashes that had yet to be washed away in the summer rains rose up in grey clouds as they galloped across the barren landscape. The once formidable defensive wall now crumbling, bricks and stones vomited out onto the ground.

Nausea rose in his throat. After all the nightmares, after all the nights sitting helplessly in his father's chair, all the childhood ambitions to fight for his country were finally coming to fruition. And in so many ways, he did not want them to.

It was not something he wished; it was something required. Something Fate required. He would be fighting his first battle here. He would wield a sword in defense of his country here, and here he would put to use all his life's training. And Fate will be looking over his shoulder the entire time.

Then, in the distance, across the horizon of the seas, he saw it. The shadow. A curtain of darkness blanketing the horizon. It was the storm of the Outerworld. And with a twinge of electric anxiety, Cary spurred Marcus faster. The Seer was right: the Outerworld would be on Juno's shores by end of the second night.

Not enough time.

Marcus' reins were thrown at the stunned stableman as Cary raced into Warken. He nearly ran straight through Dominic in the Front Hall. Dominic stood in riding gear, wide-eyed as Cary barged into the room. "Cary?"

A great silent sigh of relief washed through the Aristovin. "Good to see you." He grabbed Dominic in a fierce hug then broke free. "Where's that steward of yours?" Cary glanced around the room. "Malteau!" Cary bellowed, his voice echoed down the corridor, "Malteau!" A middle-aged man scurried out from the back recesses leading to the south wing. The man began to mouth the words 'Lord Aristovin' but Cary shouted orders as soon as the man was in sight. "Notify the entire staff that the Household is to be evacuated immediately. Move as far north as possible and expect a possibility to withdraw from Juno completely."

Dominic's eyes widened still further, "Again? When?"

"Two days, maximum." Malteau scurried off, calling names as he went. "Dominic, two pigeons, if you please, to notify the north."

Dominic yelled down the corridor and a knave in burgundy appeared at the same that The countess appeared atop the stairway, "Cary? Is that you?"

Cary nodded to the countess and spoke the message to the knave loud enough so that the countess could hear, "Two messenger pigeons, one to

Tolonel, one to Stats. Juno's Commander in Chief orders every available and able man to present himself to the Plains as soon as possible. All Warriors and Sons are to meet at Cannor."

Cary thought the word 'Sons' hung in air a little longer than it ought to. Regardless, the knave repeated the message back then retreated to the dovecote.

The countess descended the stairway as Dominic looked at Cary and shook his head. And suddenly Cary knew. He knew exactly what his friend was feeling. Loss. Fear of losing. That same feeling he had felt previously that morn and for most of his life. Only a sliver separating sanity from panic. It was all very lucid in Dominic's eyes. The Roan family had suffered great loses in the past, could they endure anymore? Could Dominic withstand another so soon after the death of his father? Admittedly, a feeling of justice passed though Cary – *let him know how it feels* – but it did not last. Nothing would make him wish that feeling upon anyone. He could not allow his friends to go into battle again without him. He could not bear their loss. He would do everything within his power to avoid that, but could he ask Dominic to allow his brother to do the same? "He's not ready, Cary."

"Dominic," Cary grasped his friend by the shoulders and looked him dead in the eye. "If we don't win this attack, Juno is no more. Frej either holds a sword now or never." Dominic's green eyes searched Cary's. The urgency grew in Cary until finally Dominic said, "He can hold his own." And then Cary knew he and his friend were on the same level – fighting not for themselves, but for the lives of others.

The countess nodded, accepting the orders of the Commander in Chief. He was sending both her sons to battle, one almost to certain death. Cary knew that none of them wanted to hear what she would say, so he stepped up to the countess and took her small hands in his. "It is good to see you all again." Cary turned and strode back out to the stables with a still stunned Dominic trailing him.

As they galloped over the sandy hills to Cannor Manor, the suns approaching their zenith, Cary could feel Dominic's eyes on him, wondering, burning with questions. Perhaps later there would be time to explain or, at least, to attempt an explanation. If there was a later.

Not enough time...

As he did at Warken Castle, Cary also charged into the Fraaml Household, but this time with Dominic close on his heels. Cary strode through the main entrance of Cannor Manor to the stunned eyes of most of the livery. Cary didn't care what the rumors were or what they were going to be – the Young Lord Aristovin returned from the dead to save Juno –he had only one thing on his mind: to save as many people any way possible.

Down the front corridor, under the grand staircase to the back of the Household, Cary and Dominic wound. If he had it right, Brask would only be in one place: his study. In an action that was probably a bit on the dramatic side, Cary threw the large, heavy study doors open. The room was a wreck. Maps and parchments littered the floor. Half the wooden shelves were empty with their contents strewn on the floor hidden under the heaps of parchments. Chairs were overturned and the hearth overflowed with ashes. And behind it all, the smell of alcohol and staleness filled the dark room. Brask didn't look up from the stacks of parchments and books on his desk. Instead, he growled, "I told you *not* to disturb me."

"Get your head about you, Commander. The Outerworld will be here in two days and I don't have time for your drunken blathering."

With that, the lord's head snapped up. His eyes were bloodshot, his appearance disheveled. Cary had figured right. The last battle had been a blow to Brask. As a Warrior, the man had an immense amount of patriotism, but as a man, his pride was bigger than his shadow. It had been a personal loss. Almost a complete loss. Enough to send the man into a panic. The same panic that was a mere sliver away in both Cary and Dominic had now gripped the seasoned Warrior.

"Well, if it isn't the Lord Aristovin. Where on Juno's green land have you been? And don't tell me you were out gallivanting either or with that fool Mentor, because *I checked*. In fact, I tore this entire country apart looking for you and that was when I wasn't fighting a losing battle with our beloved enemy!" The lord had risen and rounded the desk to raise a heavy finger and tower over Cary.

To apologize. To beg forgiveness. To hug this man who had seen the death of his best friend. But there was no time. Cary broke in, "Brask, I wasn't on Juno." He managed to catch not only the drunken lord off guard but Dominic too.

Brask wobbled slightly and moved to an upright chair to sink deeply into it. Cary turned to Dominic, "We need to get him sobered up. And get food." Dominic nodded and disappeared. Cary rounded the desk. Brask was mumbling as Cary sifted through his parchments. "I went to your Household and you weren't there. I scared your staff half to death, but that steward of yours...backbone of iron, that one. I knew a nave once who tried to tell me how to wear my sword...," Brask mumbled on but Cary was looking for something particular.

Many of the count's strategies had ended up in the history books, not only Juno's but of the nations of the Ocean Rire. Just as the count was always working on something -- new or refining the old -- the count always had a couple off the wall ideas toying around in his head. The last one, four years ago, again made it into the texts of Trium. The count had managed to find a way to divide the Outerworld force into smaller groups scattered over the Plains. With purely defensive and offensive groups of Juno Warriors, they kept the Outerworld divided and swiftly sent them back to their ships significantly fewer in number. Cary needed a plan like that and he needed it now. He needed to know that the count saw this coming.

But with Brask drunk and depressed, not without reason, Cary had a sinking feeling that either the count hadn't had that single miracle strategy written down or it had failed in the last battle.

Dominic returned shortly with a small entourage of servants. From the corner of his eye, Cary saw the new Lord Roan nod. Amidst drunken howls, several muscular servants tipped, then picked up the wing-backed chair containing Brask, and hauled him out through now open windows to the gardens. More servants awaited in the garden, each with a bucket of water. Cary had to yell over the commotion, "Dominic, had your father been working on anything before he died?"

Nodding, Dominic shouted, "He was working on a perimeter defense. He always said that if we could hold the Outerworld within a couple hundred yards of the shoreline, they wouldn't have enough room to move nonetheless attack." A maid scurried in and laid a tray of stew, bread, and cheese on the desk.

A final growl made both Cary and Dominic glance out the window. Dripping and furious but now standing, Brask had a his son's valet dangling by the collar as the others were prising on the lord's tunic and hand to release the victim.

"Was it implemented in the last battle?" Cary stuffed his mouth full of stew and bread. Dominic again nodded but it was Brask that roared, "It didn't work!" as he sent the valet flying and others scurrying.

"It was a valid strategy; we just didn't have enough soldiers to make it work. It was the best we had, though." Dominic was ashamed, but by the failure of his father's plan or by his countrymen Cary couldn't tell.

"I know he always had one or two really far-fetched ideas knocking around, like attacking through the Outerworld curtain. Did you know if he had anything like that?"

Dominic shook his head. "He didn't feel that those ideas justified the parchment. Father had many different ideas to hold the Outerworld at the shoreline: bringing the defensive wall closer, digging trenches, a double line of offensive archers....but all that requires time or a lot of soldiers. We didn't have the numbers to support the strategy and, even if we did this now, we don't have the time."

His green tunic hanging open and red hair sticking to his face, Brask glowered at the livery as they gathered their buckets and each other. "The next battle *will* be the last! There is no hope."

Cary wiped the empty stew bowl with the remaining bread and made eye contact with one of the maids. "Have you got Wigwort in the kitchen?" She nodded. "Make him a tea of it. Strong." She clutched a bucket and tore away with a determined glance back at her lord. Cary gestured to the rest of the livery who cleared up the mess and left. "Brask, we are going to lose if you think that way," and stuffed a piece of cheese into his mouth. "Eat. I need you sober, despite what you believe."

"Cary," the words from Dominic seemed strange. Cary hadn't heard his name from his friend's mouth in so long. "With respect, you don't know what you're up against. We are down to maybe fifty Warriors."

"Sixty-nine!" Brask bellowed and shook off water like a dog come in from the rain.

"No strategy works with sixty-nine men on an open Plains' fight against hundreds," Dominic concluded.

"Try thousands, Dominic." But for the first time in his life he felt like he knew what he was doing. "Maybe it's a good thing that I haven't fought my first battle and I don't know what I'm getting into," he said driving straight at Dominic's implication, but then he took hold of his shoulders. "I may not have fought an Outerworlder but I have seen the eyes of survivors. I have seen the terror and the destruction inflicted by our enemy. And until the last man falls, may he be me, I will not give up." Dominic finally nodded. Cary turned to a dripping Brask. He nodded too if only reluctantly.

"We will have more men to fight. The Sons will fight." As soon as the words left his mouth, he felt Dominic and Brask freeze. Dread crept into the room as they stared at him. Finally Brask shook his head while Dominic spoke. "Cary, Frej is enough. He can hold his own. But not *all* of them. They need to go with their families, to protect and help them. They don't know what they're doing on the battlefield and even if they did…"

"We need them all. Like I said before, Dominic, either they fight now or they'll never fight."

Brask's hand fell on Dominic's shoulder, "He's right. We need all the help we can get."

"But, Cary, you don't understand. The Outerworld…," Brask shook his head and Dominic fell silent.

"Dominic, they'd have learned eventually. Were you any different before you fought your first?" Brask knew Cary was right. If they were to have any hope at all, they had to increase their numbers.

But the sliver separating Dominic's sanity from shear panic was growing thinner. Maybe it was that Dominic could no longer protect his sibling from the enemy. Maybe it was that all this emotion -- a deep-seated fear, a relentless need to protect -- was new to Dominic. Cary had been living with these feelings all his life. He prayed that his friend would continue to see reason.

Like a spontaneous prayer for the innocence they were about to send to the Plains, they stood a moment in silence. Each one of them knew that while the chances of a full-fledged Warrior returning from a battle were only half and half, anyone else's chance would be nil. Cary attempted to wipe the guilt from his mind like lint from his sleeve, but it didn't quite work. So he instead stuffed a final piece of cheese into his mouth. In the silence, voices echoed down the hall from corridor. Juno's army had begun to arrive.

The maid Cary had sent to the kitchen returned with a large mug of tea. Brask, sobered more in the last moments, sipped the concoction as he balanced his mass on the arm of a winged chair and picked at the food platter. As the maid left, Everett and Frej, with several older Sons trailing behind, entered the study. They stood stunned and silent.

Cary nodded to the new arrivals, then continued as he leaned against Brask's desk. "Now," Dominic stood across from him on the littered floor, "Brask, have you ever known a strategy of Count Roan's to fail?" The lord shook his head.

"Do you have anything new, Dominic? Anything that we need to consider?

"No. My father taught me well but he also had experience on his side. His strategies are solid and still valid. But, as I said before, sixty-nine Warriors and however many others are no match for the Outerworld army. The strategy we used in the last battle is still the best under the circumstances, however the perimeter needs a minimum of a hundred soldiers and that's if the Outerworld can be quarantined to a specific section of the coast as soon as they land." Saying like it is. Just like his father, Cary thought.

"There are eighty-seven Sons at Trium, correct?" Nods. Cary looked directly at Everett. He saw Everett straighten. "Send the first five cohorts to their families. Nines through seventeens are ordered to battle."

Frej blanched. Everett beamed and ushered the younger Roan Son from the study with the other Sons.

Once the door closed and it was just the three of them again, Brask, still perched precariously on the arm of the chair, said, "That will only sustain the perimeter. We'll still be short. Without the other options like a rebuilt defensive wall or trenches, we'll need replacements, catapults, archers, and runners. Minimum. We're going to need a human defense if we don't have an environmental one. And we just don't have the numbers."

And with those words, an idea began to form in Cary's mind. He grilled Brask on armament supplies, metal forgers, immigrant fluctuations, and merchant prices. Then he called in every last servant in Cannor Manor and dished out orders and errands. The three Warriors exchanged weary glances. Two days. It was going to be close. Very close.

CHAPTER THIRTY-TWO

Simone flung herself into the stuffy room, her backpack onto the bed, slammed the door, and threw the lock. It felt as if J.D.'s hand still held her jacket.

Breathing. Can't stop. Stop. Can't stop.

It was like before. When she'd run into town - the eight miles into town - and didn't remember it. Almost three years ago.

Pacing back and forth, her shoes catching on the faded utility carpet of Mrs. Decker's nursing home room. Sweat beaded on her forehead; her heart raced, trying to keep up with the frantic pace her mind set. Hands red with wringing and her head dizzy with the shaking. Twitching, rubbing, shaking, plucking; stillness was nowhere.

Man with the gun. Black. Gun. Mask. Eyes. Big gun. Stop. Run.

The pacing increased, the pivots became sharper, the breathing became shallower. Shaking had overtaken her body and she couldn't stop it. It was consuming her. It was controlling her.

No. Stop. Stop shaking. Stop thinking. Stop pacing. Stop breathing.

Her breathing grew more rapid, the shortness of it surprising Simone. The objective Simone stood apart and watched, telling her to relax, just relax, what the hell is going on, this is stupid, you can stop this any time, you can, any time, why aren't you stopping this, this is stupid, this isn't happening. But the images kept flashing, kept racing. They wouldn't stop. It was out of her control.

Mom's car. Leaving. Dust. Door slamming. My fault.

"Shit. No." She tore into her backpack and dug out the wooden top.

Men. Voices. Shouting.

Jacket off, crossed-legged at the coffee table: "Breathe, damnit. Just breathe."

Hands gripping her shoulders. J.D.'s hot and heavy breath in her face. Searing pain between her legs. Cold. Alone. Dark.

She took a deep breath and attempted to balance the top on the coffee table. With an ambitious flip, it spun off and fell behind.

Hopeless.

"NO."

She flung herself after the top, bashing her head against the wall. A dull ache began a slow march across her skull and settle behind her right eye. But the pain pushed away the panic, and Simone seized the chance.

Finding a sliver of calm between the racing images and shakes, Simone spun the top and began to breathe.

Chapter Thirty-Three

Dusk drew in. Messengers were racing as fast as their horses could carry them to the City, the villages, and individual Households. Supplies and equipment were being gathered, made, borrowed, bought, and transported to the Plains. Late that night, Warriors and their Sons convened at Connor Manor. Passed the shock of seeing the Aristovin son alive and, perhaps more so, seeing him in Command, commissioned staff quieted to hear what some may have thought was their last briefing. Few objections were voiced. Then all departed to the battlefield.

Morning light cast an eerie glow. The Outerworld curtain was closing in and blocked out the suns' rise. Faint light caught on the random movements of armour and weaponry scattered over the open Plains. They were like fireflies dancing in the descending light.

Cary stood outside the canvas tent, stuffing his mouth with Mayflour Bake. The creaking catapults were being pulled into position too slowly by a number of immigrants. Battle was a novelty, but Warriors were revered. And just in front of the catapults, between the archers and the shoreline, Xan and Smal were drilling the Sons.

Five ranks of black tunics moved in unison. Smal was out front leading and Xan supervised. Though he could not see that far, Cary knew by rote that their eyes were closed.

Swords swung, dove, bodies spun, and legs kicked. Feet turned in the grass and sent a hush over the Plains. Heads bobbed as the ranks lunged and jumped, then all in one motion, feet were suddenly together and swords were sheathed. "Continue," Smal's voice carried softly over the clanking of armour and thumping of hooves. A rank of the youngest cohort left the troop. Xan led them away to their horses to begin Companion drills as the rest withdrew their swords and began anew.

Dominic came from behind him, maps in hand, with Brask and Everett. Empty bowl in hand, Cary followed them back inside. The day matured as Cary was briefed on where each foot of the previous Outerworld battle had been placed and in response to what action.

City dwellers, merchants, old men, City guards, and sailors arrived in spurts and spits to the Plains. By torchlight, they lined up for armour, weapons, and for what little training could be given in the moments before their enemy landed.

It was a sleepless night in Juno. And for Cary.

At breakneck speed across the length of southern Juno, the young Lord Commander spurred on his Companion as the blackness of the Outerworld curtain killed the stars' light one by one.

Leaving an anxious Marcus prancing in the clearing, Cary strode for the cave. In the dim light of the forest, he didn't see Dmitri sitting with his legs propped upon the desk by the cave entrance. His voice came descended in the darkness, "Mentors have not been involved in battle for nineteen generations. What you will ask will not be permitted."

Cary stopped mid-stride, foot over the cave threshold and searched for the eyes of the Mentor. "By you or the Council?" Hood drawn, the man was all but completely camouflaged in the darkness of the sheltered corner. The Aristovin felt more than saw the smile spread across the

Mentor's face. "The Council may dictate when I fight, but not how. If the Council intends to leave the fate of Juno in my hands as Commander in Chief, then I will use any method possible to ensure that Juno will have a future."

"You are not a Warrior; you are a Mentor apprentice."

"I was Crested. There is no prohibition of battle in my apprenticeship."

Cary took a deep, calming breath and continued. "We have a plan, a good one, but to make it work we need more men. I've recruited most of the Sons and all available merchants, guards, natives and immigrants alike. We lack the time to create an environmental defense and we lack the men to maintain a human one. I need something to offset inexperience and lack of skill, to protect them, and level the playing field.

"Before I left, I gave as much knowledge as I could to Simone. I sort of 'pushed' it into her mind." Dmitri's eyebrows rose. "I need to do that here, now, but with hundreds of men."

"You did it once, do it again."

"Simone and I have... had a connection. I'm certain I couldn't do it alone or as easily with the hundreds of men here."

"What you are asking was the basis of the Civil War."

"What are you talking about? Females Mentors killed their own kind in a bid to take over Juno."

Dmitri shook his head. "That's the official version. The Council saw the power of the Mentors grow and decided to divide and conquer. The male and female *Magician* kin worked in tandem to draw out and use the power of Juno to keep the country safe. The true version of history is that they did exactly what you are now proposing -- they linked all soldier and

Warrior minds to the collective consciousness to access the knowledge and power of the dead."

"No one dies; all are merely remade, reborn. That's what Master Felari said."

Dmitri nodded and hummed noncommittally. "That knowledge is vast as is the power. The Council at the time, and for many generations after, remained afraid of the power held by the Magicians. In a deft and inspired move, that Council segregated access to that power. They issued propaganda that killed off half the Magician population and confined what knowledge wasn't destroyed to only a privileged few."

"The amulet..." The pieces were slowly starting to fall into place.

"It is a tool by which those not skilled in magic may access the collective consciousness and the power of Juno. For those skilled Magicians, it increases the connection."

"There are more amulets somewhere?"

"You won't be able to access them. But as you probably now know, all Crested Warriors are granted one. Like any powerful tool, it is dangerous in an untrained hands, as you witnessed."

"So we can do this?"

"It is a risk. More than the repercussions of the Council. Some minds will not be responsive to the link. Be prepared for the immediate death or slow collapse of some minds."

"Understood."

Dmitri reached into his robes and tossed an amulet to Cary. "Then you will need this."

The Mentor's eyes broke away from Cary, his feet fell to the ground with a soft thud. Dmitri approached him and nodded a modest bow. "My Lord Commander, converge all available Warriors and Sons along your perimeter as planned, staggered with no more than three inexperienced soldiers between each. I will meet you on the Plains before dawn."

Cary would not argue with the Mentor. If that was what had to be done, then he would accept it. He would trust Dmitri. He had to. The Mentor had earned it.

CHAPTER THIRTY-FOUR

"I didn't know you were visiting today."

The voice drifted down through the peaceful fog to Simone's ears. It took a moment to register. Where was she?

She blinked, slowly regaining a sense of grounding.

Lace curtains hung like gauze against a sun. Pink flowers and ivy wallpaper. Apple pie, cinnamon. It was Tuesday. This was the Shangri-La Lodge.

The wooden top sputtered and finally faltered. It knocked into Simone's hands as they lay upon the laminate coffee table. She closed her hands around it. How long had it been this time? Stretching and taking a deep breath, Simone leaned back and tucked the top into her pants pocket. Mr. Decker stood holding his cap, eyes and eyebrows dropping in symmetry set askew by a crooked smile. "Lillian had a doctor's appointment. I didn't know you wanted to stop by otherwise I would have let you know on the ride into town this morning."

"It's okay. I just needed some time to myself."

"She's in the piano room. I just came to get her shawl. Do you want me to go get her?"

Simone attempted to move but found her legs asleep. "No, it's okay. What time is it?"

He checked his watch, "About four-thirty." Simone did the calculation in her head: she'd left the cafe about one-thirty, which meant that even if she'd arrived at Mrs. Decker's room at two-thirty, that was a helluva long time to be in meditation. No wonder her body was in perma-sit and her mind was cloud-land.

Then she remembered: "Oh, crap. Poor Sally. She's probably worried sick."

Mr. Decker pointed to the small end table beside Lillian's recliner, "Call her and I'll be right back."

Simone rolled over to the phone and suffered through Sally's tirade of concern while itching tingles raced and nipped through her legs. Sally managed to calm down by the time Mr. Decker arrived back. "I'll tell you all about Alex later. Are you home tonight?" She rung off and forced her legs to flex.

"Do you need a ride?"

"That'd be really great...as soon as I can stand. I need groceries too. Hey, I missed getting your receipts last week. You got them ready?"

Mr. Decker nodded, still clutching his cap between his hands. "Yup. I got them in the car. Just didn't ...," he shrugged and avoided her eyes, "...you know, know if you'd be up to doing my books."

"When I can manage to stand," Simone prised herself from the floor as her legs shed the last of their prickling awakening routine, "I'll be as right as rain." She sighed as the peaceful fog still lingered, shrouding her in a blanket of contentment. It felt as if the robbery was just an old dream and J.D. was just a Brothers' Grimm story told to her in kindergarten. In this state, there was no outside world, nothing was bad, and she felt as if she could float through life. Simone reached across the bed and picked up her discarded backpack and jacket. "If you can pick me up from the grocery store in half an hour, I'll see if you turned a profit last week."

The car stopped and Mr. Decker turned in his seat. "What's the verdict there, Miss Wizard?"

Simone snapped back to reality and looked around. Home. She gathered up the receipts and deposit slips, "I saw enough to know that you did all right last week. I'll get this back to you in the next couple of days. And I'll have sandwiches then too; sorry about today. Pick me up at nine-thirty tomorrow?"

"Lunch rush?"

"Yup. That's it for now." She opened the back door and gathered up the grocery bags.

Mr. Decker appeared beside her, "Here, I'll help."

With a free hand, she pulled her housekeys from her backpack and together they carried the groceries to the door. Once the door was open, Simone thanked Mr. Decker. He smiled his lopsided grin and tweaked his cap to her.

She watched him walk back to the car, pull around then down the driveway. Tires crunched on the gravel, the sound fading as the car turned toward the highway. The sun was descending, winter pulling it nearer the southern end of the western horizon. Cirrus clouds captured the decaying light and turned fuchsia. Dead aspen leaves fluttered in the late afternoon breeze; one skipped across her front step at her toes. Evergreens shivered in the incoming cold. A flash of instinct passed through her gut: shouldn't be here. But before her mind could acknowledge it, her hand snaked around and flicked on the living room light switch. She pulled in the groceries bags, closed and locked the front door, then finally faced her comfort zone.

In the fading daylight, Simone hadn't noticed that the motion sensor hadn't kicked in and turned on the yard light.

Chapter Thirty-Five

The armory tent was huge. Inside, the hearth was near the back where it could be ventilated. At the front, a series of workbenches displayed the organized pieces of amour, leather padding and chain mail hung from the walls of the tent. An older man and several younger ones were trying to keep up with the incoming soldiers. Cary struggled to keep his composure when he saw who was tying the toggles of a City guard's breastplate. "Reid! Tivas!" The breastplate of City guard slid as the toggles suddenly dangled untied.

"It's good to see you. It is *very* good to see you." Especially in Tivas, Cary saw the relief.

Cary shook his hand and grasped his friend's shoulder with an added squeeze acknowledging that he understood his friend's concern.

Tivas retrieved a breastplate that had been secreted under a workbench. Cary looked at his friend and smiled. Fitting it together with the back and shoulder plates over a chain mail tunic and sleeves, the armour was surprisingly light. With leather padding strapped securely around his legs, Cary bent and twisted to ensure maneuverability.

As he straightened, he saw Reid holding out a sword. It was his father's sword. "How? Where?" Cary cleared his throat, "You know what? I don't care. Thank you."

With his father's sword at his side, buckled to the outside of his armour, the weight of it and the situation pressing down upon him, Cary suddenly felt everything fit. Maybe, just this once, he would let Fate have her way.

They left the armory tent and rode out to the battlefield. As Xan pointed and informed Cary about personnel assignments, Brask cleared his throat and beside him, Cary felt his comrade shutter, "We have guests."

Cary turned. A silence had descended upon the Plains. For a gut-wrenching second, he thought that the Outerworld had suddenly landed, sweeping their death across the battlefield.

Instead he saw something quite the opposite. The soldiers, Warriors, immigrants, Sons and all recruits had stopped and parted. There, with robes billowing in the south sea breeze, some with walking sticks, most with grey or silver hair, strode every Mentor currently living on Juno. And the group was headed by Dmitri.

Brask was muttering, "For the love of the Juno," Xan nudged Cary's leg and whispered, "Is this also your doing?" Cary had no time to respond.

Through the parted mass and suddenly silent battlefield, Dmitri strode straight up to Cary. Cary shifted his weight to dismount. The Mentor's movement was quick and subtle. As he settled back down into his saddle, Cary caught a brief twinkle glittering in Dmitri's eyes. Cary was no apprentice here. This was not Dmitri's clearing. Here, Cary was the Lord Aristovin, Commander in Chief, and the Mentors were his to command.

Cary began, "For the first time in generations, Juno's Mentors will engage in battle beside her Warriors. While they will not wield a sword, they have another weapon: knowledge. As Sons, we were all taught to be Warriors, to think as single fighting force. Today, these Mentors will compound that which we were taught. We, *together*, will be a single fighting force. For your part, there will be no difference in how you fight. However, you must maintain this condition: no more than three soldiers or Sons between each Warrior." Cary's eyes locked with each Warrior's until he felt secure that the message was home. Lastly, he glanced at Dmitri, receiving only an acknowledging nod.

"Now. The suns are rising and we have a battle to win. Set up the line!"

Warriors mounted and rode off. The Mentors swept away in their grey robes without a glance behind. But amidst the eruption of thundering hooves, a gold tunic appeared at Cary's side. It was Lord Tolonel. "What's the meaning of this? Mentors on the battlefield?"

Cary suppressed a groan. Insinuation and intimidation rang through the lord's tone. But more so, Cary also registered an undercurrent of jealousy. Tolonel was jealous that the young Aristovin commanded Juno's Mentors.

Allowing himself to fall into focus, letting the emptiness of his Warrior's state of mind overcome him so that there were no nuances allowed into his voice, Cary said, "The Outerworld is to land any minute, likely with thousands of soldiers. I suggest that you state your alternate plan quickly and concisely." Tolonel pursed his lips then rode out to take up position.

Cary rode down the back of the scrimmage line. They'd managed to dig a shallow trench along the length of the defensive wall. Men lined the trench and the wall as catapults and trebuchets peaked overhead; a glance calculated about two hundred and sixty men. He could feel their eyes on him. If he was the reason so many of them were fighting, he wanted to meet their eyes and acknowledge their commitment.

Many of them met his gaze and nodded, immigrants and natives alike. A ruddy man stood tall as Cary rode past and met his eye. Yes. He remembered. The drunk native from the Feather in the Hat Inn at Greenspring. Aharon held his bow high. Cary nodded. At the end of the defensive line, Cary turned and rode down the front of the scrimmage line, Marcus' hooves splashing in the seawater. Cary recognized all the Sons from his last trip to Trium. They were so young and he remembered the thought that had tapped at his mind – would they be ready? He remembered it and felt Fate plucking her chords, her music floating across the Plains.

I didn't matter if they were ready.

It is necessary.

A salute, overly brave but swift, from Paklin Mal. He was the only sensible one in Langrid Tolonel's clique.

Frej Roan beside his older brother. A salute and straightening in the saddle.

Further down, on either side of Everett, grey-collared Sons fidgeted in their armour, each no more than fourteen years old. Everett grinned and saluted enthusiastically.

Ceres and Nicolas Darine were the twins of his former cohort. Black collars peaked from between their necks and chain mail. They nodded as Cary rode by.

Marcus hesitated as Cary's eyes fell upon Langrid Tolonel. A curt nod.

A couple unfamiliar faces. Mature and brave, Cary recognized the facial tattoos of the two Gallan Talls mercenaries. They saluted.

Between Xan and Brask, three Sons of varying ages. Their fear was over-shadowed by their admiration.

At the western end, nearer to FarSee than was comfortable, a Son no more than thirteen was trembling. Cary stopped. "What is your name, Son?"

"Gareth Riddinan, sir, my lord."

"Gareth, you are in charge of protecting my home." The Commander saluted and heard the Son gulp loudly behind the ill-fitting armour before taking a deep breath and saluting.

"Do not fear, Son," Arissio Silva said. "You are well flanked," he nodded to Salem Kristing on the Son's other side, "We are all in this together."

Cary nodded and turned back to the east.

The suns were rising but little light broke through the darkness: only small discs glowed on the inky horizon. Cary joined the scrimmage line and caught sight of Everett down toward the eastern end. Everett. He was his father's image in that instant. Grinning from ear to ear and armed to the teeth. He waved his sword in Cary's direction. Cary nodded back.

For Juno's sake, he hoped this worked.

For Juno, for life.

Inside his shirt, against his skin, the amulet tingled as he placed his helmet on his head and drew his sword from its sheath.

"Do as you have always done. Guard yourself. We will do the rest." It was Sesmon's voice. Cary glanced to see the Warriors also scanning to find the source of the voice. The Mentor had spoken in their heads. Outside the emptiness of his mind, questions formed -- how did he do that? -- but they were insignificant now. The emptiness grew. Singularity. Blankness. Wholeness. There was no one else. Him and him alone. Pulse slowing. Senses sharpening. Cary allowed one thought into his blank mind.

Protect.

Protect.

With that triggering word planted and reverberating, Cary knew nothing else.

A slight nausea hit him. The shoreline appeared as if seen through hundreds of eyes. He felt the hardness of a hundred saddles, the fear of a hundred of men. But, as suddenly, it tapered off and the fear fled. 'Protect' resounded in his blank mind with the force of a thousand voices. They were now connected in one purpose.

The roar was deafening. Cary couldn't tell if it was thunder or a mountain tumbling down. From the corner of his eye, he saw Gareth fidget and glance around trying to find the source of the noise. He caught the boy's glance. Taking advantage of the link, Cary reassured the Son – 'Have no fear. I am by your side.' However he knew this boy was going to die. No matter how hard Cary would try to protect him, Gareth would die like many more uncrested Sons.

Cary looked back to the water lapping at the shore first at Marcus' hooves then rolling back into the sea. Then the meagre morning light hit the first black hoof as it dug into Juno's shore and seared the earth. Two hundred and sixty-four minds focused into one objective. Cary threw up his sword and roared, "For Juno! For life!" and the line sprang into action.

Chapter Thirty-Six

Simone jolted awake. She would have normally thought that a nightmare awoke her. Her T-shirt should have been soaked with sweat. But not this time. This time, there were no figures looming in the darkness, no hands grabbing at her body, no beady eyes craving her screams. This time, she couldn't remember her dream. And she didn't know if that was good.

She sat, listening to the night breeze whistling through the crack in her window sill. Finally with the dream staying out of reach, Simone got up and padded through to the living room. The brandy snifter and her wooden top sat on the coffee table where Cary had once placed his feet. She plucked them up, reached into the dark recesses of the cabinet and pulled out a bottle of brandy. With a full glass in one hand and the wooden top in the other, Simone sipped, letting the alcoholic fire burn away the possibility of dreamtime whispers.

The sofa where Cary had slept.

The bookshelf from where Cary had plucked her favourite novel.

The front door through which her father always arrived.

Simone's eyes caught on the wall beside the front door. Under the light switch, beside the door knob and deadbolt.

The shotgun was gone. In two strides, she was at the door. Searching.

"Looking for this?"

She spun, brandy sloshing. Against the moonlight coming through the kitchen window, she watched as J.D. emptied the shells from the shotgun. They bounced, one by one, on the linoleum floor.

"Get out of my house." The words leapt from her mouth. The iciness of Fear's fingers no longer wrapped around her spine. In fact, Fear had vacated her body. Simone stood bewildered at this newfound freedom.

From the look on J.D.'s face he was surprised too. Then he smiled. The smile turned into a grin. "You know, I was starting to wonder. I thought you'd never come around. Especially when I saw that pretty little boyfriend of yours the other night."

"I will call the cops."

J.D. continued to smile. "With what? The phone's right here," he tapped the phone hanging from the wall. With a gentle hand, he placed the shotgun on the kitchen table then sighed. "We've got some unfinished business." At this, J.D. turned a predatory gaze on her. "You're gonna give in." Before she could react, J.D's fist swung down on her.

Blinding lights with darkness. Then the pain came. She was on all-fours, J.D. was bending over her, "Give it up. You know you wanna." It was all happening so fast. Too fast. Like the robbery. Like with J.D. the first time.

But unlike the first time, she was not afraid. This time, she was pissed. Anger burned a ragged road through her soul and itched to smack an annoying insect in her kitchen.

Protect.

"You are mine, bitch." A hand grabbed her hair and pulled her to standing. Searing bolts of pain shot through her scalp.

Protect.

J.D. pushed her up against a wall, one hand on her throat, another digging into her crotch.

For fuck's sake, *protect*.

Heavy breaths rained on her face as lightning began to shoot through Simone's blackening vision. She kicked, punched, and clawed, finding her one hand reluctant to let go of the wooden top. Laughter, almost giggling as J.D. pushed her further up the wall and slid his free hand up her T-shirt. "Fight all you want. I'll get you in the end."

Anger blazed through her. "Fuck off," she wheezed. A fire swept through her gut. Every nerve, blood vessel, and cell boiled with rage.

Suddenly she was on the floor, coughing, gasping for air, and clutching a hot wooden top. Screams of pain behind her. Still coughing, bolts of light still shooting across her vision, Simone pulled herself up and staggered down the hallway. In her father's bedroom, pain blazing across her skull and throat, she pulled and pushed and jostled the dresser in front of the bedroom door.

Glass smashing. Cursing. Yelling. "Come back here. We're not done yet."

From the closet she pulled the gun case and ammunition box.

Banging on the bedroom door. "You can't hide. I'll find you. I ain't leaving until you come out."

Protect, she tried again.

She loaded the .333 caliber rifle then wedged herself into the farthest corner of the room, across from the door.

Protect.

Shit. Why wasn't this working? There was nothing. She felt nothing. Where was all that training Cary downloaded into her brain? Now, when she needed it the most, no foreign memories sprang up out from her unconscious. Nothing. Her brain was empty. There was only Anger, hot and vicious.

The door rocked in its jamb with each blow. The dresser inched away from the door.

"Fine." Simone dropped the wooden top into her lap then brought the rifle up to her shoulder. Just breathe, she thought. Just breathe and aim. "Listen to your heartbeat and squeeze the trigger," her father taught.

Just like those haybales out back.

Just like that bear in the front yard.

Just like focusing on the wooden top.

Just breathe and take aim.

Then Anger receded. The wooden top began to hum and a plume of comfort spread through her abdomen.

The door burst open.

Simone breathed one last time and squeezed the trigger.

Chapter Thirty-Seven

The bodies on the ground of the Plains were becoming deep. He could feel Marcus slip over the black armour. He had caught a couple of faces he knew in that mess below. Bloodied, broken, and dead. He didn't know what time it was now but the line hadn't wavered, the shower of arrows and boulders continued. But the Outerworld kept coming. It must have been nearly nightfall but he had no way of knowing. The suns had disappeared behind the Outerworld darkness long ago. Only the fires along the defensive wall threw off enough light to see the enemy.

A break.

He had felt it more than seen it, but in that instant, he turned and it was there.

A break in the scrimmage line.

Who?

With no time to think of what happened, how or why, Cary looked to Petri. The other Warrior had felt it too. *Stay. I'm going.* Feeling the statement reverberate down the scrimmage line, the Commander noted the Warrior's nod before Cary turned to continue effortlessly, fluidly.

Darine?

Marcus' hooves slipped as the horse tried to jump over and around the metal debris. As they neared, Cary could see it. Outerworlders had also seen it. Black metal figures charged the break and were running full force into the archer's line. Secondaries stepped from around the shields drawing up bows. Runners took up swords and joined them. Some fell instantly. The rest of the offensive line, Cary knew, could not be diverted to the break. It would leave the rest of the line vulnerable. No, he had to take care of this himself.

Not Colin. Martin Darine. Eldest son. Goodbye.

Everett was further down the line and doing his best to keep the surging enemy from widening the break. The twin Sons, shoulder flank to shoulder flank, were holding their own nearest Cary.

He could not see another Warrior near the Sons.

An image of silver-grey cotton in amongst the blackened ground held a moment in Cary's mind before being pushed aside.

Marcus caught his footing and charged Cary headlong into the enemy. Adrenaline surging for the ump-teenth time, the energy flowed steadily from heart, to hand, to weapon.

No thought. No emotion.

The dagger flew and hit on target.

The black amour fell heavily against Marcus' leather-clad flank.

Upper cut to third fold under the chin.

Another fell.

Marcus spun and kicked an enemy horse as Cary's mace knocked another's helmet into the air and sent the head following it.

Two fell.

Backhanded left swing to the weak mail under the arm.

Another fell.

First movement: stabbing twist to knock away the weapon and bring the back of the neck into view. Second movement: 'Over the Rire' to slice the vertebrae and spinal cord.

Yet another fell.

Continuous. Flowing. The Aristovin's heart nearly kept pace with the bodies falling to the littered ground.

Suddenly his mind snapped and the break was sealed. Not realizing he had withdrawn from it earlier, the familiar nausea caught him off guard. An Outerworld blade came up from below but stopped as if hitting an invisible wall. Cary registered the enemy's presence and countered.

Another fell.

The Commander fell in line beside the pair of Sons.

Another fell.

And another.

And another.

He had sent Marcus off. The stallion had been stumbling and panting. Now, nearly knee deep in bodies, the scrimmage line was sparse but still intact. The curtain had ceased to birth new attackers and the arrows from the north had stopped. Former archers, runners and other soldiers took up extraneous shields and joined the line, swords now in hand. Hand-to-hand, sword-to-sword, man-to-man.

Few enemy cavalry were left. Warriors were making sure of that. Once off their horses, the black armoured enemy fell to an awaiting entourage of natives and immigrants.

It seemed the Mentors were taking turns now. Some stayed in line while others rested in the shelters to the west. Cary could see the grey robe of one ripping in the ragged wind but he couldn't make out who it was. He knew so few of them really. He just hoped they could hold on. Whatever they were doing, however they were doing it, they just needed a bit longer.

The chain mailed hands closed around Cary's throat. His mind flickered. *Protect*. He could see through the slats of the black helmet. Red eyes glowered back at him. Huge, evil eyes that hungered for his death. The fingers tightened. A cloud of dank, moist breath snorted through the Outerworld helmet into Cary's numbing face. He couldn't breathe. His eyes teared in the foul breath. His vision flickered.

Then, the grip lessened. Just a fragment, enough for him to catch a breath. Enough to clear his sight, and enough to bring his dagger under the black armour. A groan akin to a dying animal poured from the helmet then sank into the sea of bodies.

Cary stumbled and spun, his eyes searching, scanning the battlefield. He could see Everett in the distance. A bloody Outerworlder slid from his sword. Xan was next to Sesmon, placing his foot upon the ground, completing his turn as the Outerworld's disconnected head hit a shield and bounced. Sesmon pulled his eyes from Cary and scanned what was left of the scrimmage line. Cary couldn't see Dominic, Dmitri, or Brask. Lots of figures dotted the battlefield, but they were too far for him to recognise.

Had the Outerworld retreated? Unknown. But Juno hadn't. No more horses in black armour rode across the Plains. No more enemy walked upon Juno's soil.

Everett turned to Cary and waved his bloodied sword. A voice from behind spoke. It was Brask. A firm and tired hand landed on his shoulder, "You've done it. We've won."

And Cary collapsed into unconsciousness.

Voices. Whispers from across a room. Cary opened his eyes. Canvas. Tent. A makeshift healing quarters. The tent billowed in the ragged air. Medicinal herbs, broths and ointments – their smells filled the tent's air.

Cary attempted to sit up. His amulet had been placed on his chest and slid off into the blankets. He ached all over. His tunic had been removed and his trousers cut to reveal a large bandage wound lightly around his right leg. The white bandage was soaked with blood.

The whisperers were Saul and another across the tent. Cary couldn't hear above the howling wind. With considerable effort, Cary rose from the blanketed ground. Before his legs had stablised under him, Saul was there, supporting him, "You should rest."

Cary cleared the dryness and the aftertaste of whatever the Mentor had fed him, "I have to make sure Juno's safe."

Saul's hand pressed on Cary's shoulder, "Juno's safe for now."

Mild relief swept over Cary but before he allowed himself to sink back to the ground he ran a mental list through. Brask. Everett, Dominic. Xan. Petri. Tolonel. Dominic. Dominic. "Dominic. Where's Dominic?"

Saul peered at Cary a moment, then pointed to the far end of the tent. Cary hobbled over, a sense of dread filling his chest all too slowly and all encompassing. Dominic lay ashen and barely breathing, a large, deep gash marking his abdomen. Despite everything Dominic had put him through, Cary couldn't image life without him. Dominic, like Everett and everyone else, was part of his community. He was family, just as much as Denis and the Maklinaris. "Will he live?" Cary turned when Saul remained quiet. "Well?"

The Mentor shrugged with deep sympathy in his eyes. "It is hard to tell. We've done all we could. We must wait."

That wasn't good enough. Cary spun and staggered back to his makeshift bed. He drew out the amulet and threw himself back to Dominic. Saul's hands were on his shoulders before he'd withdrawn the amulet. "You don't know what you're doing. You mustn't do this." Saul was now struggling with Cary, trying to pry the amulet from his weakened hands.

Cary tried to shrug off the Mentor, "No. He's my family. He'll die if I don't help him. You don't understand."

A voice like thunder echoed through his mind. "Freeze." And both Cary and Saul did so, instantly.

Dmitri was standing in the entrance.

Cary shrugged away from Saul and fidgeted with the amulet. "Don't even think about it, Apprentice."

Cary glared up at the looming Mentor. "Why not?" Cary shot back. "Because you're afraid I can or that you can't?"

Dmitri knelt down across Dominic from Cary. His fingers closed gently around Cary's hand holding the amulet. "I know you could do it." His voice was gentle now, coaxing. Cary's rage burned because of it. "But it's *how* you'd do it that I'm afraid of."

How? This didn't make any sense. Dmitri couldn't do it. That was it. Nobody could. But Cary could. And that scared the Mentors.

"Just as fighting does not guarantee that a battle will be won, the application of power does not mean a successful healing."

"But he's dying, Dmitri. I can't let that happen."

Dmitri shook his head. "He's on the brink of death but he's not dying. See for yourself. Focus." Cary reluctantly calmed his breathing and let his mind fix on Dominic. Under the torn skin, Cary could feel the strong beat of Dominic's heart, how his lungs drew in deep breaths.

"Saul brought him from death's door but we must let him fight the rest himself. If you use the amulet you will only hurt him in the duration. We have to wait. You have to wait."

Cary threw himself upright. He grabbed the remains of his clothing and erupted from the tent with tears in his eyes.

The dark Outerworld curtain still hung over the ocean, water lapping under its edge at the sandy shoreline. It didn't seem as solid now. The wall had turned to a greyish haze but still nothing could be seen beyond it. As far as he could see in each direction, the haze hung. It was one of the few things they knew of the Outerworld. They didn't know of the Outerworld's origins or its motives, but everyone on the Ocean Rire was well acquainted with that black curtain.

The Plains were a study in shadows: dark sky above with two bright specks peering through the grey haze and a dark sea of black armour beneath. Brask wasn't wasting time in cleaning away the debris. Bonfires dotted the battlefield amongst the sea of corpses. Wagons were being loaded with bodies and debris. It took up to four men to swing or drag an Outerworlder into a wagon. Smoke drifted up from the trench at the foot of the broken defensive wall. Had the scrimmage line failed, that oil-filled trench, would have been set afire to buy them some time.

A group of Warriors stood in palaver, black, torn, and bloodied battle garb twitching in the nervous ocean breeze. Cary sighed, wiping the tears from his eyes, he slung the amulet around his neck and made his way over to his meeting. As he approached, he saw they were all from Commanding Households. His stomach turned.

Colin Darine scanned Cary's exposed body before speaking in his soft voice, "It should have been gone by now." He nodded to the hazy curtain on the shoreline. The lord, a square-jawed man with hazel eyes and straw-coloured hair, was bloodied from head to foot.

Arissio Silva, a smaller yet stockier bald man, was sporting bandages on his head and arm with a purple bruise covering half his face. "That would be strange enough, except...."

"Except that the animals, aren't burning." Durlan Tolonel's tunic hung over one shoulder as he darted Cary an icy glare. Tolonel, too, appeared to have suffered only minor injury. Blood was streaked down his face and neck, and ran through his golden hair.

Signan Stats had made the trip from the northern tip of the country in record time. He was sporting a large gash across his bearded face and his arm was in a splint. "The Mentors even tried to kickstart the fires but the bodies just won't burn."

Brask heaved a heavy sigh and plucked at the leather of his scabbard. "I don't think this is over yet, gentlemen."

Mutters flowed around the circle of men and a shiver rode up Cary's spine. He buttoned up his shirt and tunic and asked, "Has this ever happened before?" Heads shook all around the group. "When does this," he motioned to the curtain over the sea and sky, "usually disappear?"

"It usually only takes a few hours for it to blow over. It's been nearly a full day now."

"What do the Mentors think?" Cary received shocked glances before they turned away not meeting Cary's inquiring eye.

Tolonel spat the blood from his mouth. Brask leaned close to Cary, "We were waiting for you to talk to them."

He was dumbfounded. For Juno's sake, he thought. They're just a bunch of bloody Sons when it came to the Mentors.

Brask blushed slightly under his beard and the spattering of blood on his face and turned away. Cary suppressed a sigh. "I'll talk to Dmitri." He turned back to the camp on the western edge of the field, but within a couple of steps his leg gave way and he fell face first into the expanse of Outerworld bodies. Cary immediately felt hands on his arms helping him up and, as he pushed against the black armour, he looked into an unhelmeted face.

His blood froze. "Daant! Daant!" Cary clutched the black armour and shook the dead body. The immigrant's freckled face stared up at him. How would he explain to Tivas that his best friend was dead? He couldn't hear Brask calling his name and he struggled against the Lord's grasp.

Then amidst the struggle Cary turned into the face of Tivas. Dead.

A scream erupted from his throat and he thrashed to get close enough to touch it. More arms twisted around Cary. He twisted and kicked, screaming.

They were wearing black armour and they were dead.

He was thrown to the ground with Brask leaning on his shoulders and others grabbing his flailing legs. Brask was yelling, trying to calm him down, but Cary couldn't hear.

He had done this. He had caused them to be here. He killed them. And then turned his eyes to the body on his left. It was Dominic's face.

He screamed as Dominic's green eyes stared lifeless back at him. Hands grabbed his head, prising his eyes from the surrounding dead, "Cary! Cary!" A slap jarred his brain, and the pain brought his mind back to focus. Brask held him solidly, "Look at me. Focus."

Cary nodded. "I'm good. I'm good." Brask and the other Warriors rolled off him. Colin Darine gave him a hand up. "What happened?"

"The Outerworld uses some sort of ... *magic*. Makes you see friends and loved ones behind their helmets. Keep your focus and you'll be fine."

Brask continued, "It's one of the things that you weren't told about, like the amulet. During post-Test training, Crested Warriors are informed. You didn't have a briefing."

Cary cleared his throat and stepped back up to the gathering of Commanders, "It's my duty to report that there may be, um, repercussions from the unusual tactics employed during the last battle."

The Commanders shifted. Tolonel raised a golden eyebrow, "More than this?"

Brask prompted, "Meaning?"

"Watch out for signs of instability or strange behaviour in anyone who was involved in the connection. Especially in those not Crested."

Stat stood agog. "Madness?"

"Unfortunately," Cary replied. A weary hush fell over the group.

"That is an unusual price for victory," Colin Darine's soft voice fell into the silent gap.

"Two hundred and sixty-four minus sixty-nine Warriors...," Brask paced restlessly and ran a hand through his bloodied hair. "What in the Creator's name...?"

A dozen figures -- female figures -- were making their way from the edge of the camp, across the battlefield. They all wore trousers and were headed straight for the Commanders.

It wasn't until they got close enough that Cary could see that they were all women of Commanding Households. Including Brask's wife and eldest daughter. And each was wearing a sword at her hip.

The Old Ones. Cary caught Min Fraaml's eyes. She smirked and gave a slight nod.

"My Lord Aristovin," Countess Roan bowed her lean and supple body low toward him and the rest of the Ladies followed suit. Brask rolled his eyes and groaned, but Cary was flattered. The ability to resist a smile grew increasingly weak. The countess stood upright again and addressed Cary with a fire in her eyes, "We have come to aid our husbands, our Households, and our country in the battle against the Outerworld."

"Countess, do you and the others know what you're up against? I didn't."

She shrugged. "Does it matter? We're prepared to fight."

Cary stepped up to the countess. She barely came to his shoulder but her eyes could have cut any man down to a size she could handle. Unfortunately, iron looks held no ground with the Outerworld. "I once knew a woman who had the heart of a Warrior. She had no training and although she fought bravely, she would have died had I not protected her." Cary was grave. "What you would do is not just an act of patriotism, it is an act of death. Once the Outerworld attacks, your duty is to your country." And until recently, he never knew how easily this had settled in his heart.

The countess' eyes narrowed. "I do not wear this sword just to irritate the misplaced morals of Junoan society," he felt the men cringe, "I wear it because I was trained to use it. *And just like your mother*, I plan to use it to protect my country, with or without my husband at my side."

The scent of roses filled his nostrils.

A clank of metal on stone as the sword fell from a dying hand.

Against society's knowledge and custom, his mother had been trained to use a sword. It was another question that had been logged into his mind with so many others. Now, one by one, answers trickled in. Cary grasped the countess' small shoulder and hand, "For Juno may you live, for Juno may you die."

A wry smile came over the woman's face, "Your future wife and daughters will thank you for not letting them be alone." Alone. Yes. He knew what it was like to be alone. Sitting, unable to do anything but wait.

The countess' statement fell heavily upon the onlooking husbands and Warriors. Years, no, *generations* of segregation suddenly broke through the surface. All those women -- mothers, daughters, sisters -- quietly battling their resentment with real swords. They wanted to fight. They wanted to help. It was being a Warrior in the truest sense.

"Thank you, Cary." The countess' small smile turned into a grin and she squeezed Cary's shoulder lovingly. But he couldn't return it. He was sending these women into battle. *He* was doing it. Brask wouldn't, but he would. He had lost his own mother in battle and now he was sending Dominic's mother, Everett's mother, and all the others to their deaths. It was small consolation to know they'd been training and sought this opportunity. They would die whether it was on the Plains or in their Households. In that moment, that turning point in Juno's history, all Cary could do was remember his mother.

She'd held a sword and stood her ground against an overwhelming enemy. It had been hopeless but she'd done it anyway.

Just like Simone.

Simone. It seemed forever since he'd seen her face, felt her touch. That night they fended off those men from her Household flashed back into his mind. Against the odds, Simone had fought against strangers for her Household. Just like his mother.

A warmth began to grow in his chest. It was familiar and comforting.

From the corner of his mind, Cary heard Brask reluctantly give the order to arm and outfit the Ladies. His exhausted mind reached out to the bliss growing in his chest. Love. He remembered. It was beautiful. Before his mind could react, his heart had opened up and was wallowing in the fulfillment that flooded in.

A tremble rose up from the ground and through his feet. The magnetic attraction he that never thought he'd feel again pulsed through his body making his nerves itch. He was a compass being pulled in one direction.

"Simone."

Realization dawned on him. His hands ripped the chain from his neck, but it was too late. A hum continued to work through the ground and the warm glow of completeness in chest remained. Cary groaned and scanned the horizon, searching to pinpoint where he knew she would be.

"Cary?"

Cary thrust the amulet into his trouser pocket, "Do you feel it?" A sense of impending disaster settled upon him. He didn't know why, he just knew that Simone being on Juno was a very, *very* bad thing.

The Warriors exchanged concerned glances, shaking their heads. But then Brask held up a hand as if listening, "There. A hum."

Durlan Tolonel drew his sword and turned to the shoreline. "Where?"

Colin Darine was next. "In the ground."

Then one by one, the rest tuned in. "Can you tell from where?" Cary asked.

All except Brask shook their heads. Brask pointed, still straining as if to hear a whispered tune, "Over there. Somewhere."

"A new Outerworld trick?" Arissio asked, his one good eye searching where Brask had indicated.

"The madness?" Stats asked.

"This has nothing to do with the Outerworld. This is..." he didn't know where to go from there and didn't have time to think something up. Shouts rang out from where Brask had pointed. A wagon. Men fighting men. More men were running, abandoning their wagons, and joining the growing fray.

Cary cursed and broke into a sprint across the littered battlefield.

As he neared, Everett and Paklin Mal were cutting a path through the men. Unconscious bodies fell as the Commanders arrived. "Keep 'em away," Cary shouted then dove into the center of the fight.

Her closeness was overpowering, but he couldn't see her amidst the detritus of the battle. He flipped over a shield and a hand, whiter than Grenid marble, appeared in the bleak light.

He tore at the armour and bodies, flinging weapons and helmets aside. She was caught under an Outerworlder. "Help! I need help!" Paklin Mal appeared without a word and pulled the monstrous body away as Cary pushed.

She lay unconscious, dressed in nothing but an oversized blue T-shirt. A red gash ran along her temple toward a darkened and swollen eye. Her lip was split open and her throat was ringed in bruises.

Breath caught in Cary's throat. "Simone?" he whispered. With shaking hands, he felt her forehead. She was cold, so cold. "Please don't...," he wrapped his body around her, cradling her, as his soul seemed to collapse into an echoing abyss. "For Fate's sake, please don't."

A murmur.

He froze and listened, but it wasn't a sound. It was a murmur of emotion. A finger of emotion -- a flicker of panic -- hissed through his body. He waited, her face against his neck. And then it came again. "I'm here," and let his mind reach out to her.

A sharp intake of breath and a shiver. Cary fought to barricade his mind while trying to calm Simone. Despite her mounting panic, Cary broke into a grin and hugged her. "Paklin, find Saul. She's hurt."

There was no movement behind him. Cary looked up. Paklin, Everett, and every Commanding Warrior plus a growing number of men were circling him. Staring. Silent. "Brask, Everett. Someone fetch Saul." But the words had no effect.

Cary struggled to stand, Simone cradled in his weak arms. He walked through the circle of men without resistance, and as he stumbled over the battlefield of debris, they followed behind, entranced.

Within a few steps, Cary's leg gave out and stars burst across his vision. As he and Simone hit the ground, he felt the hum in the soil change. Simone's eyes flickered open. The full force of her panic hit him and he reeled. "Cary?" Her fingers curled around his tunic collar as the panic faded to the edges of his mind's wall. He could feel the blood rushing out from his injury; his leg was cold and numb. Her touch and her voice washed through, comforting him as his head grew lighter and lighter. Then suddenly he couldn't feel her, her presence or her emotions. If she hadn't been in his arms, Cary would have thought she'd disappeared.

Dmitri emerged overhead. "So, this is Simone."

Cary made to respond, but all went dark and he passed out.

Chapter Thirty-Eight

When Cary awoke, he should have been relieved: he was home, in the kitchen of FarSee Cove. A fire blazed in one of the hearths. Instead, a panic not his own raged through him. Icy terror spiked, then vanished, spiked, then faded again. Cary struggled to sit up, but found he was bound to a cot. "Relax, Young One."

Cary blurted out through a sea of nausea and blackness, "Where is she? What's happening?"

"Dmitri is with her. She is safe and close by."

"She doesn't feel safe." The words came out in more of a slur than he cared to admit. He resumed his struggle against his bonds.

"Cary Aristovin," Saul glared in a way that would have made Grand Master Sesmon proud. "You have lost a lot of blood. You will rest even if I have to club you over the head myself." Cary sank back down. He couldn't feel his leg now, only the nausea and a strange sense of disconnectedness. "We have lost too many good men in battle. We don't need to lose another due to stupidity. Especially one that united the country."

Voices from outside. Metal clanging. Horses stamping and galloping away.

"What's going on? Why am I home?"

Saul finished dressing his leg. The herbs were vaguely familiar, Cary recognised the smell. "This was the nearest place to keep you safe."

Cary started to object. The Mentor abruptly pushed a bowl to his mouth and tipped in a warm broth. "Now, rest and *don't think*." The last part was an order. Saul had put something in the broth. The dim lamplight faded from view and, despite his best efforts, Cary drifted to sleep.

"How long?" A voice from behind.

Saul stowed the herb packages in his bag then turned. Dmitri had circles under his bloodshot eyes. Saul supposed he looked little better. "I estimate he's lost about twenty-five percent of his blood. It'll take at least a week to get him back on his feet. Longer to get him back to health."

"We don't have that."

"I know. I can feel it. You sure you need him?"

Dmitri nodded and scrubbed his silver hair fiercely. "I don't know of another way. This is how I got him home."

"Didn't he get there on his own?"

"How the boy does what he does confounds me. When this is over, I intend to put him through the ringer."

Saul gestured to the hearth. "I made some broth. Drink before you return. I'll bring some food before I begin."

"**I** have seen the light! Fate has returned to Juno!" Everett moved to intercept the immigrant, a wiry man and with a few minor injuries from the battle. Everett couldn't believe he'd just fought beside this man. He'd seemed quite capable at the time.

Paklin tried again, almost yelling, "You shouldn't be here. Your help is required on the Plains. Go!" He turned to Everett, "Why can't we send these guys home?"

"I am home!" A wide grin spread across the man's face.

Everett rolled his eyes and pushed the man back from the entrance at FarSee. "This would be easier if Cary actually had a gate at his Household."

"And a wall. You would think living this close to the Plains... Here, you take one arm, I'll take the other." Together the two lifted the immigrant up and carried him back through the break in FarSee's crumbling stone wall. At the top of the hill, they set him down and walked to see him off. Paklin pointed toward the battlefield. "What is that?"

Everett squinted, attempting to peer through the blackness that still permeated the countryside. "Is that where we found her?" The skirmish that had broken out a couple hours ago had only been the beginning. Clashing metal and shouting floated up the hill from spontaneous fighting across the Plains. The Warriors and Sons now had to keep their own countrymen in check. While Everett had every respect for his friend and Commander, he had a feeling that allowing natives and immigrants to fight would be a bad thing.

"Yeah. That looks like one of those chanting circles the immigrants have outside the City. In their village."

The immigrant they'd carried out was making a straight line through the random skirmishes right toward the chanting circle. "I gotta bad feeling about this," Everett said.

Paklin smirked and punched Everett's shoulder. "You're the ranking Warrior here. You go tell the Mentors."

Everett turned to perform his duty when he spied a woman in a black robe walking from the house to the stables. He was sure she was the same one he'd seen when they brought Cary and the girl in. He'd assumed she was helping the Mentors. The cape she wore obscured her head and body, but he could tell it was a female by the sway of her hips. He waited a couple heartbeats then, sure enough, she continued walking passed the stables and into the fields.

She was leaving as everything seemed to be going wrong. That couldn't be a good thing.

Durlan Tolonel strode across the battlefield as his son used the broadside of his sword to smack the back of a man's head. A native's head apparently. The tall blond man crumpled and sank to the burned soil. His Son was displaying a bit more zeal in this task than Durlan was comfortable with. Howwever, if he worried over this, he told himself, he'd have to worry over everything Langrid did. And, frankly, all of his concern was currently engaged with the thought of his wife wearing a sword and being briefed on battle tactics.

Langrid spun to engage another handful fighting. Durlan increased to a sprint but was too late.

The Son knocked the younger of two well-muscled men on the back of the legs, bringing the man to the ground. His sword had turned and was descending blade first, as Durlan swung his own sword and caught his son's arms in mid-swing. "Stand down!"

Langrid snapped out of his focus and glanced at his father. With a nod, Durlan indicated the three attacking men. They stood beside the immigrant blacksmith and fought back the three native men; one was knocked unconscious, the other two ran away.

Durlan held out a hand, "Apologies. After so long against a single enemy, sometimes the fight makes us blind."

Reid Maklinari accepted and shook the Commander's hand. "Thank you for the assistance. Tivas?"

The younger blacksmith, the spitting image of his father in leather trousers and short-sleeved shirt, accepted his father's hand and tried to pull himself up. Durlan stepped passed his Son and helped the young man to standing. He tried not to wonder why Langrid still stood, immobile. "Thank you. I will remember not to make an enemy of a Junoan Warrior." Tivas Maklinari smiled broadly and shook Durlan's hand. He held his hand out to Langrid. Durlan nudged his Son who reluctantly shook the blacksmith's hand.

"You did well." Durlan sheathed his sword. "Perhaps you practice with the weapons you make."

Reid Maklinari laid a proud hand on his son's shoulder and accepted the compliment. "We fight for our own, that is all." Chanting continued behind them. The ring of kneeling immigrants hadn't broken and all participants appeared in a state of rapture.

"Heads up, yoos!" A young immigrant with freckles covering his face waved from across the chanting circle. "Trouble on yonder," he pointed to the west. "They're headed to Cary's place." At that, another immigrant drifted to the circle, touched the shoulder of one sitting, then, en masse, the entire circle rose and headed west toward an unheard call.

Durlan swore to himself. "You three, go."

"Call of duty, Daant!" Tivas called as he limped next to his father.

The Warrior laid a hand on Langrid's shoulder, "Round up some junior Sons on Companions and head to FarSee. I'll meet you there." Then Durlan Tolonel headed back to camp.

S imone pulled the blanket around herself. "Excuse me? Hello?" The man was in a trance, of that much she was sure. She put a finger to his shoulder and tapped. Nothing. He sat motionless in his white robes. He could give a Tibetan monk a run for his money. Even his breathing was barely audible. Was this what she'd looked like during her spinning top meditation? That would have been kind of cool if she hadn't been locked in a cold stone room on Juno.

Never in a million years did she think Juno actually existed. It was one thing to see and feel and know that Cary existed. But now she *knew* the whole thing was real. It blew her mind. Even better that she'd somehow managed to get here before J.D. burst into the bedroom.

She shivered and peered through the window shutters. It was dark outside, darker than inside thanks to a lantern hanging from the wall. The ocean roared somewhere nearby. If this was Cary's home, she'd be on the southern cliffs of Juno. But she didn't remember arriving here, wherever 'here' was. First she was in her father's bedroom, then she'd felt Cary close, then she woke up here with wizard-looking meditation-man in the corner. If she hadn't been cold, hungry, confused, Simone figured she'd likely be thankful.

The lock in the door clicked. A white-haired man with ice blue piercing eyes walked straight out of a Tolkien novel and into the stone room. Simone felt a giggle well up. An improbable escape from a psychopath to end up in a fantasy world. It was too good to be true, but Cary was real and now a wizard stood before her. What other Tolkien-like elements were on Juno? Had Tolkien dreamed of Juno too? Or, something even more unbelievable: had she created Juno or merely gained access? Gandalf the White shut the door then held out a bowl of broth and some bread. "I thought you might be hungry." His voice was resonant and seemed to bounce off the inside of Simone's skull.

She accepted the food and sat, folding the blanket around her. He watched her in a way that should have scared her. Maybe he wanted her to be scared. Thanks to recent events, Simone just didn't know what she should be any more. "Where's Cary?" There was no electrical pull in her chest and she couldn't feel his emotions or hear his thoughts.

No flinch, no flicker. Nothing. "He's unwell, but near." She didn't know whether to accept that as a lie or of evidence that something was wrong.

"Who are you?"

"My name is Dmitri."

Simone slurped her broth, "You're a... no, not a wizard...something else. I remember, you're a Mentor. You teach Cary. You helped get him home.... back..." Still not a flicker. He had the best poker face Simone had ever seen. However, if Dmitri was here, Simone figured a vote cast in the 'something wrong' column was prudent. "Are we at FarSee?" The Mentor nodded. "How did I get here?"

"I'm not sure."

Simone chewed through the tough bread. "The same way he got to my house?"

"Most likely." She got the distinct impression that Dmitri was tiptoeing around her.

Simone gulped the rest of the broth. "So why are you keeping me locked up?"

She could see Dmitri choosing his words carefully, "There was a battle. It is not safe."

"And Cary was injured." As the Mentor nodded, Simone could see the seamless linking of the story. It was neat, tidy, and too simple. She gestured to the corner, "What's his purpose?"

"He is here to protect you."

"Okay. Can I at least get some clothes? It's a bit cold in here."

Dmitri accepted the offered bowl and returned to the door. "I'll see what I can do."

The door locked clicked into place as a scream burst out and echoed down the corridor. Cary. Simone threw herself at the door. "What are you doing to him? You son of a bitch, let me out!" Cary's screaming continued in waves. With each onslaught, Simone winced and tears welled. Finally she clamped her hands over her ears and sobbed. Maybe it was a good thing she no longer felt her connection with Cary.

A shout and pointing from the defensive wall. First they'd found that girl in the middle of the battlefield, then the infighting, now this. "What in the Creator's name is going on here?" Brask pulled his Companion around. This was more than the madness Cary had warned about. This was something else and he didn't like how this was adding up.

Nicholas Darine, the younger twin, rode up as Durlan Tolonel arrived on foot. "A group of men went that way," the Son reported and pointed west. "They had makeshift weapons."

"There's more. All heading west." Ceres Darine, the older Darine twin, stood balanced on the saddle of his horse and pointed out across the battlefield.

Brask turned in his saddle. The immigrants from a recently rescued chanting circle were setting a brisk pace, picking their way across the dead. They, too, were heading west. "What is going on?" Brask muttered again and shared a look with Durlan.

"I sent Langrid to fetch some mounted junior Sons. Are all the Mentors still up there?"

Brask nodded. "Keep the battlefield secure," he told Nicholas. "Notify Commander Darine he's responsible until I return." Nicholas saluted then rode off.

Brask then gestured to the other Darine twin and his fellow Commander, "Let's go see what's going on." Durlan whistled for his Companion as Brask kicked his own horse into a gallop and continued to mutter.

Dmitri strode through the Front Room to the kitchen. "Progress?"

Beads of sweat ran down Saul's face. Sesmon was deep in concentration at Cary's feet. Saul placed the amulet on the bench next to him then rose and stretched. He nodded and wiped his forehead with the back of his sleeve.

Dmitri approached the table. "Cary. Can you hear me?" He placed a hand on the young man's chest and opened his mind. Cary's heartbeat was steady and strong. His pulse and blood pressure were much better. Dmitri withdrew his hand and shifted his focus. It was as he feared. With Cary's increased strength and health, the connection between him and the girl increased. He glanced toward Sesmon and found the Mentor shaking with effort.

"Cary," he shook the apprentice's shoulder. A groan.

Banging on the front door. Voices echoed through the empty house to the kitchen. A scream from the depths of the house.

"Forgive me," Dmitri said then placed a finger on Cary's forehead. Eyes sprang open.

"What...?" Cary tried to raise his head and groaned. "Fate's bowels, I hurt."

"I need you to stand and walk."

Cary jammed the heel of both palms into his eyes, "Haha. You're funny. I'm not going anywhere."

Banging on the front door increased in volume, then suddenly stopped. Metal clashing and shouting. Fighting. Then a scream from upstairs. "Simone. What's going on?" Cary was now sitting and fixing Dmitri with an accusatory glare.

"Saul, can you help?" The younger Mentor nodded then stepped around to help the Aristovin to standing. Dmitri felt Cary shake from effort and then from pain.

They made their way through the Front Room. Cary stopped at the foot of the stairs, gasping, "I can't. Please. Stop."

Fighting was just beyond the thick wood of the front doors. Dmitri nodded to Saul. Together they lifted Cary under his shoulders and legs. Cary yelled then passed out. A reciprocal scream called out from upstairs. A sharp bang hit the front doors, "We have come for the light! Show us, teach us, command us!"

Dmitri noted that Cary had had the front door of FarSee reinforced since the night the Outerworld broke in, ten years ago. At this moment, he was thankful for Cary's fear and resourcefulness.

He and Saul hurried up the stairs and down the corridor. Dmitri threw open the door and they let Cary slump into Simone's arms. "The amulet?" Saul handed it over to Dmitri then exited and re-locked the door.

"What did you do to him? I can't feel him." Simone's hands raced over Cary's chest as if searching for the masked connection. In the corner, Arlo shook with effort.

Dmitri dared to place a hand on the girl's shoulder. He barely managed to suppress a gasp. Overwhelming warmth and comfort. Love. Images of his first wife flashed before his eyes. Joyce. His life had been completed by her. "You are both intact. We've had to create interference because it is dangerous for you to be here." With effort, he withdrew his hand and immediately felt the loss. "I must ask that you return to your home at once."

Tears gushed down her battered face as she clutched Cary's tunic with a desperate fierceness. "I can't. Please. Oh god. I can't go back, please."

"We know how, don't worry. But I must ask that this be done as quickly as possible. The more time you are here, the more danger you bring to everyone."

"I... but,... oh god...," she nodded reluctantly. "Will he be all right?"

"Yes, child. He is healing, but will be fine soon."

Once again, Dmitri woke Cary. Curses sprang out of Cary's mouth before he saw Simone holding him. His bloodied fingers wove between hers and his voice softened. "Hey. Missed you."

Dmitri again pushed back the memory of his first wife. "We need to do this now."

Cary caught his eye, "What are we doing?"

Dmitri gave him the amulet, "Simone needs to go home. Now." He could see the rejection and disbelief crossing the Aristovin's face. Then his fingers tightened their grasp on Simone's. Cary nodded. "As before, but this time Simone will need your help." He placed Simone's hand on the amulet that Cary held. "Simone, my dear, I need you to picture your home. Smell the air, feel the comforts of it, and see every texture. Cary, place her there."

This time, Dmitri was the one to open up the door to the collective consciousness. He could feel D'Ono Felari watching from afar as Simone slipped from one door, across the dreamscape of the collective consciousness, to the other door. The Master nodded to the Mentor as the doors shut. Arlo let out a great sigh of relief from his corner. Cary cried out and curled around himself, sobbing and shaking. Dmitri rested a weary hand on the young man's shoulder, "I'm sorry, my dear boy. So very sorry."

Chapter Thirty-Nine

Red and blue lights flashing through the darkness. Voices from the other side of the house.

Simone wiped away the tears streaming down her face and threw on some jeans. Her bedroom door was ajar and her room was in disarray. Across the hall, her father's bedroom door was open about four inches. A hole in the door caught her eye -- a bullet hole. She looked behind and saw the bullet lodged into her bedroom doorjamb. Pretty good considering the circumstances.

In the living room and kitchen were Michael, Mountie Mitchell and another Mountie. Both the front and back doors were open. Dead aspen leaves and a cold night breeze were taking over the small house. Simone strode up to the men, "Can we do this with the doors closed?"

Silence.

Michael, a non-descript average guy with brown hair and eyes that had seen too much in their 42 years, snatched her up in a hug. "Where were you? What happened? Holy shit, I was scared." Then he registered the damage. "What happened to you? Who did this?"

Mountie Mitchell put a hand on Michael's shoulder and moved him away. His eyes took notes, cataloguing the damage on Simone's face, adding it to the bullet hole in her father's door. "Should I call an ambulance?"

How could emptiness feel so heavy? Cary's presence had been ripped from her body. Again. She'd been to Juno and not been allowed to explore her dream. And while these men were here to protect her, she'd never felt so alone. "No, I don't need an ambulance. I'll go in tomorrow and get checked out."

Mountie Mitchell nodded and said something to his counterpart who then left the three of them. "Do you know who did this to you?"

"J.D. Coleman, sir."

"Just him?" Michael interjected.

"He is more than enough."

"Do you have a relationship with him?"

"Except for him raping me three years ago and then stalking me for the past week, no."

Michael stiffened. Mountie Mitchell continued, "Would you be willing to come in and make a statement?"

"This time the bastard's going down," Simone said finding the Fear, once again, replaced by anger. "I'll come in tomorrow, if that's okay."

"We'll need some pictures of your injuries. And if you scratched him, we can take evidence from under your fingernails." His pen skittered across his notepad. "Do you think he's the one who robbed the cafe?"

Michael again stiffened. "No. That guy only wanted money. J.D's a whole other story."

At that Mountie Mitchell pulled a plastic bag from his cargo pants pocket. "Is this yours?"

Inside the plastic bag was a piece of paper torn from the magnetic notepad on her fridge. Written in black marker -- likely the one beside her fridge -- was J.D.'s raging taunt: You can't hide. I will find you. Your friends will help me.

Sally.

The note rattled her, breaking her body free of the anger. Fear slipped back in through the cracks its freezing numbness making her weak. Then the shaking started.

Her hands reached out for the dining room, "Sit." Michael reached behind while Mountie Mitchell guided her to a chair and took back the plastic baggie. "Stop him. Please." It came out as a whisper as Fear wrapped itself around her spine. It was so cold. Her mind was retreating, trying to find some place to hide from all of this.

"Simone," Mountie Mitchell was kneeling in front of her but she couldn't see him. "The only way we can stop this guy BEFORE he does anything else is if you make a statement."

Simone curled into herself, warming, protecting, shielding herself from the outside world. "I just... I just need time."

Michael had remained silent. Mountie Mitchell nodded and hummed noncommittally. "I suggest you get a cell phone and keep it on and with you at all times until we can get this guy. You were very lucky. Call your friends and tell them to be vigilant. Give me a call when you're ready to come in and I'll send someone out." Mitchell handed her a business card.

"No need, Officer. I'll stay here." Mitchell nodded.

"Sergeant Mitchell," her mouth blurted the words through the paralysis of her mind, "has J.D. attacked other girls?"

Mitchell turned away from them and spoke into his radio. A moment later, "He has a juvenile record but it's sealed. However, he did serve a year for an assault after he turned eighteen."

"When did he get out?"

Mitchell took a lengthy pause before finally saying, "A month ago."

Simone felt her lungs struggle against a sudden heaviness in the still air. She wanted nothing more than to wrap around herself like a snake eating its tail, slowly curling out of existence.

CHAPTER FORTY

Morning light streamed in through the bedroom window and made Cary feel he'd been birthed from a nightmare. Dmitri leaned back in the wooden chair and looked at the ceiling. "You are still alive."

"I am wounded," Cary retorted while waving a hand over his bedbound situation. "And still recovering."

"Yes," Dmitri said and looked from the corner of his eye, "but you are still alive."

Cary readjusted the position of his injured leg, "Your meaning?"

"You have accepted your father's Commanding position, you have killed in the name of your country and yet you still live, you still have your pride, and you are still very much Cary Aristovin."

Suddenly the pain in his leg began to throb.

Dmitri finally turned to him, "There is more than one way to kill an Outerworlder. And you definitely found your own way."

Too bad the Mentor was out of reach.

"Now, from the beginning. In detail." Dmitri folded his arms and closed his eyes to listen Cary's story from the past week. Cary recounted, his heart aching with the remembrance.

"That's everything?"

Kissing Simone wasn't something he really wanted Dmitri to know, so he lied, "Yes. Everything." Dmitri continued to sit, silent, and thinking. "So, Opi, huh? Is that a pet-name? How well do you know each other?"

"None of your business."

"I just spilled out my guts to you. I deserve something in return."

Dmitri grumbled and opened one eye, "Ailsene is my great-granddaughter."

"The Seer is your great-granddaughter? Geez, Dmitri, how old are you?"

"Again, none of your business." Dmitri finally stretched and opened both eyes. "Okay, where is it?"

"Where's what?"

Dmitri fixed Cary with a glare. Cary pulled his amulet from under the pillow next to him. Dmitri rose to grab it, but Cary snatched it back. "What about the next battle?"

Dmitri did not remove his eyes from Cary. An intake of breath, "What was your first lesson as an apprentice?"

"The chair." Dmitri shook his head. Cary tried again, "The flow of energy rather than the Warrior-like pushing."

The Mentor's incisive glare turned into a full smile, "That is how Mentors have done it for generations." Dmitri snatched the amulet and put it in an ornate wooden box.

Then Cary remembered turning the mug at the Feather in the Hat in Greenspring. "Why?"

"Mentors are prohibited from possessing an amulet."

"Then give me that back. I'm not a Mentor yet." The box was now on Cary's chest of drawers, well out of reach.

"No, you're treading the fine line between Warrior and Mentor, and it's a line that needs to be walked with full awareness of who you are."

"I think I'm a little past that now."

"Are you?" Cary felt himself stumbling for purchase within his slippery argument. Dmitri nodded. "I thought so. I think it's now time for you to remember."

"Remember?" The word came too late. Dmitri's hand passed in front of Cary's eyes and sent the Aristovin to the past.

After his Father had left for the Plains again, his mother had put the amulet in his hands. In hers, she held a light-weighted sword. A wall of Outerworlders crept silently down the hall, black helmets shining in the dim torchlight. They'd come in through the windows.

That tarnished sword from generations ago was magic in her hands. Cary sat spellbound, enraptured at her dance. But his mother was outnumbered, as excellent as her swordsmanship was. Cary screamed a warning. Concentration shattered by the concern for her only child, the Lady Aristovin glanced behind. Cary could almost see the sharp-toothed grin beneath the face guard of the enemy's helmet as the Outerworlder ran his mother through.

A metal clang echoed. A heavy gasp.

Then, blood. So much blood.

Focus, *a voice said.* And clear your mind.

Focused, the clarity flowed through him. Then a library of information slammed into his mind and body. He knew how to fight. His body adjusted its fighting stance. The grip on the sword altered and seemed to flash of its own accord. Without thinking, his body dove against black armour. The amulet swung from his neck as he jumped and turned and finally sliced the head from the seventh and last Outerworlder.

The black armoured body hit the floor and the clatter resounded through the empty stone corridor. The deed was done, the clarity faded and fear crept in. With one last look at his mother, he dropped the sword and ran to the only place he knew he'd be safe....

Dmitri withdrew his hand from Cary's shoulder, "You became the best in your cohort after that night. You had accessed the collective consciousness to defend your Household and kept that knowledge with you. This is how you knew you could do it with Simone and with the army."

"But you warned against untrained minds using the amulet. That access changed me."

"Since the day you were born, I -- and your father -- have known you to be tenacious and resourceful. This is why that eight-year old boy used the amulet to gain access to the collective consciousness. The Outerworld didn't determine your fate ten years ago; they merely showed you who you really are."

The smell of roses still lingered in his mind. And, like at this Test, Cary could feel Fate lurking, smiling, meddling.

A knock at the door and Brask poked his auburn head in. "Sorry. Looking to report. Also you have a letter from the Council." He waved a parchment. A wave of voices and laughter echoed down the corridor behind Brask.

Cary blinked back the new memories. "What is going on out there?"

"You have a kitchen full of immigrants. Your steward and company are back. With guests."

Cary shrugged and waved in his second in command. "I'll take the letter, but you can save the report until later." Brask stood, uncomfortable in the Mentor's presence. "How's Dominic?"

"He's recovering, confined to bed like you."

"Seems an epidemic." Cary cracked the seal on the letter. "'Congratulations on your recent victory...' blah, blah, ... 'We recognize your acceptance of the Commander in Chief posting and will be forwarding the appropriate income thus...'"

"Don't expect anything right away. The Treasury is overwhelmed with compensation to sailor and merchant widows. A month minimum."

"Good thing I still have money left from the bribe your son and Dominic gave me."

"About that..."

Cary held up a hand. "Later. I'm getting to the good part. 'The Council has been assured that the Outerworld is in retreat and will be for some time.'"

As if on cue, Brask barked, "I'll believe that when I see it."

Cary continued, beaming, "'As such, The Council is reinstating the traditional ambassadorial duties of the Commander in Chief.'"

Brask nodded approvingly. "Your father didn't do many trips because the battles started to get too severe, but he did a few when you were young and before you were born. That's how he met your mother."

Dmitri stood. "Let me see that." Cary handed over the letter.

Cary watched as the Mentor strode to the window, reading the letter with fervor. "It's not a bad thing if the Outerworld is in retreat. Is there any reason to believe it isn't?"

Dmitri thankfully picked up on the loaded question as Brask looked. "No. If that's what the Council knows, then the Outerworld is in retreat."

Brask did a double-take at the Mentor. "Um, while I'm here, Cary, about that disappearing act you did at Warken..."

This managed to catch Dmitri's attention and both he and Cary stared at Brask. "What do you mean 'disappearing'?"

"Well, that day the count died. My daughter, Minuet," he said for Dmitri's benefit, "says you disappeared right in front of her. I argued that you used smoke and mirrors to vanish and then run naked around Warken. But she's arguing for, um, magic," he whispered. "Now that you've allowed the females to fight, I can't really turn her over my knee. Her status as a, um, Warrior -- of sorts -- is also lending weight to her story. Not good, all in all."

Cary sighed. Min was the most stubborn person he knew. "Dmitri? Any suggestions?"

"The truth."

"Really? Are we ready for that? As you reminded me, what we just did in battle prompted a civil war a hundred years ago. What would knowledge of magic do for civic trust?"

"You are in the process of uniting the country and have their loyalty. You've already opened the door; the truth will come out eventually. You are in a singular position to promote the truth. The real truth this time."

Another knock. This time Denis' head popped in. "My lords, Master Dmitri. I've come to see if are needing some food."

"Yes, please! It sounds like you have half the army down there."

Denis nodded. "Aye. We might have. Olivia's cooking up a bit of a feast."

"Denis, if you are up to the task," Cary motioned to Dmitri who handed back the letter, "feel free to offer Olivia and Emil full employment." Cary handed over the parchment to Denis. "If they want it." Denis glanced over it, tucked it into his pocket, then left with a brisk nod.

"Dmitri, Brask, stay for food?"

Brask shifted his belt, "Another time. I have duties to attend while you sit with your feet up. I'll come round later with a full report." Brash leaned over the bed at Cary, "Because hearing my report is part of your duties, *Commander*. There are somethings of which you need to be aware."

Brask left. Cary turned his attention to the Mentor. "So why are you worried? Isn't this news good?"

Dmitri watched the seagulls in the bright daylight. "You are a new leader. What's the first thing you should be doing as a new leader?"

"Establishing my role and personality upon my subordinates. I need to mold the army into my own."

Dmitri nodded and turned back to the chair next to Cary's bed. "You already have the loyalty of the country including the immigrants, but it's not something that should be taken for granted, especially since you employ radical tactics."

Understanding finally dawned. "The Outerworld is in retreat and the first thing the Council does is re-instate the Chief's ambassadorial duties. You think they're aiming to undermine me."

"It stinks like dead fish."

Cary chewed his lip. "Maybe I could take some of my command with me. I could start molding my command hierarchy while abroad." Dmitri nodded. "Can you do anything to find out what's going on?"

Dmitri nodded and hummed, fingering his beard. "I intend to. And, in the meantime, we have to get going on your apprenticeship. Homework awaits!"

IN GRATITUDE

This book has been a long time in the making. Writing takes time, patience, and, oftentimes, complete surrender to the process. And it is a process. I lost faith in the process (and myself) too many times to count. There are a few people who stuck by me on not-nice days, and others who supported me while I learned to trust the process all over again.

Many huge thanks to Lauren Sapala and Lisa King for helping me learn to trust the process again. A nod to Elizabeth Gilbert and Andy Mort for unknowingly providing just the right thing at the right time.

To my dear friends, Debbie Meert, Val Gauthier, Tamara Benjamin, Brock Franklin, Shawna Thompson, Carolyn Bergen, Melanie Girard, and Eileen Stoddart, my gratitude for your endless unconditional support knows no bounds. Some of you I subjected to earlier versions of this story, others provided invaluable support and faith. Whichever you are, you helped me bring this story to fruition. Thank you!

About the Author

Yvonne is an anthropologist and creative. She grew up in the wilds of rural Alberta, Canada, and, on a good day, she may still be there. This is Yvonne's second book.

If you enjoyed this novel, visit Yvonne's blog or her Facebook Page, *The Reluctant Archaeologist*.

Her website is yvonnekjorlien.com

ALSO BY YVONNE KJORLIEN

Elise Marquette adventures

Memoirs of a Reluctant Archaeologist

Ballast (a short story)

Fate series

Waiting for Fate

The Skirts of Fate (coming soon)

Non-Fiction

Why I Quit School and Got a Life and You Should Too: Finding True Identity Outside Academia (coming soon)

Don't miss out!

Visit the website below and you can sign up to receive emails whenever Yvonne Kjorlien publishes a new book. There's no charge and no obligation.

https://books2read.com/r/B-A-TTBU-XWRZB

Connecting independent readers to independent writers.